CATCH THE KISS

L.B. DUNBAR

WWW.LBDUNBAR.COM

Cover Design: Staci Hart/Quirky Bird Covers

Editor: Nicole McCurdy/Emerald Edits

Editor: Gemma Brocato

OTHER BOOKS BY L.B. DUNBAR

<u>Sterling Falls</u>

Sterling Heat

Sterling Brick

Sterling Streak

Sterling Clay

Sterling Fight

Sterling Touch

Sterling Stone

<u>Chicago Anchors</u>

Elevator Pitch

Catch the Kiss

Parentmoon

<u>Holiday Hotties (Christmas novellas)</u>

Scrooge-ish

Naughty-ish

Grouch-ish

<u>Road Trips & Romance</u>

Hauling Ashe

Merging Wright

Rhode Trip

<u>Lakeside Cottage</u>

Living at 40

Loving at 40

Learning at 40

Letting Go at 40

<u>Silver Foxes of Blue Ridge</u>

Silver Brewer

Silver Player

Silver Mayor

Silver Biker

<u>Sexy Silver Fox Collection</u>

After Care

Midlife Crisis

Restored Dreams

Second Chance

Wine&Dine

<u>Collision novellas</u>

Collide

Caught

The Sex Education of M.E.

<u>The Heart Collection</u>

Speak from the Heart

Read with your Heart

Look with your Heart

Fight from the Heart

View with your Heart

The Heart Remembers - a sequel

Ruthie, thank you for waiting 10 years for your story.
What a crazy ride this indie-author journey has been.
Here's to hitting it out of the park one more time.

AUTHOR NOTE

Catch the Kiss is loosely based off a short story I wrote called "The Red Dress Affair". This story has seen many versions before leading to this full-length novel.

OF NOTE: *Sterling Streak* (Ford Sylver) and *Elevator Pitch* (Ross Davis) are romances that take place simultaneously to Bolan Adler's story in *Catch the Kiss*.

You do not need to read these books to experience Bolan's story but it's always fun to read about the entire team with guest appearances from others on the Chicago Anchors.

PROLOGUE

[Ruthie]

18 years old

I
t started with a kiss.

And that silly experiment.

The dating break had been all Clifton's idea. "I just need a little . . . rest . . . from us."

What he'd meant was he'd *already* been horizontal with someone else, despite our commitment to one another as high school sweethearts who'd gone to college together.

I wasn't entirely heartbroken. If Cliff wanted an out, I was happy to give him one. Maybe permanently. I needed a breather as well.

The issue was, I had only ever been with Clifton, and I wasn't confident I could so easily hook up with someone else. Forget about dating.

But thoughts of what it would be like to actually kiss someone else consumed me.

I'd entered the Psychology Department's experiment to prove something to myself.

But also, because I didn't think anyone else would willingly want to kiss me. At such a young age, my self-esteem had been wrapped up in Cliff's approval. My trust had been gifted to him, which was strange considering the daddy issues I harbored. I believed in Clifton's promises to love me, and only me, for always.

Sad. Pathetic. Yet optimistic. The decision was a first for me. A rebellious act.

A toe-dip into Reckless Ruthie.

I'd heard about the experiment from my psychology professor. The class was a social science requirement for graduation, and I'd been enjoying the section on childhood development. I wanted to be an early education teacher. Despite the anonymous participation, I could also earn extra credit toward my class.

The psychological project involved a complex questionnaire along with consent to be interviewed and filmed. A nondisclosure agreement prevented us from discussing *who* we kissed with a firm contingency about contact afterward, as in, none was allowed for one full year.

The point was anonymity.

And a kiss.

Sixty seconds, kissing a random stranger.

There could be no prior contact. No future relationship. Just a kiss.

I likened it to a moment. You know—*that moment*—when your eyes meet someone else's across a bar, or a crowded bus, or in the freezer section at the grocery store, and something clicks between the two of you. Sparks crackle. Energy shifts. For just sixty seconds, you are connected to that person.

A smile passes. An intimate stare. An extra skip in your heart.

Then *blip*. Gone.

Yet you carry that unexpected, unexplainable minute with you through all the other minutes of your existence.

Not that I personally knew anything about those precious sixty seconds. My romantic heart had only experienced them in movies and books.

Thus, the project.

The kiss experiment meant coming to the psychology department early on a Saturday morning. The only issue I had was making an excuse to my roommates about where I was going so early with fresh makeup and curled hair, plus a backless shirt I'd borrowed from one of them.

Typically, I wore jeans and flannel shirts with flat heels and scarves. Conservative. Casual. The backless shirt meant I couldn't wear a bra. I'm not flat-chested, so I was self-conscious donning something without support. My blonde hair was pulled up in a high ponytail. I wore heels, assuming any partner might be taller than me. At five-seven, I was average, just like my appearance.

I didn't need to wear anything seductive. The kiss was guaranteed. Plus, a no-groping rule was in the contract. No wandering hands. No grinding body parts.

I was a stickler for rules. And yet, I was sick of following them.

As I walked across the quiet campus, I'd checked my breath three times, blowing into my palm and sniffing. An extra mint was neatly tucked into my pocket, just in case. I'd applied deodorant—twice—and spritzed perfume on all the sensory points. Wrists. Neck. Inner elbows.

However, our lips would be the main attraction.

Once inside the empty classroom, I noticed the desks were pushed to one side of the room and the opposite wall was covered by a white drop cloth. Although we were anonymous as participants, we'd also agreed to be videotaped to capture our interaction, and ultimately reaction, to one another.

Kissing a stranger for one full minute.

After the transaction, as the experiment called the moment, we'd be interviewed, separately, of course, to discuss how we felt before, during, and after.

Standing inside the silent room awaiting my partner, I'd grown especially anxious. That double dose of deodorant wasn't working and spritzing all the important places was back-firing. The scent was making me nauseous.

Maybe this wasn't such a good idea.

The female professor conducting the project stood behind a video camera. The lights in the room were dim, but a bright photography lamp highlighted the spot where my partner and I were to stand.

Standing in the classroom, waiting, I envisioned whom I might be partnered with for this only-one-time kiss.

What if he was old? What if he had glasses? What if he didn't kiss well? What if his breath smelled?

I'd brushed my teeth so often that morning my gums had bled. I didn't want to be remembered for having bad breath. I didn't want to be remembered as a horrible kisser, either.

I wanted this moment to be a memorable experience.

A loud thud, followed by a low curse, draws my attention toward the door.

Then *he* walked in.

Broad shoulders. Solid thighs. Rusty-brown curls peeking out beneath the edges of the baseball cap on his head. He was taller than me, but with my heels on, we wouldn't be terribly mismatched.

And he was shaking out his hand like his knuckles collided with the doorjamb.

I wasn't certain who he was, only that his aura said athletic, popular, arrogant.

He approached the professor without a glance in my direction. They spoke for a few minutes, excluding me, as if I wasn't in the room. He sounded combative and I heard the words "blackmail" and "extortion". The professor responded with something about remaining on the team.

Definitely an athlete. Absolutely did not want to be here.

When he finally turned toward me, the most amazing green eyes pierced mine. Intense. Unforgettable. Moss-colored with gold flecks that twinkled beneath the focused photography light.

Then he smiled at me, instantly settling my nerves while making me restless in a new way. My body hummed. He held out a hand and I took it like he intended to hold mine, not shake it, which apparently had been his intention.

I giggled. His smile grew wider, exposing deep dimples, emphasizing the lushness of his mouth.

He tipped his head toward the professor. "Just confirming the ground rules. No groping."

Was he worried I'd inappropriately touch him? Panic pinged through me. My emotions were on one hell of a roller-coaster ride.

We could embrace, press close, tug tighter, but our hands had to stay away from the no-go zones, which included the chest area on me and below the belt. I couldn't go below his either.

The thought warmed my cheeks.

The professor narrowed her eyes at him. The glare a warning.

"So, how do we start?" He addressed her while turning back toward me. He swung his baseball cap backwards on his head, the move like he was preparing to take his mark. His rounded face suddenly became edgier, like he was locking in on his posi-tion. On his commitment.

He was determined to kiss me for sixty seconds.

Then he winked.

My heart stuttered. While I was rattling with anxiety, he exuded calm confidence. He'd probably kissed hundreds of girls, and a strange wave of envy came over me. He didn't need the practice or the research of kissing someone else. I was nothing special to him.

"How would you initiate a first kiss?" the professor eventu-ally prompted.

My partner turned toward her, while I continued to take in the lines of his face. Hard jaw. Growing scruff. The perfect Cupid's bow of his upper lip.

When he looked back at me, he said. "Just look into my eyes for a second. Breathe."

Nerves got the better of me, and I immediately glanced away. A warm mitt of a hand cupped one side of my jaw, drawing my attention back to him. The pad of his thumb brushed against the corner of my mouth. Then his lips touched mine.

The connection was overwhelming. A zap of energy, a strange electricity, a current of something I couldn't explain.

I grabbed him by the back of the neck and smashed my mouth against his in response. The kiss was aggressive at first, each of us fighting for control. He clearly wanted the lead and when his hands fell to my waist, drawing me closer to him, I snaked my arms around his shoulders, pressing myself flush against his firm chest. I adjusted to his height by rising on my tiptoes. He bent his knees to meet me halfway. Our bodies lined up in all the ways they could.

And shouldn't, according to the rules.

Our lips had to remain connected for sixty seconds. An act of the Universe could not have pulled me away. Our mouths moved, melding together, bonding us forever. He was both a stranger and familiar. His tongue quickly met mine, and a new surge of desire ripped through my body. He knew how to kiss. How to control. How to wind me up.

I rocked into him. He clutched my hips, moving me in a way only one other person ever had, and yet the motion was nothing like what I'd experienced before. We—this stranger and me—felt more in sync.

When his hand slid to my lower back, keeping me pinned against him, I held tighter, never wanting to let go.

This was no ordinary kiss.

This was more than an experiment.

This was a dream. One I didn't want to wake from.

Warm hands met my bare back, and I shivered. The shoulder of my shirt slipped down my arm. My covered breasts were plastered to his broad chest. I teased my fingers into the hair sticking out of his ball cap. His excitement pressed against my lower belly.

The thought that I'd made him hard from just a kiss sent an empowering current of desire zapping through me, threatening to electrify me. There was no doubt how my body would react if we continued longer than a minute at this kissing experiment.

With my arms around his shoulders, I used the position to leverage myself higher, lining us up better. Shifting, he practically lifted me. We moved in time with each other. A practiced dance, yet first-time partners.

"Fifteen seconds," the professor called out.

The reminder of an audience should have startled me. Should have broken the delicious tension of the moment.

The time alert only spurred us on.

One of his hands slid around my ponytail, clutching the lengthy strands in a solid fist, while the other slid to my backside. He was breaking the rules, but we did not care. Fifteen seconds wasn't enough time. We kissed with new desperation. Reinforced intensity. As if starving to swallow the last morsel of one another.

He'd be imprinted on my mouth forever.

"*And . . .* time."

As we broke apart with a rush, chests heaving, nostrils flaring, my body followed his like I was still tethered to him. My mouth practically begged for more. My heart certainly wanted extra minutes.

I was so close—*so close*—to something unique, something powerful, something I had never encountered before.

Despite time being called and the sudden break, he leaned in for a second taste.

A softer kiss. A gentle brush. A final farewell.

He pulled away first, and I bent my head, leaning into his chest, needing another minute to catch my breath.

Sixty more seconds, please?

His fingers tickled up my spine. He massaged the back of my neck.

Tears filled my eyes when he kissed the top of my head.

I glanced up at him and he grinned, cocky but sweet. With a shaky smile, I giggled, anxious and strung out, blinking back the silly tears of pent-up arousal and sudden disappointment.

The moment was over.

I tried to step away first but wobbled on weak knees. He caught my elbow to steady me.

"Any questions," the professor asked.

"What's your name?" I said.

"Can I have your number?" he asked at the same time.

"No contact for a year," the professor reminded us.

The rules.

I was a follower of them.

And I hated that about myself.

1

15 years later

You are cordially invited to
The Red Dress Affair
In honor of a celebrated life
Joanna Elizabeth Frederick
Beloved wife, mother, and cousin.

As I stand in the empty ballroom for what felt like forever, I don't know why this random memory comes back to me.

The Kiss Experiment.

Oh, to be eighteen, carefree and foolish.

At thirty-three, I am so pulled together I can't breathe.

However, The Red Dress Affair is something special to Nylah, and because of my devotion to her, I've been helping her organize the fundraiser in honor of her cousin who died of heart disease, a top contender for the leading cause of death among women.

A broken heart is certainly eating away at my life.

For Joanna Elizabeth Frederick, her condition had gone undiagnosed, and she left behind a husband and three adult sons.

The timing of this year's event is appropriate—Valentine's Day—which, in my opinion, is one of the most contrived holidays in existence.

Shouldn't every day with a partner be a celebration of love?

Ironically, Valentine's *Eve* happens to fall on a Friday this year, thus Friday the thirteenth. And while most single women my age might be out celebrating Galentine's Day with girlfriends, I'm standing here in California's Coastal Resort ballroom waiting on Nylah, who has mysteriously disappeared.

The dimly lit space overlooks the Pacific Ocean through three gloriously large, arched windows. In my lagging patience, a gin and tonic was delivered to me by a harried waitress who told me Nylah would be back soon to finalize some last-minute detail that probably doesn't need finalizing.

My mother-in-law is efficient. Or as she prefers to call herself, my mother-in-love, being that I married her son, Clifton, and she fell in love with me as well. The daughter she never had and always hoped for.

Is she technically my former mother-in-love? She's not necessarily an ex-mother-in-law, right? What is the proper term for a woman whose son had been your husband, and said husband has passed away? Either way, Nylah Jacobson has been more of a mother to me than my own, but those thoughts have no place here this evening.

Neither do thoughts of Clifton. For the past eighteen months, I've been swimming in memories.

For only a moment, I want to forget.

Maybe Nylah is right. She's been hinting that it might be

time to open my heart to new possibilities. Strange advice from a former mother-in-law, but also so typical of Nylah.

"Fuck."

My thoughts scatter when the expletive in a deep masculine grunt echoes throughout the empty room along with the distinct sound of someone tripping on the parquet dance floor in the center of the space. From my position near the three floor-to-ceiling windows, I'm obscured from his view.

"Excuse me." I scoff, giving away my presence. I've been nursing the gin and tonic Nylah sent, holding the glass in my hand despite my crossed arms. A defensive stance. One in which I can never determine if a shield to protect myself or a clamp to hold myself together.

The intruder swipes a thick hand over his head and gruffly asks, "Where's Nylah?"

He approaches my little corner of the room, and a strange vibration overtakes me. A weird energy crackles between us. I don't feel threatened, but more like a familiarity with him, like something inside me recognizes him.

Which is impossible.

The man is broad and tall, his build athletic, with a stern expression that conflicts with the roundness of his face. In the backlight of the chandelier behind him, his hair appears brown, the color not distinct, and heavy scruff covers his jaw. He could be anyone and no one of importance. In the sports management industry, I see so many athletes that their images blur together unless Imperial Sports Management represents them. Not that this man is an athlete. In his pressed suit and crisp button-down shirt, he looks more like a businessman.

"And who might you be, flower?" His gaze blatantly skims over my body, undressing me with dark eyes that might border on deep green if the light were better in the room to distinguish the color.

His visual appraisal feels nice, if a bit intrusive. In my

slim-cut pencil skirt and pearl-buttoned blouse that I can't wait to strip off myself, I'm no one distinct. It's been a long day. And I'm not certain men look at me like they really see me. The woman beneath the buttoned-up shirts and fitted skirts.

I can't remember the last time I experienced the sensation of a man's hands on me.

"Do I know you?" His thick brows cinch and that questioning voice sends a shiver down my spine. Does he feel it too? Does he sense the energy crackling between us?

"Have we been together?" His tone is sharp, and like a pin in a filled balloon, my hope-filled questions burst.

Maybe the sense of familiarity is just a result of the tension from the storm brewing over the ocean outside the windows. Rain is predicted. And this guy's insulting insinuation is a lightning strike against him.

Blinking at his brashness, I stammer, "Excuse me?"

"I feel like I know you." He snaps his fingers and points at me, like the motion will help jog his memory.

"Know me?" I choke, shifting to face him better, as if looking me directly in the eyes will jar his memory, which must be full of unfamiliar women he's *been* with. My arms remain crossed. Definitely a shield in this situation. "Is that some kind of weak pick-up line?"

Being hit on feels like an impossibility. The concept of dating is foreign. I haven't been with anyone other than Clifton. Ever.

"Do you want it to be a pick-up line?" The sudden arch of his thick brows and the way his mouth twists into a teasing smirk pops out a deep dimple, like a parenthesis on the curve of his lips. Lips that look rather full and emphasized by the punctuation of that dimple.

That spark of innocence on his face has me choking on an answer. "I . . ."

"That's what I thought." He sighs heavily, lowering his shoulders and glancing around the empty room.

The tables are covered in snowy-white linen awaiting the floral arrangements due to be delivered tomorrow. I have no idea what Nylah's last-minute detail could entail. The room will eventually be a hub of who's who among athletes and business associates of Imperial Sports Management, all gathered for a good cause. For now, the space is quiet, hushed despite its cavernous size. Like a secret tucked into a corner of this resort.

"Do you happen to know what time it is?" My purse is on a chair on the other side of the room. I should have my phone in my hand in case Nylah tries to call me, but I'd gotten side-tracked by the windows and the view.

My intruder flicks his arm outward, exposing a thick silver watch on his wrist, and reads off the time. "Ten-fifteen."

I've been waiting almost an hour for Nylah.

"Expecting someone?" he asks, bringing those dark eyes back to me.

"I was, but she's late." I take a sip of my drink as my mouth suddenly feels dry thanks to the way he's looking at me. Like he's still trying to undress me.

His eyebrows hitch again.

"She's my—"

His raised hand stalls my explanation. "You don't need to explain. Whatever wets your petals."

What the hell?

"Gotta girlfriend? That's cool." His left leg jiggles as his head nods in three short juts.

I should clarify that Nylah is my mother-in-law, but then I'd have to explain how I'm a widow, *blah-blah-blah*.

"I don't have a girlfriend." My voice comes out a little abrupt, because who is this man to be asking me such personal questions about my love life, five seconds after meeting?

"Boyfriend, then?" One brow arches.

I shake my head, the movement lessening the tension in me.

"Husband?"

I swallow thickly but shake my head again, lowering my gaze.

"Secret lover? Affair with the boss? Obsession with a hockey player?"

"What?" I stammer at the ridiculous list that reads like the tropes of a romance novel. "None of the above." I chuckle despite myself.

"How do you feel about crushing on a baseball catcher?"

"I have no feelings about a baseball catcher," I toss back at him.

Am I flirting with him?

Is he flirting with me?

"Yet." He winks.

I should ask if *he's* a baseball player, but I don't. Instead, I sort of revel in the mystery of not knowing him despite the continual crackle of recognition. Something tells me I do know him; I just cannot place him. And even though he sensed he might know me, I'm suddenly appreciative that he doesn't.

He doesn't know my relationship with Nylah. He doesn't need to know my marital status, or lack thereof.

"How do you know Nylah?" I ask curiously.

He tilts his head, assessing me. Those dark eyes have become a little more distinguishable.

"Now, that's a very long story." He offers a soft smile, one that borders on sadness, but quickly disappears as his mouth curves wider.

That smile. Those lips. Definitely something about him.

My racing heart almost confirms the strange sense of familiarity.

I lift my glass for the final dregs of my gin and tonic. The ice has melted. The remaining liquor watered down. I hold up the empty glass in salute. "Well, I'm off to bed."

There's no reason the statement should sound like a proposition, but it comes out throaty and thick. Tempting even. Or at least, it sounded that way in my head. Instead, I probably sounded like a strangling cat.

"What's the rush, flower?"

The rush is a long hot bath and a romance novel calling my name. And with this sudden antsy sensation swirling around me because of this man's appearance—broad shoulders, tempting eyes—he might play nicely in a little self-love fantasizing.

Strangers in a ballroom should make his checklist of relationship statuses.

Not that it would ever be my status.

I brush past him. Probably closer than I should be, because my long-sleeve-covered-arm rubs against his suitcoat-covered one, and a spark crackles through the layers of material. The flicker causes me to stop moving.

Or maybe it's the sudden touch of his hand at my elbow. The warmth seeping through the thin, silky fabric of my blouse. The pressure cradling, tender yet firm.

"Wait." The hesitation after he stops me has our eyes locking on each other.

A look. A moment.

His eyes come into view better in our shifted position. With his face in the light of the chandelier above the dance floor, those eyes sparkle. Definitely green. But there's something else familiar about the deep mossy color with flecks of gold dancing inside them. In the better lighting, his hair appears more rust-colored with sprinkles of gray at both his temples and along his jawline. However, I still can't dismiss this niggling sensation that suggests we have a connection.

"Have a drink with me." He isn't really asking, more like softly commanding. "It's been a day."

I know the feeling. It's been a day of days and a year of days. Hell, eighteen months of days.

"My drink is gone." I lift my glass and jiggle it, emphasizing the emptiness. "And I'm tired." Suddenly, I'm bone weary. As much as I'd like to flirt with him, deep inside, I know flirting won't lead anywhere because I'm me.

Responsible Ruthie. Always doing the safe thing.

He pouts at my excuse, blinks his eyes like a begging child, and something inside me snaps, like one of those glow-sticks they sell at stadiums. The kind you crack in the middle, and they illuminate, lighting up fluorescent and bright.

"I'll get you another one. What's your poison, flower?" He nods at the glass, before taking it from my hand, giving it a sniff, and setting it on the nearby banquet table which will hold an extensive spread tomorrow evening.

Flower. This is the third time he's called me the term of endearment. At least, I think it's an endearment. His voice turns a bit growly over it, sending a ripple up my spine, and making me feel like precious flora, delicately dancing in a breeze.

"Five minutes." He holds up his large hand, spreading his fingers to emphasize the time. "One drink." He curls his fingers so only his index points upward, long and thick, and strangely intimidating.

"And how do I know you won't go get me a drink, spike it, and then drag me off to your room?"

His brows furrow in thought. His jovial face turns serious a second, acknowledging the reality in the risk. "I like your way of thinking. Safe. But, give me a chance to prove myself. I promise not to spike anything, and we'll never leave this room." His eyes suddenly flicker, the explosion of gold flecks like an oath. Another flash of flirtation.

I chuckle, shaking my head, uncertain why I'm agreeing, disbelieving it before I say, "Okay."

"You'll stay?" His brows lift, surprised yet hopeful.

I nod as he backs up, keeping his eyes on me with each step he takes backward. Hands raised, palms out, as if holding me in place.

"Stay." His mouth curls again. One corner ticking higher than the other and that dimple sneaks out once more.

Do I have a thing for dimples? Where have I seen that dimple before? Are dimples recognizable?

The back of his heel smacks into the dance floor causing him to stumble a bit, similar to how he might have fumbled entering the room. The edge on the parquet flooring isn't raised more than an inch. A slight incline from carpet to wood surface, and yet, he's found the gap and tripped over it.

And something in that moment has me committing to stay put.

When he finally turns toward the door, feet forward and moving quickly toward the exit, I turn back toward the windows, wondering what I'm doing. What have I been waiting for?

Time has passed since Clifton's death. Hours of emptiness that existed even before his passing.

I stare outward at the rolling ocean, crashing against the large bluff. Rain has finally broken free of the overcast clouds, pummeling the glass, forming tiny streams that slither down the slick panes. The image reminds me of tears.

Too many tears I've shed over someone unworthy of my grief.

My phone pings, the sound reverberating across the room in the eerie silence, and I cross the space to check the notification.

I'll see you in the morning, darling.

Nylah. No surprise, she isn't returning.

I could be angry that I've been waiting, angry at lost time, angry about so many things. Like the rain raging against the windows, I'm a storm, bottled up and eager to break free.

Strangely, I feel lighter at the moment.

Maybe it's simply the sense of relief that Nylah doesn't need me, and I can return to my room shortly.

Suddenly, a rush of a man re-enters the room. His steps are quick as he hits the parquet flooring in the center of the space, then stalls as he stares in the direction of the windows.

"Flower?" His voice sounds . . . disappointed. Like he believes I've left.

I'm probably imagining the tone, but something inside me stirs. Quickly, I tuck my phone back into my purse and cross the room toward him.

"Hey." My throat struggles on the call, especially when he turns to look at me holding a full bottle of tonic underneath his arm, two crystal glasses with ice pinched between his fingers, and a green bottle of gin in his other hand.

Relief seems to settle on his shoulders which lower when he faces me.

Recognition strikes me full-on again and smacks my cheeks.

It can't be, can it?

The gleam in his eyes. The twitch of his mouth. Those dimples.

Now would be the time to ask him who he is. Seek confirmation. If he is who I think he is, we do have history.

Is this serendipity? I'd just been thinking about that past moment. Those powerful sixty seconds. And now I'm being presented with a new minute. Not that this is a second chance or anything. Not that he's going to kiss me, but still—

"Flower." He repeats the nickname with more confidence. "Where'd you go?"

I shake my head. "What?"

"You look kind of deep in thought there. You aren't thinking of bolting, are you?"

Would he chase me if I did? The idea is too absurd to ruminate over. My brain is already muddled between the painful memories of Clifton, the reminder of a special moment in my past, and now this. Him. Here.

I should reveal who I am. Instead, I mutter, "I'm good." My voice is still a bit shaky as I watch him step over to the banquet table and set down the bottle of gin.

"Gin and tonic?" I confirm. "My favorite."

"Lucky guess." He winks before he moves the tonic water from beneath his arm to the table as well and settles the two glasses beside it, like a minibar.

I step closer to his position beside the table.

"Exhibit A." He lifts the green bottle of gin and twists the cap. The sharp crack of the seal reassures me it's a fresh container, unopened and free from any dangerous additives.

He pours a generous amount into each glass.

"Exhibit B." He waves his hand in front of the tonic bottle.

I laugh at the dramatic display before he picks up the container and twists the sealed cap, which releases a long hiss of carbonation. He tops off each glass with tonic. As the sparkling liquid glugs over the ice, the tiny bubbles of carbonation release, and my belly fizzes like the sound.

What is happening here?

Then he slips his hand into his suit jacket pocket and pulls out a lime. He tosses the green citrus between his hands. "Shit. I didn't think this part through. I don't have a knife. Didn't want to scare you. But now I don't have a way to cut this thing."

He inspects the lime a second, then bites off the end. Removing a hunk of rind from his mouth, he shoves his thumb into the fruit to separate it, ripping it in half.

"That was . . . brutal." And yet something about it was

freaking hot. The way he bit the tart citrus. The way he forced his thumb into the fruit. The way he cracked it open with no real effort.

He shakes out his hand—something about the motion also triggering a memory—before squeezing each half of the lime into our separate glasses.

A drop of lime juice still lingers on his lips, drawing my attention to it, wondering how it might taste. How he would taste.

"I love extra lime," I offer for no reason, while my heart continues to hammer so loud I'm certain he can hear the beat across the distance between us.

"To extra lime." He lifts a glass and holds it out to me, and I take the final steps to bring us closer.

He raises the other glass and taps mine, but his eyes remain on me, waiting for me to take my first sip.

With those dark-green eyes watching me, my gut rumbles.

Tell him.

However, I don't say anything. Instead, I take a drink, relishing the explosion of tart lime on my tongue and then choking on the strength of gin.

"Whoa." I pucker and sway a bit on my heels.

"Easy there, flower." He chuckles, catching my elbow again. "Don't wilt on me yet."

The warmth of his hand seeps through the thin fabric of my blouse once more. The heat growing from a slow burn to a flaming inferno as he swipes up my arm to my shoulder where he squeezes at the joint.

Before I know it, his palm is on the side of my neck and his thumb rubs up the column of my throat to my chin. The scorching blaze spreads throughout me. If those eyes are a thicket of trees, he's just lit a forest fire inside me.

"Your skin is soft," he marvels, pausing a second. "Wonder where else you might be tender?"

Ensnared by his eyes, I've stepped even closer to him, or maybe he's come closer to me.

Again, I grapple with admitting who I am. Suggesting I know who he is. Omission is a dangerous game, and I'm so bad at playing them.

Instead, I'm breaking rules without knowing the instructions, and for once, it feels so damn good.

While his touch is strangely soothing, it brands my skin. The width of his hand is so large, his fingertips press on the back of my neck. Essentially, he's cuffing my throat and there is something tantalizing and thrilling about the position.

Would he pin me down? Hold me in place?

A rush of everything unfamiliar, and surprisingly pleasant, sweeps up my center, clogging said throat. My body thumps in a lower place. A place longing to be touched. To be spread open the way he forced that lime.

Swiftly, his hand slips from my throat and glides across my upper chest before lowering to my breast.

The shock sends a conflicting sensation through my body, and I step back, snapping the connection between us.

He quickly lifts his hand, palm outward. His brows lift, eyes wide. "Shit. Sorry. That was a bit fast."

"You think?" Despite the sarcasm, my tone is breathy, a contradiction to the harsh reprimand and leaving me questioning myself. *Am I truly offended?*

Responsible Ruthie screams *yes*. Inappropriate. Unacceptable. But the wannabe Rebellious Ruthie buried deep inside me, taunts all my uptight morals and wants to break free from restraint.

"I shouldn't have—" He points awkwardly toward my breasts with a thick finger and draws a big circle in the air with his fingertip. "That was crossing a line. One you clearly aren't interested in stepping over."

He sets his drink on the banquet table. In frustration, and

perhaps a bit of shame, he rubs a hand over his short hair, averting his gaze and shaking his head.

"Fucking idiot," he mutters to himself.

Following his lead, I set my drink down as well and cross my arms over my chest again.

"It's okay." Disappointment suddenly seems to have a hold of my throat, and I want his hands back on me. I want that thumb beneath my chin and those fingers on my nape. I want that big palm to actually squeeze my breast, where my nipples are now hard and aching for additional attention.

"I'm sorry." He finally risks a glance at me. "I'm not known for making the best decisions."

And touching me was a mistake.

Is there something deeper than disappointment? Something gut-punchingly lower than what I feel? Because I don't want to be a slip-up for him.

"Apology accepted." I risk reaching for his hand, curling my fingers around the thickness of his thumb. The one that split open a lime. I squeeze with the intention of quickly releasing him.

Only, he captures my fingers before I can pull away from him, pinning them against his heated palm. Glancing down at my trapped fingers, the sensation between us is no longer sparks and crackles but warmth and comfort. Understanding. Patience.

Could he remember me? It's clear he doesn't recognize me, but does he sense the connection? On some deeper level, does he feel a pull toward me like I feel toward him?

The thoughts feel otherworldly. Like the Universe is speaking but I can't read the script.

He surprises me once more by leaning forward and placing the lightest kiss against my cheek, softly repeating his apology, "I'm sorry."

How often have I heard those words in the past eighteen

months and yet nothing has sounded as genuine as the phrase on his lips.

He doesn't know me. He knows nothing about me, but his apology brings a prickle to my eyes. A burn of tears I fight to dismiss.

Swallowing against the thickness in my throat, the swell of disappointment before I have a right to be disappointed, I whisper again, "It's okay."

The reply is simple, innocent enough, and yet, somehow . . . permission.

He doesn't have to recognize me. He doesn't need to understand me on a deeper level. I just want more from him. Another moment.

Tipping up on my toes, I brush my lips over his. A whisper of a kiss. A breath of connection. The move is the most forward I've ever been, and I'm slow to pull back, desperate to link us together while accepting I've gone too far.

Still, heat radiates over my mouth. The brief exchange has once again turned into something electric.

I don't know who moves first but suddenly, our lips are locked. His hand returns to my throat and I'm clutching the lapel of his jacket.

He tugs me closer to him. Or maybe I pull him to me.

Nothing matters other than the explosive connection of our mouths. The reunion of our lips, because in this exact moment, there is no doubt about who he is.

Bolan Adler.

Star college athlete. Man about campus.

My sixty-second kiss experiment partner.

The tingle of recognition has unraveled into fiery longing. One deeply rooted inside me. The connection moves from electric sparks to something firework-level. Something grand finale at Disneyland. Or the symbolism of a New Year's celebration.

However, beneath the dizzying display is a little voice of

reason, telling me not to venture any further. Exert caution, it warns, because *this* moment might come back to bite me in the ass later. But I don't listen. I'm tired of listening to reason, when all I want to do is feel reckless.

I wrap an arm around his neck, still clutching the lapel of his jacket with my other hand, as if he'll slip out of my grasp once again. In sixty seconds, he'll be gone once more.

His hand presses on my lower back, plastering me to his chest. My breasts ache. Nipples peak. The softness of my bra is too much against them. The firmness of his chest sharpens the need within me.

"Fuck," he mutters against my mouth. "You taste familiar."

The limes. It must be the lime he so aggressively bit, and the gin and tonic on our tongues, which swirl against one another, sweeping deeply inside each other's mouth as if we can drink the other in.

"Want to taste you in other places."

I pull back, shocked by the brazen admission while another rush of excitement floods my lower belly and sets the throbbing at my core to a rave-worthy beat.

Yes. Yes. Yes.

I'm desperate for him to commit to his statement. Willing to let his tongue slice me open like his thumb forced its way into that citrus fruit. He must sense my desire, because he lifts me by my backside. My skirt is too tight to spread my knees and wrap around him, but no matter, as I'm suddenly seated on the edge of the banquet table.

His thick fingertips fumble with the precious pearl buttons on my blouse and he watches where he struggles with the tiny closures. "Need to see more of you."

"Yes," I whisper. *Please see me.*

"So delicate, flower." His rugged whisper is scratchy like the scruff on his jaw.

My blouse is unbuttoned to my waistband, and he slips his

hand inside the material to cup my breast over my silky bra. With his other hand, he tugs the bottom of my blouse free from my skirt. He releases my breast, and I whimper at the loss of his touch. Hastily, he finishes unbuttoning my shirt and returns to the cup of my bra, tugging down the covering, and palming the bare swell. Desperate for him to give me more, I arch my back, closing my eyes at the pure pleasure racing over my skin.

"Oh no, flower, you keep those eyes open and focused on me. Here and now."

This moment will not replace the memory of our first meeting. This time will mark me as a second encounter.

The thrill of the empty ballroom, in the quiet corner of the resort, intensifies the edge of excitement. Kissing him again. Being intimately touched by him. My whispers sound loud to me. My pleas and whimpers echo around the vacant space. My pulse is skyrocketing, caught between concern someone will walk in, and a curious interest in voyeurism. The freedom is scintillating.

But my focus is wrapped up in this man as his lips move over mine, drawing me into him while his hand continues to work my breast, kneading, teasing, plucking my nipple.

Then his fingers are on the move again, tickling down my belly and hitching up my skirt before dipping beneath the bunched-up material.

When his thick fingertip swipes across my damp panties, I nearly leap off the table.

"Holy fuck, flower, your petals are so wet." His cheeky comment has me narrowing my eyes.

"That's the worst line ever," I choke, drunk on him, dazed and mesmerized by where he's touching me, *how* he's touching me. With care and skill; firing a deep need to be closer.

He shoves aside the slip of underwear and parts those petals he's mentioned. A thick finger enters me with ease, and I cry out. My hips buck upward as I fall back, catching myself on my hands. He plucks at a spot, sensitive and swollen, greedy and grateful for his touch.

He wants me. He wants me not. He wants me.

An orchestra of wings flutter within my lower belly, scattering imaginary petals in their rapid fluttering.

Lightning flashes beyond the glass. A rumble of thunder clangs, drowning out my cries of pleasure.

The anticipation builds, spiraling like the clouds rolling across the sky and the waves crashing down below.

I brace for the final flight, knowing this moment will be unlike anything I've experienced before.

With the rush of his second finger inside me and his thumb on my clit, I jettison upward. Outward. Like lightning crackling across the midnight-black curtain in violent pink and vivid blue.

The takeoff is instantaneous, coinciding with a burst of hard rain and another tumble of thunder.

The flight is long and sweet, a soaring, chasing, freeing moment, one I never want to descend from.

However, eventually, I coast back to earth, feeling light and spent as I fall against the tabletop where a very handsome stranger is pillared over me, holding himself upright on extended solid arms

"That was beautiful." Pride laces his whispered praise before he removes my underwear and cups my ankles to place my heels on the edge of the table. With his face between my raised knees, he's staring at me like I'm a feast he's about to devour. Confirming my thoughts, he states, "Next course."

Too weak to move, the first lap of his flattened tongue turns me into a honey drizzle in warm tea. I'm melting, spreading, sinking into every swirl. Every lick. Every swipe. He leaves no drop unsavored until I blossom a second time.

Blooming like the flower he's taken to calling me.

Nothing. Has. Ever. Felt. Like. This.

Eventually, I press against his head, signaling I've had enough. *He's* too much. With a final kiss to my inner thigh, he stands and holds out a hand to help me upright.

The intensity in his eyes sends another wave of memory through me.

Just look into my eyes for a second. Breathe.

This moment feels like the first breath I've taken in years. Maybe decades.

Clasping my hand, he leans forward and kisses me, ravishing my mouth. His tongue tastes of me—salty, sweet, and pungent. I'm nearly dizzy before I find the strength to press his shoulders, pushing him back.

With his hands on my hips, he pops me off the banquet table and I right my skirt, forcing it downward and back into position. When I glance at him, before me is a wall of chest, and I skate my fingers along the buttons of his now-wrinkled shirt.

"Whatcha doin', flower?"

"Want to touch you too." I hardly recognize my own voice. Sated while seductive. I don't recognize *myself*, this needy woman, desperate to take him in my mouth, and bring him to his knees.

With trembling fingers, I travel down the front of his shirt, popping open the buttons. His jacket has already disappeared. His impatience takes over, and he tugs at the sides of his shirt, sending the buttons pinging, and exposing his solid, barrel shape.

He's unlike any man I've ever known. *Any*. Man.

My eyes catch on a silver, rectangular medallion dangling from a woven black strap around his neck.

Despite the tremor in my hands, I rub his molded pecs and rounded shoulders, pressing back his shirt enough to expose the broadness of him. Drifting over his bulging biceps, I take my time to inspect him with a light touch.

Once again impatient, Bolan cups my backside and tugs me to him. The smoldering heat of his bare torso hits the coolness of my covered breasts, and we collectively gasp.

Suddenly, the dim lights of the ballroom go out.

We both still before he glances over my head. In this corner near the windows, we remain undetected. Possibly a banquet worker turned off the lights. Maybe the storm has knocked out the power.

Whatever has happened, we are shrouded in darkness.

"I want you," he murmurs into my ear before nibbling my neck.

Another crackle of lightning illuminates the sky behind him. A momentary flash in the room.

A shiver runs through me. "I'd like that." I want to be wanted, desired, cherished. And standing in front of me seems to be a second chance at something that slipped through my fingers once upon a time.

In an instant, my back is against the cool window, rain pelting the outer side. The hammering of the drops is like an orchestra reaching a crescendo. The sound heightening, lifting something inside me once more. The chill against my skin is refreshing because his heat overpowers me.

My skirt is once again shoved up to my waist while I work at his belt and loosen his pants. My blouse hangs open. My heels remain on.

He tugs something from his back pocket and holds up a foil packet. The suggestion is clear. I hadn't thought to ask. *Reckless, Ruthie.* Risky. However, my experience is limited. And I don't want to overanalyze his preparedness.

With brawny strength, he easily lifts me, and my legs wrap around his waist. For only a second the heat of his tip rubs against tender skin, teasing me, taunting me. He hisses at the contact before he lowers me once more, taking care to cover himself.

I watch in wonder. His length. His shape. The all-around masculinity on display before me.

As I've only been with one man my entire life, I've never witnessed someone rolling on a condom. Once covered, *this* beautiful man reaches for my hand, guiding me to wrap my fingers around his heavy shaft and stroke him a few times.

Desire that hasn't dissipated spikes.

Thunder that sounds like cymbals clashing rattles the glass behind me. The echoing rhythm matches the pulse in my chest. The beat of my heart.

Once more, I'm lifted, legs easily spreading around his hips. He's quickly notched at my entrance and with a swift surge, inside me.

I gasp, blinking back tears sparked by the rushed intrusion. With my arms around his neck, I cling to him.

"Fuck, flower." He pauses for a breath, allowing me to adjust to the sudden, delicious fullness.

"It's been a long time," I admit, closing my eyes in embarrassment. I shouldn't feel ashamed but I am.

"How long?" The question comes on a strained exhale as his fingertips dig into the back of my upper thighs.

"Long enough."

His eyes seek mine, searching them a second, before something shifts in his demeanor. "Time to make up for the loss."

Another bang of thunder and a fiery burst of lightning punctuates his words. This moment will erase all others. A baptism of sorts.

Then, he moves with skill and practice, filling me, plundering me, spreading tender flesh and dipping into my ripe channel.

I've never felt anything like this sensation. Incredibly beautiful. Blissed-out overwhelm. Connectedness and freedom in one stroke.

As much as I want him to recognize me, I revel in the disassociation.

Strangers in the dark. A vacant ballroom. A storm brewing. My romantic brain gets carried away, but I quickly rein it in.

This is only a moment.

"Blossom, baby," he demands through gritted teeth. The tension suggests he's holding back, waiting on me.

For too long, I've been a dried flower. A keepsake under glass. What was once shriveled, faded and dusty, has come back to life.

Unfolding.

Reblooming.

Blossoming into color.

2

———————

[Bolan]

F
uck, is she sweet.

Her eyes are as dark as the raging sea, and while we'd been a storm of licks and limbs, fingers and fucking, her demeanor has shifted. She's almost suddenly shy, and I want to invite her back to my room more than anything.

But I can't.

Instead, I watch as she slowly stands on weak legs and her shaky fingers fumble with the buttons of her blouse.

"Here. Let me." While I've undressed plenty of women, I don't think I've ever dressed someone before, but it's evident she can't maneuver the delicate buttons that look like tiny pearls. And something inside me wants to take care of her.

I lower my gaze to focus on my own large and clumsy fingers attempting to work the small buttons.

She's so beautiful and familiar. Hiding in the corner when I entered this room, her stance was pensive, defensive even, but when she looked at me . . . those eyes. The deep, dark depth of them was aimed at me like a ball called to my glove, and I hadn't had a catch like that in a long, long time.

If ever.

I've never experienced love.

But this woman was enticing. Those innocent eyes. That pouty lip.

Like my granddad once taught me, I want to press her between the pages of a book like a precious flower and keep her forever.

But I can't.

Words I don't normally allow in my vocabulary. Words that piss me off, especially when this beautiful creature is standing before me, sexed up and scented by me. The fragrance mingles with the hint of something floral yet spicy coming off her flesh. Her perfume was most noticeable in the crook of her neck where I nibbled and quickly discovered a trigger point on her. I want to bite her again and again.

But I—

Fuck my life. And fuck the Universe for being a bitch and setting someone like her in front of me. So tempting. So sweet.

This was the last thing I expected to happen when I entered the ballroom tonight. The last place I expected to be, but Nylah wanted to see me before the event tomorrow night.

Fucking fundraiser. I get that it's for a good cause, but in Joanna's name? My presence here makes me nearly physically sick.

I needed what this precious woman gave me.

Flower. The nickname is so fitting. That bright hair. The shape of her face. The length of her body, all tender curves and soft spots.

I don't want the night to end, and in another life, I'd invite her to my room. I'd spend more time with her. At least the full night.

Hell, I haven't even asked her name.

Glancing up at her, I decide maybe it's better if I don't know it. I'll only want to chase and right now I can only run in one direction—my future.

Something tells me she and I have a past. There is something undeniably recognizable about her and yet I cannot put my finger on the connection.

Asking her if we'd been together was a bit rash, even rude, but I'm not known to make smart decisions.

In fact, most people don't believe I'm smart enough to make any decisions for myself, let alone another human being.

But as I look at this girl—this stunning woman—none of that matters. I made a decision about her. Or maybe she made the decision for me. We fucked and I won't forget her again.

The way she responded to my kiss. Like lightning bolts and thunder strikes clapped. Maybe that was the storm outside, but still, something powerful happened between us.

And the way she clung to me, like she wanted to crawl under my skin. Staring at her, I bet a woman like her could wreck me.

The slow curl of her lips. The shyness in her smile. The lazy lift of her eyelids.

I'm used to aggressive women. Ones who tell you what they want and then take it from you.

Not this one. She didn't ask for anything. Not my name. Not more. She gave and I received. Then I took—her sounds, her taste, her orgasms.

Fuck, she is so pretty when she unfolds. Again, flower isn't the wrong nickname for her. She blossomed like a spring bloom. Like an awakening, which is a weird fucking comparison but the best I can do as my sluggish brain registers that my time is almost up.

Like fucking Cinderella at the ball, I only have until midnight and the time is almost here.

My shirt is a lost cause. The buttons scattered once she said she wanted to touch me. Wanted her hands on me. I almost lost it when she ran her palms over my chest, shoulders, and arms. Her touch was tender, caressing, calming, and yet, like a lick of flames, burning over my flesh and branding me. She's made a mark. A lasting one.

As I reach for my suit coat on the floor, an awkward tension swirls around us. The aftereffect.

In the past, I might have gotten her number. Told her I'd call. Maybe I would. Maybe I wouldn't. The intention is clear tonight. This is one night only.

But fuck, I want a second one with her.

Instead, I hold out my hand. Quietly, she places hers in mine, and I lead her toward the dance floor. The ballroom would be pitch black if it weren't for the natural light filtering in from the storm outside. The rain has settled to a steady drum against the windows. The beat soothing.

When we hit the middle of the floor, I stop abruptly, still holding her hand and spin her toward me. I'm not known for gracefulness and my sudden halt surprises her. She falls against my chest.

"Sorry," she mutters, keeping her eyes lowered but I need to see them one more time.

Tipping up her chin with the side of my hand, I catch her gaze. "Dance with me."

While there isn't a chandelier lighting the floor, or music filling the room, I want a few more minutes to hold her against me.

"Here?" she struggles with the word.

"It is a dance floor." The corner of my mouth ticks upward, teasing her, then my breath catches on the look in her eyes. The questioning gaze. The hesitant stare.

Ignoring anything that would make this moment complicated, I take her hand and drop my suit coat, settling my other hand on her hip. Tugging her, the sweet swell of her breasts covered in silk brushes against my bare chest in the opening exposed by my ruined shirt.

I tuck our joined hands over my heart and rock us side to side with no melody in mind other than the rattling inside my chest.

I don't think my heart has ever hammered this hard before.

Her breath tickles my neck. Her hand fits easily in mine. Her body molds against me. I try not to think of the snug fit of my cock inside her. How she hugged me, clung to me, like she never wanted me to leave her body.

Lowering my cheek, I run it along the side of her head, inhaling her scent again.

My granddad had a garden when I was a kid. The space was his pride and joy, next to me. I can't distinguish a rose from a daylily, but *her* fragrance reminds me of the bouquets he grew. The safety of his place.

I hum, both an inhale and a tune.

Too soon, an alarm on my phone is beeping, breaking into the peaceful silence of the room like a fucking fire alarm.

"Shit," I whisper, closing my eyes for half a second and dropping back my head. "I need to go."

I'm thankful she doesn't ask why, but then instantly want to tell her all the reasons I can't stay. There wouldn't be any point, though. I'm not going to see this precious flower again.

My life is too complicated and my future more than halfway across this country if all goes well in a few days.

That's the reason this night shouldn't have happened, but I have no regrets.

I'll savor these minutes, tucking them into my pocket like a cherished talisman. Then I remember the one around my neck, wishing it was some kind of magical camera that could take a snapshot of this woman. One I could look at in the future and remind me of this memory forever.

She steps out of my embrace and offers a knowing but timid smile. "I understand."

Two words. So simple. And yet I don't think anyone has ever understood me. I don't think anyone knows me.

As much as I'd like to share myself with her, I just can—

"If you don't mind, I'd like to exit first."

I arch a brow, smiling wide as I tease. "Don't want to expose our little secret?"

A clandestine meeting in a ballroom. I only know the word clandestine from my mother. The woman embodied the term.

My mystery woman dips her head, dropping her gaze from me again and smooths her hand over her belly.

I tip up her chin, gently pinching at the edge below her lip before running my thumb over her lips. "I'm teasing, flower."

She nods beneath my hold before I drop my fingers.

I'd like another kiss. One final farewell with her, but I don't ask, feeling like I've already taken too much from this innocent woman.

She nods again, taking one step back, then another, leaving me standing beneath the dark chandelier, before spinning on her heels and rushing to a chair at a table near the exit. She swipes up a tote bag, hitching it over her shoulder then spins to face me.

One final glance.

Her hand wraps around the long handle and tugs the door forward but she pauses in the slim line of light streaming in from the hallway.

Guess the power in this resort isn't out after all.

And as I watch her, she lifts her fingers to her lips before flipping them toward me, blowing on the tips like she's extinguishing candles on a birthday cake. Making a wish on the disappearing flames.

If only I could be her wish.
And she could me mine.
But she can't.

$$3$$

[Ruthie]

The night of the actual event, my dress is red. The deep crimson shade will be one among many women wearing the color in support of heart-health awareness for women. The gown has thick straps and is tightly cinched at my waist. Layers of chiffon create a full skirt which flows gracefully to the floor. The back dips dangerously deep to the curve of my lower back. I look like a princess.

Or, as Bolan called me, a beautiful flower.

My mother-in-law picked out this dress, insisting I wear it. The material is exquisite, the fit perfect, and the price out of my comfort zone. The gift, as Nylah maintained, is a sharp contrast to the drab, professional attire I wear daily.

The dress boosts my confidence which I haven't felt in years. Or maybe that's the lingering effects of last night. Regardless, I feel desirable, even beautiful, like I'm ready to take on the world. I can't remember the last time I'd been so extravagantly attired.

My wedding, perhaps?

Glancing at my reflection in the mirror before the festivities begin, I take a moment to note the intricate style in my blonde hair. The column of my throat is on display thanks to the elaborate up-do. Mentally, I envision Bolan's hand around my neck. I even inspect my flesh as if I can find signs of his touch, but the notion is silly.

Bolan Adler. What an unexpected flash from the past. What a new memory we've made.

When our night ended, we went our separate directions again after a romantic spin on the shadowed dance floor.

He smelled like leather and cinnamon, with that hint of lime still on him.

Our farewell would have been the perfect time to tell him I knew who he was. Who he'd been all those years ago, but I still didn't speak. I didn't want to tell him that I remembered him for fear that he didn't remember me. I feared that the kiss I hadn't been able to stop thinking about for over fifteen years would be a moment he didn't recall, and the embarrassment over something so important to me, that he'd forgotten, would have been damning to my spirit.

The secret of last night would be added as another layer to my former memory.

The stark nakedness of my left hand where my wedding band once rested is the reminder of all the reasons Bolan has been only a sliver of my history. The absence of that gold band is liberating.

I'd loved Clifton Jacobson with all my heart, but I'd been weighed down by our relationship. The last few years of his life had been trying, frustrating, upsetting. And then, there was heartbreak like no other.

The time has come for me to focus on myself.

Wearing silver stilettos bolsters my confidence as I enter the ballroom and fight the reminders of my Valentine's Eve. For the first half of the evening, I avoid glancing in the direction of the ballroom dance floor as well as the arched windows overlooking the ocean. Both locations are triggers. One reckless. One romantic. Collectively, they ignite something inside me. Something red hot and cherry sweet, like the color of my dress.

Like the dichotomy of my thoughts. The responsible side aghast at the reckless one while the wild side applauds the liberating burst of rebellion.

Eventually, I need air. I'd been suffocating under the pressure of well-meaning sympathy for Clifton's absence and the delicious new memories created in this very ballroom. Making my way to a second-floor balcony, a door exits onto a veranda. Bursting into the late-winter evening, I take a deep breath and exhale. The salty scent of the ocean burns my nostrils but clears my head.

In some small way, I'm relieved not to see Bolan Adler wandering the Coastal Resort ballroom. I'd known who he was last night, but would he recognize me in the light of day? Would he acknowledge that our paths crossed? Or would he keep our *new* secret?

Either way, the foolishness of my decision to have sex with him last night tolls like a funeral bell in my head.

Stupid. Stupid. Stupid.

Slamming my hands on the cement railing, I stare out at the swirling ocean. Inky black water churns beneath a moonless sky as I inhale again. My lungs then expel a heavy breath although my body pulses with an achy need I both recognize and reject.

I want to see him again.

However, it might be best that I don't. At least, not under the present circumstances. For once, I wanted to feel like I was the one who walked away, not the one left behind. Hope filled me that last night made an impression on him, and, at least for a little while, he might continue to wonder about the mysterious woman he'd met in an empty ballroom.

Maybe, just maybe, last night will be considered a magical moment for him.

It has certainly made its mark on me.

"Lady in red," a masculine voice gruffly intones behind me. "Or should I say my beautiful flower?"

Spinning, I see Bolan outlined by the interior lights behind him.

"Looking to jump?"

He has no idea how unfunny that comment is.

"Just trying to get some air," I murmur, turning around again, placing my back to him, but not before my brief glance takes in the fit of his tuxedo. Definitely custom tailored to fit the broadness of his shoulders and the solid columns of his thighs. His entire body screams strength.

With two broad steps, he's standing directly behind me, his mouth near my ear. Leather and cinnamon again. His presence overwhelms me, and my breath quickens, my chest rising and falling as if I'm unable to draw in enough oxygen.

"Looks like fate is on my side," he murmurs to my neck.

"Why's that?" I question, facing the black night as my head tips back like it has a will all its own.

"I was hoping to see you again." He chuckles softly, gently spinning me in order to step back and appraise my appearance. His eyes roam down my body while his fingertips hover just above my skin, along my exposed throat and over my collarbone before his gaze drops, along with his hand. "You're a vision. Truly stunning."

He sighs, pausing a second, before his gaze continues to skim over the swell of my breasts and the length of my dress. "Did you know that in the Japanese culture red is a sacred color. It means strength and sacrifice. But it also means peace and joy. Luck. So many emotions in one color."

With his final words, his eyes land on mine, as if he sees something deeper inside me.

The years of sacrifice. The strength it took and the willpower I'm mustering for the next steps in my life. The peace I want to have in the future. The need to experience joy.

My eyes begin to prickle. The sensation is strange, because I'm not sad, but overwhelmed. Like for just a moment, he sees me. Truly sees me.

He steps forward and twists me once again, bringing my back to his front, keeping his hands on my hips. His nose tickles the nape of my neck as he inhales.

"You smell heavenly, too, flower."

"Why do you call me that?" I choke, hating how much I like the nickname. The anonymity of it.

"My granddad had a garden when I was child. He loved his precious flowers." Bolan quietly chuckles. "The moment I saw you, you reminded me of one of them."

His hand gently encircles my throat and tips my head to the side with a press of his thumb on my jaw. Running his nose along the column once more, he inhales again. His lips follow the trail, tenderly sucking on my skin until he reaches my shoulder.

"You look like a delicate flower." He pauses, scraping his teeth over my clavicle. "One I want to pluck and keep, treasure even." He hums. "Want to bloom again, baby?"

Closing my eyes at the sudden burst of goosebumps on my flesh, I say, "I've never done anything like what we did last night." The one-night stand thing. The exhibitionistic risk of having sex in an empty ballroom where anyone at any time could have walked in.

Thrilling yet reckless, and so unlike me.

The moment has replayed in my head on repeat, but that's all it can be—another moment.

And I should tell him who I am.

"That ballroom seems to be an aphrodisiac, flower. It makes me want you in the worst way."

"And wanting me is bad?" I ask as his lips tickle my ear. Again, I don't want to be considered a mistake. I know all about making poor decisions. I don't want to be on the receiving end of one.

"Not bad," he growls, sending shivers down my spine. "But I've never been good at following the rules."

"And there are rules?" I question.

"Ones I want to smash to smithereens."

With him cupping my throat, possessive and strong, he nips at my flesh, while his thumb presses against my pulse, and I don't want to follow rules either. And the distraction of his mouth on my skin tips me over the decision point.

Whispered like a silent prayer, I suggest, "One more time."

"One more." Bolan's hand instantly rounds my waist and lowers to scrunch up the material of my skirt.

"You have on too many layers, beautiful." He chuckles against my skin until his hand is beneath my dress and between my thighs. He pushes aside the slip of underwear and easily slides a finger into me.

"Ready to blossom, like I thought." He hums and I tip back my head, swallowing hard against his hand cupping my throat.

I'm rewarded with a second finger easily slipping inside me.

"Things are fucked up, flower." Desperation fills his voice.

I hear it, feel it in my core. I know about that sensation—feeling fucked up.

"We need to be quiet," he whispers into my neck, skimming his nose to my shoulder.

Sounds like a rule I want to break.

He removes his fingers from me, and I whimper at the

sudden loss, deflating just a smidge. The unlatching of his belt jangles behind me, instantly restoring the fever. The burning desire to have him inside me one more time.

I hike up the back of my dress while he lowers his pants enough to free his thick cock from the confines.

"Hold on, sweetheart," he coos, running his palm up my exposed back and bending me over the cool cement barrier. I hear the distinct crinkle of a package, then he's lining himself up at my entrance.

His thrust inward is sharp and quick, like he entered me last night, and I cry out at the sensation.

The fullness steals my breath. The connectedness ratchets up my heart.

In this position, he hits me in a new way. A raw, intense way. And I arch into him, attempting to keep him deeply seated inside me.

He pulls away, surges forward, draws back. In and out, the frenzy begins. My hands keep my delicate dress from scraping on the rough cement railing as he surges into me hard and deep. He cups my throat while slipping his other hand to my tender clit, teasing the sacred spot as he enters me.

Another stolen moment. The unabashed fucking. *God, I'm going to hell for this.*

As he hitches forward, I lift one knee to the railing, balancing precariously on one stiletto heel.

"Fuck, flower," he grunts as I open wider for him. He groans, "Wish I could keep you. Want to make things better."

I have no idea what he means but I'm too lost in the pleasure he's producing in my body. To the possession of his powerful thrusts. To the cupping of my throat like he intends to keep me.

Like I could be his.

Too quickly, my body reacts, and like the waves crashing below against the rocky bluff, I break, biting my lip to hold back the shout of joy. The cry of a release as strong as the rolling ocean. Wave after wave crests and breaks within me, shattering against my rock-hard heart and my soft petals as he calls them, until he stills behind me, buried deep inside me. His own swirling current of release happens.

"Holy shit." His forehead presses against my shoulder blade. His breathing exaggerated.

The time passed too quickly. Sixty-seconds, perhaps? Another minute.

Bolan kisses my shoulder before he pulls out of me. To my surprise, a cool strip of cotton swipes at the mess we've made between my thighs. Peering over my shoulder, I see him folding an honest to goodness handkerchief before slipping it into his pocket.

Slowly standing upright, my knees wobble. My legs are unsteady as the layers of my dress tumble back down to my ankles.

He steadies me with a hand on my hip, then he leans forward and softly kisses me. The brush of his lips is a goodbye. Like that tender kiss he snuck in after our first sixty seconds all those years ago.

What had he said earlier about wishing to keep me, wanting to do better? I should ask for more details, but he's leading me toward the interior of the building with a gentle but firm hand on my elbow.

When he stops just outside the entrance to the inner hallway, he turns toward me, cups both my cheeks and gives me a final kiss that is hot and desperate, heady and rushed, reminding me of that first kiss we shared more than a decade ago.

What's that saying about love in reverse? Is this a kiss on rewind? We're back to where we started.

And we cling to one another as if we won't ever see each

other again. When we break apart, I finally question him as if I don't already know the answer. "What's your name?"

If I thought asking him would trigger his memory, I'm wrong.

The moment is gone. Another set of sixty seconds is over in a flash.

Without an answer, a sad smile rests in its place. He tucks my arm into the crook of his elbow and leads me back into the building, guiding me toward the top of the staircase. Once there, he finally turns to me, something haunting and dark fills those forest-colored eyes as he unhooks my hand from his arm and gives it a final squeeze.

"I'm truly sorry," he mumbles, contrite like he'd been last night. Like he's genuinely apologetic for what we've done, but the apology feels more like a foreshadowing. Like he's sorry for what's to come.

Perhaps I should apologize. "I have something to tell you."

The distinct sound of heels on marble steps travels upward to where we stand, and I turn when I hear a familiar voice call out my name.

"Ruthie, darling, I've been looking for you." Nylah sounds both breathless and worrisome. My mother-in-law is a strikingly good-looking woman in her late fifties with flawless skin and a wide grin. She's also wearing red, although her dress is a bit more subdued, less whimsical than mine.

"Ruthie?" Bolan struggles over my name.

When I glance at him, his brows are severely pinched. He looks from me to Nylah and back.

A second set of heels follows the racing of the first, although the newer steps are more methodic, as if someone is taking her time to climb the staircase.

Click-click-click. Like a clock counting down to midnight.

"Oh, Bolan, I've been looking for you as well," Nylah addresses the man standing a good foot away from me. An invisible shield of space between us. We are no longer the couple fused together on the balcony but strangers. Well, at least one of us is, and the other is about to learn a hard truth.

"There you are." The second woman's voice is breathy, seductive and deep, unlike mine. She's tall and lanky, yet hour-glass-shaped with sleek red hair in one perfect wave cascading down her head to the middle of her back. She's intimidatingly beautiful and she comes to a full stop beside Bolan and places her hand on his chest. Her bright red nails stand out in sharp contrast to his white tuxedo shirt.

I take a second perusal of his appearance. The tailored tuxedo. Those deep green eyes. Trimmed facial hair that is still scratch worthy.

I cup the side of my neck, curious if he left marks on my skin.

He's certainly imprinted on my soul again.

Then my eyes catch on those feminine nails, filed to nearly pointed tips, and pressed against his chest, like blood stains on white cotton.

Full-on panic takes over, gripping my chest like a vise clamped around my ribs, as if my insides know something is terribly wrong before my brain can compute the issue. Suddenly, I can't get enough oxygen.

"Melody," Bolan whispers to this other woman although his eyes do not leave mine. His body stands ramrod stiff while she leans into him, evidently rather familiar with him, as she tips her head to his shoulder.

"Ruthie, darling," Nylah addresses me once more, but I can't seem to take my eyes off him. Off them.

This cannot be happening to me. Again.

"I see you've met Bolan," Nylah states, breaking into my thoughts.

I turn toward my mother-in-law, blinking, the movement lazy like I've been drugged and evidence of my confusion.

"Bolan Adler," she clarifies. "Joanna's son."

I turn back toward him, trying to identify any resemblance to his mother, Nylah's cousin, her best friend.

"That means—" I lamely point at him as my mind filters through the facts.

Joanna's son. He's practically family. He was Clifton's cousin once removed. Had he been close all this time, and yet completely out of reach? How had I not known? How was I not aware of this connection?

But then another thought slams into me.

As a member of the family, Bolan is a special project taken on last minute by Imperial Sports Management. Despite working directly with Jared, I didn't know all the details. He'd wanted to handle this "new client delicately" on his own. However, the information slipped in a conversation with Nylah.

Joanna Frederick's son.

Who happens to be Bolan Adler.

Until this moment, I hadn't connected the dots. Never knew there were dots to be connected.

"We should really be getting downstairs," Melody speaks up. She squeezes his chin, but he flinches his head away from her touch. Her eyes narrow, and she stiffens, standing straighter beside him.

"Yes. Yes," Nylah chuckles, the sound both light and tense, although I'm not certain she understands where the tension truly rests. From her next comment, her own reason to rush Bolan off becomes clear. "It's almost time. The big speech."

"You're a guest speaker this evening?" I ask, sounding dumbfounded while still unable to pull my gaze from him.

He wasn't on the roster. I didn't even know he'd be here.

"A last-minute addition. We thought it'd be nice to have one of Joanna's sons speak," Nylah clarifies.

Bolan scoffs. The sound is its own statement, but I can't

process the meaning. Joanna's other sons declined the invitation to attend tonight.

"I see," I whisper, lowering my gaze and my head when I don't understand anything.

What is even happening?

"Maybe we should make our announcement this evening," Melody adds, her voice sugary sweet to disguise the venom underneath.

"What announcement?" I look up again as Bolan closes his eyes, cutting off the forest, like he's chopping down all the trees inside.

"I'm the future Mrs. Adler." Melody nearly simpers, shimmying her shoulders back and forth, like it's the best news.

"You're married!" I shriek, jumping over the *future* part and glaring at Bolan while bile fills my throat. The same throat he cupped, only minutes ago. My stomach churns and swirls, like the violent waves of the ocean outside these walls. My breath comes hard and fast, lungs constricting with each painful attempt to drag in air.

Bolan's lids flip open. His eyes wide, panic swirling in that sea of green. His voice is strained when he says, "Not yet." He keeps his eyes focused on me and I watch them slide from that moment of fear to shuttered darkness, like he's closing me off.

His declaration does nothing to settle the nausea in my belly or make my sudden dizziness disappear.

"But you're engaged?" I clarify, my voice still shrill but quieting, as I glare at him. He has the grace to look away from me. Or is he a coward, afraid to face what he's done? What *we* did? Before he marries someone else.

"Ruthie." Nylah chuckles tersely. "What has gotten into you?"

Him, I want to scream but I can't state the truth.

He was just inside me on the balcony. Filling me up and stripping me down.

This level of shocking rejection and betrayal is certainly appropriate for an event named The Red Dress Affair.

All those scarlet gowns downstairs match the color of my shattering heart, like violent red petals scattered in the wind.

For half a second, I wonder if Clifton ever felt this way about his past actions. This searing pain of regret. The blazing brand of a giant scarlet A on my chest.

However, I don't take the time to wallow in misery. I'll do that as soon as I get away from here. From him.

And like Cinderella, I race from the party.

Saving myself with no seconds to spare.

4

[Bolan]

The second Ruthie runs off, I want to chase her. Hell, I want to run away with her.

I even take a step forward until the hand on my chest reminds me why I can't follow her.

Because I've promised to behave, when, dammit, everything about my flower makes me want to throw caution to the wind.

Of course, my mystery woman in red is none other than Ruth Avery, Nylah and Jared's beloved daughter-in-law. Or should I say, widowed daughter-in-law as they lost their son eighteen months ago, which means Ruthie lost her husband.

Fuck.

As once-removed relatives because our mothers were first cousins, Clifton and I were never close. After he failed in professional football, he'd been some fucking war hero, while I've been nothing but a failure in life despite being an award-winning professional baseball catcher. Most of those honors coming from the Japanese league.

Having proven myself time and again in the ballpark, off the field, I am still a wreck.

Exhibit A: Ruthie. Who looked absolutely crushed.

"That was unnecessary," I turn toward Melody Cross, my attorney's niece who agreed to a farce that would elevate my reputation and pad her bank account.

"What?" Her faux-innocence is not lost on me. She even places her fingers at her throat, the move intended to express her false sincerity.

"I'll find Ruthie. Bolan, get to the stage," Nylah demands, narrowing her eyes at me.

My mother's cousin is a force. She's also the wife of my new agent and she's going to *unalive* me if she learns what happened between Ruthie and me.

Then again, I wonder if Ruthie will keep our time together a secret. Maybe she'll keep the memory to herself.

Does one share with her mother-in-law when she fucks someone other than the woman's son?

Fuck!

Thoughts of Ruthie scramble through my head. The way she responded to me. The way she opened for me. Fucking blooming right beneath my fingers.

I attempt to shake the memories, knowing a simple wiggle of my head will not make me forget her.

With leaden feet, I trudge down the marble staircase with Melody at my side. Sure, she's pretty and sexy in her slinky red dress, which makes her look like Jessica Rabbit. However, she's a bit of a viper underneath, and while I might like aggressive women, Melody is more manipulative and shady than confident or confidante. Since meeting Ruthie, tender, sweet wallflowers with hidden depth and kinks might be more my speed.

I can't even think about how stunning she looks in that red

dress. Like I told her, the color represents strength, and Ruthie certainly displayed poise. Before her escape, she held her ground, keeping her emotions in check regardless of the shock. She hid her surprise and disappointment at the shitshow of my life.

"You know nothing is concrete yet," I remind the woman beside me. My attorney, Floyd Everest, is the one who thought up this ridiculous plan. Jared Jacobson, as my agent, hadn't been onboard at first, but he understands the stakes.

The Chicago Anchors want a family man, and I want the Chicago Anchors.

"It's practically written in cement," Melody scoffs, thumping down the stairs along with me.

The check might be printed, but no pen hasn't hit the paper. I still have a final say in how this so-called plan goes down.

The Reputation Repair Report. The goal is to give the impression of a family man.

And I've fucked up. If Jared finds out what I've done, if the Anchors know ... *I'm* done.

However, being with Ruthie hadn't felt like I'd fucked up. In fact, being with her felt right, felt strangely perfect, like I was where I was supposed to be for the first time in my life, and I wasn't referring to the baser desire of wanting sex.

There was something about her that felt familiar, almost like she was someone ... I couldn't live without. Which made no sense. Still, there'd been an urgency when I saw her in that empty ballroom. A need to know her, intimately and quickly, before she slipped through my fingers like a lost opportunity.

Right person, wrong moment, because the universe continues to conspire against me.

But if I don't get this contract ... If I can't transition to the States. If I can't do better for Tulane ...

Fuck. Fuck. *Fuck.*

As I hit the first floor, I close my eyes and swipe a hand down my freshly trimmed scruff to clear my head.

Tulane. I need to do better for her. *She's* my reason for all the changes that must happen.

My little girl is all that matters.

And while Melody might not be the ideal wife or optimal option for a stepmother, she is willing to help, for a fee, and the fame of being linked to my name. Bad reputation and all.

My sudden fatherhood is the question, thus a wife to dispel rumors and make me look stable. Responsible.

Because . . . Chicago Anchors.

My granddad was a huge fan, and he would be so proud if he were still alive. Well, maybe not proud because of how things went with Ruthie. Definitely not particularly happy that I'm willing to pay a woman to pretend to be my wife. And he'd probably be a little upset that I got someone pregnant, didn't know it, and didn't step up immediately because of that lack of knowledge.

Yeah, his disappointment might be more the call here.

But I'm taking control of my life now.

Everything is for Tulane.

THE SPEECH I gave about my mother nearly choked me. As the family outlier, the successful yet still fucked-up one in everyone's eyes, I don't know how I got the honor—said with all the sarcasm—of speaking on her behalf. If anything, most might say I'm the reason she had a bad heart.

However, my mother eventually became indifferent toward me.

And it's the reason I want to be the best parent I can be for Tulane.

"How was she?" I whisper, entering the Coastal Resort hotel suite after closing the door with a quiet *snick*.

"She's an angel. Went to bed at seven. No fuss." LaToya is a grandmotherly-type woman Nylah found through a vetted babysitter app to help me out over the weekend.

Last night, I'd wanted to invite my flower—*Ruthie*—back to my room. I would have done what we did earlier in the evening on repeat if I had. I would have held her longer, breathed her in better, and taken a fucking minute to enjoy her.

Instead, our night ended when she asked me to let her exit the ballroom first, like I was a dirty little secret she didn't want anyone to know about. When she hadn't known my name or my reputation. She didn't know the fuck-up, fuck-about guy practically kicked out of the professional league Stateside and shipped off to Japan for years. She didn't know anything about me, which made her all the more enticing.

Ruthie didn't want anything from me *but me*.

However, another little blossom was the real reason I couldn't bring Ruthie to my room.

My Tulip. Tulane Grace Adler. My sweet, sixteen-month-old daughter who I didn't know existed until last summer.

I am a dad. While my role as a catcher at the top of the ball-field is something I take great pride in, this new title is one that both astounds me and fills me with awe.

Tulane is a wonder, and I've made her a silent promise.

I will not be my mother. I won't even be my father.

At thirty-six, I can do this. Fatherhood. I just need a new baseball team. I don't have many years left in me to play so these final seasons need to count. And I'm grateful the Chicago Anchors are interested.

With a contingency.

Bolan Adler needs a wife.

With a tired smile at LaToya, I thank her again for her time. From my hotel doorway I watch her walk down the hallway to the elevator bank. Her payment was covered through the sitter app. Childcare is going to be an issue once I reach Chicago. However, that is a future-me concern.

I shrug out of my jacket and peel off my bow tie. With a sharp tug, I pull my shirt from my pants and lose the starchy material. Quietly, I enter the bedroom off the living room in the suite and stand over Tulip's portable crib. Her sweet little butt is in the air with her legs tucked underneath her. A shock of red curls tickles her nape. Her lips are parted, occasionally pressing together, like she's dreaming of sucking her pacifier. The one that has popped out of her mouth and rests on the mattress a few inches from her.

Sometimes, the urge to pick her up and just hold her against me is overwhelming, but I quickly learned you don't mess with a sleeping baby.

My Hiroshima teammates were amazing when Tulip unexpectedly arrived mid-season. I didn't have a clue how to handle an infant. Röki Enomoto, our star pitcher, had an elderly grandmother, Honoka, who taught me the things I didn't know, like how to warm a bottle or change a diaper. She also took care of Tulip for me. For a single parent, the life of a professional athlete on the road half the season was not ideal.

I needed a partner.

A full-time nanny, Jared suggested.

A wife, my attorney proposed.

I definitively argued they are *not* the same thing. However, Floyd clarified that a wife gave the impression of a family man, and a family man was the only person the Chicago Anchors would entertain after a recent scandal within their team.

As I stare down at Tulane, I wonder what Ruthie would think of her. What she'd think of me suddenly acting all responsible and father-like.

There was something special about Ruthie, delicate about

her. She wasn't fragile. The woman had thorns, but she also didn't look like someone out to purposely harm anyone.

I'd hurt her. Those deep dark eyes of her said it all. The wound almost like an open gash on her chest.

I'm such an asshole. I could say my dick is what got me into this mess—the attraction to Ruthie—but that hadn't been it. There was something *more* about her. That strange sense of familiarity. A weird vibe that resonated around us when I first entered that ballroom and stumbled upon her in the corner.

A lone wallflower in the vacant room. A bit poetic for a guy like me, but that's the first thing I thought of when I saw her. Like she belonged in a historical romance, but she wasn't someone who should be contained to something one-dimensional. Ruthie had other sides, curves, and angles, that I'll never get to explore.

With a heavy thud, I sit on the edge of the bed and stare at the portable crib. I'm exhausted and still working off the jetlag of traveling from Japan only a few days ago.

With thick fingers, I reach for the amulet hanging at my throat. A good luck charm, Honoka explained, slipping it over my head on the day I left her country. Leaving Japan had been bittersweet, but it was the right thing to do.

For Tulane.

I swipe a hand over my face, able to smell Ruthie on my fingers. Her flavor lingers in my mouth from yesterday evening. She was tart limes and sharp gin and fucking refreshing.

Melody, on the other hand, is the wrong woman to be my wife or act as Tulip's mother. She won't be Tulane's parent per our agreement. A nanny will be employed to care for Tulane when I can't directly. Melody would be my wife in name only, for occasional appearances. Nothing about Melody says life partner, and my concerns and doubts have grown hourly since this proposal was sent to me.

But I've run out of options and time. Catchers and pitchers

reported a week ago to spring training. I'm down to the wire and I'll be a late addition, but the Chicago Anchors need a second catcher. Opening day of spring training is this coming Friday.

And tomorrow, I have a meeting with Jared and Floyd outside of normal business hours, where the final call to the Chicago Anchors will be made, and my future solidified, one way or another.

I squeeze the medal between my fingers. The Japanese writing etched from top to bottom.

Please let my future point forward.

Chicago Anchors or bust.

5

———

[Bolan]

The morning after The Red Dress Event, I don't know that I've ever been so anxious in my life. My meaty palms sweat. My pits are damp.

This is it. The big moment. Deal or no deal.

A future Chicago Anchor or a sunken ship.

I'm being melodramatic. But it isn't just my future on the line. Every decision is for Tulane. I've made enough money over the years to keep us in good standing for a while, but I haven't had the payouts that garner endless retirement after playing. And the bigger problem is I don't know what I'll do once I'm forced to leave the sport.

I picture used car salesman or mattress seller, and my stomach twists. I'm not qualified for anything other than playing baseball.

With these thoughts rumbling around in my head, I trip over my own feet as I enter the conference room at Imperial Sports

Management. I don't typically wear what most consider dress shoes and the tight leather, plus hard soles, cause me to stumble.

The room is overly bright. Uncovered windows allow in brilliant streams of sunlight. The conference table is vivid white, reflecting more light throughout the space. But the thing —*no, person*—who blinds me is the woman standing near a sidebar setting down coffee mugs.

That hair. The shape of her hips. The curve of her ass.

Blindfolded, I could recognize her, and I saunter up behind her, chasing images in my head of her in a red dress, bent forward and hitching up her leg, allowing me to enter her.

"Flower?" I whisper, catching my breath on her nickname. Her strange mix of floral and spice, like petals and thorns, tickles my nose.

When she spins to face me, an empty coffee mug drops from her hand, but I'm quick to catch it, holding the loose cup an additional second.

My first reaction is to smile at her. A little blip inside my chest is relieved to see her again. See her whole and in front of me.

But then my slog of a brain catches up to our position.

Ruthie is Nylah's daughter-in-law. She's in Jared Jacobson's office. Which means she must have known who I was all along.

My eyes narrow, suspicion quickly settling in my head.

"Ruth Avery, is it?" I question, although we never exchanged names. She asked, but I never answered. "Why aren't you Ruth Jacobson?" Why doesn't she have her husband's name? Then again, nepotism runs in this industry and maybe the name keeps the vultures away from her. Gives her a little anonymity. After all, my little flower is tempting.

"I don't see how that's any of your business." The strength of her words and her tone surprises me, and I startle further when she hastily snatches the fallen mug from my hand.

She's so fucking pretty despite her hair being pulled severely back in a bun and red framed glasses that hide her rich brown eyes, that are soulful and bottomless. A man could get lost in those eyes. *Or be found.*

Ruthie fumbles with the collection of coffee mugs on the banquet table before pouring a cup of the steamy liquid.

"What are you doing here?"

"I work here."

I lower my gaze, shaking my head. Incredible. "So, you knew who I was?" *She fucking knew.*

And because I'm terrible at keeping first thoughts in my head and ruminating over them a moment, I blurt, "Did you fucking play me?"

Her head swings quickly in my direction. Those dark eyes narrowing to slits behind those red frames. Glasses that make me want to be a bad boy, sent to the principal's office. She's the principal. And that glare does nothing but stir my insides and pump my dick.

Fuck.

"Why would I play *you*?" She continues to stare at me until snapping her attention back to the coffee bar. "Shit."

Hot liquid has dribbled over the edge of the mug and onto her fingers, and she lifts one to suck at it.

Those red-rimmed lips wrap around her burnt digit and my thoughts race with visions of her placing those lips on a body part of mine.

She'd wanted to do it the other night. I sensed her eagerness. Saw the hunger in her dark eyes.

I'd been the one too hyped up and wanting inside her, skipping over her mouth on my dick for my dick inside her.

I slip my hand into my suit coat pocket and pull something out. "Here."

Ruthie glances down at the item and scoffs. Then those

chocolate eyes flick back up to mine. "What do you think you are doing?"

In my hand are her panties from the other night. The ones I removed from her lush legs and tucked into my suit pocket, forgetting that I had them stored there until I was checking my pockets earlier. I'd decided to leave them tucked in the pocket, like a good luck talisman. I hadn't intended to make them a souvenir of our night but I'm happy to have them, especially when I recall how I removed them down those lush thighs. How I tugged them from her ankles. How taking them off gave me a clear view of her pretty, pink—

I clear my throat. "You burned yourself." Although a napkin would really be more appropriate, I want her to know I'm not going to forget our night together and I'm not going to forget her.

I'm especially not going to forget that she knew me and acted like she didn't.

She glances around my bulky form at Floyd Everest, my attorney, seated at the conference table. Then she looks back at me.

"*You* burned me," she whispers, dragging her gaze away from me and lowering her eyes to the coffee mug on the side-bar. Despite her quiet tone, her statement stings.

"And you fucking knew who I was, didn't you?"

Her head snaps upright again and those dark wells widen as she stares at me. "I—"

A loud clap makes both of us turn our heads in the direction of the conference room doorway where Jared Jacobson enters like a strong breeze. The early-sixty-something man is silver-haired and smooth-faced with a powerful smile.

"Excellent. I see we are all present." He crosses the room to me and holds out a hand to shake mine. Quickly, I slip Ruthie's underwear back into my pocket.

"Bolan." Despite being a slightly smaller man, Jared has a

firm handshake. After greeting me, he addresses Ruthie. "Ruth."

The formal nod might appear curt if it weren't for the admiration in this man's eyes for his daughter-in-law. My late cousin's wife. A widow.

Goddammit.

I don't want to feel sympathy for her. She had to have known who I was when she saw me. I'm Imperial Sports Management's newest client. I'm her late husband's cousin. Surely, she's heard of me.

But something about the way her shoulders fall, and her head lowers tells me the moment Ruthie and I shared wasn't about recognition. Wasn't about fame or a claim to have slept with Bolan Adler.

"You should take a seat," she mutters, heading toward the conference room exit.

Suddenly, I want her to stay, like I'd asked her to the other night. When I wanted her to give me a chance to prove myself. I'm not a bad guy. Maybe a bit impulsive. Definitely reckless. But I'm open to change.

I want to do better.

The strange vibe that she's familiar spirals around me. I could chalk it up to how familiar I now am with her body, but this sensation isn't about her body. Something tells me I need Ruthie to remain present.

"Why don't you—" I'm cut off when Jared addresses Ruthie.

"Ruth, if you could close the door, please, and then join us." He rounds the room near the windows, claps Floyd on the shoulder and stops near the head of the conference table.

"What?" Ruth and I say in unison, then share a look with one another.

"I have a few things I'd like to discuss with both of you," Jared clarifies.

Does he know what we did? Fuck.

I glance at Ruthie again, but her head hangs low, as if unable to look at either Jared or me, and I don't like it. Especially the not looking at me part. I never want her to feel like she can't look me in the eye.

I made a mistake. Not her.

But like most of my impulsive decisions, I don't know how to rectify them.

I don't know how to make things right.

I can never catch a fucking break.

6

[Ruthie]

I was having a trifecta of bad luck when it came to Bolan Adler.

Working for a sports agency, I was well-versed in baseball terms, and three strikes meant I was out.

First, there had been that stupid kiss experiment back in college, where I'd quickly learned after the project who Bolan Adler was. He *was* an athlete, popular, and arrogant.

Next, I had what I'd thought would be a one-night stand turned into a two-time tryst with the man.

And now, I am sitting across from him in my father-in-law's office where Bolan is our newest client with an absurd plan to return him to professional baseball in the United States.

I hadn't typed up the report, having another, more pressing client to work on while Jared himself took over the entry of our newest case in the Imperial Sports Management family.

Ha, family! Bolan had been part of mine all these years.

And now, one ridiculous line in the unofficial Repair Reputation Report is ludicrous.

Bolan Adler needs a wife.

Equally preposterous is the gleam in Bolan's eyes as he stares at me across the white tabletop in the sunny morning conference room.

His gaze assesses me, questions me.

Dark as a forest and equally enticing, his eyes lure me into their mystery and mirth.

Fooling me once had by no means been Bolan's fault. I'd signed up for that experiment.

But fool me twice had totally been on me. I recognized who he was—as my kiss partner. He, however, did not remember me. I hadn't made an impression on the campus-popular jock who was an all-star baseball player and a relentless manwhore when he was twenty-something.

Those labels certainly explained how he knew how to kiss so well. Years later, my lips would still tingle, like a phantom kiss lingered on them, whenever I thought about that moment. A kiss that marked me because it was given by him.

The ghost-kiss could now be attributed to the kisses he'd given me in the past forty-eight hours.

I'd never been so reckless. I was a rule-follower. *Responsible Ruthie.* I was damn sick of it.

Especially with Clifton gone, I want to take back my life, whatever that might mean. I'd been his girlfriend and wife for so long, I no longer knew myself. My journey had been Clifton's adventures. NFL player. Military man. All around good guy, just not a great husband. His final years had been the most difficult.

Signs everyone wanted to ignore but me.

As I sit across from Bolan, I'm thankful there is no resemblance to Cliff. Bolan's rusty-brown hair is cut stylish, shorter up the back and a bit longer on top, with a matching trimmed beard along his rounder face. His cheeks aren't edgy, but firm and proportionate to the broad width of his shoulders and thickness of his thighs. At just over six feet, he's a powerhouse of a man in comparison to my late husband.

I am not a sports agent. I had a failed attempt at being one roughly ten years ago for an up-and-coming fighter named Abel Callahan and never wanted to look back on the experience. The forceful nature required to be an agent wasn't in my makeup. I was better as an assistant, and I'd been one to Jared Jacobson ever since the *incident* during my first assignment.

As to Bolan needing a wife, my thoughts flip back to yesterday evening, and the sexy, red-dressed brunette and her red nails on Bolan's chest.

I hated those red nails.

I hate him more.

And myself.

My inner core disagrees with the strong emotion. In fact, my body has quite the opposite reaction to Bolan Adler, who sits across from me and stares at me like he wants to devour me on this conference room table. Spread me wide and make another feast of me.

He'd fucking rocked my world. There was no less floral way to put it. The way he'd kissed me. The way he moved me. The way his fingers felt, and his tongue worked and his thick—

"Ruth?"

"Yeah." I choke, quickly turning my head in my father-in-law's direction. A man who *is* a reminder of my late husband and what he would have looked like, had he grown older. The thin face. The perfectly sculpted silver hair. The soft, brown eyes, staring at me with concern.

"Are you listening?"

"Yes. Sure. Of course." *Absolutely not.* I fidget in my seat, straightening my shoulders and smoothing down my skirt beneath the table. Today's outfit is a dove-gray pencil-cut skirt and a matching silk blouse. While the color sounds pretty, the combination is dull against my pale skin and a reminder of my even duller wardrobe. I've paired the ensemble with bright red high-heels and red-framed glasses. My little act of rebellion against both the outfit and my life lately. Perhaps I've been a little emboldened since Valentine's Eve.

"Bolan asked if there was any chocolate milk," Jared clarifies for me.

"Chocolate milk?" I repeat, like I don't understand the concept. Or maybe it's that I don't understand why a grown man, mid-thirties, wants a child-like drink.

I glance back at him, where he's casually leaning one elbow on the thick armrest of the swivel chair on the opposite side of the table from me. His fingertips brush over his lips as he watches me. Lips that kissed me. Fingers that intimately touched me.

As I continue to stare at him, the corner of his mouth curls. A knowing spark lights those damn eyes.

"I'll go find some." I stand abruptly, roughly pushing back my chair, in my need for space from him and distance from this room. If I need to drive to a suburb outside this Los Angeles office to find chocolate milk, I will. Hell, I'll even milk a cow and melt the chocolate necessary to combine the two ingredients if it gets me away from Bolan.

And the conflicting tingle on my flesh that's a combination of both the pleasure he brought me and the shame I feel that I slept with an engaged man.

"I'll help." Bolan swiftly presses up out of his chair and straightens the two sides of his suit jacket. The same jacket he'd been wearing the other night when we—

"I could use a stretch," Bolan adds.

"Is your knee bothering you again?" Jared asks. An injury is one of an athlete's greatest fears and an agent's biggest worry. A catcher with knee problems is a major red flag.

"Just need a moment to loosen up. And get some chocolate

milk," Bolan replies jovially to Jared but keeps his eyes trained on me.

On hasty legs, I exit the conference room, turning left toward the office's kitchen. I doubt I'll find chocolate milk in there, but stranger items have mysteriously appeared in the refrigerator.

"Ruthie," Bolan follows close behind me, whispering my name in the empty hallway.

I ignore him and walk faster.

"Flower," he calls next, groaning the term of endearment in the same way he spoke to me before we learned each other's names. Or at least, before he learned mine.

"Nope." I hiss, giving him the back of my hand and speed-walking what is only a few feet and yet feels like a mile to the dang kitchen area.

Only I'm not fast enough for a man who averages four point three-five seconds from home plate to first base, which is roughly ninety feet on a baseball diamond.

His hand gently cups my elbow, causing me to stop and face him.

"Rue."

"No." I shake my head. No more nicknames. No more touching me. No more looking at me with eyes that appear contrite, almost sad, when he should not feel anything but apologetic. Even regret.

Regret at what we did. Regret over who I am.

Regretful Ruth. That should be my new label.

"What do you want, Bolan?" Besides chocolate milk.

"I want to explain."

"You don't owe me anything." I glance away from him, staring absentmindedly into the vacant kitchen.

Today is Sunday, and Bolan is being given special treatment as both our newest client, and apparently as a distant family member. The deadline for a new acquisition to a major league team is the opening day of spring training which is rapidly approaching. As a catcher, he should have reported to a team last week.

While I'm saying I don't need an explanation, I'd still like one. I'm so tired of cheating men. Men who think they can get away with anything with a smile on their lips and a twinkle in their eyes. *And a damn dimple near their mouth.* Charismatic men who lure you in with promises, keep you with apologies, and then do the same thing over and over again.

Fool me once or twice? *Ha.* I've written the playbook on being fooled three times, and I'm not thinking about Bolan right now.

But he is a man, so hear my wrath. Well, the mental one. Because Responsible Ruthie does not complain. She does not speak up or cry out. She does not have sex with a man on a whim in a deserted ballroom. And then fuck him a second time on a balcony wearing a ballgown.

I close my eyes, not wanting to remember those reckless acts with him.

How many more missteps can I take with this man?

"I *need* to explain and apologize. I—"

I hold up my hand to stop him and tilt my head, certain I've heard a noise. A sound one typically does not hear in our office. The sharp strained sound of—

"Is that a baby?" My brows severely crease as I glance around Bolan's broad shoulder toward the hallway at his back.

"What? A baby? What baby? Here?" Bolan scoffs, then stiffens. His face goes ashen. He heard it too, and suddenly those moss-colored eyes are wildly shifting side-to-side.

"I think—" I step left but Bolan follows blocking my path.

"I swear I heard—" I step right, and Bolan moves again as well.

Until once more, the disconcerting wail of a young child echoes down the hallway from the opposite end of the office.

Bolan closes his eyes and then spins on his hard-soled shoes and struts down the hall with me on his tail. He snags his foot once on the carpet, curses, and then continues.

As he breaks through the entrance to the lobby, my heels skitter to a halt as I take in the sight before me.

Nylah is holding a young child in her arms. A red-headed cherub I'd put at roughly a year, year and a half old, who is crying unconsolably. Nylah Jacobsen is a pillar of strength despite her small stature. She's a force, as in she knows who she is and what she wants, and she wants it yesterday.

"Yesterday, I said. Now, would you like a chocolate or vanilla frosted donut with a sprinkle of pistachios?" Commands wrapped in kind acts are not uncommon from her. She'd make a great sports agent.

Holding a baby, though, clearly makes her uncomfortable and is the last sight I expected to see.

"Whatsamatter, Tulip?" Bolan coos. His typically rugged voice drops down to light sandpaper against wood as he reaches for the little girl who spins in Nylah's arms and tips toward Bolan.

In comparison to Nylah, Bolan Adler holding the child looks right.

And out of place.

I mean, this is Bolan. Phantom Kisser. One-night Stand Man. Fiancé to Another. With a baby.

"You're a father?" My voice comes with a squeak.

A baby. The words are a soft whisper through my head as my eyes are locked on the sweet child in his arms. The term is a soothing coo of excitement while my heart shatters in a new way which has nothing to with Bolan and yet he's a catalyst once more.

"You have a baby?" My throat is tight, the question constricting my airways, coming out quiet and strangled.

"Rue," Bolan states, although I'd just told him no more nicknames. No more soft growls and placating tones.

He glances at the bundle in his arms, jostling the crying toddler. "Meet my Tulip. Tulane Adler, my daughter."

Bolan Adler has a baby.

Despite learning that Bolan Adler was a future client, but not knowing he was a distant relative, I hadn't run an internet search on him. I'd made assumptions that he probably had numerous girlfriends, maybe eventually settling down with a wife. I suppose children were a possibility, in the recess of my thoughts, but I hadn't looked him up. Initially, I was trying to stay objective. Preserve my personal experience with him. That treasured secret in my heart.

I didn't need the rest of his life to interfere with that memory. I'd certainly lived mine.

Which causes the deep well of longing within me to open like a chasm. With tenderness and desire, I stare at the downy, red curls on Tulane's head, and the softness of her cheek, wanting to run my fingertips over that delicate skin. I bet she smells amazing. All baby soap on her flesh and special detergent on her clothes.

Everything in me wants to step closer to them, soothe her tears, even take her in my arms, and snuggle into her.

But all of that is wrong, and after a soggy smile at the toddler, I excuse myself, holding up a finger to wordlessly signal I need a minute. Spinning on my rebellious shoes, I wobble once before catching myself on the hallway wall then fast-walk toward the ladies' room, pushing the door with more force than necessary, causing it to slam against the opposite wall.

Only the resounding slam of it falling back into place doesn't happen, and I twist to find Bolan, still holding his daughter, catching the open door and softly shutting it behind him. He turns the lock. The sharp *snick* cages us in, setting off another wave of cries from his child.

"Shh, precious girl," Bolan murmurs to the side of her head, pressing his lips there as he attempts to soothe her.

I close my eyes and turn toward the sink, resting my hands on the edge of the counter to hold myself upright. My legs tremble. My feet ache in these heels. But my heart hurts the most.

Seeing Bolan Adler again like this has been too much for my already fragile mental state.

Handing me my panties. Fetching him chocolate milk. Staring with longing at his child.

I *hadn't* expected to see him again. Hadn't expected the initial sex. Hadn't expected this additional encounter. I wasn't supposed to be in the office at all when Bolan had this meeting, but I'd been called in last minute as a favor to my in-laws.

And I just need sixty seconds to compose myself.

"Ruthie." My name is a yearning plea. A deep need in the tone to speak to me, to listen to him.

Something tells me I'm not going to like what I hear, but I nod once, the motion suggesting he can talk.

He begins with, "I didn't know I had her."

7

———

[Bolan]

In the fuckups of fuckups, I was fucking up, and no one would be surprised.

Reckless. It's a word often associated with my name. Irresponsible. Inconsiderate. Burdensome.

All additional adjectives I've heard most of my life, and at some point, decided to play into them.

If I'm considered reckless, might as well act that way and sleep with random women. Not using the excuse of my profession, but as an athlete, there are benefits. As a world-class catcher at the professional level, ball chasers are everywhere. And when you were the once-chubby kid who eventually slimmed down, thus bulking up, the unsolicited attention goes to your head. And your dick.

And if I'm going to be called irresponsible, might as well knock that out of the park too, when half the issue is I'm not terribly organized and don't do well with schedules. Which earns you the label *inconsiderate* even when you try to set reminders and alarms and hire people to help you, who then call you a burden.

Because I can't follow some mysterious set of rules.

Give me a playbook and the guidelines for a baseball game, and I'm all in. My focus is narrowed.

Everything else? A shitshow.

Until Tulane.

She's the reason I'm trying to do better, be better, and I've had one little blip in the last eight months.

Ruth Avery.

"I didn't know I had her," I begin because I want Ruthie to know the truth. For some reason, I need her to understand that she—*Tulip*—was not a mistake.

"Last July, her mother came to me with an eight-month-old baby and told me she was mine."

Rachel was an American on a long-term assignment in Japan and a one-time decision like most women in my past. She'd been a hard-working, career-driven woman in her late twenties, who never wanted to be considered a quitter. When she found out she was pregnant, she figured it was one more thing she could master.

Her words, not mine.

Only, she quickly decided motherhood was not for her. With the demanding hours of her job, she didn't have time for a child in her life.

But the moment I learned about Tulane, I wanted her. A psychologist would have a field day studying how the irresponsible claimed a responsibility, but maybe that had been the issue. Tulane had been that something important in my life I didn't know I needed, hadn't known I was missing, and I was more than willing to embrace it. Embrace her. Embrace fatherhood.

The moment Tulane looked at me, she was mine, and I was hers. I am *here* for her.

"There were months of litigation. A paternity test." Although looking at Tulip's eyes, no one would deny she is mine. Her hair color also solidifies the connection. "Then the release of custody and a refusal of financial gain."

Rachel hadn't wanted monetary compensation and easily relinquished all rights to Tulane.

"She's my purpose," I state, as if that explains everything.

The need to return to the States. The desire to play for a professional level team here. The chance to end my career on a strong note, and not the decade of scandals behind me.

I might have wrecked a hotel room once. And there was that incident with a ping-pong table in a swimming pool, but I was a changed man.

Or at least, I wanted to be.

I was a dad now, and it was an honor I was not taking lightly.

Ruthie finally turns toward me and crosses her arms just below her breasts. Her hip leans against the bathroom counter. The same hip my hand coasted over, lifting a different tight skirt outlining her shape and dipping beneath it to taste—

Tulip whimpers in my arms, wrapping her tiny little limb around my neck and shuddering against my shoulder.

The memory of Ruthie, whose brown eyes are presently wide and focused on Tulip, disappears. In those dark depths, a swirl of emotion exists. First, softness while she glances at Tulane. Something sweet and almost yearning in them. The light tug of her lips pushes up the edges, like a smile is ready to bloom.

Then her gaze flits to me and those dark wells storm, like all she sees is some irresponsible guy who does nothing but fuck up. Her lips twist, clearing any semblance of a smile from existence.

I sigh and continue. "I'm not engaged."

Nothing had been put on paper yet. No ink signing the check for the woman my attorney found to pretend to be my wife.

This fucking scheme.

Between Jared and Floyd, I don't know who upsets me more. Floyd Everest came up with the plan, suggesting that a wife would dispel any rumors about my sudden single-father status and give the impression of a family man which the Chicago Anchors are demanding.

My granddad loved the team, and he'd be proud of me playing for them, even from his stadium seat in heaven.

He was the only one with pride in his eyes when he looked at me.

As for Jared, he'd agreed to go along with this ridiculous plan, as my new sports agent and the one with connections to my team of interest.

"But I need a wife, according to them." I tip my chin toward the door.

I'm nearing the end of my life span in the major leagues, and thankfully, the Anchors are interested in me. At thirty-six, my knees aren't what they used to be, and my hips and lower back bear most of the brunt of squatting for nearly half of a three-hour game, compounded with having been in that position for almost twenty years.

"I'd been on team after team before being shipped to Japan," I explain. "And now, I have a chance at making a comeback." *And I need a wife.*

Hadn't Ruthie known the plan? She knew who I was, didn't she? She must have known.

Especially with her position in this agency. With the relation to Nylah and Clifton.

Maybe that was the weird recognition vibe upon first seeing her. Being my late cousin's wife, I must have seen her at their wedding. Until I remember that I didn't attend. Perhaps at his funeral, but I hadn't been present for that either as I'd been in Japan when his death occurred.

Whatever the occasion had been, I can't shake the sensation that I've met Ruthie Avery somewhere.

You burned me. Fuck, I hate that she thinks that about me. Hate that I've hurt her.

Hanging my head, I press another kiss to the back of Tulip's as she squirms in my arms.

"Look, I'm not going to pretend I've been a good boy in the past. But all I care about now is my future." I jiggle Tulane. "And if I need a wife, or a woman to pretend she's mine, so the Chicago Anchors think I'm a family man, then that's the play I'll make."

I pause, not expecting her to understand, but still I clarify, "Because I *am* a family man now. It's me and Tulane. That's all that matters."

I'm not trying to sound like a selfish dick, but I'll be doing whatever is asked of me to continue to play professional baseball so I can financially provide the best for my girl. Another year. Two tops. Then I can retire and figure out what's next for us.

Probably turning into one of those former pros who own rundown bars or junkyards because I don't know what else I'd do.

The thought makes me shiver. So, for now, I must do what I can do and worry about the future when it happens.

Ruthie nods once, acknowledging that she heard me. She might not agree with the plan or even like me as much as she did last night and the night before, but I'm used to disappointing women.

I've been doing it since birth. My mom was at the top of the list.

Tulip shifts in my arms so that her side leans against my

chest, her head settles on my shoulder. Her gaze seeks Ruthie. Then she does something that shocks the shit out of me. She lurches forward like she wants Ruthie to catch her.

With the sudden dip of Tulip's body, Ruthie rushes toward me, but I catch my girl with my other hand.

"Hey, baby. Whatcha doin'?" Sometimes I think Tulane confuses women, any woman, with the mother she once had.

I'd been old enough when my mom left to have distinct memories of her, but Tulane won't ever know her biological mother. Not that I fault Rachel. I applaud her for acknowledging motherhood wasn't for her, and I'm grateful that she gave Tulane to me.

My life has been all the richer with my little one in it.

This morning, Nylah didn't seem overly eager to watch Tulane during our meeting, but I'd already used the sitter service two nights in a row.

The way things were going, today is going to be another long day.

With Ruthie standing in my space, I'm reminded we are in the ladies' room, and Jared and Floyd are waiting on us.

Still, I don't want to move away from her without her understanding where I'm at.

"I don't regret the other night. Or last night," I clarify. In the eight months since Tulane came into my life, I haven't touched a woman. I needed Ruthie the other night, and something tells me she needed me as well. No woman has responded to me like she did. Clinging to me. Desperate for me, in an innocent, authentic way.

Maybe she *didn't* know who I was. She certainly had nothing to gain by being with me for a few hours.

"How old is she?" Ruthie interrupts my thoughts without responding to my comment about regrets. She holds out her hand like she wants to run it down Tulip's back, then thinks twice and retracts her hand, tucking both of them behind her back.

"Sixteen months." What a riot the last eight months have been. The small changes that have been big steps for my little girl.

"She's . . . beautiful." Ruthie sighs, offering Tulane a gentle smile. I imagine my girl smiling back, though shy, maybe curious.

I'm curious, too, when I shouldn't be. Who is this woman standing before me? How I wish I could know more about her.

The two of them continue in their holding pattern, just staring at one another. Ruthie's eyes soften. She lifts her hand and bends her fingers in a wave. "Hi."

Tulane mimics the motion, her wave more like a cramping fist, but those rounded knuckles are so cute.

Ruthie and Tulane share another moment of smiles and gazes before Ruthie glances at me. Her expression grows more thoughtful, then almost stern. She straightens her shoulders and lifts her head taller.

I'm liking the red-framed glasses on her, although her blonde hair is pulled back a bit too severely. She's got that principal-vibes happening, but as often as I'd been called into a school office, no principal ever looked like her.

"Am I suddenly a page in your bad boy past?" she asks.

The sharp inhale I take causes me to catch a whiff of her scent. Floral and spice.

I'd love to tell Ruthie no. I'd love to say she isn't a page but the start of a new chapter. I would love to explore more with her. However, a relationship is not in the books for me; not with this arrangement with Melody. Heck, I'm not even a reader.

I need a wife, and I—

The gears in my head *chink* slowly at first. Then, my slog brain churns faster and faster.

"Let's head back to the conference room," I state, needing a minute.

Could I explore more with Ruthie? *Is* there a way to keep her? The sudden idea is not that absurd, is it?

Then again, I've never been known to have sound thoughts or make smart decisions.

RUTHIE LEADS us back to the meeting space where Jared is standing, facing the windows, and Floyd is on his phone, seated at the table.

Jared turns as we enter and offers Ruthie a warm smile. Floyd scowls in my direction. He hasn't liked this *new development* in my life. A daughter. He's a shark and worked hard between Japanese law and American to dot all the *I*'s and cross all the *T*'s, as he put it, to ensure Tulane was all mine, and I owe him.

Which is one reason I am willing to entertain his plan.

And another reason Melody Cross, his niece was proposed.

"Maybe the lady could take the child into the hall," he mutters, narrowing his eyes at me.

"The lady is right here," Ruthie responds, giving Floyd a glimpse of her thorns despite her delicate appearance.

Jared chuckles, brushing off the sudden tension, and waves a dismissive hand at Floyd while taking his seat at the head of the table. "Let Tulane stay. This meeting concerns Ruthie as well."

"It does?" Ruthie and I say in unison again, reminding us he'd said something similar earlier. I'm curious if Jared has the same sudden idea I do.

As I step toward the side of the table where Ruthie had been seated, Tulane drops forward again as if she wants Ruthie to take her.

My flower reaches out for my daughter, like it's instinctual to take her from me. We stand in this awkward moment of Tulane leaning forward and Ruthie standing with her hands up, ready to catch my girl again.

"I don't mind holding her, if you don't mind." Her voice is soft, her offer hesitant. Her eyes are wild while eager.

"Of course," I state reluctantly, as I've become a bit of a helicopter parent when it comes to Tulane. A hovering father but not one who intends to smother my girl. She'll be allowed to be whomever she wants to be. On her terms.

As I shift Tulane toward Ruthie, I narrowly miss a brush of my knuckles against her breasts in the pass off. Ruthie easily pulls Tulane to her chest, and the girls focus on one another again. Tulane's small fingers fiddle with the buttons on Ruthie's blouse, which is closed at her throat. Ruthie smiles, stroking her finger around Tulane's cheek. Then Tulane settles her head against Ruthie's shoulder.

Dammit. I shouldn't like how good they look together. A simple bouquet of red and yellow.

"Shall we take our seats?" Jared directs, although he's already seated.

I pull out Ruthie's chair, placing my hand near her lower back to help her take a seat. Then I lean across the table, setting my fingertips on my copy of the report, and slide the file across the table toward me. I settle into the chair beside Ruthie where Tulane can see me, and I can keep my eyes on both of them.

"We left off where you need a wife," Floyd begins. "A family man is more attractive to the Chicago Anchors in light of what's recently happened on the team."

One of their new-to-them players last season slept with a fellow teammate's wife. *Scandalous, indeed.* I'm aware of Romero Valdez's reputation, and at one time, worried mine equals his, but I've never, ever so much as look at a teammate's wife or girlfriend other than in a friendly manner.

I do have boundaries.

I nod at Floyd, acknowledging my understanding, although my gut has told me his choice will never make a good wife nor a decent stepmother for Tulane.

I need a partner.

Tulane needs someone compassionate and caring to act as her mother.

This is the part that concerns me most. Would any woman want to mother my child? And what would that do emotionally to Tulane when the year is up, and that woman is no longer contractually bound to us? What damage will she have done if Tulane grows close to her? What damage will be done if Tulane *isn't* close with her?

My own experience with a mother who flitted into and out of her role is the background for my concerns, and I wasn't comfortable with Tulane having a similar type of mother-figure.

Melody Cross is an issue for me.

"You will secure a full-time nanny," Jared adds, as if reading my internal worries. If I have childcare, I don't need a mother for Tulane. For appearances, I simply need a wife for me.

"And finally, I'm promoting Ruth to be your new agent."

"You're what?" Ruthie barks, leaning forward, clutching Tulane tightly in her arms.

"Why?" I choke, watching as Tulane slowly closes her eyes as if comfortable in Ruthie's lap. Or maybe she just feels the sudden tension in the room and wants to shut it all off. I know I'd like to pretend none of this is happening.

Pretend I'm not agreeing to someone random being my wife.

"You'll need someone full-time to coach you through appearances and monitor your behavior. Ruthie is being assigned to you."

"Jared," she groans. "No." Her eyes widen, and an entire

conversation ensues between them. Is it me? Am I the problem? Does she not want to be assigned to me? Then again, I don't know that I can have Ruthie close to me, with another woman *pretending* to be my wife.

Eventually, Jared speaks again, his voice soothing. "This won't be like the last time, Ruth, darling. You're older, wiser, and better experienced. You can handle this assignment."

What *last time*?

Ruthie falls back in her seat, still clutching Tulane who has closed her eyes and nestled her head into the space between Ruthie's neck and shoulder.

I won't think about how I nipped Ruthie there. Nope, not allowing those thoughts to enter my thick head.

Instead, I clear my throat. "Actually, I've been thinking about the assignment. The Reputation Repair Report. I'd like a new plan."

Floyd groans and tosses his phone on the table. "You're out of options, Bolan. You have a reputation as a loose cannon. And now this."

He waves toward my baby girl in Ruthie's arms, who looks like she's holding Tulane even tighter, as if protecting her from the insult.

This. My child.

"A marriage is the best solution," Floyd adds.

My earlier thought, the one that popped into my head while staring at Ruthie in the bathroom, tumbles forward.

"Then I don't want Ruthie as my agent. I want her for my wife."

8

———

[Ruthie]

Have I entered some alternate universe? Was I living *The Handmaid's Tale*? Were these men not aware I am in the room, and this is my life they are discussing as if I am not sitting here?

"Of course, that's if Ruth would agree," Bolan adds, trying to dig himself out of a deep pile of manure.

"What about Melody?" I snap, singing over her name, certain the jealousy I don't wish to display just rang out in my tone.

I glance in Bolan's direction but can't see him well-enough over his daughter's head on my shoulder. His sweet baby girl who has settled against me and must have drifted off to sleep if the weight-shift of her body tells me anything. She's suddenly a brick in my arms. The most amazing, wonderful, welcome brick.

Jared is staring at Bolan, wide-eyed and surprised. Floyd's

weaselly eyes narrow at me. He already has strikes against him for suggesting *the lady can take the kid out.*

"I hate to say she's no one, but she's no one." Bolan states.

Yikes. Harsh.

Even Floyd flinches, clearing his throat and sitting straighter in his seat.

"And if you think I need tending to"—Bolan glances at Jared and then at Floyd—"a babysitter of sorts? Who better to keep me in line than my wife?"

I snort. I'd hardly kept my late husband in line, what would make this time different? While the term *wife* should equate to loyalty and dedication, to some men, it did not always mean those things. Let's not forget love and attraction, too.

However, a rush runs up my middle at Bolan's suggestion.

I don't want a rush. I don't want to be married again. I am looking forward to being an independent woman.

Plus, Bolan cannot be serious.

"And you said it yourself, Jared. I need a nanny for Tulane."

"A nanny and a wife are not the same thing," I defend, shifting the rotating chair so I can look more directly at him. A mother and a nanny aren't the same thing either, but I don't feel like dipping into that argument yet.

"Of course not," Bolan eyes me.

"And I wouldn't be engaging in any so-called wifely duties," I state, as if I'm considering this preposterous decision.

Am I considering it?

"Absolutely not," Jared interjects.

I swivel my chair, so I face him. Does he mean absolutely not to being Bolan's wife, or absolutely not to sexual activities? Either way, is his objection because of who I am?

His daughter-in-law. The daughter Nylah and Jared never had. In some ways, I'd become closer to them than Clifton. For me, *they* have been better parents than my own and I never want to disappoint them.

But I want my own life.

Tulane shifts in my arms and Bolan leans forward, scooping her out of my hold and settling her on his chest, the practiced move of a loving father. Her body instantly curls into his. She looks so peaceful. So safe. So protected by his large arm around her small back.

"The decision should be up to Ruth," Bolan states, his tone a little firmer. Those mischievous green eyes on me again.

Did he mean the decision for conjugal experiences? Been there, done that.

Or did he mean, the choice to be his wife?

I've already had *that* experience as well, and it wasn't always that great. There are secrets I'll take to the grave because I don't want Nylah or Jared to ever think poorly of their treasured son. They've already suffered enough heartbreak from him, and I would never add to their pain.

Still, I'd been set free and I'm looking in a new direction. The future me.

For eighteen months, I've been moving in a bubble. One protecting me against the sympathetic comments and looks of concern about Clifton's passing. Before that, I'd been numb, keeping myself together as best I could under the circumstances. The final act of betrayal from Clifton. The loss of a future I'd so desperately wanted.

But since that moment in the ballroom with Bolan, I feel charged, energized . . . alive. The sensation comes from more than amazing sex but from the tender moments when I sensed Bolan saw me. The me I am. The me I want to be. He won't be my happily ever after. I'll be certain to protect myself better in the future.

No more *Responsible Ruthie*.

The thought hits me hard. The very opposite of acting responsibly would be to do something reckless. To do something unexpected. To have sex with a man in a dark ballroom.

Or kiss a stranger for sixty seconds and then never see him again.

Or marry him.

I turn back toward Jared, who is a good man, but a hard one. He's been overly kind to me, but I'm reminded of the requirements set in place when I agreed to work at Imperial Sports Management. The pity-employment. The job I hadn't ever wanted but took anyway. The position meant buttoning up in these constricting blouses and wearing knee-length skirts. Slipping into killer heels and donning my glasses instead of contacts, to appear more serious, more severe.

It did nothing to prevent an incident. My first and last foray into being an agent.

And I was so tightly wound, I was afraid I'd suffocate.

For the past eighteen months, I've been living the grieving widow role, with every reminder of Clifton a little more of a farce. I don't want to hurt anyone, but I've been craving some space and distance from this city, these amazing people, and ISM.

When I glance back toward Bolan, the final stitch in my resolve is knotted in place. It's hard to resist a man wearing a suit holding a sweet baby. And it's hard to deny that an answer to my prayers is sitting beside me.

"What would it look like . . . to be your wife, in this arrangement?" Maybe he already had a plan for all the sexual positions he'd practice with Melody. The thought makes my blood run cold.

Not with fear. With envy.

"Y-you can't be serious, Ruth," Jared stammers, surprise lacing his tone.

"I am," I say, surprised myself by the conviction in my own voice.

"You are?" He gasps.

"You are?" Bolan's eyes widen, the gold flecks sparkling among the green base like fireflies flitting through dark woods.

"I'd like to think about it."

"Think fast," Floyd interjects, sarcasm thick in his voice and reminding the room that Bolan is on a time clock.

Bolan narrows his eyes at Floyd before he brings his attention back to me but speaks to the other men in the room. "Can you give us a minute?"

Floyd is hasty to stand but Jared lingers a second. "Ruth, are you sure about this?"

I've never been more unsure of something, but at the same time, I think this is what I might need. My gaze drops to Tulane, cradled in her father's arms, sleeping like a major deal isn't going down around her.

Her presence sweetens the possibility of this arrangement. To be able to protect her, nurture her, care for her, would be an honor, a blessing even, and the bonus is I wouldn't have to be concerned for Bolan. He wouldn't get close enough to break my heart like Clifton had. Like my father repeatedly did.

"I've got this," I state, sounding more confident than I feel.

Jared excuses himself, stating he'll be right outside, as if I'll need him. And isn't that part of the issue? For too long I've relied on my in-laws. Leaned on them for support. It was time to veer off the path they've paved, with good intentions, for me. I want a road less traveled. One that's just for me.

Bolan sits upright, adjusting Tulane so her head rests on his broad shoulder. Looking at me over her, he says, "Thank you." Breathlessly spoken and full of sincerity.

"I haven't said yes," I remind him.

"There's no pressure." He licks his lips. "For anything."

Conjugal experiences. Wifely commitments.

"Maybe we should discuss some terms." Again, I sound more powerful than I feel.

"Name them."

No sex is on the tip of my tongue but then I reconsider. That's a mighty bold declaration to make considering I've already had sex with him. However, I also don't want sex to be an assumption.

"Patience," I state. Maybe sex will happen. Maybe it won't. I wouldn't take bets on the outcome yet.

Bolan's eyes widen. "O-*kay*."

"Faithfulness."

Those green eyes narrow to slits. "Of course." Then he adds, "And same for you."

"Of course." I softly agree. He has no idea how committed I can be to someone.

"A year at least," Bolan adds.

"The season," I counter which could run roughly eight months.

Bolan twists his lips, considering the timeline. "Fine."

"Fine." I pause a beat. "What do you want from me?"

Bolan assesses me a long minute. To my surprise, his gaze doesn't wander down my body in some lewd appraisal but holds on my face. My eyes. My nose. My mouth.

"Willingness to renegotiate terms at any given time."

"O-*kay*." That suggests our situation remain open-ended. "But faithfulness is still a hard limit."

Bolan tilts his head, assessing me a second. The secrets I hold are buried deep, though.

"Deal." He holds out his left hand which would be awkward to shake, so I place my right in his, and for half a second, it feels like the first time we met.

That awkward moment when he held out his hand to shake mine, but I took his hand like he intended to hold onto me.

This time, Bolan does not tighten his grip but does hold fast. He leans forward and wiggles his thick brows. "Should we seal the deal with a kiss?"

"Don't press your luck," I tease, scowling at him, but when that damn dimple pops out, I know I'm screwed. Resisting him will be half my battles. Wondering if he'll really want me, is the other half.

I'm used to men with pretty promises that end up bottomless and false.

"So just to confirm. Will you marry me, Ruth Avery?"

"I will."

He squeezes my hand in wordless gratitude. "I'll get your number and call you later with details."

He stands with Tulane pressed to his chest and steps backward, but his foot catches on the extended wheels of the swivel chair. He stumbles a bit, dropping my hand and clutching Tulane tighter, as he wobbles.

I stand abruptly and reach out toward him, as if I'll catch both of them before they fall.

Bolan smiles tightly, cautiously stepping backward a second time. When he nears the door, he stops. Pressing his fingers to his lips, he blows me a kiss.

And I stand there staring at him.

"Come on, Ruthie. You didn't even try to catch it."

I blink, confused by what he's doing, what he's saying.

"The other night when you left the ballroom, you turned back and blew me a kiss."

I did? I don't remember that. Was I sex-drunk? Was I really that flirtatious? Was it a punctuation mark on our time together?

I've certainly re-opened what I thought was a closed door.

"Try again," Bolan says, his voice playful. He presses his fingertips to his lips and watches me. Then he tips his hand forward and blows, like he's sending fairy dust or imaginary glitter in my direction.

This time, I raise my hand like I'll catch the kiss. Only, I feel awkward and don't know what to do with my upright palm. Do

I place the imaginary kiss on my lips? Tuck it in my non-existent pockets? Swipe my hand on my hips?

Instead, I just stare back at him.

"Better. Not a strike. I'd call that a foul ball. It means I have another chance."

"Chance for what?" I scoff quietly.

"Chance at a hit." He clicks his tongue in his mouth making a knocking sound, like a bat hitting a ball. Then, he sails his hand through the air, mimicking the trajectory of a hit ball, watching his fingers sweep before him. Finally, he glances back at me. Those eyes like a private firework display.

"A chance to win you over."

Was I a game to him? I'd already said yes. I don't know what more he'd want, but I don't get the opportunity to ask as Bolan turns toward the closed door, opening it, catching it on his toe, and watching it bounce back into place.

Tulane shifts and Bolan presses a kiss to her head, then shuffles to attempt opening the door again.

The clumsiness was only mildly present the other night. A cocky seducer was present instead. Someone who laid me on a banquet table and ate me like a feast. Someone who held me up against a window and hammered into me. Someone who swayed with me on an empty dance floor as a final gesture.

Yet, the bumbling man, holding his daughter, is more charming than any of his alter egos.

And I might be happy to catch his kisses.

Someday.

9

———

[Ruthie]

"**I** do."

Within forty-eight hours, I'm standing across from Bolan in a Vegas chapel, accepting a list of promises with two little words.

There's something a little seedy about our location, but I don't comment on my surroundings. I've hardly had time to think since agreeing to be Bolan's wife.

In the interim of my acceptance was Jared's concern and Nylah's objection. She's aware of Bolan's reputation and I'm aware that his mother Joanna was not an active part of his life.

Her objections included her worry. "Is this a grief thing?"

A grief thing? Like I'm rebelling against the emotion. Little does my mother-in-law know that I grieved Clifton and his love long before he died, and it was something I wasn't willing to discuss with her.

"I'm just ready for a change of scenery." My response wasn't a total lie. I'd be getting out of California and away from ISM, at least physically.

Thanks to my agreement to be his wife, Bolan got the three-year contract he wanted with the Chicago Anchors. I got a way out of Los Angeles. A chance to escape people I adore but need a break from.

When I answer the officiant, Bolan's smile widens, and his broad shoulders hoist him taller. Like the weight of the moment had been pressing down on him, but with this simple phrase I've lessened the pressure.

When I first entered the chapel, Bolan stood at the end of the short aisle, looking rather anxious. His left leg jiggling. Nylah and Jared are present as witnesses. Floyd is here as well with a woman beside him holding Tulane. She's dressed in an innocent white dress like a miniature cherub. A part of me wanted to demand the woman hand that sweet baby over to me. Tulane did not look happy being confined by someone who was clearly a stranger to her.

As I strode down the aisle, Bolan didn't take his eyes off me. That deep emerald gaze called to me, like it had done on a few occasions, not knowing the power of their pull.

When I reached the end of the aisle, he finally smiled. A bit crooked. A lot pleased. Dimple present.

"You wore white?"

"I did."

Bolan and I had minimal interaction in the whirlwind of events leading up to this moment, but one thing he asked me was what my dress looked like. Originally, I'd planned to wear a dress I'd only worn once before for some other special occasion hosted by Imperial Sports Management.

When I told him it was light pink, his responding text was simple. **Oh.**

The single word led me to doubt my decision. At first, I thought he might want me to wear something vibrant, like the scarlet dress I wore to The Red Dress Affair. Then it occurred to me that Bolan might want his bride to wear white. Even if this was all pretend, it's still his first wedding.

"You look beautiful, flower."

White didn't exactly scream exotic or enticing, but the way Bolan looked at me, I felt beautiful. Like that whimsical flower dancing in a breeze.

My dress isn't half as stuffy as my first wedding dress. This one floats to my knees with a fuller skirt and a tight-fitting bodice that culminates at my neck with a giant bow wrapped just off center around my throat.

Bolan looks stunning as well in the same tux I saw him wearing the night of the fundraiser.

The night he bent me over a balcony railing and slid into me from behind.

Despite it being my wedding day, there is no place for reminiscent thoughts like that. This is an arrangement.

The deal *will* be sealed with a kiss like Bolan teased roughly forty-eight hours ago in Jared's office, because the officiant ends the ceremony with the suggestion that Bolan may kiss his bride.

He leans forward. My mouth waters.

He chews at his lower lip. I lick mine.

Then he presses a butterfly-soft kiss to the corner of my mouth.

Disappointment floods my belly. *He didn't kiss me.* It's our wedding day and he didn't kiss me.

Bolan pulls back, watching me, assessing my expression, which I'm certain shows shock and discontent.

With a soft smile, he offers, "Patience." He pauses and his grin grows, the tweak of his dimple showing. "I haven't earned the kind of kisses I want yet."

What kind of kisses? A wedding kiss? A seal that binds me

to him? Or one of those over-the-top displays that border on making out at the altar?

I want over-the-top!

But the disappointment in me turns to butterflies, wondering what Bolan will do to earn kisses from me.

Ones that would leave me breathless and craving more, like when I was only eighteen.

10

—————

SPRING TRAINING

[Bolan]

Ruthie and I don't have the pleasure of a wedding night as I'm a late addition to the Chicago Anchors and spring training games begin in days. Pitchers and catchers reported to the Anchors' spring field in Arizona a week ago Monday.

The afternoon of our wedding, we fly to the Scottsdale location.

The wedding chapel in Vegas was not how I pictured my wedding day. Hell, I hadn't ever pictured such a day for me, but there Ruthie stood, looking breathtaking and nervous in a white dress.

One she'd worn for me.

One I wanted to untie by the bow at her throat and kiss along the column I haven't kissed enough.

When she told me she planned to wear pink, our situation

being an arrangement hit home. My new bride wasn't even going to wear white to our ceremony.

And I'd only be doing this once.

Ruthie was not a virgin. She'd been married before, plus we had our interlude during The Red Dress Affair. Still, I wanted my bride to wear the traditional color that marks the significance of a wedding.

What Ruthie is doing for me is important.

I left Floyd and Jared to hash out financial compensation for Ruthie and settle on a one-year marriage commitment compromise. The timeline will hold off suspicion that the marriage was only for gain. Of course, part of the agreement was that the team never find out our marriage is a sham.

I assume Ruthie is all-in because of the money. The Chicago Anchors signed me with a three-year deal, with a payout that wasn't as high as the highest paid catcher, but still substantial money. Happily restored to the major leagues in the States, I will retire with the iconic team.

I can almost hear my granddad cheering from the heavenly bleacher section.

But could Ruthie be proud of me, too?

I don't have time to contemplate this big question before Ruthie and I arrive late-afternoon in Arizona as a newly married couple.

Players often bring their wives and families to spring training to live in a compound-like setting, renting homes near each other or condos in the same building. A sense of community grows and helps players and their families transition to the long months ahead when our time at home will be cut in half, spending the other half on the road.

When Ruthie and I enter the condo rented for us, we collectively take in the couch and recliner chair in the living room. A small round table that seats four stands in a dining space beside the narrow kitchen.

Ruthie wanders down the hallway holding Tulane in her arms as I carry our bags up to this second-floor apartment. She stops in front of one bedroom with two twin beds.

"We need a crib," she says quietly, glancing down at Tulane and jostling her a little bit. My little girl stares into the stark room as well.

I've rented a duplex in Chicago and can't wait to set up a space I can call home for my Tulip, and now Ruthie. For the next month, this place is home, though.

Ruthie turns toward the open door at the end of the hallway and pauses at the entrance to the larger bedroom. I stand behind her while we both stare at the king-sized bed.

"I can take the couch." I clear my throat, not liking the idea. My hips and back can't handle a lumpy set of cushions, but I don't want Ruthie to feel uncomfortable. She's been quiet since departing Vegas and I'm worried she might have doubts about her decision to marry me.

I won't make my wife into a foregone conclusion, even if I have already slept with her. Ruthie's doing me a favor, not turning into a kept woman.

"I can take the couch," she counters, still staring at the bed.

"Absolutely not." I can be a gentleman, or at least try to be. Which proves nearly impossible every time I see Ruthie interacting with Tulane. I've heard of breeding kinks. Is there a mommy kink? Because watching Ruthie with Tulane revs my engine and embarrassingly gets me hard.

I swipe a hand down my face and clear my throat again. "So, I gotta head out. Check in with the team as I'm already late, and—"

"Of course. Go. *Go*." Ruthie turns toward me. Her dark eyes unreadable. "I've got this." She jiggles Tulane in her arms. "We're going to be fine."

I don't doubt Ruthie can handle my child. Hell, she'll probably be better at nurturing her than I am. The issue is . . . I want to stay. I want to be with them for a little while. I want to know more about Ruthie and I'm cognizant that I'm basically dumping my new wife and new-to-me child in a rented condo and leaving them to fend for themselves.

"I can order groceries. Or have a meal delivered."

"Bolan." Ruthie softly chuckles. "I've got us covered."

I'm sure she does. She's more capable than I am. Definitely more punctual, as I was almost late to my own wedding. Thank goodness for alarm-reminders on phones. It's not like I would have forgotten, I'm just not good with time management off the field.

With a final glance at Tulane, I swipe my left hand over her downy red hair and catch sight of my silicone wedding band. I gave Ruthie a thin gold band I bought hastily in Vegas. She bought me a package of three athletic-safe rings.

Very efficient of her.

I kiss the top of Tulane's head. Then I have a momentary lapse in judgement and lean toward Ruthie, intending to give her a quick peck. She flinches back from my approach. Our mouths never connect.

Shit. I'd promised on our wedding day I'd use patience. I'd earn her kisses.

Because make no mistake, I intend to be kissing my wife.

"I'll see you later." I pull away, stamping down my disappointment at Ruthie's rejection.

"I'll be here." Her voice is light but strained, implying *where else might she be?*

I have no idea what her life was like outside of Imperial Sports Management, but I'll learn.

∽

As far back as I can remember, I've been a part of a baseball team. At the professional level, an unspoken hierarchy exists between veterans and rookies. Then there are seasoned players who become newbies on a team, like me, and time is necessary to establish a place in the current dynamic. Like the new kid at school trying to fit into an established friend group.

The team bench manager, Dalton Ryatt, handles introductions when I hit the practice field where my new teammates and coaches are in a variety of positions. Warming up. Batting practice. Individual lessons.

There is Ross Davis, the newly assigned head coach.

Kip Garcia, a pitching coach.

Ford Sylver, the long-time centerfielder and a current captain. Roughly the same age as me, Ford appears preoccupied. He has reasons to be standoffish. His wife slept with another team member, Romero Valdez, who has dubbed himself Romeo, and remains the shortstop for the Anchors this season despite the scandal.

"You want to be an Anchors, *cha*?" the shortstop asks in a thick Hispanic accent upon meeting me. "Got to play with your balls." He grabs his crotch, turns his head and waggles his tongue at someone nearby like that guy understands the reference.

"You got a wife? Girlfriend?"

I narrow my eyes at him. "Why?" Does he think he'll get in the pants of my significant other? Not a fucking chance.

"She can't have a grip on you." He squeezes his fingers in front of his dick again. "You need to lay it all on the field." He waves his arm outward, addressing the brilliant green field within the spring training stadium. "You come out with us. I show you, Bad-ler."

I bristle at the mention of a long-ago nickname. A combination of my name and reputation. Only, I'm not here to relive my wilder days. Valdez might consider his advice sage, like I'm some rookie, but I'm not interested in his thoughts.

And I'm not going anywhere with him or any lackeys who

follow him. He's a fucking prick for taking advantage of a teammate's wife, or whatever the case might have been. Wives are off limits. Girlfriends, too.

And being the new kid on the block, I do not want to be affiliated with the known troublemaker in the sandlot.

I'm bigger than Valdez, so I'm not half as worried about an altercation. I don't trust him, though. While most rumors are exaggerations, some contain hints of truth. No one understands that better than me as the source of gossip in the past.

By marrying Ruthie, I'm here to keep my reputation clean, not tarnish it, so I reject Valdez's invitation. "Thanks, but I'm gonna pass for now."

"You don't know what you're missing. Ball chasers are everywhere down here."

Spring break desert dwellers. Baseball fangirls. I know the gig but I'm not in the market anymore, and relief hits me harder than a ninety mile per hour fastball.

I don't need to play games to win over some random woman for a night.

The only score I want is getting my wife to open up to me.

For now, I don't have time to concentrate on the anxious silence surrounding Ruthie as my introductions continue with the bullpen of pitchers, who will be my partners on a rotating basis.

Catchers and pitchers go, well, glove-to-glove.

Finally, I meet Cyrus Sawyer, who is the current catcher for the Anchors. We'll essentially flip-flop between games. One on for him. One on for me. Cyrus comes from a small town in Georgia and seems like an all-around good guy from first handshake.

I'd like us to be friends, but I don't need new buddies. I'm here to prove myself.

Prove something *to* myself.

And from there, I begin practice.

11

[Ruthie]

The next two days, Bolan and I pass one another like we're tag-teaming. Sometimes, I expect us to give each other a high-five as we cross paths.

While he has practice and meetings, I order items for Tulane and take us shopping. A portable crib arrives but then we need sheets and a changing pad, plus diapers and seasonal clothing. During late February in Arizona, the mornings are cool while the afternoons might be warm and then the evening temperature drops again. The desert is fickle.

All Tulane's needs are met with the help of Bolan's credit card, yet I try to be conservative. This place is only temporary. However, active toddlers need items to occupy their attention. I splurge on a small library of board books and a few educational toys, plus a baby doll and miniature stroller for Tulane to push along the sidewalk.

At night, Bolan takes over, and I make myself scarce to give them one-on-one time. He gives Tulane her nightly bath and reads to her before bed. I'd love nothing more than to be part of their evening rituals, but I don't want to intrude on the precious time Bolan has with his daughter, knowing soon enough he'll be missing out on days and nights collectively.

As an outsider looking in, Bolan is a good father.

And I'm not Tulane's mother, even if for all intents and purposes I'm her stepmother. I am Bolan's wife. But I remind myself to keep my distance, or I'll be sucked into loving Tulane more than I should.

She is not mine. I will not get to keep her when Bolan and I separate, and the idea is like a sliver wedged beneath my fingernail. I hadn't considered the ramification when I said yes to Bolan.

A part of me worries about Tulane, though. The innocent child of a professional athlete. I don't want to see her left with random sitters or endless nannies, or worse, carted from game to game as a show piece.

The experience of being a child with parents in the limelight is familiar to me. I know all too well the position of being pulled forward for photographs and social engagements, then returned to the corner with nursemaids and tutors. I was the daughter of people who had no business having children.

Watching Tulane curled up in Bolan's arms in ISM's office, I didn't want her to be me. Not that I thought she would. Not that Bolan didn't act like he loved her unconditionally, although a bit awkwardly. Like he is still learning how to care for her. Parenting does not come with a manual, though, and Bolan is doing the best he can.

He explained how he's only been a father to Tulane for eight months. Every day is something new for both him and her. Her budding independence shines brightly.

Like now, when she runs naked through the rented condo,

fresh from a bath, with Bolan chasing after her, bath towel spread wide between his hands like he's a giant bat.

"Tulip," he groans as her little legs move fast and she rounds the corner to the kitchen to bury her head in my knees.

I've been holing up in the primary bedroom each night to give them space, and I'd stepped out of the room to make myself a mug of calming tea.

"Whatcha doin', baby." I dip down and pick her up. Her damp body shivers against me. She's also a little slippery.

With his T-shirt soaked, Bolan comes up behind her and drops the towel over her back. "Gotcha," he growls like a pirate. When he tucks the large towel around her lanky body, the backs of his hands brush my breasts, and I gasp.

"Shit." Bolan mutters. "Sorry about that." He tugs Tulane toward him while she squirms in his arms, her body trapped in the towel while she leans toward me.

My heart swells but she needs to spend time with her dad. She should have the chance to be a daddy's girl. My hope is she will always be one.

Bolan peppers the side of her head with kisses while her legs kick forward like she's a mermaid. Then he dips her to the side and flips her around, so she's like a wingless airplane. She squeals as he flies her back to the bathroom.

Within minutes, Tulane is back, dressed in a pink, short pajama set. Her hair is slicked back, combed a bit unevenly, and I smile knowing Bolan is trying.

Tulane wraps her arms around my legs again and I bend down to pick her up, inhaling the freshly bathed scent only toddlers have.

"She's a slippery one tonight," Bolan says, entering the kitchen once more, his previously soaked T-shirt removed.

My breath hitches at the brush of hair on his chest and the firmness of his abs. He isn't washboard tight as much as barrel broad and solid. He also wears that woven black strap around his neck with a silver, rectangular medal dangling from it. While I've touched his chest, I hadn't seen him fully divested of a shirt.

My eyes drink him in. The strength of his arms. The width of his shoulders. The comfort a chest like his might offer.

Bolan has worn mainly T-shirts since our arrival in Arizona. Much different than the suit and tux I'd previously seen him in. I haven't missed a giant bear tattoo that runs up his forearm. The creature is not storybook-friendly looking but frightening, and I'm curious about it. What it means. What it represents.

But I don't ask.

He glances down at his arm and then looks back up at me. Those green eyes narrow. His lips cock upward. He runs his hand from his pecs to his waist, that bear flexing, and my gaze follows the trail he blazes. A thick line of hair peeks from the waistband of his shorts to his navel.

"Huh." He huffs.

Snapping out of my trance, I blink and flick my gaze upward to meet his. He knows what he's done. He knows how I'm responding.

My husband is too good looking for his own good. Or mine.

Busted. With the tweak of his lips, that damn dimple appears. His sudden cockiness is like a neon sign in a bar.

"Hang out for a bit while I put Tulip to bed." He isn't asking as much as inviting me to wait for him. After a kiss to the side of her head, I set Tulane down on the floor and she scampers off to the living room.

"I should probably answer some emails." The past two nights, I've scrambled to fulfill the responsibilities I have with Jared and ISM. As Bolan's personal babysitter, I've given him the first few days of practice to get acclimated. How much trouble can a grown man get into when he's new on the job?

Bolan isn't a rookie to professional baseball. He's a seasoned player with a long rap sheet of incidents behind him. *His wife* is here to keep him in line.

"Just give me a few minutes," he pleads, dropping his gaze to my bare feet.

"I guess I could wait," I state, lifting my warm mug of tea.

Bolan watches the motion, his mouth slightly opening as mine perches on the rim of the cup. After a hot sip, I lick my lips like I've missed a drop. He swallows thickly, like watching me drink tea is some kind of turn on for him.

Then he spins on his heels and scoops up Tulane, rushing off for the remainder of their bedtime ritual.

Like a creep, I slink down the hallway and listen. The rough, low voice of Bolan. His little girl's laughter. The sound is infectious while heart shattering. A reminder of all I'll never have.

With my spine against the wall, I allow the torture to continue as Bolan reads a book to Tulane. I tip back my head and close my eyes, listening as he tells a story but doesn't follow the words written on the pages. Since I've read her the same story, I know how it goes.

Too soon, Bolan's rugged voice softens, and I picture him pressing a kiss to his little girl's head before setting her down in the portable crib.

I rush back to the kitchen, not wanting to be caught listening, and metaphorically kicking myself for acting like a voyeur, desperate to hear their laughter and shared voices. Two sounds that equal love.

When Bolan enters the kitchen, I'm leaning against the counter, one foot on top of the other, like I've been standing here, casually waiting on his return.

In the momentary silence that ensues, with him simply staring at me, his eyes are a little intimidating, and I give myself away. "Wild imagination you have." I tilt my head toward the hallway, indicating Tulane's bedroom.

Bolan hangs his head and cups the back of his neck. Thankfully, he put on a fresh T-shirt. "Yeah. About that. I'm dyslexic. It's still kind of an issue and I don't read well. I use text to talk and talk to text messaging a lot."

Instantly, I feel bad and set down my tea mug. Straightening when I look at him, I say, "I'm so sorry. I didn't—"

Bolan quickly cuts me off with a forgiving hand. "My only concern is if Tulane is going to struggle, too. If she'll be like me." His voice lowers again, gaze dropping to his bare feet.

He clears his throat. "I was never good at school. Not great with time management. And I have a bit of ADHD. I set myself reminders for things, but even then, I'm not great about getting where I need to go on time. On the field, I'm different." Bolan tilts his big head. "Maybe I do need an assistant." He doesn't sound arrogant as much as reflective. The cocky man without a shirt from moment's ago has disappeared.

"Want to hang out? Watch a movie?" He sounds hopeful.

I can't remember the last time I simply hung out with someone. Just enjoyed shared company. I also don't want him to feel obligated. "I don't want to intrude on your alone time."

"I'm not great at being alone, either."

Was this another reason he caused so much trouble, especially with women?

"I've got some emails to catch up on," I remind him.

"Are you still working with other clients?" His thick brows lift.

"I'm always working on whatever Jared asks."

Bolan tilts his head again. "Do you like working for Imperial Sports Management?"

"I'm grateful for Nylah and Jared in my life," I answer. I *am* thankful for the amazing, loving, accepting couple that they are.

"That's not what I asked." The corner of Bolan's mouth ticks upward, the cockiness returning like a slow drip.

"Still, sticking to my answer," I snark, not willing to explain how much I really don't like working for ISM. How I never wanted to work for them.

Clifton liked the idea. While I'd wanted to be a teacher, he didn't think education was a very glamorous profession. Shortly after we graduated college, he entered the NFL and his father agreed to hire me, without any experience in sports management or agenting. I failed my first assignment. After that, I'd been given the role of an assistant, with lots of leeway to allow me to follow Clifton around the country in those first years. When Clifton entered the military, I followed him once again, until long-term assignments put him overseas, and Jared offered me one of two positions as his personal assistant. I've been working beside him for roughly four years. While grateful for the work because it offered me some socializing and a little money for myself, in general, I hated the job.

Bolan's mouth turns into a full-on smirk, similar to the one that got me in trouble in the first place. "My wife has some sass."

"No one would ever say that about me."

He chuckles, shaking his head like he doesn't believe me. "I like it."

And I hate how I like a little too much his vote of confidence in me and the way he calls me his wife.

Like he really means I'm his.

12

———

[Bolan]

"What's this?" In the morning, a large calendar with the remainder of February into March hangs on the refrigerator.

"A calendar," Ruthie casually states, like it's obvious. But then she steps closer to where I stand, staring at the schedule of days with times written all over it. Her nearness gives me a whiff of her freshly showered scent, that combination of floral and spice, and I wish I'd been able to experience a shower with her.

My wife is damn tantalizing but aloof, disappearing each night like a mouse skittering into her hole. I hate it.

As promised, I've taken to sleeping on the couch, feeling a little stiff and sore already from the sagging middle cushion, because I don't want to do anything to make Ruthie uncomfortable.

Last night, I'd really hoped she'd just hang out with me. I

was getting itchy, anxious even, about the game today. My first one with the Anchors.

I fight the pull to look at her and keep my eyes on the rectangular page held by magnets on the fridge door.

Ruthie points at the paper. "These are your home games." Written in red. "These are away." Written in blue.

"You have really nice handwriting." Her printing looks like a professional font.

"When I was younger, I wanted to be a teacher."

The casual toss of what she once wanted to be turns my head. Even in profile, she's so pretty. The length of her eye lashes. Her perky nose. The puff of her lower lip, slightly larger than the upper one.

Lips that kissed me and wanted my cock and—

Fuck. I pull my eyes away and stare back at the color-coded sheet.

"But you don't want to be a teacher anymore?" I ask because she hadn't directly answered my question last night about working for ISM.

Ruthie can be whomever she wants to be, but something tells me sports agent, even sports assistant, isn't her first job choice. For one, she's too quiet for the position which typically includes strong personalities with loud voices.

She shrugs, keeping her gaze on the calendar. "I'm just not a teacher."

Another vague answer and I hate it.

"Anyway." She points at the calendar. "For some people, a month at a glance is too much information. But for other people, they need to see the big picture." She spreads her hands wide to exaggerate the scale of the next thirty-something days. "I don't want to overwhelm you, but I thought maybe seeing this on the fridge each morning might jumpstart your day. Let you know where you need to be when. If it's too much, we can cover the rest of the weeks and look at this schedule week by week, or even day by day."

"Like task by task?"

"Exactly." Her tone says she's pleased, and goddamn, I feel like a kid who got a question right in a classroom.

"I once had a coach who did stuff like this for me. Taught me step by step how to be a better catcher."

Despite my father's criticism of how I played, Matt Kincaid fostered my love of baseball. He was a model coach. He took the time to work with me on my stance. On my catch. On my throws. And my batting. He'd been an instrumental cog in the wheel to get me where I am today.

Ruthie smiles. "I've also included practice times, podcasts and interviews, and team meetings. I've made a digital copy, too, if you'd prefer that instead."

"This is amazing." I glance back at her, staring in awe, and struck again by how pretty she is.

She must feel me watching her because she slowly turns her head toward me. "What?"

"This was really thoughtful of you."

Ruthie shrugs. "All in a day's work. All puns intended." She chuffs a giggle. "But that's what I'm here for. To take care of you."

My eyes widen and my mouth falls open just the slightest bit. No one has ever taken care of me.

"I mean . . . you know . . . it's part of the job description."

"Right. The job." I look back at the schedule with the reminder Ruthie works for me. She's my wife in title only. She's my assistant and personal babysitter. And nanny to my kid.

My stomach sours.

"Can you do me an extra favor?" I slip my phone from my pocket. "Can you put this in my phone for me?"

Ruthie stares at the device in my hand like she's never seen a cell phone before. Slowly, she lifts her gaze. "You trust me with your phone?"

"Yeah, why not?"

Ruthie stares at the device another few seconds before hesitantly reaching for it. I tell her the code, and she taps in the digits while I peer at the calendar, staring at today's date.

"First game today," I say, finding my throat thick as I tip my head toward the calendar. "I should probably get going."

I wouldn't say I need to rush out, but suddenly, I don't want to stand here inhaling Ruthie's intoxicating scent, remembering I'm just a paycheck for her.

There's nothing wrong with getting to the stadium early. I'm not worried. I've been playing ball for decades, but every game comes with a touch of apprehension. Being new to the team, a pinch of unease mixes with the excitement of a new season.

The Anchors are a good group of guys, minus Valdez, and I want to prove I'm worthy of them.

"I know," Ruthie says, her voice kind, drawing my attention back to her. Another smile curls that lush mouth of hers. "It's on the calendar."

Yeah, the calendar.

I take another look at the spread sheet, with evenly spaced squares for days, seven across, four rows down. Job or not, it was still nice of her to create this calendar to organize my days for me, even if I'm not certain it will help me keep things straight.

My phone dings and I glance at the screen as Ruthie hands it back to me. A notification has popped up.

> Game Day. Need to leave in ten minutes.
> Catch all the catches.

The extra sentiment causes my lips to curve. Those little words of encouragement mean more than she'll ever know.

Tulane wanders into the kitchen from the living room

where she's been pushing around her baby doll, and anything else she can pile in the fragile stroller Ruthie bought her, and stands between my bare feet, her little arms raised upward, signaling she wants to be lifted. She's still wearing her pink pajama set from last night. Her hair is a riot of curls.

"Up." I state, setting my phone on the counter, and lifting Tulane high above my head. My large hands are still bigger than her belly. "Tulip. Do you know what today is?"

I wiggle her between my outstretched arms as she stares down at me. "Game day, girl. You gonna bring Daddy good luck?"

So far, Tulane has been my special charm. First, her coming into my life; then us coming to America.

I lower her and press a raspberry kiss to her covered belly. Tulane giggles, a sound I never knew I needed in my life and feel grateful every time I hear the rippling tinkle.

I catch a glance of Ruthie watching us with a weird expression on her face. One that looks like someone pinched her hard. Her brows cinch. Her eyes are sad a second.

"Oh." She shakes herself from whatever thought she had. "And there is chocolate milk in the fridge for you. I didn't know if you had a game day ritual about it or something."

Fucking thoughtful.

As I reach for the handle of the refrigerator, my phone buzzes again and I glance down at where it still rests on the countertop. Then I arch a brow at Ruthie and laugh. "Really? Every minute."

Ruthie shrugs. "Don't want you to be late on your first big day."

My first big day *with the Chicago Anchors.*

Hope my wife brings me luck as well.

~

THE ANCHORS SPRING training stadium is not as grand as their home field in Chicago. Still, the scaled-down baseball arena has nostalgia about it with a red marquee sign that mimics their home one and raised lawn seats that run from left field to right like their iconic bleacher section.

I can't wait to walk into Anchor Field for the first time as an Anchor. But that's a month away, and for now, I need to take things day by day.

In my new uniform of royal blue and Anchor red with the number 12 on my back, I'm ready for the opening game. The sky is cloudless. The temperature is moderate. And I've had a nice warmup in batting practice. Until I prove my worth to the team, I'm lower in the batting lineup. However, my batting average is one of the things that keeps me valuable.

I'll never admit that I'm getting slower on the uptake from squat to stand behind home plate. My hips ache a little more. My knees sometimes throb with pressure. I don't know what I'll do without the game, so I'll continue to power through any twinge or tweak. Ice baths after games. Heat treatments. Massages. Stretches.

The one thing I do not want to rely on is pills, knowing all too well the lure of addiction.

With my head focused and a little swagger in my step I take my position behind home plate, nod at the umpire who I'm going to get up close and personal with for spring training games and settle into my stance, squared up with the first batter, knee down in the dirt in hopes to convert low pitches to strikes.

Flynn Royal is on the mound. As a rookie, these first games are all about testing who works best where. Only a few veterans are in today's lineup, including Ford Sylver and Romero Valdez.

The tension between these two has been high but Ford is an exemplary captain. He ignores Valdez most of the time, which is difficult to do when you're supposed to be teammates.

The opening pitch happens, and the stadium erupts. The excitement of a new season fills the air.

But in the third inning, the craziest thing happens.

A ball hit by the second baseman from our Chicago south-side rivals, the Agitators, goes high toward left center. Valdez hightails it backward on nimble feet from his position at short-stop while Sylver rushes forward from centerfield. As the ball begins to drop, both players have their heads up, gloves up, and then they collide like kids in a tee ball game. Ford falls over, clutching his shoulder which he had surgery on last season. He's been looking good in practice, even getting a few balls from mid-center to home plate but seeing him on his knees concerns me.

Like Ford, I've crossed the line of thirty-five, which makes us nearly geriatric in baseball terms.

Standing, I sling back my protective face mask to give myself a better line of sight to the outfield as our coach heads onto the field behind the medical trainer.

Words are exchanged.

Once Ford is standing, the crowd goes wild in support of one of their favorite players.

When we finally get out of the inning, Ford tosses himself on the bench in the dugout.

"You okay, man?" Maybe he feels the signature clock of Anchor Field is ticking for him and his career. I certainly feel that way.

"I'm good." His answer is tight, his jaw clenched.

Standing at the railing along the dugout, I pay attention to the field, watching as the lineup starts at the top again. If their pitcher goes three up, three down, I won't be batting this round, but I'm hoping that doesn't happen. We need a win at this opener.

I consider myself a good team cheerleader and I easily shout out words of encouragement to my teammates.

Suddenly, Ford is standing beside me at the rail, but his concentration is directed toward the lawn section. The grassy area that runs along the curve of the outfield is full of people plopped on the grass or seated on spread blankets. Ford stiffens and stands taller beside me, and I glance in the direction of his focus, where a slight commotion happens among the lawn patrons.

A woman in a ball cap stands among three little girls I assume are Ford's kids. I haven't interacted enough with the team to learn all their wives and girlfriends, kids and pets, yet.

However, my attention falls on the woman sitting in the grass beside that bubble of commotion. The woman with a blonde ponytail and a little girl with vibrant red curls seated on her lap.

My ribs constrict like my chest protector is fastened too tight.

I'm never one to peek into the crowd in hopes of finding someone there for me. Someone rooting for me.

My granddad had been my biggest cheerleader.

But Ruthie brought Tulane to my game, and I can hardly breathe from the rush of appreciation in my lungs.

I'd like to think Tulane is my number one fan.

I'd love to grow my personal fan club members to two.

13

[Ruthie]

As I have a job to do, I go to the game with Tulane. However, sitting in the lawn section, Tulane and I both bare foot in the grass, my position doesn't feel like work. I'd thought the lawn area would be easier with a toddler versus the stadium seats, but the hill imitating the Anchors's home bleacher section is steep and I constantly keep my eyes and hands on Tulane to prevent her from tipping down the slope.

We are seated next to an older Hispanic couple with three young girls under the age of ten, and they are a great source of entertainment for Tulane, who can't possibly concentrate on a baseball game. Somewhere around the third inning, though, another person joins their party. A woman wearing a worn Chicago Anchors ball cap pulled low over her face. She also has Aviator sunglasses perched on her nose to cover her eyes.

The girls instantly recognize her, and I swear one of them

calls the newcomer Cadence, a world renowned country music singer I adore. However, it doesn't seem possible someone of such fame and acclaim would be among the superfans on the lawn.

When the centerfielder, Ford Sylver, hits a homerun, the three girls cheer extra loud, and I quickly learn they are his daughters. Because of our continued interaction with the girls named Zelle, Winnie, and June, I take the liberty to introduce myself.

"Hi. I'm Ruthie Av—" I stumble, then correct myself. "Uh. Ruthie Adler." The name feels foreign on my tongue. I've been Ruthie Avery all my life despite being married to Clifton Jacobson. Cliff's father thought it was best to use my maiden name in the office so people wouldn't think he was playing favorites, although everyone knew who I was and how I was related to him. He also didn't want the last name of Jacobson to infer nepotism.

The irony is in the significance of my last name remaining Avery.

"Nice to meet you, Ruthie," the woman in the ball cap states without introducing herself. Eventually, I learn the names of the couple are Ruby and Javier.

Tulane and I continue to interact with them as strangers do when you share a common interest. We're here for the game, but more importantly, two specific men who play for the Chicago Anchors.

When Bolan hits a double in the fifth inning, I jostle Tulane on my lap, forcing her hands together to clap. "Yay, Daddy!"

The cheer tingles on my tongue. *Daddy*. How I'd yearned to call Clifton such a term. Longed to be a mother hearing a small voice call me Mommy. To my dismay, it never happened.

Momentary thoughts of Cliff bring back Bolan's request to load his phone with the calendar I'd designed for him and my surprise at how easily he handed over the device. Clifton didn't let me near his phone, knowing what I'd undoubtedly find. The device was conveniently lost upon his death.

Beneath the bright sunshine of an Arizona afternoon, I chase away the memory and focus on the little redhead in my lap. Tulane hardly wants to sit still and begins to get fussier and fussier. We've interrupted what should be her nap time, but I don't want to leave the game quite yet.

Unfortunately, the Anchors lose.

As fans file out of the spring training stadium, I follow the crowd until Ruby speaks to me in a thick accent. "Do you know where to meet the players?"

"I didn't know we could." I assumed Bolan had been too busy focusing on the game to notice us in the lawn section, which I'm certain was a blur of people. It never occurred to me to seek him out afterward, especially as I don't hold a special pass as his assistant or any identification that I'm his wife.

"You follow us," her husband, Javier says, as the ball cap-disguised woman, whom I'm pretty certain *is* Cadence, carries the youngest Sylver girl on her hip. Ruby and Javier each hold a hand of one of the other girls and I follow their lead out the side of the stadium to a walkway that leads through a practice field that currently doubles as a parking lot. The pathway ends at a second building on the property.

I easily find Bolan in the crowd of players and families, and he rushes toward us.

"Flower. Tulip. You came." Excitement and surprise etch the roundness of his face. His dimple is like an extra ray of sunshine shooting from the corner of his wide grin.

"Hey," I awkwardly reply. "Great game."

"Hey, baby girl." Bolan runs a hand up Tulane's back and she shifts to lean toward her father. Bolan easily takes her from me, kissing her nose before squeezing her to his chest. "Did you see my hit?"

Uncertain if he's speaking to me or Tulane, I answer. "Yeah.

It was great." One would think I could find better descriptors in my vocabulary, but I'm addle-minded by Bolan's appearance.

Up close, I can better appreciate him in his uniform. The fit of his jersey. The hint of that woven black strap around his neck. The strength of his arms, and the snug curve of his baseball pants over his backside when he twists to thank someone passing by and congratulating his efforts. Add in the backward baseball cap on his head and . . .

I dig my teeth into my lower lip in appreciation of his body which I'm already acquainted with but would like to know better.

When he spins back to face me, I'm caught ogling him. But he's looking at me like he might ravish me right here on the sidewalk. Those moss-colored eyes are nearly solid gold in the brightness of the late afternoon. Something hungry, almost savage, in them as his gaze roams from my face to my breasts and down to my toes.

I'm wearing sandals that expose my bright red toenail polish. It felt good to run my toes through the grass in the stadium earlier. I'm also wearing denim shorts, and I slip my hands into my back pockets as Bolan takes in my shirt. The Chicago Anchor emblem is over my left breast.

"Whose shirt you got on, flower?" His voice is grizzly, like the appetite in his eyes is rumbling in his throat.

I bite the corner of my lip because I'm unsure with how he's going to respond when I twist to show him my back.

"No." Bolan gasps, the no almost an echo. "Fuck no." He states louder. "No, no, *no*, Ruthie."

Valdez is printed across my back, arching over the shortstop's number 6.

My shoulders fall, not appreciating Bolan's chastising tone, even if I'd been expecting this reaction.

"It was the only shirt they had at Target." With a quick trip before the game, Romero Valdez's shirts were the only ones on the shelf. When I arrived at the stadium, I went into the Anchor Shop, but Bolan is too new to the team to have a T-shirt there yet.

"I don't fucking care." His irritated voice doesn't express anger *at* me, but he's definitely upset with the shirt.

As he glares at me, two dark haired girls rush to Bolan's sides forcing me to take a step back. They jump up and down excitedly, startling Tulane, whom Bolan squeezes between the two women to hand back to me.

The women separate only enough to allow Tulane to be passed over and then close in again like giant castle doors, shutting out anyone else, narrowing in on their focus.

"Adler," one cries out in a thick Asian accent.

His face goes ashen as he looks at the first one.

"We come all the way from Japan." The other breaks into giggles, covering her mouth, pleased by the surprise they've sprung on him.

Both women are beautiful. Exotic with perfect pale faces and gorgeous large eyes. Their hair is sleek and midnight black with faint highlights of neon blue. And they are clearly smitten with Bolan.

His head swivels side to side, taking in each woman with stunned confusion before his eyes take on a wild, caged look.

"Um . . . hey . . . girls."

Are they girls? They look young but not too young to have crossed an ocean to see Bolan Adler.

The Scottsdale, Arizona area is a mecca for baseball fan enthusiasts in late February and early March, luring many families and college kids on spring breaks to the desert.

"You remember us?" Number One Girl's voice rises, like she's both happily shocked and pleasantly relieved that Bolan might recall their names.

The look on his face says he's drawing a blank and those once heated eyes glance up at me in panic.

I'm of no help. And I'm not liking how close they stand to him, one taking the liberty to clutch his forearm while she continues to bounce on her toes, bringing her pert, little breasts a little too close to him.

The other one really flips the switch for me, though, when she says, "You go boom-boom with us, again. Yes?"

My gaze snaps up to Bolan's face. His eyes are practically the size of baseballs. The liquid gold drains from the green which swirls like a windstorm as he stares back at me.

"No. No boom-boom." He swallows thickly and I cannot decipher if his distressed tone is because I'm standing here witnessing this moment. Or disappointment that he can't leave with them and *boom-boom*. With. Both. Of them.

Bolan promised faithfulness, and it's evident the vow is a struggle. And I feel sick.

Jealousy hits me like a giant gong. A warning blare that a man who so easily had sex with a stranger-to-him woman in an empty ballroom, and then a second time on a secluded balcony, would definitely have sex with two women. At once. He'd want to do it again. He'd miss the opportunity to do it again.

"I'm going to-to take Tulane home," I stammer, pulling her closer to me, like I don't want her to be a witness to Bolan's infidelity. A crime he has not committed, but once burned, forever branded, and Clifton permanently scarred me. My father had been no better.

"Tulane needs a nap." I spin with her tight to my chest and take off on quick feet. The slap of my flat sandals is like imaginary puffs of air, emphasizing my haste to get away from him.

"Flower," Bolan strains behind me. He could easily catch me. His legs are longer, stronger, and I've seen him run bases. He has speed.

"Ruthie." His voice distantly follows me, but he doesn't chase, and I make my get away, rounding the back of the stadium and heading for the parking lot on the opposite side.

I'm shaking by the time I reach the SUV Bolan rented for me and buckle Tulane inside her car seat. Finally, I pull into line behind all the other fans eager to exit the stadium parking.

If I thought I'd get away with it, I'd keep driving. Head for anywhere but Bolan's home.

THE SHARP SLAM of the apartment door lures me from the main bedroom.

"Shh," I warn Bolan with a stiff finger against my lips when the hard thud of a full duffle bag hits the entry area floor.

"Tulane is sleeping," I whisper. The late afternoon timing isn't great, but she's had a long day. A long few days, between arriving in America, the rush to Las Vegas, and then a hasty turn around to Arizona. Poor baby is exhausted.

And I'm tired as well.

Tired of cheating men and stolen moments.

"Why did you run away like that?" He immediately asks, hands in fists on his hips. He's wearing a pair of loose athletic shorts in Anchors royal blue and a long-sleeved athletic shirt with the sleeves pushed up to his elbows. That bear inked on his forearm is practically glaring at me. A baseball cap covers his head, forward facing this time, like he means business.

"How can I help keep your reputation clean, playing the dutiful wife, when I, and everyone else nearby, had to watch women so enthusiastically admire you? Offering sex like Tulane and I weren't even standing there." I swallow the sudden lump in my throat, fighting the desire to correct myself. Admire *my husband*. The dryness of my mouth matches the Arizona desert. "A threesome, Bolan. Really?"

He stares back at me before swiping the cap off his head and running his palm over his scalp. Back and forth his hand moves against his hair, making it stand up a bit before he sets the cap back on his head, this time flipped backward.

"Look, I never said I'd been a good boy."

Nope. He's admitted a few times he's been bad. An entire report was written about his bad boy reputation and a plan devised to correct it. That's *my* purpose here. To shield him from errant decisions.

Yet, I hadn't expected something like two excited fans in his face. *In my face.*

He's going to have fans. Admirers. People who crush on him. I'll have to accept it, and I get it. Bolan Adler is hot. Even if he's covered most of the game in protective gear, the strength of his thighs and the power in his arms is on display. Plus, that firm ass. Then he removes that mask and those damn dimples appear.

I tell myself to brace for the next time because there will be more women. Innocent admirers. And fanatics. And ball chasers. Those women who are willing *and wanting* to sleep with a professional baseball player for notoriety.

The trouble is I don't want to witness it, remembering all too well Clifton's infidelity because of the same type of attention.

"Those girls were nobodies."

That's what Bolan casually said about Melody Cross. The woman he was momentarily engaged to. How many others will he claim as insignificant? How many people will he tell *I'm* of no consequence? Did he even mention to those women he has a wife?

"Did you even tell them you are married?" Does that hold any weight with him?

Bolan blinks a few times, like the thought hadn't occurred to him. His expression suggests he's either shocked that I've reminded him or repentant that he hadn't mentioned it. While

I want to believe he's sorry, I just don't. Not with my track record, not with his.

"Well, what about you?" he snaps, lowering his hands and glaring at me. "*My wife* was wearing some other man's name of her back."

"I told you what happened." Blaming the retail store's availability is a bit weak but I truly hadn't had other options, and I'd been in a rush to have *something* that showed my support of the Chicago Anchors. I removed the T-shirt as soon as I got to the apartment, and I'm currently wearing a solid white tee.

"Where is the shirt?" His tone turns glacial as he eyes up and down my torso.

"In the bedroom."

"Go get it." The sharpness in his words pisses me off and I should argue back.

I don't take orders from him.

I don't have to do what he says.

He isn't my husband.

The last one catches me up, though, and I spin on my heels, the petulant stomp of my exit emphasizing I'm as angry as him.

I snag the shirt from the top of the hamper. When I re-enter the hall, Bolan remains by the front door, head lowered; his shoulders drooping. At the forceful pad of my feet on the tile flooring, he lifts his head again. His eyes narrowed.

Standing three feet away from him, I fling the shirt in his direction. My aim is even better than I intended as the tee lands on his head, covering his face. I have to bite down on my lip to stifle the release of a startled laugh. I can't believe I threw it at him. Nor can I believe the hot glare aimed back at me when he swipes the shirt off his head.

He holds it up to read the back one more time, and then rips the cotton right down the center.

"Bolan!" I shriek, louder than I should with a napping

toddler down the hall. "I hope that's not superstitious or something." Baseball players are notorious for being superstitious.

"It's probably sacrilegious." He scoffs, then mutters under his breath. "Wearing another man's jersey." He tosses the shirt to the floor. "And I don't want *that* guy's name on you. Or anyone else's but mine."

He bends down for his duffle bag, struggling to hastily unzip the closure. When he stands upright, he holds up an official team jersey and flips it around so I can read the back.

"Adler," he barks at the custom print of his name on the back of a royal blue jersey. "Number twelve."

He lowers the jersey just the slightest bit as he narrows his flaming gaze at me. "Know what that number means, flower?"

Silently, I shake my head as I'm ensnared by those eyes again. The ones with the heat of a forest fire in them.

"It means I'm twice the man he is. Because I'm patient." He drops one corner of the jersey and slaps his chest hard. "Waiting."

"Waiting for what?" I swallow thickly, meeting eyes I can't read but that swirl like a storm again. One crackling with lightning strikes and gray clouds.

"When you're ready for me." He gulps. "Because I'm right here, baby."

He's waiting for me to give him a signal that I want more. That I want him.

I lick my lips, my mouth still dry, and take the jersey from him. Bringing it to my chest, I tuck my chin and inhale the fresh newness of the shirt.

Bolan bends at his waist again and retrieves a second item from his bag. "I also got this."

In his hands is a miniature jersey, also in royal blue, with ADLER in small print across the back. "Want both my girls wearing *our* name."

He points between us. "Adlers." Like we're a package deal. A family.

Something I always wanted. One of my own.

Tossing the larger jersey he purchased over my shoulder, I reach for the smaller one. Spreading it between my hands, I stare at the tiny size and small font. The giant number twelve is centered on the back.

Tulane is going to look adorable in this mini-me jersey.

Slowly, all the steam seeps out of me, and I lower the shirt. "I'm sorry."

Bolan had been bending to pick up his bag, but his head snaps upward, and he slowly stands, leaving the duffle on the floor.

I lick my lips again, uncertain I should say what I'm about to share, but suddenly feeling like the truth needs to be let out, if only a sliver of it.

"Clifton." I swallow thickly. "Cliff. He . . . uh . . . he wasn't exactly faithful to me."

"What the fuck?" Bolan mutters. His hands immediately come to his hips again.

"In fact." I clear my throat. "He wasn't faithful at all." My voice strengthens. "We'd been high school sweethearts and took a little break in college. That was the first girl."

The secret I'm holding about Bolan and me hits hard, but this moment isn't about *my* sins.

Instead, I power on with Cliff's history. "It happened a second time when he played professional football."

The life of a professional athlete, he'd said. *The attention. The temptation.* As if either was an excuse. Like a little extra interest or the momentary enthusiasm of a fan excused his behavior.

He wasn't even that great of a player. Not one people would readily recognize. He'd been a second-string wide receiver.

"Second time?" Bolan scoffs, his brows severely creased.

Fool me twice, shame on me.

"The third time, though . . ."

Cliff had been away for six long months on an Army mission. I'd been waiting for him, as a wife should. Holding off on my own dreams. Pressing pause on having a family. Working for his father when being in sports management was the last thing I wanted to do.

The third time. I'd asked Clifton for a divorce.

"Third time?" Bolan barks, stepping closer to me.

For some reason, I step back, afraid of his touch. Afraid of how much I secretly crave it, want it to be real, yearn for it to mean something to him.

Forcing down the pain of that final time and brushing past the rush of hurt on Bolan's face, I barrel on, keeping my gaze on his eyes. "Nylah and Jared don't know."

"Why the fuck not?"

"Because I don't want them to." I didn't want to ruin their image of their son. Their precious, perfect boy who is gone.

I also hadn't wanted to lose them as better parents than my own.

Bolan licks his top set of teeth and turns his head a second. "Who does know?" He looks back at me, hands restored on his hips.

"Only me. And now you."

His hands fall from his hips. His fingers spread wide before relaxing. He stares back at me. "You're trusting me with this secret?"

I tilt my head. "I'm trusting you." With this secret. With my heart. I don't want Bolan to shatter it like Cliff did, and cheating is a hard limit for me as I told him when we negotiated terms for this arrangement.

Real marriage or not, I don't want a wayward husband just because we are together for false pretenses.

Patience. I need it in order to trust him with more of me.

Plus, I still have another secret I'm keeping from him.

Bolan nods before closing the gap between us. The rush is so quick, it startles me, but I don't flinch away this time when he gently catches my upper left arm and leans toward my right ear.

"I'm sorry that happened to you." His voice is a whisper of sincerity. "And *I'm* sorry, too, flower. That you thought, even for a second, that I'd step out on you. That you had to witness a sliver of my past. I told you I've been bad, but I'm promising . . . on my heart." He leans back and paints a giant X with his fingertip over his chest. "That I'll be good to you."

Then he kisses the tip of his finger that crossed his heart, and he cups the back of my hand, lifting it palm upright. He sets that kissed fingertip against my inner hand, like he's branding my love line. Marking me with that promise. Stamping me with a kiss he's being patient to give me.

Patient to earn.

14

[Bolan]

When Ruthie comes to my game on the second day, she is wearing the jersey I had made for her, with my mini-me in tow wearing her Adler jersey as well.

After the awkward interlude with the two women I couldn't remember, I rushed to the Anchor shop, hopeful to get a jersey custom printed with my name on the back until the official jerseys arrive.

I hate that my past catches up to me at times. Hate that Ruthie has a rough past with Clifton.

My cousin is one of those guys people hail as a hero but forget that he was only human. His death elevated him to sainthood, but it's evident the halo people like to place above his head slipped, and slipped, and slipped.

What a fucker.

I'm not a fan of cheaters. As in, I hate them. My mother

cheated on my father and ran off with another man. I might have messed around with a lot of women in my past, but I was always crystal clear about my intentions. No strings attached. No hard feelings. So, I wasn't committed to someone, then dipping my wick into some side piece.

The thought angers me even further when I think about Clifton. How inconsiderate he was and a fucking moron. He didn't treasure what he had with Ruthie, in Ruthie, and I'd like to bury him all over again for being the reason behind the sad, insecure look in her eyes.

I'm more determined than ever to do right by her. To prove that she deserves of better.

After Ruthie shared her story, Tulane woke up and Ruthie's demeanor shifted. She went into mom-mode, which reminded me that, for all intents and purposes, she *is* Tulane's stepmom. Ruthie is amazing with my little girl, who adores her as well.

Like I do, and I'm biding my time with Ruthie. *Patience.* It's becoming nearly painful.

I can control my impulses, but I'm a sexual guy. Not making excuses for myself, but I crave physical connection, and I'd been in a drought until Ruthie and our two times. I'm not looking to touch just anyone either. I want my wife, and it's been torture living with her. Smelling her shampoo in the shower. Watching her wear those sweet denim shorts. Knowing she sleeps just down the hallway from me. She's all I want. All I think about. All I see. I *feel* her, too, because I still have this strange sense of familiarity with her.

Maybe the sensation is as simple as how easily she fits with Tulane and me.

However, Ruthie remains distant, when her eyes tell a different story. I think she wants me, and I don't like the separation. It makes me itchy, like she'll bolt any second. Something tells me Ruthie is more responsible than a runner, though.

She wouldn't leave me, would she?

The most important thing I'd taken away from the information she shared about Clifton was that she trusted me. She shared a dark part of her history with me. And I want to know all her secrets.

Spring training for the Chicago Anchors is not starting off strong. The gossip mongers and rumor mills are spinning early about our team, especially after a guest appearance by Cadence. The world-renown country singer slipped into the lawn section on day one.

I'd asked Ruthie if she met the superstar, knowing they sat near one another. Ruthie said she introduced herself to the famous singer, but didn't make a big deal of the other woman's notoriety. Ruthie's met tons of stars in her profession and something tells me she isn't impressed by fame.

After the game, I linger outside the stadium waiting on my girls. Two games, and I'm addicted to seeing them directly afterward.

When Ruthie approaches, she kindly offers, "Tough game." We lost and as I'd played the opener, Cyrus Sawyer caught today.

"Yeah, it was a rough one." I tug my ball cap off my head and spin it around, setting it backward now that the game is over. Then I reach out for Tulane who lunges toward me. Tugging her close, I pepper the side of her head with kisses.

"Did you see my hit?" I mutter to Tulane while really asking Ruthie. I went in as a designated hitter in the seventh inning for a rookie who got hurt earlier in the game. Was she watching the game? Was she paying attention to me? Even thinking such thoughts makes me sound desperate, needy even. But for two days in a row, she's been at the games, for me. That's two more professional games than anyone has attended for me.

"Nice one," she states.

The double I'd hit landed me on second base. Unfortunately, I didn't get home as Valdez followed me in the batting order and struck out.

"Thanks." I set Tulane down on her feet and stand upright, keeping my eye on my little one. "Thanks for coming again today."

My throat catches on my gratitude. I remind myself she's here because of the arrangement. She's been assigned to be my agent, which essentially means she's babysitting me. She agreed to be my wife which brings its own level of confusion. When I dig deeply, nothing in our situation settles well in my gut.

Then Ruthie says, "Of course, Bolan. I'm here for you."

How I want that statement to be true.

I take a deep breath, turn my head to the side and squint in the bright sunshine. "Never had someone come to my games before."

"What do you mean?" Her voice is light, like she thinks I'm kidding.

I bring my attention back to her. "My dad stopped coming when I was younger. My mother never showed up for me."

"Bolan," Ruthie softly whispers, stepping closer to me.

I glance down at Tulane, who is looking around at all the people exiting the stadium. Her little arm is wrapped around my knee like a buoy. Safety in a sea of people.

"My mom left when I was ten," I begin, wondering where this information is coming from. Why I'm telling her this now, and here, in the side lot. "She'd been having an affair. Left to marry the guy. Had two more boys with him. They are the favored ones."

Hunter and Miller Frederick aren't bad guys. Hunter and I are eleven years apart; Miller and I thirteen. We're not exactly close as brothers go, but I check in on them occasionally. When I went to Japan, communication became even more limited.

I scoff. "Which is why giving that speech during The Red

Dress Affair was a joke." My voice hardens and I clear my throat.

Ruthie doesn't take her eyes off me.

"My dad was another story. He drank a bit too much." A lot too much. "And he'd make a scene. One time, he got kicked out for unruly behavior." I glance down at Tulane. "I was in high school."

One of the most embarrassing moments of my life. My father so drunk, hollering at the coach, taunting me with how to play better. A bad catch. A missed hit.

Finally, the school security removed him. I asked him never to attend one of my games again, and he didn't. Not a college one. Not a professional one.

"I never want Tulane to feel that way. Unwanted. Unworthy." *Dammit.* My eyes prickle, but I'll deny tears and blame the sunshine for the burn. I clear my throat again. "Anyway, I just want to say thanks again for showing up. For being here. It means a lot to me."

My gaze drops to where her fingertips brush the thick hairs on my forearm.

"I totally get it," she whispers. "And I—"

"Adler, man, quit flirting with all the ladies and get your ass in the locker room." Romero Valdez claps me hard on the shoulder as he's passing me.

The moment with Ruthie was getting a little intense, although she was on the verge of telling me something. Something probably important.

"I don't flirt with all the ladies." My gaze lands on Ruthie, holding on those dark eyes, willing her to believe me. She's the only woman I want to flirt with.

Turning toward Valdez's retreating back, I become defensive. "She's my wife."

Valdez stops, the abrupt clomp of his cleats on cement cut

short, like he hit the brakes. He does an about-face and turns back toward us.

"Damn." He hums in appreciation, looking Ruthie up and down. "I didn't know you were married." He winks at my wife. "You're one lucky man."

Holding out his hand, he approaches her. "Romero Valdez. Around here they call me Romeo."

Everything in me wants to step between Ruthie and Romero. I want to tell him he can't touch her. Keep his hands off her and his eyes away from her. Instead, I growl, "Now who's flirting with who?"

Ruthie chuckles. "Ruthie Adler. Nice to meet you."

My head swivels toward her. *Ruthie Adler.* While I know it. While I've heard it. This is the first time I've heard her say the name in her sweet voice, and my chest puffs up.

Valdez is right. I'm a lucky man. *That's my wife.* She's smoking hot. Blonde hair in a ponytail peeking through the back of an Anchors ball cap, wearing a jersey that says our name on the back, and denim shorts with frayed hem. The jersey is long, and those shorts are a tease beneath the length of the shirt. Ruthie looks good and my gaze drops to her feet. Red toenail polish peeking through her sandals.

Fuck. Those toes. That color. Reminds me how badly I want my wife. She'd been wearing heels that first time. The spike poking into my ass when her legs wrapped around me. We'd been lost in the moment then and I relished the pain. But something in me wants to take her sweet and slow, tuck those feet around my back and feel her wrapped around me, skin to skin.

"Down boy," Valdez claps my shoulder again, and I'm jostled from my salacious thoughts.

Ruthie smiles softly before bending to pick up Tulane and set her on her hip.

And my wayward thoughts run rampant again because

nothing makes me hotter for her than watching her interact with Tulane.

Mommy kink? I swipe my palm down my face. I need to get myself together.

"I'll see you at home." There's hesitation in Ruthie's voice, like she's questioning I'll be there when I don't want to be anywhere else.

"Of course." I'm here for her, too, she just doesn't know it yet.

15

[Bolan]

Our opening spring training run includes a three-game series with the Agitators, Chicago's crosstown rivals, and ends in a losing streak. The black, white, and green are as mean as their mascot, a Tyrannosaurus Rex. Tomorrow, we start a new series.

After admitting how important Ruthie's presence at the game is to me, there's been a little shift between us. Nothing tectonic, but a swing, nonetheless. She didn't hole up in the back bedroom but lingered while I gave Tulane a bath and read to her before putting her down for bed.

When Ruthie plops down on the couch while I watch the replay of another spring training game from the recliner, I'm thrilled. We don't talk until I ask her about working at Imperial Sports Management.

"How'd you end up working as a sports agent if you wanted to be a teacher?"

"You remember that?" Those dark eyes sparkle in the glow of the television set from her seat on the couch. Her eyes are like the cosmos, a mystery of darkness with the hint of stars in them.

Sitting in the recliner, my feet are propped up, head tipped back but turned in her direction. I might need to get one of these chairs for my new place.

"I remember lots of things about you, flower." I wink.

Her eyes only momentarily flare at my flirtatious memory. Her responding smile is weak. "Clifton wanted me to work for his dad. *He* thought it was a good idea."

I adjust the chair to sit upright and lean heavily on the armrest. "Why?" Every story I hear about my cousin makes me dislike him a little more.

Ruthie shrugs. "I'm quiet. Shy even. He thought it would bring me out of my shell." She scoffs. "Teaching wasn't glamorous to him. When we graduated college and he was recruited to play for a national football team, he thought it'd be cool for his wife to work in the industry."

What the fuck? "First, you can be whoever you want to be, Ruthie. For you. Teacher. Sports agent. Hell, a belly dancer."

She snorts.

"Your profession should reflect your passion, and it isn't being a sports agent." I recall how adamant she was not to be assigned to me, and something told me it had very little to do with me. Ruthie didn't want to be an agent, as she told Jared.

"Also, I wouldn't call you shy, flower." I stare directly at her, recalling a woman a little thorny upon first meeting, but still sweet. She didn't seem shy when she kissed me like her life depended on it. Nor when she spread her knees, allowing my head to drop between them.

"Maybe a bit reserved." I choose my words wisely when I'm not really a smart guy. "But that's not a bad thing. You're cautious." And I'm willing to wait, like I already told her. I tap my temple. "A thinker."

She's definitely smarter than me, but also thoughtful. The calendar on my fridge says so. So does the stock of chocolate milk in said fridge. And she came to my games.

"And just *what the fuck* about wanting his wife in the industry? You see how Valdez responded to you yesterday? You're fucking hot, Ruthie."

Her eyes widen at the strength of my voice. Her skin flushes pink at the compliment.

"That blonde hair is like honey to most men. Plus, you've got those doe-eyes looking all innocent and sweet." I hum, dragging my gaze around her face. "I'm going to have to disagree with Cliff on this one, and if I had a say, which I don't . . ." I pause to level my eyes on hers. "The last place I'd want my wife working is in the industry where horny, egotistical assholes exist. Athletes can be sharks." Circling a beauty like her.

I pause again, realizing that's exactly where *my wife* does work. "If you don't want to be a sports agent, if you don't want to work for Jared anymore, quit. I got you, Ruthie." I pat my chest.

I'm financially sound, and she'll be financially well-off once our contract is up in a year. "If it's about money—"

She softly lifts her hand and shakes her head. "It isn't about money."

"Then what is it about? Why are you still with them?"

Her shoulders drop. "Because they're family. They've been good to me."

"Do you feel obligated to them? Nylah and Jared adore you, and if they truly love you, they aren't going to be upset that you want to leave their company."

"It isn't that simple."

"Yeah, Ruthie. It is." We stare at each other a long minute, the tension between us building.

She breaks away first, narrowing her eyes at the television, but I'm certain she isn't watching it. "Nylah and Jared are like second parents to me. Better parents than my own. I don't want to disappoint them. And I'm not actually an agent. I'm an assistant."

She glances back at me. "I don't know why Jared called me your agent. I sucked at being one."

I laugh, sharp and loud at the word choice. "I'm certain you didn't suck, flower. You couldn't suck at anything." Then I dig my teeth into my lower lip. Well, I could think of a few ways she could put that term to proper use.

She laughs. Not full-on but soft and delicate. "Is your mind ever not thinking dirty thoughts?"

"I'm a guy. A twelve-year old at heart." And I'm horny for my wife, but back to the conversation at hand. "I'm serious, though. Baby, if you want to still be a teacher, teach. Go back to school or whatever it takes and live life for you, Ruthie."

Her expression slowly morphs from teasing me about a dirty mind to something close to crestfallen.

"But I'm not living my life, Bolan. I'm living yours." Her eyes are soft, compassionate even, until they lower completely, dropping away from me.

Dammit. She's right. She's stuck with me, like she might have felt stuck with Cliff.

"Why'd you marry him? He sounds like a dick." The question is harsh, expressing my envy of a dead guy. He had her first and he didn't appreciate her quiet beauty, not shyness. Her sensual strength. Then again, maybe she wasn't with him like she is with me. One could hope her eagerness, the way she kisses, is only about me.

"Don't they warn you not to speak ill of the dead," she counters, thorns prickling out of my flower again.

"What's he going to do? Haunt me?" I make a spooky sound because I don't believe in that shit, only Ruthie glances back at the television. That far-off look she sometimes gets in her eyes tells me he might haunt her.

"Hey." I slide off the chair and walk on my knees over to her, stopping in front of her, so she'll focus on me. I want her full attention, so I place my hands on her knees, spreading them to allow my wide body between them, and instantly noting how soft her skin is.

"I'm a dick sometimes, when I don't mean to be. He was your husband. You obviously loved him and it's none of my business why." I'd still like to know what the attraction was. How did a guy like him end up with a girl like her? But then I could ask the same question about myself. How did I get so lucky as to have her give up her life for a year to be with me? I'm no better than Cliff.

I lick my lips and swallow tightly. "If you want out of our agreement, Ruthie, I'll make it happen." I'll let her go. I'm on the team. Surely, I'm proving myself useful to the Anchors and they'll see me as a worthy player, with or without a wife.

"No." She shakes her head, pulling her gaze from my hands on her knees to my face. "No, I don't want you to let me go."

She doesn't want me to let her go? She wants to stay? My heart races, palms sweating on her kneecaps. Does she want me? Will she let me kiss her? So many thoughts collide, and as I don't think before I act, I lean forward, wanting to steal another kiss from her, whether I've earned it yet or not.

I swear she leans toward me as well. Her floral and spice scent tickling my nose. Her eyes are on my lips and my gaze drops to her mouth. That puffy lower lip. The curve of the upper one. Her teeth nip at the corner and I can taste her before we've even connected.

Her slight inhale tickles the coarse hairs around my mouth. My beard needs a trim, but something tells me Ruthie likes the scruff. She certainly loved it between her thighs, and I want to dive between them again.

But first, I want to kiss her.

On my knees. Happy she wants to stay. Thrilled she's giving me a chance.

I lift my hand for the side of her neck, wanting to pull her closer—

Tulane lets out a sharp cry.

Ruthie and I both turn out heads in the direction of the closed bedroom door.

While my heart is hammering, I'm holding my breath.

Please don't cry again. *Please don't let her cry again*, I pray.

But another sharp wail drifts from behind the door and Ruthie shifts, forcing me to fall back on my heels. My knees crack, catching up to kneeling on a tile floor.

"I'll get her," she says quietly. I want to hear disappointment in her voice. Swear I hear it, but I can't be certain.

As Ruthie stands, her hips are eye level, and I stare after her. The hourglass shape of her. The sweet swell of her ass. The back of her toned legs.

She opens the door to Tulane's room and disappears inside.

I bend forward, resting my forehead on the couch cushion where she just sat.

So close. So close to kissing her again.

Fear catches up to me. Fear she might never want my kiss again. Fear she feels trapped with me and the last thing I want to do is make her feel like she has to do anything she doesn't want to do.

I want Ruthie to work where she wants, or not work at all, if that's her jam. I'm happy to have her as my wife, and as a stepmom for Tulane. She doesn't need Imperial Sports Management.

She has me.

I want to be enough.

~

As the Anchors losing streak continues, I'm out of sorts. I'd fucked up in the sixth inning of the new series, missing an easy catch thrown from second to home plate which went over my head, allowing in a run.

I hate when I make simple mistakes.

However, my mind has been circling around what Ruthie told me. How she didn't want to be an agent. How she'd made decisions because of Cliff or for his parents. Hell, she's doing something special for me.

Add in the near kiss between us, and her absence from today's game after I've told her how important it is to me that she attends, and I'm a curve ball just waiting to be released from the pitcher's clutch.

My irritation level is near .246, my batting average, which is actually on the high end for spring training.

When I'm finally back at the apartment, rushing to open the door, I'm vibrating with agitation, prepared not so much for a fight, but an inquisition. *Why didn't she attend today's game? What was more important?*

I can be a hothead, and I know this about myself. I've worked myself up into a full lather, as my granddad would say, until the front door pops open and I see Ruthie pacing the living room with a subdued Tulane in her arms.

"What's wrong?" Spidey senses I didn't have before Tulane came into my life prickle under my skin, knowing something isn't right as I close the door behind my blustery entrance.

Ruthie presses a kiss to the side of Tulane's head. "She has a fever. She's been extra fussy today. Didn't want to nap but doesn't want to play either."

"A what? How?" I drop my bag, which causes a heavy thud when it hits the floor. In my haste to reach Tulane, I stumble over the bulky bag, catching myself before faceplanting. Eventually placing my hand on Tulane's back, heat emanates through her thin shirt. "What's the matter, Tulip?"

Instantly, my girl shifts in Ruthie's arms, reaching out for me, and I scoop her up. She's a little bundle of gooey warmth.

Panic escalates. "Did you call a doctor? Give her medicine?"

"Didn't you get my message?" Ruthie stares up at me, brown eyes wide with concern. She also looks exhausted.

"I haven't checked my phone." *Why hadn't I checked my phone?* It should have been the first thing I did when I didn't see them at the game. I'm not used to people checking in with me or checking in on them.

I shake my head. "What did the message say?"

"I called a local pediatrician. They said for now to simply monitor her. Liquids are a must. If she doesn't eat, that's okay. Baby Tylenol to help reduce the fever."

I nod, prepared to ask if I even have the fever reducer, but then remember I do.

"I also felt a little stupid, not knowing Tulane's medical history, when I'm supposed to be her mom."

"Supposed to be?" I stare at her around Tulane's head tucked against my shoulder. It's been roughly a week of marriage, but it feels like Ruthie has been part of Tulane's life for months. She *is* her mom, right now.

My own mother hadn't known when I broke my ankle or injured my knee. Didn't know when I had the flu or even a common cold. My dad had been the one to tackle all those things, and I wouldn't say he handled them well. He wasn't exactly a compassionate man.

But Ruthie has enough compassion to fill the Grand Canyon.

"Okay. Good point. I'll find all her records and share them with you." Tulane had to be up to date on all immunizations before she could enter the United States. She'll eventually have dual citizenship being born in Japan but parented by Americans.

Later that evening, Tulane won't stop crying. Every single time I set her down in the crib, she wails.

"Okay, baby. I've got you." But I can't keep hanging onto her. I have a game tomorrow and need some sleep. It's bad enough I'm sleeping on a couch that's too small for my body, not to mention, not great for my back.

By ten o'clock, Ruthie exits the main bedroom, having holed herself up again after a failed attempt at feeding Tulane dinner.

She whispers my name in the dark apartment. The glow of the muted television set is the only light in the place. "You need your rest. I can take her."

Ruthie is a vision in pajama shorts and a thick-strapped tank top. She's wearing those red-framed glasses, and her hair is piled up on her head. She looks young and hesitant. Like I might not appreciate her offer of help when I'm growing desperate.

I step closer to her, handing over Tulane who feels like she's finally nodding off to sleep.

"If it's alright with you, I'd like to take her to my room. Give you some privacy and hopefully some quiet." Ruthie runs her hand down Tulane's back and presses a kiss to her downy hair.

"Yeah. Of course. Whatever you think will work." As I watch Ruthie walk down the hallway and disappear into the main bedroom, I feel like a failure. The soft *snick* of the door might as well be as loud as a metal gate, locking her away. I don't like this underlying tension between us, and I especially don't like how I'm not a great dad.

With a heavy sigh, I collapse on my back on the couch, kicking my feet up on the armrest. I stare at the flash of color coming from the television, a replay of today's game, and my error. I curse my body. The crack in my knees. The ache in my lower back. And despite the exhaustion of trying to placate a sick child, I suddenly can't sleep.

Especially when I hear Tulane crying again and then abruptly stop, like all the gas ran out of her.

Scrubbing a hand down my face, I glance up at the ceiling fan, swirling in a slow circle.

What the hell do I think I'm doing, trying to raise a kid on my own while being a professional ball player?

Moments like tonight remind me how lonely I've been, but I'm not alone. I have Ruthie, holed-up in a large room with a king-sized bed and my kid. I should be in there with them. It should be me soothing Tulane's aches, but I won't be selfish. I won't deny her love from all angles. A multitude of people loving on her, like my Hiroshima family had.

Maybe I'd been wrong to return to the U.S. Thinking here was better than there. Thinking I could do this on my own. While I have Ruthie, I only have her for a year. Long enough for my sweet Tulip to fall in love with her and for Ruthie to break her little heart when she leaves . . . like my mom left me.

Not quite the same thing but still the same sensation. A broken heart is a broken heart.

IN THE MORNING, I hate to leave them. Ruthie looks even more exhausted. Tulane doesn't look any better. Her little nose is running, and she has a barky cough.

"I'm going to take her to an urgent care," Ruthie tells me. Dark circles curl underneath her eyes. She's wearing her glasses again. Her hair is still piled high on her head. Last night she had on shorts and a tank top. Now she's wearing a sweat-shirt and sweats, covering up every inch of her skin.

I nod, grateful but feeling guilty. "I don't exactly have a nine-to-five job. One where I can take the day off."

"That's why I'm here," Ruthie assures me, weakly. Her voice is groggy.

"You okay?"

"Yeah, just a little tickle in my throat."

"Oh boy. Are you sick?" *Are both my girls ill?*

"Haven't built up the mom-resistance yet, I guess." Her smile is timid as she glances at Tulane who lies on the couch, eyes forward toward the television where a kid's program is playing at a low volume.

Ruthie would make a great mom.

"Why aren't you a mother?" I blurt before realizing how insensitive my question is. I know all about women struggling to have children and how difficult the subject can be. I also understand Ruthie is Tulane's stepmother, but I mean why hasn't Ruthie had children before now.

She shrugs, her motion almost as sad as the sudden dullness in her eyes. "Just never got pregnant."

Her monotone answer reveals only one thing: she's lying. Another secret. One I don't press because she looks too worn out to talk.

"I promise I'll come right home." So far, I've attended practices, participated in games, and come home every night. The actions are less about being a dutiful husband, but more about keeping my promises and coming home because home is where I want to be. Duty has nothing to do with my position. I'm thankful trouble hasn't found me, but then again, I'm not out looking for it either. The only kind of trouble I want involves my wife, and trouble is the furthest thing I'd call her.

Within minutes, I'm dressed, gear collected, duffle bag full of snacks and an energy drink, and turn back when I'm at the front door, hand on the knob, but not opening it yet.

Ruthie is sitting on the couch with Tulane in her lap, both girls staring at the television as Ruthie softly sings some kid song I don't know.

Everything in me wants to stay. Wants to take care of my girls, but I need to go.

"Hey, flower. Call me if it's anything more than a fever, yeah?" I'll be checking my phone as often as I can today.

She turns her head, leaning it against the back of the couch. "Of course."

I nod once and then turn the doorknob. While facing the door to exit, Ruthie calls out to me. "Hey Bolan?"

Spinning around, the door whacks me in the knee because I'm startled by the sudden call of my name.

"Yeah?"

"Catch all the catches." She further shocks me by placing her fingers on her lips and blowing me a kiss.

I lift my hand, spreading my fingers wide to catch that kiss in my palm before squeezing my fingers tight to close my fist.

"Got it," I call out, like I'm racing for a pop fly that's gone behind home plate, hoping to catch the ball for an easy out.

Only, I don't want to strike out with my wife.

With her kiss in my hand, I make a big show of tucking it in my pocket, patting over the spot to emphasize where I'll keep it safe.

Ruthie softly chuckles which is the first happy sound I've heard from her in days. "Anyone ever tell you that you're ridiculous?"

"Yes. And from you, I'm taking it as a compliment." Just like her tossing me a kiss made my day.

Especially when the Anchors lose again, and I come home to find Tulane tucked on Ruthie's lap, both girls bundled under a blanket on the couch.

Both of them sick.

[Ruthie]

I have no idea why I blew him a kiss. Perhaps I felt saucy. Maybe I'm just delirious.

I'm running a low-grade fever, and my throat is on fire. I just want to close my eyes and sleep for a week, but Tulane is as ill as I am.

She has a double ear-infection, and the 'pink medicine' was prescribed for her. I texted Bolan the details. When he finally responded with concern, he mentioned a mandatory team meeting he hadn't known about, and he would try to skip out on. Because I'd designed his calendar, I knew about the meeting, and I also knew he couldn't miss it.

Little things, like skipping team meetups, were the types of situations that snowballed Bolan's bad rep and sent him to Japan in the first place.

The numerous bigger issues for him include ones like an incident with a Mini Cooper and an opposing team's mascot.

As the afternoon turns to evening, the sky grows darker, and I feel guilty that I've missed two games in a row. However, with Tulane as my sidekick, she cannot keep up with this pace, and I've notified Jared that either a nanny needs to be hired, or Bolan needs to be trusted.

I'm rooting for option number two. He needs to be allowed to make good choices on his own, without me hovering over him. I believe he can do it. Plus, I'm enjoying my time a little too much with the little one sleeping on my chest. I should set her down but I'm afraid her ears are still bothering her despite giving her antibiotic and baby acetaminophen to manage the ache.

It also might be that I simply don't want to put her to bed yet.

Because my father called. Of course, I ignored any message he left, but even the idea of him calling me adds to the weight of my illness and I just wanted to snuggle Tulane a little longer. My personal reminder that I'd never let anything happen to her. She will know love.

Sitting on the couch, my legs are stretched out with my back braced on the armrest, and Tulane on my lap. A blanket is draped over both of us. The hum of the television is just that—soft background noise. My eyes have fallen shut.

Earlier in the day, I had the Anchors' game on the set. Bolan is an incredible catcher, but he also had some great hits today. I feel awful that Tulane and I have missed his game. It broke my heart when he said no one ever attends them for him. I like being that someone there for him, cheering him on, talking with him about the games afterward. He has someone rooting for him now, and that someone is me.

I've missed him today.

When the apartment door bursts open, like Bolan raced up two flights of stairs, the suddenness sends a woosh of air into the room, and my lids fling open.

Bolan startles when his gaze catches on me.

"Flower, what's wrong?" His voice is filled with the same level of concern he expressed yesterday when he walked in and found me pacing the room with Tulane in my arms.

"I'm not feeling so great," I admit. "But Tulip is doing better."

Bolan's eyes widen and then soften. His smile grows next. "You just called her by her nickname."

My cheeks heat. "Should I not? I know that's your special name for her."

Bolan sets down his bag and rounds the couch. "It can be *our* special name for her."

The thrill that rushes up my middle shouldn't exist, especially as my throat burns when I swallow, but Bolan has made repeated comments with *our* in them.

Our last name. Our home.

He's making it too easy to slip into a reality that doesn't exist in this fantasy we're building by playing family.

"You should really stop calling me flower, though."

"Why? Because you don't want me thinking about your delicate petals? Or the soft sigh you make, like a leaf in the wind, when you—"

"Bolan," I snap, jostling Tulane against my chest as I chuckle. "Don't make me laugh." *Or turn me on.* I'm too sick to think about him touching me intimately or making any sigh he says I make.

Bolan twists his lips. Fighting a smirk or feeling chastised, I can't tell. There is so much about him I still cannot read.

Then again, I'd known Clifton most of my life and hadn't been able to understand him either.

"You're right, though," Bolan interjects, erasing my thoughts of Cliff. "Flower is too generic, which is why I wanted to call you Rue. It's more specific."

"How do you even know what rue is?" Bolan does not strike me as a man who propagates flowers.

"My granddad had a flower garden." Bolan lowers to squat beside the couch. "He loved those flowers more than almost anything. Except me."

The look in his eyes expresses both love and loss.

"He sounds like a special man."

"He was. My number one fan."

I don't have grandparents, but I appreciate that relationship. I'd longed for it as a kid. Longed for any semblance of family, which is why falling into Clifton's had been both easy and dangerous for me.

I also fight the admission that I could be Bolan's number one fan. Instead, I swallow against the fire at the back of my throat and shift Tulane. "I should probably get up."

Twisting my body, I intend to stand when Bolan catches my knee. "What do you need?" He stands and toe-kicks out of his shoes while he asks.

"I should put Tulane to bed." Her nap was short again today. She needs more rest.

When Bolan reaches downward, I assume he's going to take her from me. Instead, he scoops both of us up.

"Bolan," I whisper-scold. "What are you doing?"

He steps over to the recliner and takes a seat, setting me on his lap before tipping the seat back. I fall against his chest, Tulane still tucked against mine.

"I'm taking care of my girls."

"I weigh too much," I say as I wiggle to settle better on his thighs.

"Never say that." He presses a kiss to the top of my head which rests just beneath his chin on his shoulder. "And you're burning up, baby."

"I'm freezing." The last half-hour I might have been using the heat of Tulane on me to try and warm up.

"Did you take anything?"

"Tylenol. About thirty minutes ago."

"Tell Dr. Adler what else aches, flower?"

"Now you're a doctor?" I tease, my voice scratchy.

"Let me heal you."

I hum, closing my eyes. He has no idea the ways he could heal me. On the flip side, some wounds might go too deep.

"Is this about petals again?" I flirt when I have no business, as a sick woman, flirting.

"Do you want it to be?"

I hum again, not certain if I do or don't but leaning toward *yes*. I don't know why I'm resisting my husband. Bolan Adler seems like a good man, trying to do the right thing for his daughter. We could have fun together although I'm not known for fun.

Responsible Ruthie versus reckless, spontaneous, adventurous Ruthie. Then again, I did marry him on a whim.

"How long have you been holding her?" he mutters to my hair, and I realize his lips linger on my forehead.

"A while."

"I think she likes you better than me," Bolan states quietly.

"Never say that," I chide, parroting his words when I made my weight comment.

His relationship with Tulane is solid for now, and as long as Bolan never does anything to crack that bond, she'll always love him more.

"But I'm definitely falling in love with her," I admit. Dangerous. So dangerous to love someone else's child. "How could I not? She's so sweet."

At sixteen months, life is an adventure. So many discoveries. So many developments.

Bolan hums next, his lips still at my hairline. "Tell me again why you aren't a mother." He pauses a second. "The real reason, this time."

"I didn't get pregnant," I state again. My eyes close as I relax into the rhythm of Bolan's chest lightly lifting and lowering with each breath he takes. The thud of his heart through the thin material of his shirt is soothing.

Keeping my eyes closed, I breathe deeply. "Clifton and I didn't work." I shouldn't feel comfortable talking about my late husband while I snuggle into my new one, but Bolan asked.

And when he doesn't speak, I fill the silence. "I thought it was me." *My body. My fault.*

I swallow thickly, fighting the burn in my sore throat, a combination of illness and melancholy memory. "But it was him."

In the eight years of our marriage, discussions about having a baby came and went. Eventually, per a doctor's suggestion, we committed to six solid months of trying to get pregnant. If I hadn't been pregnant naturally by the end of those six months, then we'd talk about alternatives.

Six months came and went. At the nine-month marker, I demanded Clifton and I each be tested for infertility issues.

The results showed Clifton's sperm count was low. The idea sent him into a ridiculous rage. His sexual drive was a badge of honor, although stamina and sperm numbers are not the same thing. Eventually, he joked about being impotent. Called himself a dud. The humor was a coverup for deeper emotions. For what he considered another failure.

He hadn't been the football star *he* thought his father wanted him to be.

He hadn't been a faithful husband.

He wouldn't be a father.

For me, the final blow came when I went to the doctor thinking I might be pregnant, despite this new development, to learn I had chlamydia.

Clifton's *third strike.*

"It wasn't meant to be, I guess," I say, realizing I'd been lost in painful memories.

"What about adoption?"

"It wasn't an option." I'd asked Clifton for a divorce. My final secret from Nylah and Jared. "Then, he ... passed."

I always stumble on the word, as if *passing* implies Clifton hadn't had a choice. Like cancer or a heart attack claimed him.

"Tell me again how he died."

I'm thankful my eyes are already closed, and I swallow once more, the pain in my throat from more than my current ailment.

"He killed himself," I whisper. "Walked right into the sea and—"

I hate the ocean now, though it isn't the natural wonder's fault my husband took his life. I'll never know what thoughts were running through his mind; how he could choose to walk himself into the roiling waves of the sea, rather than fight for our marriage. He chose to step out on me. He chose to break us. To break me, over and over again. Yet, when I finally decided to fight back for myself, Cliff decided to end it all, breaking me for the final, most excruciating time.

I'd begged him for marriage counseling. Even suggested he get therapy on his own. The stigma around mental health was not the same as it was ten years ago. Not for athletes. Not for veterans. But Clifton refused. He saw therapy as an admission to failure. Me. His parents. Himself.

When I told him I thought we should divorce, he walked himself into the ocean.

Bolan squeezes me tighter. His lips press more firmly against my forehead. He doesn't tell me he's sorry. Doesn't offer condolences, and I'm grateful. I've heard the words so often in the last eighteen months, and anger brewed within me with each new set offered.

People wanted to hail Cliff as a hero. He wasn't. Not a saint of a man nor husband either. He was simply a sad, disturbed human who refused to get help.

Through my own counseling, I've learned not to blame myself. Some days were harder than others. Most days, being around Nylah and Jared were difficult.

The secrets I kept, preserving their memories of him, slowly chip away at me, and I don't want to be whittled down any more than I am.

"Is that what you want, Ruthie?" Bolan's tone is the most serious I've ever heard it, breaking into my memories and the silence that has lasted minutes. "Do you want a baby?"

Yes. "I don't foresee that happening," I whisper, the thickness in my throat once more a combination of soreness and sadness.

And for now, I had Tulane.

Bolan doesn't speak again, tightening his arms around me once more. Securing both Tulane and I to him in this boat of a chair, where we drift for a little while.

Safe. Secure. Words I wouldn't ever have used with Cliff. Concepts I'm afraid to accept from someone else.

With the low murmur of the television and the warmth of Bolan's embrace, I'm lulled to sleep in his lap, where my fever-induced dreams include Tulane being mine forever.

And Bolan, too.

IN THE MORNING, Bolan tiptoes around the bedroom. At some point, he carried me, with Tulane on my lap, to the main bedroom and set us on the bed. He took his spot on the couch for the rest of the evening.

He stumbles against one foot of the bed, jostling the entire thing, and my eyes spring open.

"Shit. Sorry," he whispers, standing beside the bed,

towering over me. "I didn't want to wake you but wanted to know how you were feeling before I head out."

"Yeah, I'll be okay." Another day of fever reducers and lots of tea, and I should be on the mend. I'd love to stay in bed, but the option isn't present. I need to take care of Tulane.

Bolan lowers his head, slipping his hands into the pockets of black joggers. He's wearing a generic Chicago Anchors tee.

"I'm sorry, again, that I don't have a job where I can call out sick." Sincerity fills his voice along with a lingering concern on his cheeks.

"I'd never ask that of you." My voice is groggy, and I'm not certain if it's sleep-laden, or dishonesty, choking me. I once asked Cliff to leave professional football. After I caught him cheating during our marriage. He agreed to quit, then held it against me, when the truth was he'd been unable to handle the pressure of the sport.

"I'll be fine," I add, shuffling to sit upright. "Today might be a lot of couch and television time, though."

Bolan hasn't set limits on screen time for Tulane, giving me full reign to monitor her how I see fit. Watching children's programs is rare, but I still want Bolan to know my plan.

"Of course. Whatever you need." Despite my greasy hair and need for a shower, he brushes his hand gently over my head and I close my eyes, relishing the tender touch. "And if you need something, and it can wait, text me. I'll pick it up on my way home."

What I need is my husband to climb into this bed and hold me, but I don't mention that desire.

Instead, I smile timidly at him and tell him, "Catch all the catches."

17

[Bolan]

I like how Ruthie says *catch all the catches*. But what I'd really like is something else.

"Toss me a good luck kiss, flower." I cup her chin. Wide innocent eyes stare up at me, glassy-eyed, fever-riddled, and yet beautiful.

"I don't want to get you sick," she says, like she'd really kiss me on the mouth.

I saw the disappointment on her face during our wedding. When I didn't kiss my bride on the lips but stamped a soft peck to the corner of her mouth instead. The seal of a promise that I'd wait until she was more comfortable with me. Until she gives into me again without the coercion of gin and tonic and an empty ballroom.

We almost had that moment the other night, when she was leaning toward me until Tulane cried out. That wail was the first sign that my baby girl might be sick.

"Just blow me a kiss." My teenage brain wants to simply tell her to *blow me* but that wouldn't have sounded right. Even thinking the word 'blow' has a chuckle rumbling up my throat. "I feel lucky when you do."

Yesterday, I'd had a good game despite Ruthie and Tulane not being present. On a pop-up, fly ball that went behind home plate, I shucked my mask and raced for the hit, catching it and spinning for home plate, where the pitcher, Flynn Royal covered the base when a Cleveland player stole for home, diving toward the plate.

Out is a satisfying word when it's on the other team.

"You can even put it here." I pull the medal I wear on a woven black strap forward and bend at the waist to give Ruthie a better view.

Her hair is piled on her head again. The rings beneath her eyes fading only a little bit.

"What is that?" she asks.

"It's called an *omamori*," I explain. "When I was in Hiroshima, my teammate Röki Enomoto was a good friend, and his grandmother, Honoka, babysat Tulane for me whenever I had games."

Awkwardly bending toward Ruthie, I glance down at the charm.

"Most *omamori* are cloth with a little pouch in them. They are considered an object of higher power that brings protection to the owner. They need to be given as gifts, and Honoka gave this one to me the day I left Japan."

I smile at the fond memories I have of the older woman who didn't speak much English and yet understood how to raise a child and how to teach me to take care of one.

"Inside the pouch is a letter. More like a directive. A wish, maybe."

Ruthie looks from the *omamori* pinched between my fingers to my eyes. "What's it say?"

"That's just it. I don't know. I'm not *supposed* to know. It's simply a statement. Protection, like I said. Or willing something to happen, like success, employment." *Or even love.*

Honoka gave me this charm before I left for the airport, and I haven't taken it off since. I was wearing it the night I met Ruthie. In hindsight, I wonder if she was my destination. Is she the request inside the amulet? Was she sent to me by some higher order?

She's certainly been the answer to my needs. A wife. A mother for Tulane. She's giving more than she's receiving.

I recall what she told me last night. The horrors of Clifton's death. The ache of her not having a child.

A new flame of desire burns inside me. I want to give this woman everything. But first, I want her to get well.

"I could open this, like a locket, but I won't." I sigh, standing taller as my back aches from bending like I was. "I'm letting Fate direct me. Plus, baseball players are notoriously superstitious, and I've determined this thing has brought me luck."

"Really?" Ruthie arches a brow. "How?"

"It brought us together."

Ruthie chuckles, the sound rough, like when I teased her about petals and sighs yesterday. "How is that lucky?"

"Because I met you. Then met you again." I wiggle my brows suggesting the two times Ruthie and I came together. "Then saw you again. Three times. Lucky number. And now, here we are."

"I'm sick. In your bed."

"One out of two isn't bad." Now if she'd only allow me in that bed next to her . . . "So set your kiss on the *omamori*, flower, and I can wear it all day."

"Why does this feel like I'm kissing the ring of a mafia don?" she jokes, but then reaches for the charm, reverently placing her hand around it, and cupping it in her palm, before tangling her fingers tighter into the leather strap and tugging me toward her. Our faces come closer together and I reach for the headboard to steady myself.

"Consider me your king." I do my best impression of Marlon Brando from *The Godfather* but note the tremor in my voice. I want to kiss my wife. "I'll make you my queen."

Ruthie laughs, breaking the sexual tension between us, before rising to her knees in front of me. In this position, her head comes to my chest, and my brain goes haywire, wanting her in this position again, only my pants are lowered, and my dick is long and hard, and pointed in her direction.

Which it kind of is doing right now, confined in joggers that reveal exactly what she does to me.

Ignoring my stiff dick, though, Ruthie lifts the *omamori*, sets her lips on the Japanese etched letters running top to bottom on the talisman, and raises her lids so she can look up at me while kissing my good luck charm.

"Ruthie," I growl, wanting to tell her how good she looks on her knees before me, gazing up at me, mouth so close to where I want her.

She blinks once and slowly pulls away. "What?"

The innocence in the question contrasts with the knowing gleam in her eyes suggesting she's well aware of how she affects me. And I want to push her back to the bed, climb over her, and show her all the ways I want to affect her.

Only she's sick and my phone dings with a notification that it's time to leave.

"Saved by the bell?" she whispers.

Fucking damn bells. "Yeah." I shift my ball cap to the forward position and straighten to my full height, keeping my gaze on my wife, kneeling in front of me. I dig my upper teeth into my lower lip, wanting this woman something fierce.

Especially after what I've been learning about her late husband, and the one thing Ruthie wants most, despite saying otherwise.

A baby. Ruthie wants a child, and I want to give her one. I want to see her pregnant with my kid, which I missed out on with Tulane. I want to rub her feet and run my hand over the swell of her belly. I want to see her body expand and know my heart will as well, because this time, I'll get to experience everything from the start.

I want to be the one to give Ruthie everything she's ever desired and share in the adventures with her.

"I should get going," I whisper, struggling to find my voice with all the thoughts rattling around in my head. Like balls tossed into the air and I'm trying to catch them all when I only have one mitt.

"Take it easy today," I suggest, when I want to be the one to take care of her.

18

[Ruthie]

Later that afternoon, Tulane fell asleep next to me. Her little body erupted in a burst of energy this morning before collapsing in a nap. Instead of placing her in her crib, I set her in the large bed beside me, propping pillows around her body on three sides while I was a wall along her fourth side.

My eyes were beginning to close when my phone rang. Without a glance at the caller ID, I answer, not wanting the loud ringtone to wake Tulane.

Before I can even say hello, the sharp tone of a familiar male voice fills my ear. "Ruth Anne."

I close my eyes and swallow hard around my still sore throat. "Graham." For as long as I can remember, I wasn't allowed to call Graham Avery Dad, even though he is my father.

"What have you done now?" he begins like I'm some rabble-rouser. Like I've ever caused him trouble other than by being born.

"I'm sorry?" I wasn't apologizing for anything, though.

"You married Bolan Adler."

Now, I wondered if there is a question on his part. It isn't a secret that I am Bolan's wife, but there hadn't been a public announcement. Sports news cared more about Bolan as a new addition to the Chicago Anchors, not his marital status. Still, my father knowing this development was strange, especially as he rarely cared about me. Rarely acknowledged me.

"Yes." No further explanation was required.

"For money, no less." The heavy accusation in his voice is clear and he pauses for effect. "If you were so desperate, you should have contacted me."

The lies in that request are plentiful. I am not desperate. I'd also never contact him. He wouldn't have helped me.

I am Graham Avery's dirty little secret. The daughter he had with a girlfriend while he'd been married. While sowing his seed as a young baseball player. In contrast to Bolan, my dad tried to ignore his one responsibility while Bolan is embracing fatherhood, like it was a calling he didn't know he had.

My mother hadn't been much better, allowing my father to pay for nannies and private schools for me, while he sent her all over the country to be with him.

I don't respond to Graham. What is there to say? Correcting him would lead to him making me feel bad about myself. Silence was golden. I'd mastered it as a child.

"How much is he paying you?"

The question gives me pause. How would he know the arrangement involved money?

"If he were paying me, I don't see how that's your business." I'm not certain I've ever been this bold with him. I don't openly share much with my father as he doesn't often ask much of me.

But this kind of question has me protecting myself and my personal situation.

"You're my business."

I snort. "I haven't been your business in forever." I'm thirty-three. I can't even claim I speak to my father once a year now. He attended Clifton's funeral, but I ignored him then, the circumstances a blur of faces and comments.

"Do not be flip with me, little girl." The words make me bristle. Not in fear but anger. I was never his little girl, and I'd argue, why not? But arguing led nowhere with a narcissistic man who loved himself more than anyone else.

"You're in Arizona." Again, more confirmation than question of my whereabouts and I bristle once more. He doesn't need to know my location, but professional baseball spring training is not a secret.

With a panicked glance at Tulane beside me, I shiver, hating that with one simple call he can get underneath my skin. A call I'm wondering if it has an actual purpose.

"Now isn't a good time, Graham," I counter, using words often spoken by him to me.

When are you coming home? Will you be at the school concert? Are you coming to my birthday?

The response was always the same, even in the offseason.

"I'm sick," I add for some unexplained reason. I don't, however, hold my breath waiting for him to ask me what's wrong. He doesn't.

"Behave yourself, Ruth Anne."

The warning comes as no surprise. What the man fails to realize is I've behaved my entire life, mainly because I was taught to be seen and not heard. When he wanted to appear like a doting father but wasn't. When he tugged me forward for photos, and then pushed me aside once the cameras lowered.

I was constantly pitted against my father by my mother. Neither wanted me.

"Bye, Graham." I hang up before he can respond, and power off my phone before curling up beside Tulane and falling into a fitful sleep.

WHEN BOLAN FINALLY ARRIVES HOME, after the Anchors win their first game, he's a mix of jubilation and trepidation.

"Why didn't you answer your phone?"

I'm seated on the couch, Tulane at my side. We've been flipping through the same book for twenty minutes while I identify every item on the stiff pages. Bolan's question causes me to remember I turned off my phone.

"I didn't want it to wake Tulane." There is no reason to burden Bolan with the truth. My father is not a threat, just a nuance lingering in the recesses of my life. Another man who treated me poorly, walked all over me, making promises and reneging without apology. I should have learned my lesson from the first man in my life. Instead, I made similar mistakes with the second.

Tulane slides off the couch and rushes to Bolan who picks her up with one arm and kisses the side of her face multiple times before setting her on her feet again. I shift on the couch, crossing my arms over the back of it to watch this display of fatherly love.

"I'm surprised you're home. You won." My smile is my congratulations. The Chicago Anchors were on fire during their afternoon game. "I thought you'd go out and celebrate with the team."

I hold my breath waiting for him to tell me he's leaving. Just coming home for a quick shower and change of clothes, like Clifton would say.

"The Anchors won." He smiles, proudly acknowledging the game. "Seems kissing my *omamori* did the trick." He tosses me a wink and laughs. "As to going out . . . nope. I'm here to take care of my girls." Bolan puffs up his chest, pride vibrating outward.

I huff in disbelief until Bolan sets a plastic bag I hadn't noticed on his wrist on the dining table and empties the contents.

"Soup." He holds up a can in each of his large hands.

"Crackers." He points at a box big enough to feed six people for a month.

Then he sets down the soup cans and pulls out the final item. "And flowers. Well, actually, it's a plant. A cyclamen."

The dark green, heart-shaped leaves are variegated, and delicate red flowers bloom above the thick plant.

"I missed Valentine's Day," he remarks, although we are into March.

I don't remind him we spent Valentine's Day together because this gesture is too sweet.

"I was also hoping they might brighten your day."

My smile grows to a beaming grin. "They certainly do," I respond. *He* brightens my day, polishing up everything, especially rubbing away my father's earlier call.

"Now." He claps his hands once. "Chicken noodle or chicken with stars?"

I giggle as he wiggles each can in my direction.

"I don't know." I hum then glance down at Tulane. "What do you think?"

"Nope. This is all for you tonight. I've got Tulane." Bolan walks around the couch and scoops her up. "First, a bath for you." He points at me before kissing the side of Tulane's head and walking toward the bathroom. When the water starts running to fill the tub, I rub my hand over my hair, which hasn't been washed in two days, and wince. He must think I'm a mess.

When he returns, he sets Tulane down and catches me by surprise by scooping me off the couch. I squeal in his arms, wrapping mine around his neck.

Laughing, I say, "You don't need to carry me."

"Ruthie." His tone is rather serious. His gaze latches on my eyes. "Let me take care of you."

My throat thickens and it has nothing to do with the ache in the back of it. "Okay," I whisper.

He carries me into the bathroom, where he sets me on the closed toilet lid and checks the bath water. When he stands to his full height, he runs his eyes down my form, then bites the corner of his lip and wiggles one brow. "Need me to undress you?"

Yes. Strip me down to nothing and join me in the tub. But already thinking he finds me a mess, instead I say, "No, I think I can handle it from here." Still, I can't fight the smile I give him. Surprised by this additional gesture. Grateful that he's here.

"Let me know when you're finished, and I'll start the soup." He winks before stepping out of the small room and closing the door. I hear Tulane happily squeal on the other side.

Quickly, I undress and sink into the deliciously warm bath, realizing Bolan added a scoop of bath salts I'd purchased but haven't used yet.

With my eyes closed, I hear Bolan's quiet murmurs and the jabber of Tulane, and I smile to myself despite the burn of tears.

He's here. For her. For me.

Thirty minutes later, I step out of the bathroom to the smell of chicken soup. When I approach the kitchen, Bolan is pulling a large soup mug from the microwave. He smiles at me when he says, "It felt like a stars kind of night."

Then he tips his head toward the couch. "Take a seat."

As I'm not used to being so taken care of, or so pampered, I feel a bit awkward curling up against the corner on the couch, but Bolan follows me, draping a blanket over my lap and handing me the soup.

"Be careful. It's hot."

At the gentle reminder, I blink away the threat of more silly tears, telling myself I'm just tired and exhaustion is catching up to me. There's no room to be sick when you're taking care of a little person who is also sick. And while Tulane is on the mend, I'm still a day behind her.

Bolan scoops up Tulane, tipping her over his shoulder. "Okay, matey. You're next." He does his best pirate impression again. "Bath, books, and bed for you."

He winks at me again, giving me space and silence to eat my soup while he tackles the nightly routine.

Only after Tulane's bath, he brings her out to the couch, collapsing beside me and holding her in his lap.

"I thought you could read to her, if you don't mind." He knows I don't mind at all, but then he adds, "I like hearing your voice." His own is timid, sheepish even, suggesting his comment isn't about me reading better than him.

The corner of my lips curl. "I'd be happy to read to you." To both of them.

Three books later, Tulane curls into her father's chest and he carries her off to bed. Returning to the living room, he snags up the remote and turns on the television. "Okay. So what are we watching? Hallmark? Lifetime? Netflix?"

I bark out a laugh. "You don't need to—"

"I'm going to stop you right there." He holds up his firm palm with the remote in his hand. "I *want* to." Then he aims the remote at the television, flips to Netflix and picks a movie.

I settle on my side while Bolan picks up the soup mug I set on the floor, and takes it to the kitchen. When he returns, he tugs at the cushions behind me, removing them from the couch and dropping them on the floor before he slips in behind me.

"Is this okay?" His voice is rough and low at my ear while I feel the solidness of his chest at my back.

"Yeah," I whisper, keeping my gaze on the opening scene of what is certain to be a cheesy rom-com.

Within seconds, Bolan's arm is over me. The forearm with the bear tattoo tugging me tighter against him. His chin rests on my head, cocooning me in.

"I've never done this before," he finally says to me. His voice is exceptionally quiet, almost like he didn't intend to say his thoughts out loud.

"Take care of someone?" He does an excellent job with Tulane. This evening, he's been wonderful with me.

"Cuddle." He squeezes my midsection.

I swipe my hand over the bear tattoo on his arm, the ink looking a little less scary as this creature appears to be keeping me safe, offering me comfort, holding me tight. I melt deeper into him.

I don't know what happens in the rom com, because I drift off to sleep, dreaming my own mental movie, starring Bolan and me, and the easy comfort of him.

19

———

[Bolan]

y Tulip appears to bounce back rather quickly from her ear infection. Ruthie struggles another day or two before she looks more like herself again and she's ready to leave the house.

It occurs to me that my wife and I haven't had a proper date. Instead, we're a family of three as we enter a local barbecue restaurant, known for their brisket. I'm pleased to learn Ruthie can put away the meat, as she eats a chicken leg-quarter, fries, and coleslaw. While I enjoy Japanese food—sushi, udon, and tempura—I've missed the hearty meats and potatoes of America. Like blackened brisket and mashed potatoes.

With my belly full, and a smile on my face, I suggest we drive somewhere to watch the sun set over the mountains. A quick search finds a place close to Phoenix with an easy climb. Our timing isn't the best as it's still late winter in the desert and the sun lowers early, but I've been told the clearness of the sky makes any place ideal for observing the overhead color change.

When we pull into Papago Park, I notice I'm not the only one with this idea. Still, we take our time to walk through the crowded parking lot and hit the gravel-like dirt common to the area. Tulane alternates between walking on her own, exploring as we go, and being picked up by me, to speed us along, especially as the sky continues to shift. Walking through the desert landscape of cacti and low brush, we don't climb the highest peak, but a large mound where I take a seat facing west and settle Tulane in my lap. Holding out my hand, I assist Ruthie to sit beside me on the dusty rock.

I'm not much of a hand holder, having big hands that are often clumsy. Still, I clasp her hand and start to sweat a little bit when she doesn't pull away either. Eventually, Ruthie scoots closer to me, so we sit hip-to-hip. Then she sets my hand on her knee, and her hand over the back of mine.

We sit in silence a few minutes before Ruthie starts pointing out the colors in the sky to Tulane.

"Orange." She points at a stream of rusty red and then tugs at Tulane's hair. "Like your hair."

She aims her finger at another strand of light. "Yellow. Like mine." Her hair hangs down, stick-straight, and she winds a few strands around her finger.

"And pink." She pokes Tulane in the belly, emphasizing the color of her shirt and then points once more at the sky.

I'm not certain Tulane fully follows the direction of Ruthie's finger or understands the correlation between the streaks in the sky and the comparison to hair color, but it's amazing how Ruthie makes everything a game while also a learning experience.

"What's your favorite color?" I ask, then quickly cut her off. "No, let me guess. Red?"

Ruthie laughs. A genuine rumble that I'm not certain I've heard before. "Red feels too reckless for me."

"Really?" I arch a brow, looking over at her. "A color can be reckless?"

"Definitely. And red is a reckless one."

"Perfect for Reckless Ruthie."

"Ha." She snorts. "Not something someone would use to describe me."

"Why not?" She had sex with me within an hour of meeting me. That's pretty rash, all things considered. I recall feeling that sense of familiarity with her. Maybe it was a sense of rightness, which made the decision not quite so irresponsible. "You're always wearing the color. The dress at the event. Your glasses. Your toenails."

"My—" Ruthie glances down at her feet which are covered by her gym shoes. "How do you know that?" Her voice lowers to a curious whisper.

"I pay attention." Not always. My ADHD can get in the way, but when I'm focused, I'm hyper-focused. And she has my interest piqued.

Ruthie straightens a second. Her shoulders back and her eyes aimed forward. "Well, thank you for noticing, but red is not my favorite color. What's your favorite color?"

I shrug, having not really thought about it but I glance up at the sky again. The blue darkens as the sun lowers. The color matches the royal blue of Chicago Anchors uniforms, and the color *feels* lucky.

"I'd say blue today."

Ruthie hums. "Blue is nice. Said to be a calming color."

"You disagree," I tease, bumping her shoulder with mine.

"I'm finding I'm partial to green lately." Ruthie turns her head to face me. Her gaze locks on my eyes. "Green feels . . . safe." Her voice lowers a bit. "And that's a little scary."

My eyes widen, taking in her meaning. "How can something be safe yet frightening?"

"It's unfamiliar," she states, still looking at me.

With us staring at one another, the sun setting off in the distance, and Tulane on my lap, I understand her sentiment. This moment feels like a warm hug. An embrace you didn't know you needed and then don't want to let go of. Deep down inside me exists the fear that nothing this comforting can last. And I never want Ruthie to feel uncertain about me.

I sling my arm around her shoulders and tug her into my side. With my lips at her temple, I mutter. "Whenever you're scared, flower, cling to green."

Cling to me.

SPRING TRAINING DOESN'T OFFER many days off. Most games are played in the afternoons, so evenings are open for downtime or nightlife, depending on who you are.

Lately, I'm priding myself on being a family man and decline Valdez's repeated invitation to attend nights out, chasing women already chasing ballplayers.

But when the Anchors win our second game, roughly a week after our first victory, it's cause for celebration, and I long to go out with my team.

As I'm standing outside the stadium waiting on Ruthie, as I've grown accustomed to doing, Cyrus Sawyer claps me on the shoulder. "Come out with us tonight."

Just as he asks, Ruthie appears before me, holding Tulane's hand. They are the cutest Anchors fans I've ever seen.

I glance back at Cyrus. "I can't."

Cyrus peers from Ruthie to me and back. I look at Ruthie then Cyrus.

"You should go," Ruthie says, her voice encouraging while a little off.

"Bring your wife," he says at roughly the same time.

"My—" I'm dumbstruck a second. Despite calling Ruthie my wife in her presence, I don't talk about her much during practice and games. Games are often too serious, but practices can be a time when players shoot the shit a little more. While other guys talk about their wives and girlfriends, I don't speak up about Ruthie, mainly because I don't feel I know enough about her.

We've been married roughly two weeks.

Cyrus nods toward my left hand and I glance down at the silicone ring on my finger, the visible sign that I'm a taken man.

"We're going to a country bar. They have line dancing."

I snort. "Do a bunch of city players know how to line dance?" Doesn't matter. I love to dance.

Cyrus chuckles. "I'm a country boy at heart." His accent thickens, the Southern twang growing more predominant.

"Ruthie," Cyrus turns toward her. "Tell him he should come out with us. You both should come."

The invitation doesn't offer the one-on-one that Ruthie and I need for a date, but it would give her a break from Tulane and get us out together. Being my wife, she should meet the significant others of my teammates. Those ladies might be key support for Ruthie once the season hits full-on.

I arch a brow at her, and she fights a smile, nodding once toward me.

"Yeah, man," I address Cyrus, while still looking at *my wife.* "We'd love to go."

"Excellent." He slaps my shoulder again. "Tonight. Eight o'clock. Gus Mackers. I'll text you the address."

He's already walking away backwards and pointing at me with a finger gun, before spinning on his cleats and heading for the locker room.

"I don't have to go with you, if you'd like time with your team."

Team building is important, but I want bonding time with my wife. Turning toward her, I say, "Nah. I think it will be fun. We haven't been out together . . . ever."

She slowly nods, not pointing out the obvious that we won't be alone, but this is a good first step.

I have a date with my wife.

20

[Ruthie]

Bolan is quick to find a babysitter for Tulane. To my surprise, it's Ruby, Ford Sylver's nanny. He isn't going out like the rest of his teammates and Ruby is available.

I've told Bolan a few times he really doesn't have to include me tonight, even though Cyrus asked me directly to attend.

"Stop," he eventually says as we clean up the kitchen after dinner. "I love to dance. This will be fun."

I am not much of a dancer. The last time I danced was with him and before that, I can't remember.

"You can hardly walk across a flat surface without tripping," I tease him, chuckling at how often this big, sturdy man is a little unsteady.

He kicks up his heel behind him like he's reacting to a first kiss and laughs. "These flippers are hard to flip some days, but dancing is different. There's no structure. You just let loose."

He does the White-man's overbite and sways his hips, snapping his fingers to imitate his skills.

I laugh. I don't know if everyone would agree there isn't structure to dancing but who am I to argue with him. Plus, he's very excited about the prospect of going out.

Which worries me that I'm holding him back. Having a wife might be cramping his style of hitting on random women and having one-night stands. Then again, he's been home every night after his games, hanging out with Tulane and me.

Slowly, Bolan stops dancing. "I can almost hear the gears clicking in your head. What are you thinking?" His shoulders droop while his brows pinch. "We don't have to go, if you don't want to."

Disappointment fills his rugged voice.

"No. No, I want to go. It's just—" I wasn't certain how to explain myself, without making me sound needy, or him sound seedy.

Bolan steps closer to me and cups my shoulders. "Look. Let's go for a little while. If you're uncomfortable for any reason, we can leave." His eyes scan my face. "Tonight's a green, Ruthie. You're safe with me."

My eyes widen, but then soften. Being safe is half the problem. The good half . . . where I feel comfortable with Bolan. The bad half—I'm tired of playing life safe. I want that moment of reckless red back.

Instead of admitting the truth, I nod.

Bolan releases my shoulders and claps once. "Yes. Now get dressed, beautiful."

When I enter the living room forty minutes later, Bolan is seated in the recliner. I swear he loves that chair. Tulane is in the corner of the room that's become her play center with buckets of toys and books.

Bolan's attention shifts from the television to me as I exit the hallway and quickly turns back for the game on the set.

Then his head snaps back in my direction, and his feet kick down on the lifted portion of the chair. He slowly stands, keeping his eyes on me while rubbing his hands down his dark-wash jeans. He's also wearing a plain short-sleeve, button-down that makes him look like a cowboy-wannabe.

"Holy shit, Ruthie. You're a fucking knockout."

My cheeks heat at the compliment while I press a finger to my lips and glance at Tulane. "Little ears," I admonish before swiping my hands over my hips. "Am I underdressed? He said line dancing."

"You want to stay home and get undressed? Because that's what I heard. That's what I want," he rambles, letting those safe eyes of his shift to dangerous as his gaze roams down my body. The appraisal heats my face again but another place on me is hot and bothered as well.

"Bolan." I chuckle, assuming he's joking with me. He wants to go out. He wants to be with his team, his new friends, and in the time it took me to get ready, I'm excited to go out as well. I love Tulane but I need some adult conversation.

He digs his teeth into his lower lip and steps closer to me. "Seriously, Ruthie. You steal my breath. White looks good on you."

I glance down at the fitted cropped top that leaves a sliver of skin exposed above my high-rise jeans. The collar fits tight to my throat while the shirt is sleeveless.

"White?" I chuckle. "Really?"

"White means commitment." His tone turns serious, forcing my gaze to meet his again. "You wore white when we got married, and I swear I could breathe for the first time in a year." He exhales as if emphasizing his statement. "Maybe the first time ever."

"Bolan," I whisper. All the compliments. All the comments. If I wasn't careful, being safe was going to get reckless, even dangerous like those eyes of his, because I could fall for him.

The man I'm learning he is, not the college guy who kissed me or the clumsy yet cocky man who entered a ballroom.

The thought reminds me that I still haven't told him we'd met once upon a time. Some days, I think the secret will never matter. Other days, I know secrets are the devil and I should just tell him.

When a sharp rap on the front door turns both our heads, my thoughts scatter. Tonight is not about the past. Tonight is for the present and living in it.

Bolan opens the door for Ruby and gives her a quick rundown of phone numbers and medical information for Tulane.

If I had any concerns about leaving Tulane for the first time, I'm put at ease because Tulane seems to remember Ruby. She walks right up to the older woman and hands her a plastic toy cow. As if we aren't even in the room, Ruby leads Tulane to the scattered toys on the floor and folds down to play with her.

Bolan and I meet eyes, and he shrugs. "Guess we'll be going."

He steps over to Tulane and picks her up, pressing kisses all over her face before finally landing one on her nose. "I love you, Tulip. Bed at eight. No parties," he teases.

Everything in me wants to tell Tulane the same thing. That I love her as well and promise her we'll be home later. She won't ever have to worry if we'll be back.

Instead, I silently think my thoughts and give Tulane an extra squeeze before pressing a kiss on her cheek. "Be good, baby girl."

Bolan offers Ruby a thank you for her time and I give her a final smile before we exit.

Once we leave the apartment, Bolan places his hand on my lower back, leading me to the staircase.

"You're so good with her," he states, as he's told me many times.

"I adore her," I state, afraid to admit my true feelings.

Bolan thunders down the stairs but I take my time in low heeled booties which causes him to stop and pause on the landing in the stairwell. He glances up at me again and those eyes shift once more.

"Ruthie, I—" He swallows like he's trying to contain words. His shoulders lower when I stop one step up from him. "I just want to thank you again for all you're doing for us."

Something tells me that wasn't what he was going to say, especially when he glances away but takes my hand giving it a squeeze.

"Let's just have fun tonight, yeah?" I reply.

"Yeah."

~

GUS MACKERS IS a country-western themed bar with a tall stage overlooking a large dance floor and comfortable sitting areas made for groups of patrons. Dining tables are on the opposite side of a square bar that divides the dancing area from a restaurant. A band plays live music.

And the place is packed for a weeknight in early March.

"Tourists," Cyrus explains after waving Bolan and I over to a set of couches in an L-shape with a low, square table in front of it.

"Baseball lovers," another team member corrects before Cyrus introduces me to everyone, eventually landing on the only other woman in the group.

"This is Lacey." He waves toward a woman with sleek black hair and a welcoming face who pats the space beside her.

"Come sit by me. Us girls gotta stick together with this bunch."

Bolan's hand has been on my back, the heat of his fingers finding that sliver of exposed skin. For a second, it feels like his palm stiffens, like he doesn't want me to sit by this Lacey person, but then he says, "Lacey is Cyrus's wife."

I turn my head from Bolan to Lacey, questioning why Cyrus didn't introduce her as such. Ignoring my thoughts, I accept what Lacey said. *Us girls need to stick together.* So, I round the table and take the space she patted on the couch. Bolan remains standing, chatting with Cyrus and another teammate.

"Welcome to the club." She lifts her glass toward me and notices my empty hands. "And we need to get you a drink. Pronto."

As if hearing Lacey's comment, the waitress arrives. I open my mouth to order when Bolan points in my direction and says, "She'll have a gin and tonic."

"Actually." I point at myself. "I'll have a margarita. Classic. On the rocks. With salt."

"Damn, girl. Way to put him in his place," Lacey chuckles, nudging me with her elbow.

Bolan blinks, and then turns back toward the waitress. His pouty lip expresses my order is *my* order.

"Actually, I'm not offended," I admit to Lacey, finding small pleasure in Bolan remembering fine details. Like my toenail polish color. And one of my favorite drinks. "We met over gin and tonics."

Not the truth. Not exactly a lie.

Lacey shifts in her seat. "Do tell. Everyone's been wondering about the elusive Adler."

"Elusive?" I snort. No one seems more like an open book than Bolan.

"Cyrus says he's quiet. Focused. Driven. But a great team motivator. He isn't getting into the drama on the team with Romero." Lacey nods in the direction of another set of couches on the opposite side of the dance floor.

Romero Valdez and a collection of additional players are gathered there.

"Didn't take them for line dancers," Lacey mutters to herself.

"Why not?"

"Think *clubbin'* is more their scene." Lacey keeps her eyes on the other group. "Don't know why they are here."

"Team bonding," I suggest positively.

Lacey chuckles. "I've never heard of a team more divided. I don't know how Anchors' management could keep him on the team after what he did to Ford."

I heard about the scandal. The situation was one reason Bolan needed a wife. The Anchors only wanted a family man.

Lacey continues. "Never been more shocked than to learn Felicity slept with him." She nods in the direction of Romero. She also sounds disappointed.

"Is she your friend?"

"Had been." Her eyes narrow on a woman seated across the way, then those blue eyes shift back to me. "But one thing I can't stand is a cheatin' man. And I don't hold a double standard, so it goes for women as well." Her gaze flicks from me to Cyrus, and there's a story I'm not certain I want to hear.

The waitress returns with a tray of drinks, handing me a margarita and Bolan a beer.

"Anyway," Lacey draws out, lifting her glass again. "Here's to the wives."

I lift my glass and tap against hers before taking my first sip. My eyes lift and I find Bolan watching me as the salt on the rim hits my tongue and my mouth gets a burst of lime and tequila. He doesn't take his eyes off me, even while someone speaks to him.

"He's got it bad," Lacey mutters beside me. "Must be nice."

"What?" I turn toward her.

"Your man looking at you like he wants to be that margarita."

I laugh. She has no idea, but then I think back to his

comments earlier. How seeing me in white, he felt like he could breathe for the first time. Staring back at him a second, I recognize the feeling.

Being here, tonight; being with Bolan, in general, has felt freeing. He's the fresh breath I've been longing for.

"You're ridiculous," I state, taking another sip of my drink and winking at her.

"And you're my new best friend." She clinks her glass against mine again. "Lacey and Ruthie. We have a nice ring to us."

As I haven't had a best girlfriend in . . . ever, I wasn't certain what to say, but I could use someone in my corner.

Wives for the win.

Within minutes, the song "A Bar Song: Tipsy" by Shaboozey is sung. Bolan sets down his beer and starts clapping in rhythm to the beat.

"This is my song." His hips sway and he stomps a foot. He's walking backward toward the dance floor and pointing at me with finger guns that he shifts to beckoning fingers. "Come on, flower."

Lacey snorts beside me. "You better go, *flower*. He looks like he wants to pluck your garden."

I laugh, setting down my drink and shaking my head. "I don't dance," I say to Lacey while watching Bolan. I want to dance, I'm just not comfortable enough in my own skin.

"If your man wants to dance, girl, I'd dance. Before he finds someone else to be his partner."

While I wouldn't mind being Lacey's new friend, her negative energy is making me itchy. Still, her speech motivates me to stand and skirt the low table to approach Bolan, who is still clapping his hands and stomping his foot more than dancing in the space closest to our area.

As I approach, he reaches out for my belt loop and tugs me closer to him, lining up our mid-sections. My hands crash on his chest, firm beneath a lightweight cotton shirt. Then he's guiding me side-to-side with his hips and his finger in that loop.

"I'm not much of a dancer," I shout over the music.

Bolan glances down between us, where there isn't much space. "Yeah, you are, flower."

I recall that slow dance in the dark ballroom again. Another moment with Bolan. *How many moments will I get?*

The question makes me realize I need to make the most of the ones I have with him, so I let Bolan lead me in his chaotic rhythm, laughing as he exaggerates our movements like he's Patrick Swayze in *Dirty Dancing*.

Three songs later, the band slows down. I'm thirsty and breathless from laughing so hard.

As the first strum of the next song suggests it's a slow one, people begin to exit the dance floor, and I turn for our section, but Bolan catches my wrist.

"Where you goin', flower?" He gently pulls me to him, circling his arms around my lower back. My hands land on his broad shoulders. We haven't been this close, this often, since that first dance, since that night.

Slowly, I lift my lids. "What are we doing?"

"Dancing." His eyes widen like it's obvious.

But I'm aflame from the heat of his body, and the rise and fall of his chest as his heart settles down from the previous gyrating. I can also sense the width of his hips and the expanse of his abs, solid and tight. As if my hands have their own will, they smooth down his biceps, enjoying the strength in them.

"Flower?" Bolan groans.

When I look up at him, he tugs me closer. Our hips move in sync with each other, like a lazy wave brushes the beach.

And I'm wet and hot and needy.

He lowers his head and runs his nose along the side of

mine. His breath kisses my lips and my mouth waters for a connection.

Kiss me.

We came so close about a week ago. As much as I'm certain it isn't a good idea, I also can't promise I won't kiss him back.

I want another shot of him. *Make it a double.*

Bolan continues to torture me, brushing his cheek against mine. The trimmed stubble on his face tickling my tender skin. His mouth comes near my ear, his breath another invisible kiss there.

Then he turns his head, his lips so close to my flesh, yet hovering over it. He inhales and I shiver, hitching my shoulder to my jaw.

"Something wrong, flower." His voice is all-knowing.

"Tickles," I admit.

"I seem to remember you have a sensitive spot." He pulls back, pressing two fingers to his lips before placing them near my pulse point. "Right here."

How can something so seemingly innocent have such an effect on me?

"Bolan," I whisper, our eyes locked on one another.

"Want to drag you to a corner of this bar and just have my way with you, Ruthie."

God, I think I want that as well.

"But I'm not tucking us in a corner again." A tender reminder of that storm-lit ballroom.

"Or hiding us in the dark." A gentle prompt about the balcony.

Bolan cups my jaw. "Stop me now or forever hold your peace."

"My peace?" Something tells me I've been peaceful too long. Complacent really, and I need the chaos Bolan might bring me.

He pulls his head back. "That mean you're choosing stop?" His brow twitches upward. His eyes questioning me.

Breathlessly, I beg, "Kiss me."

With his lips suddenly on mine, I cling to him like I did in that darkened ballroom, clutching his shirt in my fists while his hands stay on my jaw. Our mouths move with their own practiced dance. Down to the corners. Sip at the lower one. Lick through the seam. Tongues meet in a frenzy of connection, swirling, twirling, like a full-body skirt spinning out of control. Or a flower opening up, blossoming.

Too quickly, the kiss is over. Bolan pulls back, but his forehead comes to mine.

"Still want to take you to that corner, beautiful. But I'm promising to behave myself."

Don't behave, I want to scream. Don't hold back. But my responsible side supersedes the desire to drag *him* to a dark part of this bar.

Instead, we hang out for another round of drinks and another hour of dancing before I'm not certain I can feel my legs. Whether that's from the exercise, or the alcohol, is to be determined.

When we get back to the apartment, Bolan sets his hand on my lower back again, holding me steady as we climb the stairs to the second floor. Once we near the door of the apartment, I stop just outside it.

"This is my place," I tease, pointing at the number like I live separately from him. Like this is a date and he's dropping me off.

"Funny that. This is my place, too." He smiles at me, eyes sparkling that green-gold combination. He's the one who is breathtaking. Or is it breath-giving, as I'm reminded how much I've laughed tonight. How free I've felt.

"I had fun tonight," I say.

Bolan leans on the wall, just outside the door. "Yeah? Me too."

"Well, good night." I stick out my hand like I intend to shake his.

Bolan laughs, pressing off the wall, and taking my hand. Then he tugs me to him, pulling me into his chest, and hugging me.

We stand like this a moment, his arms around my shoulder and neck, and mine looped around his back.

Slowly, he releases me and cups my jaw like he did earlier. "Look me in the eye and tell me you don't want me to kiss you."

Just look me in the eyes. Breathe.

Déjà vu, but I don't have time to answer, my body doing the responding, as I cling to his shirt again and bring him to me. Or maybe he leans forward and takes what he sees in my eyes.

Yes. *Kiss me.*

One of his hands scoops around the back of my neck while the other finds the middle of my back, slipping his fingers just under the hem of my cropped shirt. I arch toward him, pressing my breasts to his chest and sliding my hand to his neck as well, fingers brushing over his short hair.

As our lips meet with urgency, a rush to connect, he tightens his hold on me, allowing me to feel what I'm doing to him. The bulge in his jeans presses into my lower belly, where I'm fluttering with my own arousal.

Bolan bends his knees a bit, like he intends to line us up and I hitch up my leg. He catches the back of my thigh in his hand and pulls me tighter against him.

Our lips move. Teeth nip. Tongues collide and crash.

Everything in this moment brings back memories of another one and Bolan abruptly pulls back.

His gaze pings back and forth at my eyes before his brows severely pinch. "Ruthie?"

Without asking, I know the question and I open my mouth to answer just as the apartment door flings open.

Bolan and I both turn our heads although we don't shift from our position with my raised knee at his hip and his hand on the back of my raised thigh. I'm still holding onto his neck, and he still has a hand on my lower ass.

Ruby clears her throat. "My apologies. Thought I heard a noise in the hallway."

An awkward few seconds passes where I'm hoping she'll close the door and forget what she sees, or rather, shuts the door and lets us continue where we left off.

Where I was about to reveal myself to Bolan.

Instead, Bolan releases my leg, and I stand on my own two feet, smoothing my hand over my belly which still flutters like a flock of birds are in there. He shifts to stand behind me, certain to be hiding his reaction to me. He slips an arm around my waist and kisses the top of my head from behind me.

"Can't keep my hands off my wife," he admits to the babysitter.

Ruby smiles. "I remember those days." She sighs, swooning a bit. "And I hate to interrupt but you did promise by eleven and it's eleven-fifteen."

Bolan releases me and places a hand on the door to open it wider, allowing me to enter the apartment first. Quickly, he's on his phone sending Ruby money through an app.

She gives us a brief overview of the night, praising Tulane as an angel, before closing the door behind her exit.

The moment outside that door is suddenly lost.

Bolan scratches at the back of his neck, lowers his gaze, and mutters to me. "Well, good night."

And we both break into laughter as we'd just been caught making out by the babysitter.

21

[Ruthie]

The next afternoon, I'm rushing out the door, hoping to make Bolan's game, when my phone rings. I almost ignore the call for fear it's my father again. The second I see the caller ID, I answer.

"Ruth," Jared says through the phone.

"Ruthie, darling," Nylah echoes him.

"Hey," I stumble over the simple word, setting the phone down to use the speaker function as I work to put Tulane's shoes on her.

Guilt hits me square in the chest. Like they know I went out with Bolan last night. Know I kissed him again.

However, I *am* married to the man.

"We just wanted to check in on how Bolan is doing," Jared continues.

"How are *you* doing?" Nylah counters him again. I spoke to Nylah roughly a week ago when I wasn't feeling well.

Without seeing them, I can picture Jared glaring at Nylah and her waving at him, like she can erase him, despite them having a rather loving relationship. Jared's tone, however, is a reminder of the pressure Clifton put on himself to please his father.

"Bolan is great. I sent a progress report the other day." I've been keeping up with his stats and sharing them with Jared who wants a running record of Bolan's highs and lows. Bolan has been hitting exceptionally well.

"How are his knees?" Jared adds.

After strapping one of Tulane's shoes closed, I pause. "Is there something I should be worried about? I don't recall any injuries in his initial report."

"How about his hips or back? Those are more prone to issues as a catcher, especially as he's reaching the end of his life span in baseball."

Immediately, I consider how Bolan has been sleeping on the couch every night. Having my own experience lying on it while I was sick, the furniture is comfortable but a little too soft for nightly rest. Considering Bolan's bulk and weight, plus the exertion of professional sport, he must be miserable on that thing.

Not mentioning any of my concerns to my Jared, I snort and say, "You make him sound geriatric."

"In baseball years, he almost is."

The thought hits me hard. Bolan has mentioned how baseball is his life, but he hasn't mentioned what he'll do afterward. He has three years to decide because of his Chicago Anchors contract but time goes quickly.

"And how are you, dear? Your knees, hips, and back." If I didn't know my mother-in-law better, I'd swear there was innuendo in her asking. She's teasing Jared, and in my mind's eye I can see her give him a saucy glance.

"My body parts are all intact." I almost said well-cared for, but going by innuendos, that would certainly say a lot, and a few body parts are not well.

After our kiss last night, I collapsed on the bed and had my hand between my legs quicker than a pitcher releases a fast ball from the mound. It didn't take long to get where I was going, and it was sadly lackluster as most orgasms I've experienced in the past few years have been. Because I'd gotten them on my own. Alone.

While Bolan had been right down the hall.

I should have invited him into the bedroom. Should have told him I wanted to be reckless red again. Instead, I let another moment with him pass.

Even still, Bolan should be sleeping in a bed if there are concerns for his physical well-being and performance. Proper rest is necessary, and the worn couch cannot be good for Bolan's body.

"You'll keep me updated on any concerns, right?" Jared interjects. "He's staying out of trouble." It isn't so much a question as a declaration. As in, he better be.

"He's been home every night after games. Goes to practice on time and attends all team meetings."

The heavy silence that follows leaves me wondering what Jared is thinking. His son appeared dutiful and responsible and yet somehow snuck other women into the cracks in our marriage. In the everyday crevices, where every minute could not be accounted for.

I'm reminded that Jared and Nylah do not know about Clifton's infidelities, and my love for them, as his parents, prevents me from tattle-telling on my deceased husband.

His secrets went to the grave with him.

"And you?" Nylah interjects. "Are you okay? No trouble for you."

"With Bolan? No. I'm good." *But am I?* I could be better, if I didn't feel this incompleteness. Like we have unfinished business. Like taking our kisses to the next level.

"Hey, I hate to cut us short, but I've got to run. I'm trying to make it to Bolan's game."

"Have you found a nanny yet?" Nylah asks.

"I thought we decided against a sitter. *I'm* here."

"You're there for Bolan," Jared states.

"Which means being here for Tulane," I defend.

"You're his agent," my father-in-law reminds me.

Which I didn't ask for, but I don't have time to argue with them right now. With Tulane's other shoe on and fastened, I stand and collect her diaper bag—a backpack with all the toddler essentials.

"We'll see you in less than two weeks," Nylah adds cheerfully, and I halt my hasty movements. I've hardly gone more than two days without seeing my in-laws, and honestly, the reprieve has been nice. I adore them as a couple. I love them as people. But I've struggled to be near them so often because of Cliff.

"Two weeks?" *What's in two weeks?* I wrack my brain for anniversaries or birthdays.

"I assume you'll come back and pack up more items for Chicago."

"Chicago." *Right.* I'm moving across the country, and I have a home to sell or rent, and more essential belongings to collect. In the hasty two days between decision and wedding, I'd only packed for a month away. Chicago's weather will be quite different from the mild temperatures of Arizona.

"See you in a few weeks," I say, hoping to end this call, as I pick up Tulane and struggle to hold the phone while opening the apartment door.

I don't have time to discuss how leaving Bolan might not be optimal. Who will care for Tulane?

"We look forward to it," Nylah states, her voice still positive.

"Look forward to an updated report, too." Jared's gruff demand rankles as it follows Nylah's pleasant tone.

The reminder is clear. I'm here for Bolan. Like I was there for Clifton, someone who took advantage of my steadfastness and dedication to him.

I'm also here for Tulane, and I kiss the side of her head before mumbling goodbye to my in-laws.

"I've got you, baby girl," I whisper to her, knowing better than anyone that a sports-centric parent isn't always a win.

22

From the moment I saw Ruthie in that ballroom, I sensed something familiar about her. Even flippantly asked if we'd been together because my memory is shit.

Last night, I didn't know if that sense of recognition was heightened because I knew I'd only kiss her.

Or if it had been the kiss itself.

Or this strange sense that I'd kissed her before. Before the hallway, and the balcony, and the ballroom.

A dusty memory came to me while we were kissing. College and that damn kiss experiment. The professor blackmailing me, telling me if I didn't participate, she'd flunk me in psychology, a required credit for graduation. Poor grades were also not acceptable to the team and could lead to a probationary period, or worse, removal.

And if I didn't have baseball, I didn't have anything.

The idea of Ruthie being that girl was silly. Surely, she'd remember me, right? Then again, that moment probably hadn't made an impression on that girl.

She probably isn't that girl.

I could shake the thought, but not the strange vibe humming through my body, and the constant desire to kiss Ruthie again.

Ruby's interruption had been a bit of a buzz kill, but I could have picked us back up. Could have pressed my wife to the wall and ground into her some more. Could have taken her to the couch, or better yet, that damn king-sized bed.

But I didn't want alcohol to be involved again in a moment with Ruthie.

Not that we were drunk the first time, or even last night. We were riding a high of good company, clean fun, and dancing, and I didn't want anything that would spoil that buzz.

Still. *Is she that girl?* The one from the experiment? The girl I wasn't allowed to contact again and eventually pushed out of my thoughts.

For weeks, she'd haunted my dreams, and I looked for her on campus, hoping to randomly run into her. Maybe the cafeteria. Hell, I'd even gone to the library a few times. Hoping. Wishing.

But when my mysterious kiss girl seemed to disappear, I moved on.

Just like I do when the game begins.

And when the Anchors have a two-game winning streak, I'm definitely thinking kisses from my wife are the lucky charm.

Of course, I don't share that with the team. A player does not give away his superpower.

"Did you have fun last night?" Typically, I don't think I'd worry, but Ruthie isn't some random woman I don't plan to see again. She's my wife, and I want her to like me. Like my team-mates. "Liked the guys? Enjoyed meeting Lacey?"

We're sitting at our small dining table after the Anchors' second win in a row, lingering despite dinner being finished. Ruthie picked up take out on her way home, and we ended up arriving at the apartment at roughly the same time.

She scoops a section of her blonde hair behind an ear. Her face turns a soft shade of pink, and I wonder if she's remembering our kiss like I do. That hot moment in the hallway. Even holding her on the dance floor had been a grand slam.

"Yeah. Lacey was a bit . . . intense." She lifts her head. "Did Cyrus cheat on her?"

My brows lift. I'm kicked back in the dining chair, legs spread wider than the seat and outstretched, heels digging into the floor. I've overexaggerated the sprawling position so my leg brushes Ruthie's beneath the table. "Not that I know of. He's always saying he wouldn't be anywhere without her. They have three little boys."

"Huh." That's the only response I get, and as much as I'd like to know more, I'm more concerned about *my* wife.

"I spoke to Jared earlier today."

"Jesus." I scrub down my face. "He's worse than my dad was."

"Really? What was your dad like?"

"Overbearing."

"And now?"

I shrug. "We don't talk as much. When I went to Japan, he told me a different country only meant different issues. When he heard about Tulane, he was less than pleased."

When I'd called my dad to tell him he was a grandfather, I thought he might finally be happy for me. Even proud of me for manning up after I hadn't known about Tulane.

Thought he would be like my granddad, but my dad was not thrilled.

"*You've just ended your career. Kids ruin everything,* he'd told me." I mock his tone.

"That's awful."

"Yeah, well, he's a bitter man because of my mom."

"I still can't believe Joanna did that to you. Nylah never mentioned it. Hardly mentioned you, actually." Ruthie's brows pinch, possibly disappointed in her mother-in-law, definitely a little confused by the omission.

"Didn't like to discuss her transgressions, I guess. Or the black sheep." I pat my chest.

"Don't talk about yourself like that," she counters.

"You already know I'm trouble."

"Maybe you *were* trouble. *Before*. But now you're not." Her gaze roams over my face.

"Are you calling me your good boy?" I tease.

"Do you want to be my good boy?" She arches a brow, and I dig my teeth into my lower lip. She can call me anything she'd like but her tone turns a little more serious when she continues. "I mean, look at you. Family man, having dinner at home. Hanging with your wife and child. So domestic."

She pauses a second. "You must be so bored."

I shift in my seat, pushing it back and twisting so I'm facing her better. I lean forward and rest my elbows on my thighs. My fingertips trace a circle on her kneecap. "I'm not bored. Not one bit."

Surprisingly, I'm enjoying domestic life more than I thought I would. When Tulane came along, her presence was such a life adjustment, but I fell in love with my child. I want to be around her, making up for the time I missed.

And now, I'm falling in lo— I like my wife a lot.

When she softly smiles at me, I realize I'll never be bored with her looking at me like she is. Like she's a little thirsty for more kisses. Maybe even desperate for them, especially when I consider how she clings to me, like I'm not close enough. She wants me closer.

"How about your parents? You don't ever mention them." I sit back but keep my body sideways in the uncomfortable chair. I wish we were hanging on the couch, but I don't want to burst this little bubble of conversation.

I don't want to stop tracing over her skin.

"Oh, my parents weren't the type who wanted to be parents. I was an oops."

I smile until I realize Ruthie isn't teasing. "They didn't really tell you that you were a mistake, right?"

She ducks her head, shoving hair behind her ears again. "Not in so many words. But I spent a lot of time with babysitters and nannies and tutors."

"Tutors?"

"Traveled a lot." She doesn't explain but continues, "When I was in high school, I was often left alone which suited me. I was quiet and shy, but then I met Clifton."

My fucking cheating-ass cousin.

Ruthie smiles weakly. "Your typical mouse-girl and big cheese jock story."

"Don't call yourself a mouse." I reach for her hand and link our fingers together in a playful handhold, realizing too late that I once compared her to a mouse, scurrying off to the larger bedroom each night when we first moved in. My wife is nothing like what I thought of her then.

"Anyway, I got swept up in his attention. His life, actually. And I fell in love with his parents." She sighs, looking down at our joined hands. "I didn't want to lose them."

I squeeze her fingers. "I get that. Wanting to find a substitute family. Wanting any kind of parent. But did you stay with him because of them?"

Ruthie glances at her plate, covered in scraps and a paper

napkin. "In some ways, maybe, yes. I was alone once again when Cliff played football. He was always busy. Then he joined the Army."

I swallow, knowing our life is about to get even busier. I'll be gone. She'll be alone but I don't want her feeling lonely. I'll still be present for her, dedicated to her, wanting her.

"I was immersed in every part of their lives, right down to the family business." Ruthie snorts. "But I am no fucking agent."

"Whoa." I sit up straight, squeezing her fingers. "I don't think I've ever heard you swear. You got a dirty mouth, flower?" I wiggle my brows because I definitely want to hear her talk naughty to me.

"No." She giggles. "But I'm just saying . . . I'm not an agent and I told Jared that again. I feel silly being called your agent as I'm not doing anything but writing up a few reports."

Wiggling my brows again, I tease. "Am I getting all As? Extra points for good behavior."

"You're a solid B-plus for Bolan. And no extra points needed for good behavior. You're amazing."

I sit taller, prouder, wanting her to always think so. I won't even argue that I want an A for Adler. I'll take any grade she gives me as long as I'm not failing her.

"Jared did seem concerned about injury."

"Worse thing that could happen, especially at my age."

"That's exactly what he said." She taps her chin teasingly. "I think he used the term geriatric."

"Hey now."

"But seriously, I've been feeling guilty about that big bed." Her cheeks twinge sweet pink. "It seems silly to sleep in it alone when there is plenty of space for two."

Holy fast balls, yes. But that would not be a good idea. I can't sleep next to her. I'd want to cuddle her, which would lead to wanting to touch her, which would lead to wanting to please her.

I mean, *If You Give a Mouse a Cookie* and all, one of Tulane's favorite books. I want the cookie and all that comes with it.

"We both know if I get in that bed with you, I'm gonna want to do things. Things I'm not certain you're ready to do again."

Ruthie chews at her lower lip, her eyes light with possible desire but definite hesitation.

"I promised patience, flower. And I'm willing to wait for you to get there with me."

Her head tilts. "Get where?" She could be flirting but I'm serious.

"You just asked me about Cyrus cheating on Lacey, and I know how Clifton treated you. Sounds like you had shitty parents, like me, so I want you to see I'm not like any of them. I'm committed." I focus on her eyes. "I'm the color white."

She smiles softly. I like this color game we've started, but I'm not playing with her feelings. I'm committed to Tulane and baseball, and now Ruthie. I'm not going to fuck this up.

Which means I'm definitely not mentioning that kiss experiment and the girl.

Ruthie drops a bomb next. "I need to go back to California before heading to Chicago."

"What? Why?"

"I have a house there. I need to figure out what to do with it."

I'd love to tell her to sell it, especially if she once shared it with Clifton, but I don't feel it's my place to say such a thing.

"Plus, Nylah and Jared want to see me. Proof of life," she jokes, but she video calls them at least once a week. They've seen her. She looks good. She's fucking beautiful.

"It will only be for a few days."

"The turnaround between our leaving Arizona and heading out for our first away series is quick," I remind her. The season starts in St. Louis for the Anchors before opening day at the iconic Anchor Field in Chicago.

"I know." She hangs her head.

"What about Tulane?"

Her head lifts again and her eyes soften. Her voice is hesitant when she suggests, "I could take her with me."

I trust Ruthie. Trust her with Tulane. But there is something I don't like about her taking Tulane to California with her.

I'm afraid Ruthie won't return *for me*. She'll go back to California and realize she's made a big mistake. She'll beg Jared to get her out of our contract, and Tulane and me will be a party of two again, when I'm enjoying our family of three.

"No," I say softly. "I'll figure something out." I don't know what or how, and I realize I've become too reliant on Ruthie. I'm a project for her, when she's becoming so much more to me. And to Tulane. I have no doubt Ruthie loves my kid and maybe likes me a lot, but I have my doubts about her falling in love with me and wanting to keep our commitment for more than a year.

Maybe I'm just a dumb jock thinking of us in terms of forever.

"I don't want to put you in a bind. You'll be gone for those first few days anyway, and Tulane won't be any trouble."

"No, I got it. She's my kid." I stand abruptly, hearing a sharp gasp from Ruthie, but not acknowledging it. I'm frustrated. I don't want her going back to California, and I wish I could go with her if she must, but I can't.

With my back to her, I set my plate in the sink and rest my hands on the edge of the countertop. I need to remind myself it's always going to be Tulane and me against the world, and I should be working on finding a nanny in Chicago. I've been spoiled with Ruthie pitching in and so easily taking care of my little one.

Her hand comes to my lower back, and I stiffen. "Bolan?"

"It's nothing." I twist my head to look over my shoulder, hating how her face looks stricken and confused. "We'll miss you," I say, only half-heartedly, when my whole heart feels a little raw. I turn to face her and pull her to my chest, wrapping my arms around her shoulders, loving how she falls against me. Her arms circle my waist.

"I'll be back," she says, her voice quiet, almost like she isn't certain.

It's only for a few days. I can do this. I lived without her before, but the issue is I'm becoming used to living with her.

23

[Bolan]

When I consider Ruthie's return to California, even for a few days, I'm not happy. Jared and Nylah don't need to see Ruthie in person, and I start to think maybe Ruthie just wants a break from me.

The insecurity escalates in my head when I see Ruthie standing outside the stadium after one of our final games, waiting on me but chatting with Romero Valdez.

From a distance, he's standing too close to her. Her head is bent forward, hair shielding the side of her face. She has Tulane in her arms, like my catcher's chest protector around her midsection. Tulane's head is tucked into Ruthie's neck and her legs dangle on either side of Ruthie's hips. She looks fragile compared to him.

As my pace picks up, I note how Ruthie's shoulders hunch forward as well, like she's cornered by him, closing in on herself. A shell around Tulane. Her feet shuffle like she's uncomfortable and wants to get away from him and she shifts Tulane against her front. Romero reaches out for that long loose hair and Ruthie flinches back, taking a step away from him. His hand stalls in mid-air, and I race to close the final distance between us.

"What the fuck?" I hiss as I skid to a stop in my cleats between Ruthie and him. We're teammates and I'm trying not to cause additional trouble for Romero. But I don't trust the guy. Our team already has a slim crack in it, and he and I are going to have a big problem if he thinks he can touch my wife.

"Just having a little talk with your pretty girl," Romero says, shifting his gaze to look around me at Ruthie.

I glance at her over my shoulder, sensing she's uncomfortable. Puffing out my chest, I stand to my full height which is a good six inches taller than my shortstop.

"You got something to say to *my* wife, you say it to me." I narrow my eyes at his dark ones. Ones that dance with mirth. He's a fucking instigator.

"Think Ruthie can speak for herself," Romero glances around my shoulder again, but I shift my body to block his view.

"Everything alright here?" Ford Sylver's soft mountain drawl comes from somewhere beside me.

"Just getting to know the family members of my teammates," Romero says, turning his gaze from me to Ford and smiling extra wide.

"Get the fuck away from my family," I mutter, lowering my voice as others are nearby. The warning in my tone is clear, though.

"Bolan," Ruthie quietly states behind me, but I don't move. I want him away from her. Away from me.

Dalton Ryatt approaches next, placing his arm around Romero's shoulders and not so gently moving him along.

"What a fucker," Ford murmurs as Dalton guides Romero toward the clubhouse. "You okay, Ruthie?"

I spin to face her, placing my hands on her shoulders before scanning down her body, like Romero actually touched her somewhere.

I'll kill him.

"I'm okay," she answers Ford with a shaky breath, and she shivers beneath my touch.

"What did he say? What did he want?" I demand.

"He just asked me about Tulane. How old she is. Told me how cute she is." Ruthie turns her head and presses a kiss to Tulane's head, flicking her gaze toward Ford.

I'm sensing that isn't all he said to her, and Ford pats my shoulder, before walking away to give me the privacy I need with her.

"It wasn't a big deal."

"He tried to touch you." I slide my hands from her shoulders down her arms. "That's a big fucking deal."

"My hair blew in my face."

"Flower." I stare at her. "Never lie to me."

She exhales and glances away from me. "He also said he couldn't believe I had Tulane less than two years ago. Not with a body like mine."

He's dead. We're in the middle of the desert. No one will find his body.

Ruthie's eyes are full of pain. His words a pinch at the truth. Tulane is not her child, biologically, and I'd said something to the same effect the other night.

"Shit, Ruthie. I'm so sorry." I tug her to me, sweaty uniform be damned, and lower my lips for her head.

"I'm fine. It's fine." She pulls back too soon, trying to reassure me but her eyes are cloudy.

"Baby, you don't look fine." I brush my thumb along her cheek and pinch her chin.

"It happens." She shrugs. "It's not like it hasn't happened before."

My entire body goes rigid, realizing we aren't talking about motherhood and Tulane anymore. "What do you mean it's happened before? What did he do?"

I'm going to bury him so deep in the earth even a coyote won't find his remains.

"Not him."

The fine hairs on the back of my neck rise. There's a story here and I want to hear it but not in the middle of the back lot of the stadium.

"Tonight, you'll tell me everything." Then I lean forward and steal a kiss, knowing I might need it more than her.

24

———

[Ruthie]

Romero's words could have rolled off my back, but then I remind myself that it's not acceptable to make uncomfortable or unwarranted—and highly suggestive—comments to a complete stranger. Or even someone you know. A shiver ripples down my back when I recall the way he looked at me. His eyes scanning my body like he could see all my assets, like I wasn't wearing clothing. It wasn't like he was going to throw me down on the asphalt and hump me, but I had an eerie sense that dragging me off behind the nearest tree wasn't out of the question. I was just about to walk away from him when Bolan stepped up to us.

The energy coming off my husband was enough to settle the nerves caused by Romero, but a new wave of anxiety crested because of Bolan. He looked like he wanted to strangle Romero. Instead, he blocked Romero from my view and shooed him off like an insect.

And now, I need to reveal a sordid moment from my past.

As I don't feel like cooking, I'm relieved when Bolan offers a chicken dinner take out. Despite little ears at the dining room table, he digs into the topic we put on hold earlier.

"Tell me what happened."

With a heavy sigh, I set down my fork and lean back in my chair. Bolan's foot slips around my ankle beneath the table as we sit across from one another. The gesture is comforting. An anchor to steady my rising anxiety as I reveal this part of my past.

"Jared hired me after graduation. Like I told you, the idea was Clifton's." I take another deep breath. "I'd gone to school to be a teacher, but I hadn't found a job, and Clifton wanted me available to follow him everywhere."

I hate how it sounds and, in hindsight, hate how much of myself I gave up for him. But teaching wasn't an option because it meant I couldn't travel with Cliff. At first, he wanted his wife at every game. Quickly, he decided a wife stifled his ability to bond with his team, thus going out, meeting other women.

"Anyway, my first, and only agent assignment was for an up-and-coming fighter named Abel Callahan."

Bolan lifts his head at the mention of the prizefighter who left the ring a few years ago.

"I didn't need to do much for him. Just schedule interviews and keep him in line. More assistant than agent, really." My gaze flicks to Bolan. My current assignment through Imperial Sports Management is no different.

But Bolan and I feel like so much more than a job, and it's getting complicated.

"Abel wasn't any trouble. He didn't even want an assistant." He might have *acted* like he was coming onto me once, but I recognized the cockiness. The assuredness of a rising star. Cliff behaved the same way.

Abel had a girlfriend, now his wife, Elma. She was the light in his eyes, and he didn't want to lose her. He'd even teased me that he'd fire me if she was ever jealous.

He didn't need to let me go.

"One night after a fight in a hotel in Vegas, I was wearing this professional, feminine suit that Nylah picked out for me. And a new pair of glasses. High heels that pinched my toes. My hair was brown at the time." I gave the appearance of a serious, studious assistant. I also stood out like a sore thumb in that Vegas night club.

"Blonde isn't your natural hair color?" Bolan eyes my hair before lifting his water for a sip.

"That's all you're taking from this story?" I chide playfully, pouting my lips. But his question has lessened the tension growing in me. "*Anyway*. I tried to play the tough assistant with the club manager. Really give the guy an evil glare and a dressing down."

I narrow my eyes to slits and try to hold my mouth in a straight line.

Bolan chuckles at my face and smiles crookedly. "Really scary."

"Yeah, well, he took it as an invitation."

Bolan falls back in his chair, watching me from across the table. "He what?"

"Didn't like being put in his place. He followed me out of the club. Cornered me. Told me he wanted to wipe the smirk off my face and paint my lips with his . . . you know." I circle a finger in the air toward Bolan.

"Are you fucking serious?" Bolan leans forward, bracing his thick forearms on the tabletop. "Where the fuck was Clifton?"

I shrug, twisting my lips before answering. "Off playing football."

"What happened with that guy? What happened to you?"

Bolan stares at me, both anger on my behalf and concern warring in his eyes.

"I shoved him as hard as I could and ran. I told Nylah the next day. She'd told me these things can happen, but it wasn't like she was telling me to accept it. She sensed that I couldn't handle that kind of attention, *those* kinds of situations, and she demanded Jared remove me as Abel's assistant."

Bolan continues to stare at me, like he's lost for words.

"When I finally told Clifton, he said I was too pretty for my own good. Thus, the suits and glasses. I needed to tone down the cuteness and up my fierceness." Thumb down for one; thumb up for the other. Then I wave around my face. "And it's just not a look I can pull off."

Bolan closes his eyes and his fingers curl into fists. He mutters under his breath, "Motherfucker."

I glance at Tulane, hoping she doesn't pick up such a word in her growing vocabulary.

Bolan shakes his head and reaches across the table for my hand. "I'm so sorry that happened to you, flower. Sorry Clifton wasn't supportive. Wasn't loyal. Wouldn't let you be who you want to be."

I simply shrug.

"I'm no better," he whispers, lowering his gaze and squeezing my hand before releasing it. Instantly, I miss his touch and the comfort it offered. "You're trapped with me now, aren't you?"

He lifts his gaze. "When you go to California, you should ask Jared to break the contract."

"What?" I sit up straighter.

"Tell him you want out." Bolan swallows hard. "I'll give you a divorce right now and set you free."

"No, that's not what I—" My throat closes. "I mean, if that's what you want."

Bolan sits forward once more and reaches for my hand

again. "It's not what I want. But I want you to have what *you* want. I want you to feel free to make the right choices for you. Not me. Not Tulane."

My gaze drifts from Bolan to Tulane and back. I have what I want. Him. Her. And when we move to Chicago, I'll be truly free. I love Nylah and Jared, but we are too close in proximity, and I need space. A new location. A fresh start.

"Bolan, you're my ticket out." I stare at him, hating how harsh that might sound but being with him is my excuse to leave. "No more California. No more ISM."

He lets go of my hand again and slips back in his chair. "The job." He pauses a second. "Right."

Slowly, he stands and takes his plate with him when I haven't even started eating. Suddenly, I'm not hungry as he looks so hurt for some reason.

"Just so you know," he pauses, standing beside the table. "If you ever gave me that look, I'd be frightened of you. I'd be very afraid." He softly winks but his smile doesn't reach his eyes.

In the time it's taken for me to explain my story, Tulane has finished eating, and Bolan takes her from the booster seat on a chair.

"I'll give you some time to finish your dinner in peace."

With that, Bolan takes Tulane toward her bedroom when being alone is the last thing I want to be.

THE EVENING PASSES SLOWLY, but finally Tulane is in bed and Bolan has taken up his nightly position on the recliner.

"Mind if I sit?" I point toward the couch. Earlier he said he was giving me space but maybe he needed the distance. Bolan and I keep having these mishaps as we navigate who we are, what we are.

Am I the nanny? The stepmom? Definitely *not* Tulane's mother.

Is he a project or a person? The answer is easy. He's someone I could really fall for when I'm scared of falling.

Bolan pops the chair into a seated position from the reclined one, and then reaches out for my hips, tugging me into his lap. Then he kicks back the chair, and I fall against his chest. His arms loosely wrap around me, and he kisses the side of my head, lingering there.

"I don't want you to ever think you are too beautiful for your own good. You're beautiful. Period. Is that a good thing? Sure is. I like to look at you, flower. But you're also radiant on the inside. So sweet. So kind. Being beautiful is who you are. For you. Not for some asshole to take advantage of in a club. Or your fucking husband to downplay." He sighs and his chest heaves beneath my side. "I'm so fucking angry."

I rub my hand over his chest and tip back my head. "Thank you."

"I don't like you going to California alone. I can't protect you if I'm not there."

I chuckle softly. "You don't need to protect me."

"But I want to." His voice lowers. "I'm here for you." He shifts so he can better see my face. "And not because some contract says so. We're *married*, Ruthie. You're my wife. I want you to be happy."

He sounds so sincere. Like he's really taking the position of marriage to heart and he's protective of me as his life-partner. He genuinely sounds like he wants me to be happy with him but more importantly, with myself. What I want to do with my life. Where I work. How I look. All decisions I need to make for me first.

I feel like a lighthouse coming to life after a long blackout. A brightness inside my chest illuminating and seeping through my pores. I need to shine in whatever capacity that might be.

"I am happy," I admit, a smile breaking out across my lips. "I love spending time with you and Tulane. I like playing your wife."

Although playing may not be the correct word. I'm not acting. I don't need to pretend. I truly enjoy hanging out with Tulane and treasure the time I have with Bolan. The way I feel safe with him. The way I can be open with him. The way he listens to me.

His eyes turn serious. "I don't want you to play. This isn't a game for me."

"It's not a game to me, either."

There's no score or tally or collection of points to be won. Bolan is the prize and I'm grateful for this time with him. More grateful than he'll ever know. He's exactly what I needed when I didn't think I needed anyone else but myself.

"Fuck. I want to kiss you. I want to show you how special you are, but after what you just told me, I don't know that you want me to ever touch you."

I'm already in his lap, but I don't point that out. Instead, I say, "Kissing sounds good."

Right now, I just want his mouth on mine, erasing the bad memories and making good ones.

His lips against mine are soft at first, taking his time to kiss the corners before sucking tenderly at the delicate skin. Slowly, we move from light kisses to heavier ones. Ones that involve more of our lips. Our tongues tracing. Even teeth tugging.

Not breaking the connection between us, I shift on his lap. The movement isn't graceful, but Bolan guides my hips as I straddle his thighs. My hands come to his shoulders.

"This isn't what was supposed to happen," he says against my lips as I settle over him. The thick bulge in his athletic shorts against the achy center between my spread thighs. "It feels dangerous."

"Reckless?" I arch a brow while still kissing him.

"Everything with you feels reckless, baby." The sparkle in his eyes says it's not a bad thing. Maybe dangerous for our hearts but not our bodies.

And I need him. I need the rush he gives me when he kisses me. And the compassion in his heart when he listens to me.

With the slightest dip of my hips, I brush against his stiff length, the sensation delicious.

Bolan hisses.

"Want me to stop?" I murmur against his mouth.

"Never," he growls. "But we also only go as far as you want. No pressure for more."

I nod, before running my cheek against his. The stubble on his jaw is prickly but exciting.

"You like that." He chuckles. "Liked it between your thighs, didn't you?"

His question makes my hips thrust forward, dragging my hot center over him again.

He grunts. "Fuck."

I hum and repeat the motion again and again, as his hard cock stimulates my sweet spot. With my hands on his shoulders, I glance down at where my center rocks over him. My hips rolling forward and back. I close my eyes and tuck my head.

"Gonna come like this, flower? Gonna bloom for me?"

"Oh God," I whimper, as my body suddenly spirals out of my control. Sensation takes over. The feel of him between my legs. His hard to my soft. I grind harder, move faster.

"Bolan," I whisper, knowing I'm close. "Please," I beg, clinging to his shoulders.

"Not gonna move, baby," he admits, holding onto my hips as I rock over him, taking from him, needing him.

Until I'm a burst of energy. A seed bursting into a bud, breaking through the earth. I dig my nails into his shoulders and still, letting the rush take over. I come unraveled, like something inside me snapped, shredded, drifted away. I lunge forward, cup his cheeks and kiss him with everything I have. Telling him without words how I'm right where I want to be. With him. With Tulane.

Then, there's a sharp ping, like a spring popped somewhere and I pull back just as the chair collapses on one side. Bolan wraps his arms around my lower back, and we awkwardly fall back with the release of the recliner. He does a clumsy roll and I'm on my back against the armrest. Then he flips us, so he's on his back and I'm over him again.

"What the . . ." Bolan lifts only his head, cocking it to the side to look at the broken recliner.

"Oh my God." I chuckle. Then I outright laugh, dipping my forehead to his shoulder as my body lays over his.

"Well, that was a mood killer." He presses on my hips, and I sit upright, straddling him again. I rock once, hoping to restore what we just lost. But Bolan jackknives upward, wincing and reaching for his lower back.

"Shit. Are you hurt?" I scramble off him, worried I've unintentionally injured him. Kneeling beside him, I wave my hands around his body, afraid to touch him.

"I will be." He winces again. Placing a hand on the broken armrest, he gingerly lifts himself. Only when he stands, he remains bent forward, holding onto his lower back.

"You know guys always say they could die buried deep in their woman."

"Bolan," I snap.

"But no one is going to believe I hurt my back making out with my wife."

I chuckle before realizing this could be serious. "I'm so sorry."

"Don't be. That was one of the best moments of my life."

"Falling out of a chair while making out?" I counter, crossing my arms and glaring at him.

"Kissing my wife until she came."

"You're ridiculous," I joke, placing my hand over his on his back.

"That's why you love me."

He has no idea, I'm almost there.

25

———

[Bolan]

Ruthie absolutely refused to let me sleep on the couch that night, practically pushing me down the hallway and onto the bed.

"We just talked about injury and now I've hurt you."

"I'm not hurt," I lie but there's definitely something pinching my lower left side.

"I'm only sleeping in that bed if you're sleeping beside me." I'd been trying to hold out, giving her the patience she needs. At the moment, I'm in too much pain to think about sex.

"Okay," she softly says, standing beside me as I gingerly lower to the edge of the bed and then twist to lay flat on my back.

Fuck. It hurts.

"What can I do for you?" Her voice still sounds sexy, sated and willing, without intending to sound as such. And as much as I want to joke about what she *could* do for me, I'm not in a position to enjoy it.

"How about an icy-hot patch?" I keep them on stand-by, and I roll over, hoping Ruthie will place the patch on my lower back.

When she does, she remains standing beside the bed.

"Get in," I mutter to the pillow, the side of my face smooshed in the luxurious fluff. I've missed a bed.

"I don't know that that's a good idea," she counters.

"I promise to keep my hands to myself, flower." I've already tucked them underneath the pillow, not only for safekeeping, but as a way to stretch out my spine.

Ruthie softly chuckles. "What if I can't keep my hands to myself?"

I huff. *Dammit.* Why is she still so tempting? "Words I've never said . . . Not tonight, baby."

Ruthie laughs harder. "Give me a minute."

As I hear her step into the ensuite bathroom, I reflect on how only I would break a chair with my girl on my lap. It was worth it to see the smile on her face and hear the stuttering hitch in her breath as she came.

Plus, we were kissing again.

Kissing Ruthie is an experience. Like a full-body, soul-entrancing, heart-filled experience. Her mouth sweet while hungry. Her hands clasping at me, begging with her touch to be closer to her. And the way her body moves, like she was made for me.

When I consider how she kisses me, I don't think about our arrangement. She isn't my assistant. Or a nanny to Tulane. She's my wife and mother to my child. She's everything I need, and I'm struggling to make her see how I feel. Breaking a chair with her in my lap doesn't exactly say I'm stable.

But I want to be. I don't want her to ever feel unsafe with me or uncertain about my intentions. I'm here for her.

I'm hers.

And I want her to be mine.

When I hear the soft click of the bathroom light being turned off, I'm in a drowsy state. Too tired to move a muscle, but still conscious of her movements in the room. Her presence stands beside the side of the bed I've fallen on and for a moment I worry she wants me to slide over. Like she's claimed this side as her side.

Instead, gentle fingernails come to my back, and she scratches along my spine.

Holy shit, does that feel incredible. I mutter into the pillow what I think is something similar to my thoughts as goose-bumps break out on my flesh. I want to tell her how much she means to me. How grateful I am that she's here for me. For Tulane.

But the magic of those fingernails scratching down my back has me passed out in a matter of minutes.

26

[Ruthie]

When the Chicago Anchors have a doubleheader, I take a pass on a double dose of baseball. Instead, Lacey Sawyer invited Tulane and me to visit the local aquarium with her and her boys.

Surrounded by three rambunctious boys under six, Lacey doesn't mention any concerns about Cyrus and his fidelity. She's less intense than she was at our first meeting, with her focus presently on her sons. She's a great mom, and I hope we can be friends as I'll need some when I get to Chicago.

We spend a good portion of our time together chatting about raising children.

"You know how it is," she eventually says to me, with the assumption that I'm Tulane's biological mother and I've been raising her since birth. Since I don't know how Bolan wants to play my relationship with Tulane, I simply nod in response to Lacey's comment.

But I consider how, biological or not, Tulane feels like mine. We have a wonderfully exciting day, pointing out the fish and sea life, giggling at how they open their mouths or flip their fins. Watching her take in this new experience will go down as a highlight of my life. I'm honored and fortunate to share these moments with her. I truly love this child.

We went to the aquarium first thing in the morning and stayed until late afternoon, which means Tulane's nap time is messed up again and she falls asleep in the car. When I get to the apartment, I make as little noise as possible and lay her down in her crib in hopes she'll stay asleep a little longer.

But I almost let out a scream when I see Bolan sprawled out on the king-sized bed, face down, arms and legs spread like a giant star fish.

Then I slump against the doorframe and take in the curve of his back. His defined muscles are apparent as he isn't wearing a shirt. My gaze lowers for his backside covered by loose-fit athletic shorts. There is just something about baseball players. Bolan in those famous pants is something. Bolan out of them is also something.

I chew at my lower lip, feeling like a voyeur watching him sleep. Poor man misses a mattress and a good night's rest.

The night of the recliner incident, I'd kept my distance on the massive mattress, afraid my nearness would hurt him again.

While I'm watching him, Bolan lifts his head, rubs his nose against the bed cover and then lies flat again.

I should really step away, but I don't. Instead, I witness him roll over to his back and wince.

"Are you okay?" I rush forward.

He lifts his head again to look at me, but he also lifts his leg, bending his knee toward his chest and then rotating it outward, like he's working his hip flexor.

"Cramp," he grits through a clenched jaw.

"What can I do to help?" I'm not a physical therapist or

personal trainer, and Bolan has an entire regimen of exercises after catching to stretch and relieve his muscles, but he's clearly in pain.

He does the same motion again, this time holding the back of his knee and tugging his leg higher against his chest.

Instead of remaining at the foot of the bed, I climb onto it, positioning myself between his spread legs.

"Grab my ankle." He winces.

I follow his instructions, keeping a firm grip on his thick ankle as he pulls his leg toward him once more.

"Now push. Resistance might help."

I do as he asks, leaning into his bent leg, but he grits, "Harder."

Putting all my weight into it, I shove his leg, placing my other hand on his inner thigh to stabilize myself. Only my hand slips and I narrowly miss a part on him I shouldn't be touching.

Bolan lifts his head again, gazing at me between his spread legs. My attention falls to the definitive bulge in his thin shorts.

"See what you do to me, flower," he grunts.

I try to ignore it. Him. His dick. Instead, I rotate his leg like he'd been doing before. Placing my hand on the inside of his thigh, I have better control of the movement, rolling his hip flexor and bringing his leg back to the bed.

But I'm still between his thighs and when I go to remove my hand from his inner leg, Bolan claps his hand over mine.

"Fuck. flower." He drops his head back to the bed and drapes his arm over his face.

"I'm sorry," I mutter, releasing him with my free hand.

Bolan moves his arm and lifts his head once more. "Don't be sorry. This is what you do to me." His voice strains. "I'm so fucking hard for you."

Just looking at him. That thick bulge in his shorts. The length of it. The fact he claims *I* do this to him spurs something inside me.

"May I touch you?"

Bolan snorts. "So fucking sweet when you never have to ask me for permission."

I slide both my hands up his inner thighs, digging my thumbs into the solid muscles, before reaching the weight of his balls. I wrap my hand around his covered dick. With a sharp tug, I slip up the length and Bolan hisses.

His head has fallen back. His eyes close. "Yes," he chokes, as I start to stroke him faster, squeezing harder.

Touching him turns me on in a way I hadn't ever considered. He's hard because of me. His body is reacting to my touch. And I feel powerful with his dick in my hand.

I squeeze and pump, and then take the liberty to dip my hand beneath the waistband of his shorts. No underwear. Bolan groans as he lifts his hips to help shove down the athletic wear. I'm not sure if it's the pain in his back or the eagerness of knowing his cock is destined for my mouth.

In the early evening light, I have an excellent view of his length and girth. The strength and stiffness. And I remember the powerful thrust of this appendage into my body. Memories of him surging into me, taking me up against a cold window, send tingles between my thighs. I want to straddle his thick thighs. Instead, I squeeze my thighs together as I work him.

"Just like that, baby," he groans as I jerk him faster, watching where the tip is swollen and leaking. Then I lower and give it a lick. Bolan's hips thrust upward.

"I'm sorry. Sorry," he mutters as his hand comes to the side of my head. "Don't stop. *Please* don't stop. Do anything. Mouth. Hands." His breath comes in short bursts between each command.

Opening wide, I take him in, taking my time to suck along the length that fits in my mouth. My other hand cups the rest. My tongue circles the rim of the crown, and then I draw him in again, hollowing my cheeks. With the increased suction, Bolan's hips rock again, gentler this time.

"That's it, flower. Take me. Take all of me."

I cup his balls with my other hand, gently rolling them. While I'm thrilled with his responding moan, I'm equally surprised by my own body's reaction. I slip my leg over his thigh and press my center against the firmness, keeping my mouth and my hands on him.

There is something so virile about Bolan. Something that makes me want to be a little wild. Something that gives me permission to be reckless.

Both his hands come to the sides of my head. "Ruthie. Flower." He grunts in warning, like he'll pull me off him, but I double down.

"F*uck*." Bolan goes off like a river let loose from a dam.

When I finally drag my mouth up his length and kiss the tip, I glance up at him. Head tossed back. Eyes aimed toward the ceiling and blinking.

"I see silver stars. Do you see silver stars?"

I chuckle lightly and sit back, my center notched on his kneecap. Bolan jackknives upright, startling me, and with one smooth movement, he rights his shorts and then grips my hips, flipping me to my back beside him. He twists, settling on his knees between my legs, forcing them to spread for him.

"How about you, Ruthie? How are your hip flexors?" He grabs my ankles.

I could tease him that mine are out of practice, but I don't need to speak as Bolan presses my legs upward, forcing my knees to bend and come to my chest. He tugs my legs apart, spreading my knees wide. In denim shorts, I can only rotate so much.

"Felt you on my thigh. Tell me you've been achy for me, like I've been aching for you."

I lick my lips and answer. "I've been achy."

"Dr. Adler is here to help."

His silliness makes me chuckle again, but the laughter quickly drops off when he reaches for the clasp on my shorts, then unzips them. With a sharp tug, he drags them down my legs and off my feet. He leans forward, placing his face directly between my legs and inhales.

"God, I've missed you," he says to the intimate part of me covered by my underwear.

I've missed him, too, but I don't say that as he licks over my damp panties. Then he hooks his finger in the material between my thighs and pulls my underwear downward. He takes his time to remove them and then drags his gaze up my legs until he's reached my center. He stares a second, inspecting me, admiring me. Then a finger brushes against my clit, and my breath hitches. That same finger dips inward and I arch off the bed.

"So ready for me. So responsive to me." He pulls his finger back and adds a second, diving into me, and taking my breath once more. Back and forth, he works me, alternating between watching his fingers and glancing up at me.

At one point he says, "Look at you soaking my fingers. Fucking them." He hums, then adds his thumb to the rotation, pressing my clit.

"Never gonna be the same," he mutters, but I'm not certain if he means him or me. Because I've never felt this before. This undivided attention. This rush of desire. This powerful sense that I'm beautiful, special, important to him.

"Bolan," I whimper.

"Is my wife needy? Does she want me to fill her up? Stuff her full of my fingers, and then my cock?"

"Oh God," I cry out, fisting my fingers in the duvet beneath me.

"You're kissing me," he whispers, watching where his fingers disappear. "Marking me."

My cheeks heat but I have no time to be embarrassed because my lower belly flutters and my legs begin to shake.

"Bolan," I whisper again, the quiet tone desperate for him.

He curls his fingers inside me, and something clicks. I go off like the perfect hit. A line drive to centerfield, only I'm headed out of the ballpark. This is so much more than a grand slam. It's fireworks over the stadium.

I cover my mouth with my hand to prevent the scream that would surely wake Tulane. I arch into Bolan's touch, dragging out the sensation until I have nothing left and collapse back to the bed.

"Yes," Bolan whispers, finally removing his fingers and then dipping them into his mouth.

"You're so bad," I tease, my voice unrecognizable as I twist my head to see him better. His large body still between my spread legs.

"And you're such a good girl." He presses a tender kiss to my lower lips, and I shiver at the intimate touch.

Then he shifts his entire body, pouncing onto all fours over me, until we hear a small cry.

Bolan and I both stiffen a second until another cry tells us this sexy interlude is over.

He hangs his head a second before glancing up at me. "I'll get her." Then he leans forward, kisses my nose, and hops off the bed, like he didn't just have aching hips, hadn't just rocked my world.

He goes into dad mode and there is nothing sexier.

27

[Bolan]

The second half of spring training sped up. We had a rare day off and Ruthie and I spent the morning at the Phoenix Zoo. In the afternoon, while Tulane napped, Ruthie and I cuddled on the couch which we hadn't done before. It took everything in me to ignore my dick springing to life, and just enjoy the time holding onto my wife. Ruthie's back was snuggled into my front, and I couldn't remember the last time, if ever, that I'd simply spent an afternoon hanging out, holding a girl.

Ruthie was changing everything about me. For the better.

Her fingers tickle up my forearm. "I keep meaning to ask you what this tattoo means. I get that it's a bear, but why a bear?"

I could give her some cheesy explanation, like bears are attracted to honey produced by bees who are attracted to flowers, thus my attraction to her. Instead, I give her the deeper meaning which I've never told anyone before.

"My granddad. He told me this story once about how bears love to fish, and they are notoriously good at it. Snap and grab." I imitate the motion with my hand. "A bear felt like an appropriate tattoo to get for someone wanting to be able to easily snatch and catch"—I imitate catching a fish with my bare hand again—"a ball."

Not that baseballs are like fish, but catching a fish bare-handed is all about timing and concentration.

"My granddad laughed when I got it. Told me he thought I'd done it because bears are a bit reckless." The sluggish swagger of a bear can be deceiving. There is strength and power in a bear and fierce devotion to their cubs. The tattoo has taken on new meaning in the past year.

Ruthie hums. "Remember that night you pulled Tulane and me into your lap. The night I was so sick."

"Yeah?"

"Kind of felt like a giant bear was holding onto us then. Someone fierce and devoted."

I smile against her hair, my eyes closed by the lazy way she runs her fingertips over my tattoo.

"Since you call me flower, I should call you bear."

"Funny, that had been a nickname of mine a while back." Before I left for Japan. "Valdez called me the name on the first day I met him." I don't want to give too much credit to Valdez, but it did feel like The Bear was back once I stepped on that field for the Anchors. The right side of the nickname, not the old reputation.

"You're like a giant Teddy."

I laugh into the top of her head. "I don't think anyone would ever call me that."

"I would. You bring comfort and give great hugs." She wiggles her body against mine and I grit my teeth again, forcing my dick not to react to her. Melting in a new way around her.

Wanting to be that bear which comforts her, protects her, keeps her safe.

WHEN THE FINAL day of spring training arrives, Ruthie attends our last game and then it's a whirlwind of activity. She's scheduled to fly out to California at roughly the same time Tulane and I leave Phoenix. I couldn't take a child on the team plane, and I needed permission to travel separately with Ford Sylver and his girls as he doesn't have a traveling nanny. Ruby will remain in Arizona with her family.

Ford helped me secure childcare for the days Ruthie will be absent. He gave me the name of someone he'd used in the past. She'll be available for team practices the next few days and then spend the weekend with Tulane as I'll be in St. Louis and Ruthie will be in California.

When Ruthie and I get to the airport check-in, I look like a hunchback, with the car seat in a carrier strapped to my back, Tulane in my arms, and our suitcases, Tulane's stacked on mine. Ruthie is pulling her own bags.

"I feel so bad I'm not traveling with you to Chicago."

We've already talked about this. How it was silly to fly to Chicago and then turn around for Los Angeles. The flight is shorter from Phoenix to LAX.

"I've got this." I traveled from Japan to California with my child. I can handle this much shorter jog across the country.

I'm more upset that I'm not getting a proper goodbye with her. Weighed down with all the bags and holding Tulane, there's no way to lean over and kiss my wife without risking that I tip over.

And Ruthie needs to get to a different terminal.

"We're going to miss you so much," I say, jostling Tulane in my arms after checking in our bags. I keep my attention on my baby girl because I'm afraid to look at Ruthie. Afraid she isn't going to miss us.

"I'll miss you, too." She reaches out for Tulane's leg and gives it a little shake. "But it's only a few days."

We'll need to get used to goodbyes.

She tips up on her toes and plants a kiss on Tulane's cheek, then settles back on her feet and rubs her hand over Tulane's red curls.

"You'll call me when you get there?" she says to me.

"Definitely."

Then she tips up again and kisses the corner of my mouth, missing my lips. I don't like the sinking feeling in my stomach.

And as she walks away, I call her name. She spins quickly and I catch the glisten in her eyes. Shit.

"Flower," I rush forward. Still holding Tulane in my arms, I cup the back of Ruthie's head and pull her to me for a real kiss.

A better goodbye than this lame one we're tapdancing around.

She pulls back first, her smile soggy. Her eyes still watery. "I've got to go." She walks backward a few steps, keeping her eyes on us, then presses her fingers to her lips and tips them forward, blowing on them.

"Catch it, Tulip." I jiggle her in my arms.

Tulane reaches out her little hands and claps them together, giggling that she's caught air in her tiny fingers.

"Now pat Daddy's cheek," I softly command.

She smacks my cheeks a few times, then wraps her arms around my neck. I glance back at Ruthie, who waves one more time, then turns away from us.

"Tell Mommy you love her," I whisper to Tulane as Ruthie picks up her pace, rushing through the crowd until I lose sight of her.

Tulane waves, although Ruthie is long gone.

28

[Ruthie]

As soon as I can, I duck into a bathroom stall and let the tears fall. I'm going to miss them so much. It's only for a few days, like I said, but it somehow feels bigger than that. Separation is never easy. With my history of distrust with Clifton, I don't want to project on Bolan. I want to believe he'll behave.

However, my heart races. I'm scared. Scared of how I feel. Scared of missing them.

Scared of loving them.

Within minutes, a text pings on my phone.

Miss you already.

A video is attached with Tulane blowing a kiss to the camera and the tears start again, along with laughter. She's so stinking cute.

He'll be fine, I tell myself. We found a temporary sitter who can watch Tulane during the next few days. She's an older woman Ford Sylver previously used and approved, and it brings small comfort to know someone who had experience with her.

This is the best time to do what I need to do, which is ship my belongings to Chicago and decide on the house.

"Do you really want to sell?" Nylah says to me, after picking me up at LAX and arriving at my home. The cute little house I had to have once upon a time. A place I thought would be full of children and fond memories.

"This is the house you and Clifton purchased together." Nylah sighs nostalgically, looking around the small living room. The mantel is now empty, pictures which used to be there now absent. There was a time I could no longer look at photos of Cliff and me. Reliving the happier times along with the grief was too much. Out of sight did not make him out of mind, but it helped.

"I think it's best," I tell her, setting my keys on the small table by the staircase and stepping into the living room, doing a slow spin to face her. "It's time."

"In this market, you might not find a house so easily, so cheaply, when you return."

Nylah glances around the space once more before her gaze lands on me. Her eyes are somber and worried.

"Maybe I'll stay in Chicago."

"Oh?" she arches a perfectly sculpted brow. "Things going that well with Bolan."

I smile and chew at the corner of my lips. "He's a good man."

Her brows lift higher, and I'm reminded that her best friend, and cousin, was Bolan's mother. The woman who abandoned her child after having an affair with another man.

Nylah's mouth opens to argue and then snaps shut, stating, "I didn't know him well."

"That's unfortunate." I smile kindly, but think about her son, whom Nylah would claim she knew very well, and yet didn't. I'm not certain anyone saw the depth of his demons. Only in hindsight did I recognize the signs.

"Speaking of Bolan, though, there's a few things I'd like to discuss with Jared."

IN LESS THAN A WEEK, my house is on the market. The belongings I want to keep are packed up and picked up to be moved across the country, along with my car. There had been a heavy discussion with Nylah and Jared about making rash decisions, but for once in my life, I am leaning into being impulsive. It's time to leave California, and Clifton, behind, and I finally make my farewells to Nylah and Jared.

"Don't forget to write," Nylah teased recalling the old-fashioned form of communication: letters.

"Call if you need anything," Jared reiterated, concern in eyes that match the color of his deceased son.

I know they feel like they are losing a child again, but I'm an adult, and I'm not Clifton. I'm only half-way across the country and a phone call away.

With every step I take through LAX headed for Chicago, anticipation blooms inside me. This is the fresh start I've needed for years.

And no matter how Bolan feels at the end of the baseball season, I'll have a new place to call home, a new future ahead of me. I won't be returning to California.

Excitement crests when I arrive at the address Bolan provided. I'm days early, having rushed through the packing of my house. I've made it to Chicago on opening day for baseball, but the Anchors first series of games is in St. Louis.

The place is a white, clapboard, four-story building with two front doors on a raised landing. One door enters the first floor and belongs to a duplex that includes the garden space below it. The other door leads to the second-floor duplex which includes the top floor.

I take my bags from the driver and climb the steep stairs to the outdoor landing, before entering a code into the keypad on the doorknob. As the lock zips open, I feel a zing rush up my middle.

Home.

Opening the door, I'm faced with a broad wooden staircase with a long child-proof safety gate across the top of it. The soft sound of Tulane's jabber comes from somewhere up there.

"Hello," I call out.

Tulane rushes to the gate and waves at me over the edge of the barrier. "Mama."

I freeze, nearly dropping my bags and tumbling backward. "What?" I whisper, tears instantly prickling the back of my eyes.

When an older woman appears, I blink back the well in my eyes and smile up at her.

"Hi. I'm Ruthie Adler."

And I'm home.

I DISMISS THE SITTER, because she's no longer needed, but pay her in full for her promised time. I'm here now and I have no intention of leaving anytime soon.

After she leaves, I wander with Tulane in my arms to inspect the duplex. The first floor has an open concept living room and kitchen combination with space for a dining table to the left of the kitchen and directly in line with the top of the entry staircase. The place came with four high-top stools along a large peninsula counter but not much else. Bolan sent me a video of the empty space when he finally arrived after a snowstorm delay set back his flight to Chicago.

He'd promptly ordered an L-shaped couch and set up a large screen television on the wall opposite it, sending me a second video when it arrived.

The place has three bedrooms, although the third one is located on the first floor and remains empty. Bolan told me how he'd become a minimalist in Japan and gave away any furnishings he had before he left the country.

On the second floor of the duplex are two bedrooms with a bathroom between them. Tulane's room is rather sparse with only a crib and matching dresser that doubles as a changing table.

"We definitely need to spruce up this room," I jostle Tulane on my hip as we stand in her space. My mind already races with ideas for a pretty rug, bookshelves, and a basket for stuffed animals, plus pictures for her walls.

In the final and largest bedroom is a king-sized bed with a box beside it, doubling for what looks like a nightstand. A book sits on top titled *The Toddler Years*.

I chuckle to myself as I flip through the pages.

"Well, baby girl." I jostle Tulane on my hip. "This is home." I press a kiss to her cheek. "How about we have some lunch and send Daddy a video?"

Tulane holds up her little hands, palms out, like she's questioning something. She glances around and says, "Dada." She's just the cutest little thing.

"Don't you worry, Tulip. Dada will be home soon."

29

THE SEASON

[Bolan]

Nothing surprises me more than a short video of Ruthie and Tulane together in our duplex. Both girls are smiling through the screen and waving at me, saying, "Hi Dada."

My chest pinches. I miss them both and can't wait to call Ruthie when the game is over. She's home early and nothing makes me happier.

"What are you doing there?" I chuckle when I eventually lay on my back, staring up at the ceiling of my hotel room. Cyrus and I chose to room together, but he's down at the bar with a few of the guys.

"I thought I'd surprise you," she says.

"Best surprise ever."

We're both quiet a second.

"It's good to hear your voice," Ruthie finally says, hers not more than a whisper. It's late, and I wasn't able to see the video until after the game. Now is the first chance I've gotten to talk to her today.

"It's nice hearing yours, too." I scoot lower on the bed, settling in with my ankles crossed and my hand behind my head.

"Makes me feel like you're here."

I hum. "And where are you?"

"In bed."

I chuckle lightly. "That would be *our* bed," I clarify.

While Ruthie and I were eventually sleeping in the same bed back in Arizona, because I finally gave in after hurting my back and her noticing the crick in my hip, we haven't had another moment like that afternoon after my doubleheader. And as far as I'm concerned, we aren't going back to sleeping separately. We'll already have too many nights apart as it is.

This week has been rougher than I thought without her present. I hate sleeping without her. And I especially hate that she came home and I wasn't there to greet her properly. To welcome her into our new place.

"Our bed," she whispers, as if convincing herself.

"What's mine is yours, baby," I tease.

"But am I yours?" Her voice is still quiet, hesitant.

Does she worry that I'm on the road not being faithful to her? I'm not upset by her concerns. My douchebag cousin did a number on her and she has deep trust issues, but I want Ruthie to trust me.

"Flower," I groan. "I'm yours, and I wish I was there to show you how much I'm yours."

"What would you show me?" Her voice shifts, sounding less sleepy and more seductive. Is my wife getting turned on in our bed? Without me? Fuck that.

"Ruthie, what are you wearing?"

She chuckles, light and carefree, breaking the sudden tension winding around my body, turning it into something not unwelcome. The sound sends shivers over my skin with a need to touch her, to be close to her.

I move my hand to my belly, beneath the waistband of my joggers, but stops short of touching myself despite the sudden hardness of my dick.

"Just my pajamas."

"The white set?" I ask. She has this pair of silky white shorts and matching tank top. Too often, I've imagined her wearing the set without a bra. Nipples peaking against the soft material. The bottoms revealing a sliver of her fine ass.

She giggles. "Actually, no. It's a bit chilly here for that outfit."

"Hmm." I'm already lost in my head with images of her despite what she isn't wearing.

"Bolan." She pauses. "What if I told you I was naked with just layers of blankets over me?"

"Are you telling me that sweet body of yours is rubbing against our new sheets and I'm not there to see it?" I choke. "Flower, you're killing me."

My hand slides down my stiff length then tugs up my hard cock to thoughts of her naked and writhing against the sheets, turned on and needy for me.

"Let me see," I moan.

"You want to see me naked in our bed."

"Absolutely." My voice stresses, my resolve straining. I squeeze my cock harder, giving it a slow, steady pull.

"I've never—" I can almost see her lick her lips, hear it in my head. Her nervous habit. Her innocent eyes. "Clifton didn't—"

"Do not speak another man's name in our bed." That might have come out a little harsher than it should, but my patience cracks. I need to hear her call my name, knowing she's in our bed, in our home, waiting for me.

"Flower." I gentle the demand in my voice. "Let me see you."

A heavy pause fills the phone before she says, "Give me a minute?"

"I've got time." I've waited a long time to see her fully naked, and I'd planned to continue waiting until I was home, but my wife is just too tempting.

The call gets dropped, and for a moment, I think she's not going to play along. I don't know if I've ever done this either, and suddenly, I'm nervous.

But then a Facetime call comes through, and her face appears on the screen with a dark shadow behind her.

"Hey."

"Hi, beautiful." My entire face lights up just seeing her. I feel my cheeks heat and my smile grow. "Let me see all of you, baby."

She flips the image, giving me a shocking, but stunning view of her body from breasts to toes. Those fucking red painted ones.

"Ruthie," I choke again, knowing she's giving me something special here. Not just a view of that luscious body of hers but her trust. There's something intimate about visual phone sex or watching another person self-love. A level of vulnerability involved.

I'm vulnerable in a lot of ways with Ruthie but this is not going to be an area I hesitate. I want her to feel confident, respected, desired.

"Show me how you pleasure yourself, flower. Let me see those petals."

She giggles again, most likely at what she considers my ridiculous name for a sacred spot on her, but she has no idea how pretty and pink she is down there, how she swells and drips, blossoming like a dewy flower.

I watch as her fingers skitter down her midsection and disappear between her legs. Her breath hitches, and I squeeze my dick harder, tugging a little quicker.

"That's it, Ruthie. Show me those fingers touching you."

Ruthie sits up and positions the phone between her raised knees, propped against blankets rolled to her feet.

"Fuck, baby," I groan, a little surprised how easily she followed my instructions, but also loving how the woman who hasn't done a few things, easily does them with me. I never want to break Ruthie. I want to help her mend her fractured parts. I want her to give me the broken places and trust that I'll hold them together. Like the Japanese art of Kintsugi, Ruthie and I form something beautifully imperfect and rare.

With heavy lids, I watch as she slides her fingers up and down her seam, stilling on her clit before rubbing in slow, delicious circles around that tender nub.

"Right there, baby. Feels good, doesn't it? You're turned on, knowing I'm watching you give me this little show, this precious display."

"Bolan." Her voice quietly squeaks.

"I'm between your legs, baby," I remind her. "And just look at that pussy. So ripe. So needy." I lick my lips although she isn't watching me. "I want to lick that slit. I want to taste you again."

Her back arches a bit. The phone jostling just the slightest, but I still have a clear view of my wife pleasuring herself to the sound of my voice. My own arousal builds. My dick tight. The tip seeping.

Ruthie purrs, the sound salacious and greedy.

"Would you like that, baby? My tongue back on that pussy. Slicing you open and drinking that sweet honey." My mouth falls open like I can taste her. That nectar on my tongue. Her musky scent at my nose.

My dick is so hard, it almost hurts. My balls tighten, my back pinching. "Flower," I grunt.

And then I hear the soft, sweet cry of her calling my name, and I watch as she releases around her fingers, spilling down toward her fine ass, marking our sheets.

"Watching you, I'm going to come," I announce, ready to burst myself knowing she's safe in our home, tucked into our bed, there for our daughter.

Her phone is moved, and suddenly, I can see her face. Her eyes bright despite the darkness. "Let me watch you."

Quickly, I angle the phone in a way she can see me fisting myself, thinking of her, feeling those eyes on me, and I spill over, bursting like a fountain opened in spring, coating my hand in sticky substance and falling back at the relief.

"That was hot," Ruthie states, her voice full of awe and innocence.

Oh, the ways I could corrupt her. But there are so many ways she's changing me.

A family man. Thinking about home. Wanting to be with my wife.

THE NEXT NIGHT, I'm eager to get to the hotel room and have a repeat of the night before, but Ruthie sounds tired. Again, it's late. But she also sounds serious when she says, "I need to talk to you about something."

I'd called my girls in the morning, where Ruthie made the video time more about Tulane, so I could see my bubbly redhead and listen to her babble about her plastic farm animals.

"Okay." I'm lying on my back, similar to last night's starting position. Ankles crossed. Hand behind my head, but I've settled in to listen. "Let's switch to Facetime."

I need to see her if we're going to discuss something serious.

Within seconds, we flip over to the video call and Ruthie offers me a soft smile. She's so beautiful, it's like I haven't seen her in days, when it was only this morning.

"So, Tulane called me Mama."

My lips slowly start to curl.

"And I don't know what to do about it. We haven't really discussed my position. With her."

My smile instantly drops. "Sounds like Tulane has determined your *relation* to her."

"I don't want you to think I've been coaching her to call me that or—"

"I'm going to stop you right there." I sit up, propping myself against the headboard with pillows at my back, realizing this conversation needs better attention. "You *are* coaching Tulane. That's how I view parenting. You're teaching through repetition, guiding her to discover things, and helping her develop her skills for life. That's what a parent does. What a mom should do."

Ruthie and I once had a talk about all the learning phases of a child and while I didn't know the first thing about rearing a kid, Ruthie knew a lot of technical jargon and science behind development.

Basically, it's like coaching, I'd said and got one of her approving smiles, like I'm the only kid in the class with the correct answer.

"But you also love her. I see it in the way you look at her. Unconditional. Unfiltered. Just love. And I'm okay with that. Who doesn't want their kid to be loved by as many people as possible?"

We're both quiet a second as I recall neither of us had parents who came across as loving.

"You never talk about your parents."

"There isn't much to say. They aren't really in my life." Ruthie shrugs. "My dad called me when we were in Arizona."

I sit up straighter. "Why didn't you tell me?"

"There isn't much to tell." She gives me that look that suggests she isn't telling me the whole truth. She's been elusive about her folks, and I don't need to know the people who haven't cared enough about her. Still, I'm here for her if she needs to vent.

"Want to talk about it?"

"Not really."

I watch as her lids lower. Her head shakes slowly side to side. She's quiet another second. I want her to open up to me, but I don't want to push her either.

"I'm here when you're ready," I remind her. But I want her to know I'm beside her every step of the way forward.

The promise is returned by the corner of her mouth ticking upward.

"Well, I like to think having shitty parents makes us . . . you and me . . . realize how we don't want to behave as parents. Thus, making us work harder to not be like those negative experiences in our lives."

"Yeah," Ruthie softly replies.

"So, I'm honored if Tulane calls you Mama. I think you're amazing, and I've already told you I think you'd make a great mother. You *are* a great mother, to her." My throat thickens, because holy shit, Ruthie really is a good mom, and this little arrangement we have isn't just between us but the three of us.

Although, I'm no longer thinking of our situation as an agreement, or a contract, but a life. For all of us.

"You don't think it might be confusing for her?"

"While I'd like to think she has some memory of her mother, I just don't believe it's a memory she'll retain. For the longest time I worried she was missing her mom, definitely confused about how the big *oaf* was suddenly in charge of her."

"Don't call yourself that," she chides.

I scoff. "I'm sure it was strange that she was suddenly being watched by an older Japanese woman who didn't speak much English. I'd be gone a few days, but I'd always come back, and that's the thing I want to instill in her the most. I'm here for her whether she sees me or not. And I'll always return home to be with her. Always."

I'm not running off like my mom. Not disappearing into alcohol like my dad. And not putting my daughter in the hands of others until I can leave her alone as a teenager or whatever the hell happened with Ruthie and her parents.

"We're a family, flower. The three of us."

Ruth sniffles through the phone and I'm afraid I've made her cry.

"Tell me those are happy tears, baby." My voice lowers, fear lacing it. Maybe she doesn't like the idea of the three of us as a unit.

"Happier than I feel like I have a right to be."

"Aw, flower. You have the same rights as everyone else. We all deserve to be happy. But happy is so hard to define. I just want you to find joy in each day and love on us. Tulane and me."

I hold my breath thinking I've gone too far, asking her to love me.

Ruthie chuckles, soggy and rough. "I do love you guys."

Not exactly a declaration for me directly, but close enough for now. "I love you guys, too," I snark, snorting to cover what I really want to say.

I love her.

I love my wife.

"So, let's circle back to Tulane. If she calls you Mama, and you're comfortable with that, I'm comfortable with that. I think Tulane has made the right call. You're her mom." The only one I ever intend for Tulane to know.

Ruthie is definitely crying harder. "Thank you, Bolan."

"Baby, you do not have to thank me. I'm the one so grateful for you in our lives." I lift the *omamori* around my neck and press a kiss to the medal. Thanking the stars or the Universe or the mysteries of the unknown that brought Ruthie to me.

"I'm grateful for you, too. So thankful."

Grinning wide, I accept that this night turned out pretty great after all.

30

____

[Bolan]

Getting home late the next night and actually seeing Ruthie standing in the kitchen is the visual reassurance I hadn't known I needed. Like that night of watching each other had been a dream, and not reality. Like Ruthie was more a mirage than something physical in our duplex.

"You waited up," I whisper as I crest the top of the entry stairs and see Ruthie leaning against the peninsula island. Her hair is in a messy bun on top of her head. Glasses on. One foot on top of the other in that way she stands. She reminds me a little of a flamingo, but she'll always be a flower to me.

Slowly, she smiles while I drop my bag and close the distance between us. She steps away from the counter and falls against the refrigerator opposite the peninsula as I rush to stand right in front of her. Bracing my forearm on the cool surface of the appliance beside her head, I lean over her.

"Hi." I smile back, taking in her face. Those deep eyes. The swell of her lips. The slope of her nose. I don't even know where to start. I want to kiss her everywhere.

"Hi." She giggles, and I further lean forward, kissing her softly at first.

"Welcome home," I murmur to the corner of her mouth, although she's been here for three days.

"Same to you." She smiles again and I capture her lips, kissing her more soundly this time until she squeaks and presses into me. She breaks the kiss and glances over her shoulder where a stream of water dribbles from the water dispenser on the refrigerator door.

Ruthie swipes at her backside. "You got me all wet."

I chuckle. "That's exactly what I like to hear." I bend my knees to wrap my arms around her ass and lift her. Her hands land on my shoulders, and she spreads her legs around my hips while I spin us to set her on the peninsula countertop.

My lips travel along her jaw to her neck where I drag my teeth over her flesh. She shivers before she runs her hands over my shoulders around to my back, pulling me closer to her. I slip my hands underneath the hem of the cropped sweatshirt she's wearing.

"Your skin is so soft," I mutter to her shoulder, pushing the loose fit collar over the curve and down her arm.

Ruthie hums as I slip my hands further underneath the sweatshirt until I hit the underside of her breasts. No bra.

"Flower," I groan as she arches forward, inviting me to continue my exploration. I cover each of her breasts with a greedy palm and squeeze, tugging at the tender swells and pinching her nipples in tandem.

Ruthie gasps and I swallow the sound, needing to breathe her in. Like I've told her before, she feels like the first solid breath I've taken in years.

I slide my hands around her sides and cup her ass next,

where one cheek is damp from the water dispenser. Tugging her to the edge of the countertop, I line us up. My hard cock to her soft center, covered in baggy shorts. Massaging down her thighs, I stroke over her knees before breaking the kiss to glance down to where we meet in the middle.

"I want to touch you," I groan.

With her arms loosely around my neck, she purrs, "Yes."

I skim her inner thigh again and sweep into the edge of those loose shorts, finding her wet in other places. Quickly, I push aside her underwear and slip one thick finger into her heat. *Home.*

Clinging to my neck, Ruthie whimpers as her head tips back.

"I remember touching you like this on that banquet table," I murmur as I run my nose along the column of her throat, inhaling her floral and spice scent. "I wanted to devour you that night."

Ruthie hums. "As I remember it . . . you did." Pleasure fills her voice, the memory fond for both of us.

With my free hand, I gently press her backward, breaking her hold on my neck. This kitchen counter looks like another perfect place to savor her. Swiftly, I remove her shorts and underwear, lifting her heels for the edge of the counter, and staring down at my feast. The swollen lips. The pink flesh. She's a flower eager to bloom and I don't plan to disappoint her.

Seeing her in person is so much better than the other night.

With my head between her spread knees, Ruthie whimpers as I slice my tongue through her seam, dipping into her creamy center and savoring her essence. Her hands come to the back of my head, running her fingernails over my scalp which causes me to shiver. However, nothing deters me from bringing her to the brink and then tipping her over the edge.

A line drive to center and a base stolen.

She's so beautiful, all spread out on the counter, panting my name, and taking what she needs from me.

While I hadn't planned our night to go this way quite so quickly, a homerun is my greatest desire, but I won't push her. There are so many other things I can do to please her.

With a kiss on her inner thigh, I tug her upward and into my arms again. She wraps her arms around my neck once more. Her legs around my hips.

"Where are we going?" Her voice is quiet, sated and soft.

"I'm going to carry you over the threshold."

"You're going to take me down the stairs and outside, like this?" She pulls back to see my face. Her mouth gapes.

I chuckle. "How about if I take you upstairs and carry you over the threshold of our room." Because this is our home and after losing nights with Ruthie, I've decided I don't want to spend the nights we have together without her in our bed.

There's no pressure to do more than kiss her breathless and then hold her all night long. But when I set her down, I slip my hands underneath her cropped sweatshirt and guide it over her head. "I just want to look at you."

I want to see her, in the flesh, spread out and naked on this bed, solidifying the vision in my head. A photograph etched in my brain forever.

"I've missed you," I whisper, looking her directly in the eyes while running my fingertip over the peak of one breast, around the tip of her taut nipple, and down the other side.

I drop our locked gaze as I coast my hand between her breasts before laying my palm over her belly, pausing above that soft mound of hair at the top of her legs. "I don't think I've ever missed anyone the way I've missed you."

The ache for her isn't just about her body, though. I've missed her presence. Her laughter with Tulane. Her smiles at me.

Ruthie softly gasps before cupping the side of my face. Her

thumb strokes over my jaw which is in need of a shave. "I missed you, too. More than I can explain."

Her brows pinch like she's puzzled by how she missed me, but I don't need her to explain herself. Tonight, I just want to worship her body, and I continue my intentions by slipping my finger into her warm center while we stand toe to toe.

Ruthie moans and slides her hand over the front of my pants. The heat of her hand seeps through the thin material as she gently squeezes where I'm stiff and desperate for her.

"Let me show you how much I've missed you."

I blink in the dark room as my wife turns into a vixen, dropping to her knees and fumbling with the removal of my pants. Hastily, I remove my shirt, wanting to be as naked as she is. Free to any exploration she wants to take with my body.

Ruthie wraps her delicate fingers around my hard cock, and I hiss at the sizzle of contact. *God, have I missed her.* It's been a week without her. Three weeks without her touch. More than a month since I've entered her.

When her mouth surrounds me, I swear I see heaven.

After only one long suck up my length, I'm tugging free of those sultry lips and hoisting her upward, tossing her onto the bed. Ruthie scrambles backward and I follow her retreat over the blankets and up to the pillows, wedging my large body between her legs.

"I just want to feel you against me." Her heat. Her skin. I hold my dick, placing the tip at her entrance, and sliding the head through her slick folds. There's no pressure to do more. I could naked-cuddle this woman and be happy. Kiss her all night and be happy. Be in her presence and simply be happy.

But we both groan at the electric connection between us.

With strength I didn't expect her to have, Ruthie presses at my chest, forcing me to my back and sliding over me, straddling my lap.

At the contact, I hiss again. The pleasurable crackle of her wet heat against my hard cock is a welcome spark. She glides up my length, coating me in her creamy essence until she notches on my tip. Back and forth she moves, grinding against me, and my hands land on her hips, guiding her along my dick from head to balls.

"Ruthie," I groan, keeping the pace at her speed.

"I want more."

My eyes ping open, staring up at her face above mine, reading her desire for me. Fuck, I want to give her everything.

Reaching for her hair, I tug at the elastic holding up her messy bun, freeing her hair to hang down in a lush curtain over her shoulders and around her cheeks. Taking a second to admire how beautiful she looks over me. Her eyes sparkling. Her mouth gaping. Then, I roll us again, flipping her to her back. My dick is so hard, weeping and begging, to be enveloped in her warmth, but I don't want to pressure her.

However, because I'm reactive instead of reflective, I blurt, "I want to give you a baby."

She stiffens beneath me. "What?"

I realize a little too late that I've said too much too fast. My damn brain, which can be slow to chug, picked up speed, and barreled forward like a runaway freight train, and I can't seem to stop myself.

"I want to give you what you want most. Let me be the one to do that for you. Let me make a baby with you."

Although we've discussed Tulane, and I'm thrilled to consider Ruthie her mother, I want to give Ruthie something else she's wanted. Another baby. A houseful of babies.

"I . . . I don't know what to say." She swallows thickly, enough that I hear the gulp, and I inch back. Her legs are spread, my hips cradled between them.

We can stop right here.

"I understand." I'm deflated but I get it. I've said too much too soon. This is a conversation we should have outside of a moment like this one. One where it might appear I'm just caught up wanting to give her that *more* she asked for earlier. When what I want is to give her the world.

"I just want you to know that I haven't been with anyone in over nine months. Not since I met you. You can trust me. You're safe with me." I stare into her eyes, willing her to understand without mention of her past experience. "You will never have to worry about me straying from you, because I want to give you everything. You mean *everything* to me."

Breaking eye contact, I scoot back, lowering my face and pressing a kiss to her shoulder, preparing to push up and off her. Condoms are inside the makeshift nightstand which is still an upturned box.

But Ruthie wraps her ankles around the back of my thighs. Her hands cup my ass, and she tugs me upward again.

"You'd really do this with me? For me?" Her dark eyes blink up at me.

"For us." I kiss her quick. "I'd do anything for you, Ruthie."

What feels like the longest moment of my life passes between us before she nods once. "Okay." Her voice is featherlight.

"Yeah?" I whisper, choked up a little. The pressure slowly rising inside me. She's trusting me. She's giving me this honor. I'm going to father a child with her.

"Yeah." The happiness in that single word is the best sound I've ever heard.

With my tip at her entrance once more, I press forward, wanting to take my time, wanting to remember this moment. Every inch forward. Every hug of her tight channel. I've never been bare with anyone. Not ever.

And my breath hitches as I first enter her. The sensation is almost too much. I'll blow before I've fully seated if I'm not careful. And I want to be careful. I want to take care of this woman who takes care of me and our little girl.

I want to see my precious flower bloom and grow our family.

As I slide deeper into her warmth, her body hugs mine in a new way, and I'm overwhelmed. Emotions ping around inside me, like a fast pitch pitching machine.

Finally, I'm to the hilt and I breathe deeply. "Just give me a second." My voice is thick, and I lick my lips. "God, Ruthie. I've never felt anything like this." Her. Us. Love.

"Me neither." A single tear slips from the corner of her eye.

"Oh, baby. I've got you."

"I know," she whispers.

"Green," I remind her. The color of safety for her.

"Green," she says, her mouth curling in a soft smile. "But I wouldn't mind a little red."

Buried inside her, I chuckle. "Nothing feels more reckless and wonderful at the same time." I kiss her with a broad sweep of my tongue before sucking at her lower lip.

Then I move. Back and forth, I go slow until I can't keep the tempo steady any longer, because Ruthie moves with me, like she was made for me.

There isn't any rush like the minutes we had against a window in a ballroom. We have all the minutes in front of us, in our bed, in our home, expanding our family.

The thought spurs me faster and I press up on my hands, my hips pistoning harder. Ruthie matches my pace, sucking me into her sweet body. The sound of us fills the room.

"Never felt this," I stammer. This need to fill her. This need to love her.

Ruthie tips back her head, a smile on her lips as her eyelids lower.

"Keep those pretty eyes on me. I want to see your face when I plant my seed inside you."

She huffs. If she could laugh, she might, but I dive deeper

inside her, cutting off any words from her. Our bodies speak the only language we need right now.

Until I feel her squeeze me in a new way. A tight embrace. A swell of warmth. Her release triggers my own.

"Flower," my voice hitches as I fall apart inside her, her shattering around me. Nothing has ever felt so right.

Those silver stars she sets twinkling dance before me as I try to catch my breath. I collapse over her a second, smothering her, but she doesn't protest. She clings to me like she does, like she never wants to let me go, and I don't want her to ever release me.

Eventually, I tip to my side, taking her with me, keeping us connected. Not quite as intensely as a moment ago, but still as one.

"I think you just got me pregnant," I tease.

Ruthie laughs harder, covering her mouth to stifle the sound. "You're ridiculous."

Her laughter causes her to clench around me, and I press a kiss to her nose. "That's why you love me."

She doesn't respond; maybe one day she will. In the meantime, she rushes to kiss me, and I have the only answer I need for now.

I love her.

Eventually, Ruthie excuses herself to clean up and get ready for bed while I'm too tired to move. She's drained everything out of me, and I doze as Ruthie tiptoes around the room. On my belly, hands tucked underneath the pillow, my head is turned in her direction when she finally returns to bed.

Something light tickles my arm. The touch is soft, though, hesitant. Slowly, the pressure running up and down my forearm deepens until her hand finds mine and I link our fingers together beneath my pillow.

"Think we made a baby?" I mutter.

"It might be a little too soon to tell." Her tone is more somber as she stares at me.

"I'm looking forward to the practice, if you aren't."

Ruthie softly smiles, her thoughts possibly catching up to reality. We might have made a baby.

"I'm happy you're here," I add, my voice sleep-laden and low. Happy that I'm married to her. Happy she's the mother of Tulane. Happy to make more babies with her.

"I'm just happy," she whispers.

With that, I shift, scooping her into my chest and holding her against me, wanting her as close as I can get her. Still holding her hand, our position kind of reminds me of dancing with her. Ruthie would think I'm ridiculous, but I'm ridiculously content.

Savoring this unfamiliar sense of happiness.

ANCHOR FIELD IS an iconic baseball stadium known for the ivy wall running the length of the outfield beneath the bleacher section. A giant scoreboard is manually operated by managers who hang out inside the ancient thing, adding numbers or switching them as needed when teams score. Everything about this setting screams history and nostalgia for one of the greatest games to be played in one of the greatest stadiums to play in.

Standing in the friendly confines on opening day is a dream come true.

My granddad would be so proud. I can almost hear him cheering from heaven.

Could also be the roar of an overzealous crowd happy to have their team home and kicking off a new season at their beloved field.

After warmups, I take a quick peek into the stands, seeking the WAGs section off to the left of the dugout. In the sea of people, I find my redhaired girl wearing an Anchors knit cap to ward off the cold. With the sun shining and the temperature low, it's a perfect day for baseball but my personal fans are bundled up against the chill.

Ruthie catches me watching them and shifts Tulane while pointing in my direction. I wave and Ruthie holds up Tulane's hand, forcing her to wave back. Then Ruthie presses her fingers to her lips and blows a kiss in my direction.

With my catcher's mitt raised, I jump up to catch the kiss, then scoop it out of the leather like I'd remove a ball. Only I don't toss this kiss away but slip it onto my *omamori* tucked inside my jersey for safe keeping.

One of the great things about the Anchors is how they allow walkup songs for their batters during home games, and I've picked a new one for mine.

When it's my turn up at bat, Katy Perry's "E.T." cuts to the refrain begging someone to kiss her, and I'm ready to take on the world.

Or at least, the ace pitcher from New York.

I twirl the bat in my hand, focus on what I assume will be a curve ball, and watch my hit soar through the sky, having a good feeling about it.

Yes! First at bat in a new stadium for me, and it's a fucking homerun. I feel like the alien Miss Perry is singing about. Just out of this world.

From there, our home opener is chaos.

Sylver and Valdez have another showdown in centerfield, which leads to what looks like a more purposeful altercation. On the big screen over the bleachers, the replay shows Ford pointing a finger at Romero and Romero twisting Ford's arm. The one with a bad shoulder.

The crowd boos. Whether their jeers are a response to the overall show of poor sportsmanship from men on the same fucking team, or an insult to Valdez who has injured a fan favorite, it's hard to tell.

Either way, after the game, the locker room is somber not only from the final score which resulted in a loss for the Anchors, but the loss of Ford due to injury and Romero under suspicion of suspension. Post-game interviews are a shitshow. Questions run rampant about the stability of the Chicago Anchors and the new management under Ross Davis.

Personally, I like the guy. He's roughly a decade older than me but solid. He loves the game. He knows our team. He values our worth. And he knows Valdez is a fucking dick, but like any good leader, he isn't slamming the weakest link. At least not openly.

In general, I'm pissed off by the loss. Undeniably, we should have played better but we for damn sure should have looked like a unified front, not a ragtag gang of boys on a sandlot where two guys are fighting over the same girl.

Not that Ford wants his wife back. She was in the wrong. Valdez was in the wrong. And Ford can do so much better than all this bullshit.

Still, tensions can run high on a ball field. Although, it's typically between *opposing* teams, not the same team.

When I eventually toss myself into bed, Ruthie is sitting up beside me on her side of our new bed. A new comforter covers the bed, which I hadn't noticed last night. The overhead light is on because we don't have any lamps yet, or nightstands for that matter. Ruthie is reading from the toddler book I bought.

This will be my win for the day. This moment right here.

"You okay?" she asks me, having asked me the same question twice already this evening.

Tucking my arm behind my head, I lie on my back and stare across the room at the empty wall. "Yeah." I sigh.

"That's a heavy sound."

"Ford might be out for the season." I twist my neck so I can look at my beautiful wife, who remains silent, waiting on me to say more.

"It's a reminder that at any time I'm an injury away from forced retirement." At my age, recovery would be difficult. That's the position Ford is in. If he needs surgery, then he'll need rehabilitation, and he won't be the same player he was. He'll have too much time off the field as he inches closer to being too old for the game. Being washed up in your late thirties is a daunting thought.

"I can't retire yet." I shift my head, returning to stare at the wall opposite our bed.

"What do you want to do after baseball?" Ruthie's tone is cheerful, like I have an entire list of possibilities. She's also trying to sound positive about the next page in the playbook of my life when I'd like to keep my cleats firmly planted in the current chapter.

"Fuck if I know. I can't even joke and say I'd be a farmer, living a simpler life, because I don't know the first thing about growing plants or raising animals. Farming looks like fucking hard work."

My heart hammers, panic rising that I don't have any other skill than playing a game. Catching a ball and hitting one with a bat is the only *field experience* I've ever known.

"You could go into broadcasting. You have the charisma and face for it."

I turn my head in her direction again, pinching my brows, despite the compliment of my face. I'd be hell at reading a teleprompter.

"Or coaching?" She stares at me, almost like she isn't certain herself if leadership would work for me. But she's commented in the past about how animated I look in the dugout. My penchant for cheering on my teammates, even that fuckwad Valdez.

Finally, she says, "You'll figure it out. You have time."

I snort.

"What about you?" I ask after a few seconds. "You gave everything up to be here, but when this year is over, what will you do?"

Ruthie blinks a few times, the movement rapid, like something is in her eye, or I've caught her off guard. Was it something I said?

"I . . . uh . . ." She glances back at the book on her lap. "I haven't thought about it."

Funny thing. I've learned to tell when my wife is lying, and Ruthie is a thinker, so I have serious doubts she hasn't considered what she'd like to do a year from now.

Maybe there will be another baby pattering around our house by then. But I don't want Ruthie to think motherhood is the only thing that defines her. She wanted to be a teacher. She followed her late husband's wayward path and her in-law's direction. I want her future to be what she wants for herself.

But suddenly, she's tossing back the covers over her legs and swinging them out of the bed, taking the thick book with her as she stands.

I sit upright. "Where are you going?"

"I'll let you sleep." She lifts the book, her fingers wedged inside it to mark her place. "I'm going to read. Downstairs."

She quickly circles the bed and while I want to reach out for her and tug her back to bed, because I don't have a clue what just caused a shift in her, I'm too tired, too sad, to react.

31

———

[Ruthie]

I don't know why I am so upset. His question was innocent enough.

When this year is over, what will you do?

But wasn't it only last night we were talking about a baby? A baby is more than a year commitment. A baby is for life.

He'd been the one who said *for us*. Doesn't that imply a future? A forever? Together.

Like everything else about Bolan Adler, he's a storm. The unpredictable kind that trips into a ballroom and seduces you into something you've never done before. Or kisses you breathless when you've only just met.

Or mentions things like love and babies, but then tosses out things like *when this year is over*, suggesting an end date on all the things we're pretending. The things that don't feel fake.

Like kisses and orgasms. Laughter and quiet moments. Tulane.

My eyes water at the flash of memories and the instant sense of rejection.

It wasn't like I hadn't thought about a year from our start date, focusing on what I'd do with myself once the calendar flipped, and our contract was fulfilled.

I'd considered returning to school and started researching local colleges. Chicago has five city colleges, several of which offer master's degrees in education. My plan had been to revive that dream of being a teacher and head into a classroom with twenty or so little Tulane-like beings, all needing guidance and education.

But I also really enjoy being Tulane's mom, as Bolan so easily and generously deemed me, while claiming Tulane was the one to pick me. Spending time with only her feels like a once in a lifetime experience. She'll never be the age she is again, and I want to soak up being the sideline coach to her life as she develops.

So, Bolan's question pisses me off, especially after decisions I made during my short jaunt in California. I imploded my life to be here in Chicago. Exploded everything for him.

In many ways, that's not the full truth. In other ways, I'm damning myself again. For falling so easily into a familiar pattern. Clinging to a man, following his path instead of my own.

Bolan had been my ticket out, like I'd once too harshly stated to him. But it is time to be my own ticket master. I am in charge of the show, or more appropriately the game, and it was time for me to step up to the plate and swing.

With a heavy sigh, I sink into the couch, holding the toddler book on my lap while staring at the blank television screen across the room.

Change is frightening, and I lift my gaze to the dark staircase leading to the second floor, knowing how Bolan feels. His fear that he's one injury away from never playing a game he loves again. One wrong hit or bad catch and he's facing a future he hasn't thought about yet.

Within seconds, I hear his large feet pad down the wooden staircase until he's standing beside the couch. I'm seated in the deep V that joins the two sides of the L-shape.

Bolan reaches over me, tugging the cushions at my side free and tossing them to the floor. Once finished, he climbs over me, collapses to his side, back to the cushion-free couch, and wedges his head underneath my arm, forcing me to lift the one, so he can settle his head on my chest. I set my book on the cushions on my other side. He wraps his arms around my waist, and lugs one heavy leg over both of mine which are now outstretched before me.

"What the hell?" I chuckle despite myself, feeling like a giant labrador has just weaseled his way onto my lap when he isn't a lap-sized dog.

"I don't know what I said to upset you, but I don't want to sleep without you." He presses his head into my sternum, rubbing his nose back and forth before settling his cheek against me. He squeezes me tighter.

"We're going to have too many future nights apart, flower. I need to soak up all the nights we have together."

I blink, startled by the honest admission and set my arm loosely over his shoulders. My fingers find the back of his head and massage his scalp.

He hums, appreciating the touch. "What'd I say, baby?"

"You asked me what I'd do when the year is over." I swallow the tiny lump in my throat, feeling it travel down my esophagus and lodge in my chest.

He shifts his head, so he can look up at me. "Poor word choice? You know I'm not known for making smart ones."

"Bolan." I cup his face. "You are smart. You're beautiful and kind."

He scrunches up his face. "Isn't that from a movie?"

"It's the truth, but it still hurt me that you asked."

His brows lift. "That I want to know what you want to do in the future?"

"That you asked what I want to do in a year. When our contract ends."

Those brows press firmly together. His tone turns hard. "What contract?"

"Bolan." I chuckle bitterly, knowing he knows.

"Fuck the contract, Ruthie. Fuck the entire arrangement. I told you I'm yours. You're mine. We're going to work this out. You and me. Tulane and more babies."

He lowers his head and presses a kiss to my belly.

"Are you sure you weren't just saying that about more babies? Maybe caught up in something?" *Like amazing sex.*

He lifts his head again, arching back to look up at me once more. "I wasn't *just* saying anything. I wasn't caught up in some moment."

For some reason, those words strike deep as well, because I believe in moments. Those sacred sixty seconds. And I assess this one. The fact he came down the stairs. Sought me out after a misunderstanding. He's wrapped around me like his mitt holds a precious baseball, treasuring me. He's being expressive and open-minded, something he asked me to do when we made our arrangement.

Willingness to renegotiate terms at any given time.

The terms have already been renegotiated. I'm here because I want to be with him. With Tulane.

"This is what I want, Ruthie, but if you don't want to have babies with me yet, there's no rush. It doesn't have to be today, or this month, or even in a year. *No end date,*" he emphasizes. "I just want to make you happy. I always wanted siblings, and while I have Hunter and Miller, we don't have that connection I see between others. I'm so much older than them and our lives were lived too differently."

The reminder of his mother's transgression and the siblings he hardly mentions hurts my heart. As an only child, an unwanted child, I'd always dreamed about siblings as well and I want to foster the kind of relationship I've seen among siblings for Tulane.

"I'm sorry if I hurt you, baby. I just meant that you can do whatever you want, be whomever you want. If you don't want to stay home, what would you do? If you want to stay home, be a mom, and do something else later, that's cool, too." He presses a kiss to my chest then places his forehead to it but says something I can't hear.

Cupping his cheeks, I lift his head. "What did you say?"

He licks his lips and stares up at me, those green eyes full of vulnerability. "I just want to do whatever will make you stay. With us. With me."

The truth hits. He isn't forcing me out in a year. He isn't even suggesting I leave. *Ever*.

"I'm not going anywhere," I whisper, leaning down and giving him a quick kiss. When I pull back, Bolan lowers his head to my chest again. With his arms around my middle, he squeezes me once more.

"But you left our bed, to *read* down here." He snorts, catching onto my excuse to leave our room. "So I'm here to snuggle into you while you *read*. And when you're ready to head back to bed, we'll go up. Together."

I could be upset that he's not allowing me the space to be upset about his poor word choice, but I'm also tickled at how he's willing to let me be upset, *a.k.a. read*, if I need to be, but he isn't leaving me alone to stew. He's letting me know by his actions that he's here for me. He's literally wrapped all around me, settled in to let me do my thing, but letting me know he's right here beside me for whatever I decide to do.

"I'm still a green, Ruthie." He's still safe.

That's why I'm here. That's why I made the decisions I made.

And I realize questioning my love for this man is too late.

I'm already in love with him.

32

[Bolan]

For the remainder of the nights that I'm home, Ruthie and I are in bed together, learning more about each other's body. Our likes and dislikes. I only want to do what pleases her because she pleases me in so many ways.

After our talk on the couch, I learn I need to speak with intention. Take a moment before I blurt things that might hurt my girl. I'm not always going to be perfect. I'm still probably going to say the wrong thing more often than I want, but at least I'll be better aware and try not to misstep.

Our home game series is short, and we will be back on the road for another full week stretch. Ruthie and I have already spent almost a week apart when she went to California, so I'm feeling pretty confident about this future separation.

I got this.

But there is something about this second stretch of time apart that has me on edge. When the first set of games was in

Milwaukee, Ruthie surprised me by driving up for the day game at the end of the series. Unfortunately, the team had to catch a bus that drove us directly to the airport for a flight to Cleveland.

When Cyrus enters our hotel room after our first game, I'm sulking on the bed because I haven't been able to reach Ruthie yet today.

"Come out with us. One drink. It will take your mind off whatever's bothering you." He watches me, waiting on me to explain why I've been itchy all day.

"We won," he reminds me.

We did win and I should be celebrating with my team, bonding with them. I'm still the new guy, and I'm reshaping my reputation as the happy-go-lucky teammate. The one with a cheer or encouraging word for everyone else. Maybe that's what's draining me today. I didn't catch well but I hit like a monster, taking out any frustration on that ball connecting with my bat. I hit another homerun.

I have no idea if Ruthie saw it.

"You played hard today," Cyrus reminds me, pulling me from my thoughts.

I exhale. "How do you do it, man?" I blink while staring up at the ceiling. "When you miss them so much, how do you do it?" I shift only my head, catching on Cyrus staring back at me from his seat on the edge of his bed.

"You call home. Text a lot. Video chat with the kids. Have phone sex with your wife." Cyrus chuckles, the sound a bit off. "At least, you used to do some of those things."

"You guys okay?" I ask, swinging my legs over the edge of the bed and sitting upright, remembering what Ruthie once asked me. If Cyrus had cheated on Lacey.

Out of all my teammates, I'm closest to Cyrus as I've only been on the team for less than two months. However, that doesn't mean we're diving deeply into our pasts or divulging secrets. Still, I'm concerned for my newest friend.

Cyrus sighs, scrubbing a hand down his face. "Some days are just harder than others, right?" He speaks like I'd have any clue. I haven't been married as long as him. Don't have three rambunctious boys at home.

Still, I nod, like I do know what he means. I'm just off, I guess, and realize I'm not being very supportive if I sulk in my room like some lovesick lackey.

"One drink," I state, holding up a finger. I'll call Ruthie later.

We don't go farther than the hotel bar and I'm already having regrets. The place is packed, and I'm lucky to find a stool along the counter, not really interested in interacting with anyone, but being present for that one drink I promised Cyrus. Who has already disappeared in the crowd.

I order a whiskey neat then twirl the glass on the edge of its base, watching the liquid slosh around the ice cubes.

"You gonna drink that, or just play with it?" The feminine voice coming from beside me is salacious with a low chuckle wrapped around her second question.

Turning only my head, I find a woman standing a little too close to me. I tug my spread elbows closer together on the bar and glance back at my glass. I'm not trying to be a dick, but I'm not interested.

"Strong silent type. I like that in a man."

My head whips in her direction again. *What the fuck?* I'm used to women coming onto me. In Japan, I stood out like a sore thumb being taller than the average man over there. Everything about me screamed American, and probably, available for a good time.

But that's not me anymore.

I glance down at the ring circling my finger on my left hand

and then look back up at the brunette standing beside me, leaning a little closer to me, despite having tugged my arms in tighter. She's pretty enough. Long eye lashes. Wide mouth. Sultry dress.

But again, I'm not interested.

I drop my arms from the bar completely, placing my hands on my thighs as my left leg begins to jiggle. I don't want her standing so close to me. I don't want her even talking to me. Sadly, I don't know how to get rid of her, other than ignoring her and hoping she'll take the hint.

"You played well today."

As if she didn't already have strikes against her, this is the final one, because the last thing I want is someone coming onto me because she knows who I am. Because she sees a baseball player, and she wants to chase balls. Mine.

When her hand lands on my shoulder with her compliment, I stare down at it, starting to sweat. She has no right to touch me. Nothing about me says willing. I'm not talking to her. I didn't initiate anything. Didn't even glance in her direction at first.

Still, a bead of sweat trickles down my back and another along my brow. The idea of a panic attack brewing causes me to further panic. My breath is like shards of ice pricking my lungs.

Another hand claps my other shoulder, squeezing tightly, and drawing my attention to the firm, masculine grip.

"Adler," Cyrus says, keeping his eyes on mine, like he senses what's happening to me.

"Sawyer," I counter, keeping my attention on him.

An entire conversation ensues between us with only our eyes.

Do you want this? he asks.

Fuck no, I counter.

"You should go call your wife now." His gaze leaps from me to the woman whose hand slowly drags off my shoulder.

I'm married. And while some men don't respect that status, I do.

My left leg continues to jiggle beneath the bar almost uncontrollably. "I wasn't going to do anything." My throat knots. "I swear. I wasn't going to go off with her."

Cyrus pats my shoulder. "I know." He continues to look at me, assessing my face, catching on the bead of sweat rolling along my hairline. "Go call Ruthie."

"I—" I nod once, knowing I should have been doing that in the first place. Hastily, I stand, knocking back my stool which Cyrus catches before it hits the floor. My hands are trembling. I haven't done anything wrong. I wasn't looking at another woman. Don't want another woman. But suddenly, I'm a mess.

I fumble with my wallet, struggling to retrieve my credit card for my drink.

"I've got it. Just go."

Cyrus and I meet gazes once more before I nod again, unable to find my tongue to speak. To thank him.

I would have turned that woman down. I would have told her I was taken and shown her the ring on my finger. Because I do not want to be unfaithful to my wife. I would not do that to Ruthie. I am not Clifton.

As I rush into my hotel room, my phone is already in my hand, and I fall against the closed door as if that woman literally chased me.

I press Ruthie's contact and hold my breath, waiting on her to answer.

"Ruthie." I breathe her name, like the air I need to exist.

"Bolan?" Her voice is groggy.

"Flower." I choke on the nickname as I slide down to the door and swipe at my forehead, then hold my elbow on my knee and rest my forehead against my fingertips.

"Are you okay?" Concern fills her voice, and I breathe another sigh of relief.

"Ruthie," I whisper. "I just need you."

She's silent a second, and I hear rustling, like she's adjusting herself in bed. Our bed.

"What do you need?"

"I just needed to hear your voice." I lean my head back against the door and stretch out my legs. "I just need to know you're still there."

"Of course I'm still here." Her laughter is light, not having known what just happened downstairs. Not knowing that another woman touched me without my consent. I wouldn't be giving consent to someone else. I only want Ruthie.

"I don't want to fuck this up."

"*Okay.*" Her voice shifts, growing deeper, growing more concerned. "What did you do?"

"Nothing. I didn't *do* anything." I exhale and swipe my hand down my face. I sound guilty when there's nothing to be guilty about. "Just talk to me. How was your day?" I just want to hear her voice.

She's quiet for a moment, maybe contemplating the crazy edge in mine. I should just tell her what happened, but I don't want her worrying about me. Don't want her thinking I might have gone off with that woman. I'm *not* Clifton.

"My dad tried to call me again today." Her voice drops, quiet and sad.

I still don't know a single thing about my in-laws. Not their names. Not their locations. In my head, I keep thinking of Nylah and Jared as her parents, which makes them my in-laws when they are actually Ruthie's in-laws. That's just confusing.

"Maybe you should take another call from him." The man obviously has something urgent he wants to talk to her about. "What if someone in your family died? Left you a ton of money? Or maybe you inherited a cat?"

Ruthie laughs and the sound soothes my soul.

"No family members. No financial inheritance. And I don't want a cat."

I chuckle, finding further relief in releasing the sound.

"I still think you should answer his call." I'd be crushed if Tulane stopped answering mine when she is older. Then again, I hope I never do anything to warrant my daughter ignoring my phone calls. Like being a shitty dad, making my daughter feel unwanted or unloved.

"Let me tell you about Tulane instead." Ruthie changes the subject by diving into her day. How her phone was dead this morning and then she couldn't find it because Tulane kept taking it, walking around the house with it, like I would magically appear on the screen.

"She misses you."

"I miss her. I miss both of you." I knock my head back on the door, realizing the hollow ache in my chest is because of how much I miss them. And I'm missing out on all the little moments with Tulane. The mundane ones like her stealing a cell phone and acting like it's a magic machine.

Ruthie once told me I'll make my own mundane memories with her. Have my own moments, and she never means to make me feel bad that I'm missing out. She only wants to fill me in on all the other minutes.

"Saw your game today. Nice homerun."

"I didn't catch all the catches." I lower my head, plucking at my jeans on my outstretched legs.

"You did fine, Bolan. That throw was over your head."

Our new centerfielder, the replacement for Ford Sylver, has quite an arm but his aim was off, and the ball went a good foot above me.

"I still hate when I suck."

"You don't suck, bear."

I tip back my head again, taking a deep breath, holding in the sound of her voice in my ears. "You just called me bear."

She quietly laughs. "Guess I did. Everyone else around here has a nickname."

Tulip. Flower.

"I need something that fits the garden theme." She chuckles a little harder.

"Yeah, grass doesn't exactly cut it." I snort. "Did I just make a dad joke?"

"Neither does plow or hoe." She snorts, breaking into deeper laughter. "Is there such a thing as mom jokes?" She snorts again. "I'm sorry. I'm so tired today, I think I'm a bit delirious."

I glance at the time on my phone.

"It's late, and I should probably let you go."

Ruthie ignores my suggestion and asks, "You're still happy you signed with the Anchors, right?" She knows all about my granddad and wanting to play for Chicago because he'd been a lifelong fan.

"I'm happy, baby." For more reasons than simply signing with my team of choice. I wouldn't have her in my life without the Chicago Anchors and their demands.

"I'm glad." Her tone is quiet, the hint of a smile present. "Do you feel better?"

"Yeah. I feel a lot better. Just hearing your voice has changed everything." Everything about her has changed everything. She makes life better.

"Get some sleep," she says.

I press up off the floor, wincing after sitting for so long on the hard surface. I don't want to hang up, but she needs rest as well. "Sorry I woke you."

"You can wake me at any time."

"Miss me in our bed?" I tease, walking deeper into the hotel room.

"Yeah, Bolan. I do."

My heart begins to hammer in a new way, and I want to ask

her if we can pretend I'm there now. I want to make her feel better, give her confidence in me, or maybe that's just reassurance in myself, feel better that she's here for me, making me feel confident she isn't going to leave.

But phone sex doesn't exactly feel appropriate.

"I'll call you in the morning."

"Okay, honey. I'd like that."

I chuckle. "Bears like honey, let's stick with that. Get it? Honey. Stick. Another dad joke."

Ruthie laughs, the sound light and refreshing and putting me at complete ease.

"You are ridiculous."

"I've heard that a time or two before from you, but like I say, that's why you love me."

"Mmm. Maybe."

Not a full confession but not a denial either. I'll take it.

"Talk to you tomorrow, then, baby."

"Tomorrow."

33

———

[Ruthie]

I just needed to hear your voice.

I hadn't known how much I needed to hear his as well. His proposal to have a baby came out of left field, and in the throes of passion, I wasn't certain he meant his suggestion. However, Bolan was attentive the remainder of the week. Very interested in the practice of making babies.

Last night, his phone call rattled me. The tremor in his voice. The quiver of hesitation. The adamant resolve that nothing happened to warrant such a stressed call, when something clearly happened. He needed me and I hadn't been there, to hold him, to calm him, to care for him.

So, I make a bold decision.

Tulane and I head to Cleveland. A six-hour drive and a last-minute ticket to the game set us just off center from the visiting team's dugout.

Before the game starts, I wasn't certain I could grab Bolan's attention. He once told me how he drowns out most of the stadium, especially as no one was present to see him specifically. *Before.* No immediate family. No former girlfriends.

The second Bolan is looking in our direction, I wave. Then blow him a kiss, hoping he catches sight of us. His feet stumble over the sandy strip running down the third base line as he crosses it toward the visitor's dugout. Then he lifts his hand, jumping in the air to catch a kiss that went over his head.

A smile breaks out on his face. One that pops that dimple as bright as the stadium lights.

During the game, Bolan hit like a champ, bringing in a run and scoring one. When the game ends, he comes to the netting that protects fans from fly balls, and motions for me to come to the edge of the field. With his fingers through the woven protection, I slip mine over his.

"You came to my game."

"We came to your game." I jostle Tulane in my arms, glancing at her before looking back at her dad.

He blinks a few times, looking from her to me and back again. "I need to fucking kiss you."

Leaning as close to the net as I can get, Bolan gives me a quick peck that isn't enough for either of us.

"Why didn't you tell me you were coming?"

For half a second, I worry that I've made a mistake. That Bolan doesn't want us here. That I've ruined some plan he has. But I quickly shake the thought.

"I just wanted to see you. Surprise you. You seemed pretty upset last night."

"Best fucking surprise ever." He wiggles his fingers toward Tulane.

Someone calls his name, and he glances to the side, brows furrowing before he looks back at us. "I've got to shower and head back with the team. I share a room with Cyrus." Those furrowed brows deepen.

I knew I couldn't stay with him. I'm hoping he'll stay with me. "I got us a room in your hotel."

His smile grows wide again. "You're just full of surprises." Then he turns a little serious. "But you should have told me. If something had happened. A car crash. A choking issue. A snake bite. I wouldn't have known because I would have thought you were home."

"Well, good thing I wasn't planning on roaming the desert in Cleveland." Said tongue in cheek.

"Flower," he admonishes.

I jostle Tulane on my hip. "We're safe."

"You're beautiful." His gaze shifts to Tulane. "Both my flowers are lovely." He glances back at me. "I'm so happy you're here."

"Yeah?" The niggle of doubt needs extra reassurance.

"Of course, baby. I'll see you back at the hotel. Give me about an hour." He tugs at the netting, forcing me to come close to him again and kisses me through the square of rope.

I giggle at the feel of the net around my lips and the way Bolan doesn't care that he's kissing me in public.

BY THE TIME I arrive at the hotel where the team is staying, Tulane is heavily asleep, and I set her in the portable crib. With her in the room, Bolan and I aren't going to do anything sexual. Still, I want to comfort him, hold him, like he's done for me so often in the past month and more.

When a quiet knock comes to the door, I jump, even though I've been anticipating his arrival, and I let out a low, nervous giggle. Leaping up from my seat on the edge of the bed, I cross to the door and open it.

"Hi," I say, taking a deep breath at the sight of him, like I haven't seen him in years when it was only an hour ago.

"Hi." Before the door is even shut behind Bolan's entrance, I'm plastered against the wall and his lips land on mine.

We kiss like we haven't kissed in decades, instead of a week. Like that kiss all those years ago, when a clock was ticking, and sixty seconds was all we had.

Bolan pulls back, breathless a second, before he moves along my chin and down my neck. "You are such a sight for sore eyes. And my heart."

"Bolan," I quietly moan. He can be so sweet.

His mouth meets mine again, his large body still pinning me to the wall. His hands quickly roam over my shoulders to my chest, cupping one breast and pinching my nipple, peaked against my bra.

"Bolan," I whisper. "Tulane."

While I'm not saying no to sex, I am saying no in the shared room with a child. If all we do is kiss and he holds me all night, that's the reassurance I need that everything is fine.

Bolan breaks the kiss and turns his head toward the crib in the corner of the room. Then he shuffles us into the bathroom.

"What are you doing?" I chuckle as he hits the light, blinding both of us with the sudden brightness and closes the door.

"I need to see you." He spins me to face the mirror and returns to sucking along the column of my throat.

In the harsh light of the bathroom, my eyes are dilated. My skin pink where Bolan's scruff has tickled it. His fingers come to the buttons of the jersey I'm wearing. The one with his name on the back.

Our name.

"Want to fuck you with this jersey on, baby. But also want to see every inch of you again."

My knees give a little, and I catch myself on the edge of the countertop as he continues to pop all the buttons until the two sides separate. Pressing my ass backward, I catch on the front of him, where he's long and hard and eager for me.

He slips his hands inside the jersey, where the length covers my waist, and pops the button on my jeans. In seconds, I'm out of my pants and underwear. Bolan even has me remove my bra but leave the jersey on. With the front panels separated, a slim line of skin is exposed right down the middle of my body.

"Bolan," I whimper as his hands skim over my ass and hips, rounding to the front of me. One dips between my thighs.

"Watch us," he demands as he palms me, then slips a finger easily inside me. My head tips back, and my eyes close.

"Watch," he commands, nipping at my neck. "See what I see."

I open my eyes and meet his gaze in the reflection of the mirror. "What do you see?"

"The most beautiful woman I've ever known. My wife."

A second finger joins the first and my breath hitches as he fills me up. He smiles against my neck before nipping me once more. His other hand slides up my middle, cuffing my throat. That inked forearm on display. I swallow against his tender hold.

"Bear," I whisper.

Bolan chuckles but doesn't break his attention on my body. His fingers slip and slide. The build inside me climbs. The flutters collide like a storm.

Suddenly I'm soaring, head tipped back, mouth wide, free-falling through the sky. Like the hits Bolan makes out of the park. Then I drop.

The orgasm came too fast. The end too soon, but Bolan isn't going to quit at one.

"Sure like seeing my number on your back, flower." He slowly removes his fingers from me and presses at my back, causing me to bend forward. He traces over the number bracketing my spine. "And I know this isn't a romantic moonlight balcony, but I need to have you like this again. Where I can see my name draped over you. See my cock entering you, stuffing you full."

He kicks lightly at the inside of my ankles, spreading my legs in a new way. He tugs off his shirt and I watch the show through the mirror. The clink of his belt buckle follows, and the soft thud of his jeans hits the floor.

His gaze is lowered, aimed at where he's stroking his tip through soaking folds.

"Want to put a baby in you, flower. Want to bury my seed deep inside you and plant a new life."

I'd snort at his metaphor if I wasn't so turned on by the possibility.

With an easy glide, he slips inside me, buried deep within seconds, and stills. He meets my eyes in the mirror.

"Still good with that?"

"A baby?" I choke. I want that more than anything. A piece of him I'll always have. Because I'm still not certain where we'll be in a year, but for now, we're here, taking pleasure in one another.

"*Our* baby."

"Bolan." My eyes prickle as I struggle with his name, and then he's moving, quickly picking up the pace and distracting me. His hands spread over my back. His palm splays over his name stitched on the jersey. He grips my hips, pistoning into me like he can't get deep enough, and I meet his thrusts, like I can't pull him far enough into me.

He slides one hand around my front, his fingers finding that trigger spot. My skin is slick. The sound of us echoes in the small confines.

"Bolan." My voice hitches, and he moves faster. His fingers. His hips. The glide in and out of me.

I cover my mouth to prevent the scream that would bounce off the walls in this tiny space and wake a sleeping toddler, as I spiral out of control, releasing a ripple up my belly and a trickle of down my inner thighs. The orgasm is so powerful my knees buckle, but Bolan holds me upright.

He tugs me back, my ass flush with his pelvis, and he stills, jettisoning inside me. His groan is deep and throaty. A vein bulges along his neck but his eyes catch on mine through the mirror, and he smiles like he did earlier. With that dimple bright and beautiful and full of promise.

Like he's truly happy to see me.

He leans forward, keeping himself seated inside me, and wraps his arms around my belly.

"I'm still green for you, but I sure like you in Anchors blue." He chuckles as he presses a kiss to the side of my neck.

I giggle, shaking my head at how ridiculous he can be. How ridiculously romantic without meaning to be.

I shift, prepared to release him, but he tightens his embrace, looking at me in the reflection. His chin on my shoulder.

"Not yet," he whispers. "Just another minute."

Another moment between the two of us.

OUR SPENT bodies wrap around each other as we snuggle in the hotel bed.

"I need to tell you something." Bolan's voice is serious, tight even, which is so unlike him. "I don't want any secrets between us."

I stiffen beneath his hold, swallowing thickly as I worry that he's found out the secret *I've* been keeping from him. The innocent slip of truth I haven't revealed yet.

However, as he prefaced this conversation by saying he had something to tell me, my skin prickles, goosebumps forming and not the good kind.

"*Oo-kay.*" I hesitate, shifting in his arms, attempting to pull away from him, but he holds me tighter, like he's afraid I'll slip away.

He rolls me to my back, positioning half his body over mine. His leg between mine. His arms at the sides of my head, brushing back my hair. The weight of his broad chest pins me in place.

The room is dark except for a sliver of light coming from the bathroom where the door is almost closed by not quite. Tulane is used to a night light and I didn't want her to wake up and be frightened, especially in the unfamiliar surroundings of the hotel.

"When I called you last night, I really needed to hear your voice."

I swallow the sudden lump in my throat. The prickle of tears almost instant, as if my body knows before my head can catch up that something happened. Something I don't want to hear. Something I won't be able to handle, especially after what we just did in the bathroom.

"It was nice to hear your voice, too," I counter tersely, my voice quivering. I squirm beneath him, preparing to flee.

"Something happened before I called you, and I just want you to know."

My body goes cold. I'm stiff as a board beneath him. My hand had been on his bicep, but it slips free, fingers clutching the sheets instead. My breathing starts to exaggerate.

I nod. The only motion I can muster.

"Someone hit on me." His admission slams me in the chest, and I can't help the strangled gargle that escapes. The rush of pain up my throat and out my mouth.

Bolan continues, the words in a speeding stream of confession. "Nothinghappenedwithher. Ididn'tinitiateanything. Didn't hardly speak to her. Didn't do anything."

My breaths come faster. My heart hammering, the rattling enough to knock me over if I wasn't already lying down. I don't know how to respond. Instead, I look away from him, but he gently pinches my chin, forcing me to look at him.

"I want you to know because I'd never do anything to hurt you like that, Ruthie. I am not tempted by anyone but you. I—"

He cuts himself off and I'm grateful that he's stops his tongue from saying something he'll regret. Something I don't want to hear in the midst of a confession about someone trying to pick him up.

"I swear I didn't touch her. The second I got away from her, I rushed to my room and called you. You can ask Cyrus."

Because his friend will cover for him. The situation was too familiar. The ache in my chest almost worse than I remember.

Bolan continues to hover over me, keeping me in place. "I just wanted you to know. I made a commitment to you. You're my white. And we promised to be honest with one another. I'm still your green."

I nod, but I don't feel safe. Suddenly, I'm spent in a totally different way than having sex with him in a bathroom. I'm drained, but the tears leaking from the corners of my eyes cannot be withheld.

"No, baby. No, don't cry. I swear nothing happened." He leans forward to kiss my lips, but I can't find it in me to respond. He takes my hand instead, lifting it to his mouth and lingering against my palm. His eyes close. "Please believe me, Ruthie."

I lick my lips. I want to believe him. Deep down, I'm certain I do, and I attempt to tease him about the situation, but my throat constricts around the words. "You can't help it that you're irresistible."

Bolan lifts his head. "But I did resist. I didn't want her. I don't want anyone but you. Only you."

I nod, still struggling to find my voice. "Why didn't you tell me last night?" Before I dragged his daughter across three states.

"I didn't want to worry you. I didn't want you to doubt me

like you do right now. I can feel it. That distrust. And last night, I wanted to hear your voice. Knew you'd calm me down."

And he didn't want to tell me the truth.

But he's telling me now.

Cliff was repentant. He'd beg for forgiveness. He'd assure me it meant nothing.

Bolan isn't doing that. He's only asking me to believe him, trust him, that nothing actually happened.

"Shit. I'm just fucking this up." He lowers his forehead to mine. "I just wanted to be honest, but instead, I'm hurting you."

"No," I squeak. "No, I appreciate the honesty. I want the truth. Always the truth."

"I don't want you to worry about me on the road. I only have eyes for you, baby. Your eyes." He rubs his fingertip over my brow and around one eye.

"Your kiss." He presses one to my lips, the sensation featherlight.

"Your heart." He lays his hand flat against my chest.

"I'm all yours, flower. Only yours."

Slowly, I run my hand up his arm again, tracing along the ink before coasting over his shoulder and around his neck, tugging him down on top of me. He relaxes a little, drifting to his side but keeping me pinned to his chest.

"All I can do is trust you," I whisper. Until he proves otherwise. "But, if you ever feel tempted—"

"I won't. I swear." He clutches me harder, pressing his face into my neck, inhaling my skin where I smell like him and me.

"Green, Ruthie. Always green." He continues to hold me, smoothing down my hair and all I can do is hold on tight in return, and hope he means it.

34

[Bolan]

When the Anchors return from Cleveland to Chicago, a weird tension exists between Ruthie and me.

I'm afraid I've spoken a little too much truth to my wife.

Two steps forward. One step back. It's my least favorite kind of dance.

I appreciate her concerns. Clifton fucked her over. But I'm not him and I need her to see me. I'm different, not only from him, but from who I used to be.

And I'm willing to prove it, I just don't know how.

On the final game of our first home series, I remain on the field an extra minute after we win, easily finding Ruthie and Tulane in the stands. The weather is unpredictable in April, and my two girls are bundled up because of the threat of rain.

As I stand on the edge of the field, I toss Ruthie a kiss. It's been a great game for me again, and I'm attributing my batting average to the changes in my life.

A new team. A new home. My wife. My family.

Ruthie lifts her hand, palm up and flat, similar to how she awkwardly raised her hand back in Jared's office that first time. Then she makes a fist like she caught my kiss.

Smiling, I motion for her to come down to the field. We only have a few minutes before post-game interviews and cooldown routines, but I want to hug her. I need to hug her.

As the security guard lets Ruthie onto the grass, with Tulane on her hip, I pull both into my arms. "Hello, family."

"Say hello Daddy." Ruthie tickles Tulane's belly, and she giggles before reaching for me. Her smile is so sweet. Her eyes the same color as mine. I love everything about my mini-me, and I want to give her more.

I want our family to grow. I want Ruthie and me to have the baby she desires. I'm not pretending with her anymore. She needs to know how I feel, and I almost slipped up the other night in Cleveland. Almost laid it on the line but held back, reading the temperature of the room for once, which was icy cold.

But as I'm riding the high of a win, the words are on the tip of my tongue when Coach calls out, "Gentlemen, locker room."

It's then that I realize Romero Valdez is on the field, chatting up a woman. Ford Sylver's ex-wife, maybe. I turn back to Ruthie, stamping the corner of her lips with a quick kiss, then turn toward the tunnel.

Ignoring Valdez, I walk a few paces behind Ross Davis. The clomp of our cleats echo through the tunnel to the locker room the second we hit the pavement.

"Got a girlfriend, Coach?" Valdez calls out behind me.

I've seen Coach glancing into the stands on occasion, and I've wondered if he has a woman. He's a private guy, keeping himself mainly to the coaching staff. Kip Garcia, our main pitching coach, is a former pitcher himself who once played against Ross. Then Ross was under Kip for a while when he played for the Anchors a few years back. Now they coach together, but they are also friends.

Coach doesn't answer Valdez, ignoring him like most guys on the team do. People are sick of his shit. His attitude mainly, but also these little digs about girlfriends and wives.

Trying to defuse the situation, I respond. "Ah, give Coach a break. We can't all be the Romeo you are." Not that I think he's a true romantic in any sense. More like the tragic character Shakespeare wrote about.

"You were once a Romeo, too," Valdez reminds me of my former reputation. The dig a little too close to the bone, all things considered back in Cleveland.

"Now you've got that ring weighing down your finger," Valdez continues. "I don't know how you handle such a mouse in your bed."

I'm on Valdez in an instant, slamming his body against the cement wall. "Don't even *think* about my wife."

Valdez lets out a strangled laugh under the pressure of my forearm at his throat, pinning him to the tunnel wall at his back.

"Don't speak about Ruthie like that. In fact, don't even look in her direction."

Coach slips his arm between us, saying something, but I don't hear him. My ears are ringing louder than a gong and I see red. Valdez's blood on this pavement if he so much as breathes Ruthie's air.

"You're a shit stirrer," I continue, shoving my forearm harder beneath his chin. He's only recently been reinstated from his suspension after the incident with Ford. "And no one likes you."

"*Ohh*, you hurt my feelings." He falsely whimpers his taunts at me.

"That's enough," Coach demands, still attempting to wedge his body between us. "Adler, back up."

With a final shove against Valdez's throat, I press off my teammate and take a large step back. My chest lifts and lowers. My heart racing. I'm itching to finish this fight *he* started, but Coach steps between our bodies. Facing me, he acts like a wall, blocking Valdez from my sight.

"Maybe what your little wife needs is a real man in her bed," Valdez says.

I rush forward again while Ross spins between us, becoming a blanket of protection over Valdez. A flimsy blanket, because if I have to go through Ross to get to Valdez, I will.

"You're fucking toast," I yell, pressing up against Coach, preparing to push him out of the way.

Only someone is suddenly pulling me off Coach's back and I'm plastered to the opposite wall, held back from killing my teammate.

Ross speaks low and steady to Valdez, who glares at me over our coach's shoulder. His nostrils flare like a bull ready to charge. *Bring it on.* I'm a fucking stampede waiting to trample his ass.

Valdez sharply turns his gaze to Ross, who punctuates whatever he said with, "Watch me."

"Get your ass in the locker room," Dalton Ryatt yells at Valdez. It's only then that I realize the bench coach is present, along with Kip Garcia and Cyrus, both of whom are holding me.

Ross presses away from Valdez who only holds his head higher as he turns toward Ryatt. Then he spits in my direction, narrowly missing my feet.

"*Pendejo*," Valdez mutters. Asshole.

"Fuck you," I snap, although the words are lost in the tunnel, and I tip back my head, feeling the cold cement blocks against my thick skull.

Ross spins toward me once Valdez is down the tunnel with Ryatt at his back.

"Coach, you need to do something about him." This bull-shit needs to stop. It's not good for the team to have such a loose cannon. One so full of himself. Thinking he can go where he wants, say what he wants.

"I'm handling him," Coach replies, but I have my doubts. He's new to the team, like I am, and that means tiptoeing around issues. I don't want to question my coach's ability to lead, but I'm starting to.

"Are you calm yet?" Kip asks, stepping back but holding up a hand, prepared to push me against the wall again, if necessary.

"Yeah. I'm good." But I'm fucking not. I want to strangle Valdez for what he said about Ruthie. She's not a mouse. And she has a man in her bed. Me.

Even if the past three nights we haven't been together, and I miss my fucking wife.

"Let me know what you need. For Ruth," Coach finally says to me.

"What do you mean?" My tone is still sharp. My emotions raw. If Ruthie needs anything, she has me.

"If you're worried about her . . . him getting anywhere near her, I'll file a restraining order myself, if you need me to."

I huff, the sound bitter. "Yeah, I don't think that will be necessary." I appreciate the gesture, though. "He's just talking shit. But that shit needs to stop."

I want to believe words are cheap and all Valdez is doing is flapping his lips. But I still don't want him talking about my wife.

WHEN I GET HOME, I'm still rattled. The afternoon game means Ruthie and I have the night together with Tulane still awake, and I was looking forward to spending quality time with my family. But I can't shake what Valdez said.

Maybe she needs a real man in her bed. I'm man enough physically, but have I been present enough emotionally for Ruthie?

"You okay?" she asks as soon as I enter the duplex.

"Yeah. I just . . ." How do I tell her I got into a fight with my teammate? "I had an issue with Valdez."

Ruthie chuckles good-naturedly as she sets something in the microwave. The soft hum of the appliance fills the kitchen. The scent of something spicy wavers in the air. Children's music is coming through the television while Tulane walks from the ottoman to a basket of toys and then back.

"What now?"

I shake my head. "He was just running his mouth." I comb my fingers through my hair, pulling my gaze from Tulane to find Ruthie watching me.

"What'd he say?" Her lowered tone expresses her concern.

"Just making comments," I state, brushing off the insult although it's still circling around me. Then I glance at Tulane again and wonder what the hell I'm worried about. I have my daughter. I have Ruthie.

Delicate fingers come to my hand fisted on the edge of the peninsula countertop.

"I still want to know."

I nod and purse my lips. "He made a comment about you. Then us. Saying I might not be man enough in bed."

Ruthie laughs. Out right guffaws until she reads something in my expression. "You can't be serious."

I lower my gaze and twist my lips from side-to-side. "As a kid, I was bullied a lot. Fat kid." I run my fingertip along the counter's edge, thinking back on years of rejection and then years of over-attention. "And I guess, just sometimes, I do wonder if I am enough."

"Bolan." Ruthie steps closer to me.

"But more so, I wonder if I'm enough emotionally." Slowly, I lift my head. "Like have I told you lately how much I appreciate you still being here. Taking care of Tulane. Looking after everything." She's not asking for anything. Not money. Not even a baby. I'm the one putting that suggestion out there.

Suddenly, Ruthie is in my space, wrapping her arms around my middle.

"You're enough, honey."

Circling my arms loosely around her back, I drop my chin to her head. "Say that again."

"You're enough—"

"The other part."

"Honey?" She mutters to my chest.

"Yeah. That part."

"Honey," Ruthie says softly, pulling back to look up at me. Her cheeks turn a sweet shade of pink.

I trace a finger around her face. "This might be my new favorite color." The perfect one to match other places on her body.

"I'm so going to get you pregnant," I tease, lowering for a quick kiss because Tulane is present.

Ruthie chuckles against my lips. "We should probably talk about that. What it means for you?"

"What do you mean, what it means for me?" My earlier irritation slowly returns.

"Like, if I get pregnant, what will that mean for you? Do you want to be—"

My fingertips come to her lips. "I'm going to stop you right there before you say something that pisses me off. I want to get *my wife* pregnant because she wants a baby. *I* want a baby with her. You. Us."

I stare at her, wondering what her train of thought is, and then realizing, I don't want to know. Respectfully.

"This isn't fake for me, Ruthie. I'm not certain our relationship ever has been. You're my wife. That means I'm yours. And we . . ." I point between us. "Are forever. Not a year. Not a season. Not a contract. For life."

Until death do us part and all that.

Ruthie blinks at me a few times. Then her eyes water. "I just thought . . . I mean, you mentioned a few weeks ago that when the year was over . . . so I thought . . ."

"You thought *my God, my husband is an idiot because who talks about when a year is up.*" I do my best impression of a female voice. "I also apologized for being a dumb ass."

She chuckles, shaking her head and places her forehead against my sternum. Maybe she still thinks I'm counting down the days or checking off the months. Maybe she still thinks I'd step out on her, but I won't.

The microwave beeps and Ruthie pulls out of my arms, leaving me with this strange sense of loss.

"I talked to Jared. He'd like you to call him."

"Really?" Why would Jared want to speak with me? Ruthie works for him. I assumed all communication would be through her.

"He wants to talk to you about an opportunity."

I tilt my head, waiting for her to explain but she doesn't. Instead, she says, "Maybe you should call him now. Dinner will be ready in ten."

THE PHONE CALL with Jared is not what I expected it to be.

"We have a promotion opportunity for you. Ruthie told me

you love chocolate milk, and we reached out to the National Milk Campaign."

I fall back in the chair Ruthie bought for the third bedroom slash office. While sitting there, I glance around the room, noting all the little things she's done in here. A computer and two plants on a simple white desk beneath the window. A rug on the floor. This chair. And pictures on the wall of Tulane and me. I lean forward, narrowing my eyes, taking in the images.

Tulane and I pressed cheek to cheek. Her smiling wide. Our eyes are the same. Her hair brighter than mine, but she's my kid, and she looks so happy.

As I glance from image to image, I wonder when Ruthie took all these pictures and when she made them into photos for the wall.

"Bolan?"

"Yeah." I can't take my eyes off the photographs, realizing Ruthie has made this room homey. She's making this temporary living space feel permanent.

"So what do you think?"

"I've never done commercials before." Never been approached to act as a spokesperson.

"It'd be great for your image. Family man drinking milk with his kid. Plus, you'd send the message that athletes enjoy milk. Your body alone would suggest milk made you grow big and strong, and that's an angle the campaign wants to take."

"Would Tulane be in the commercials, too?" I'm not certain I want my baby girl splashed across television, print advertisements, and the internet.

"Not likely. They'd use a slightly older child actor. One who can talk." He chuckles. "It's a great deal, Bolan."

Next, he tells me their offering fee, and I almost fall out of the chair.

"Okay. Yeah. Sure. Sounds great." I cough to clear my throat before he thinks I'm a bumbling idiot and won't be able to handle the promos. "You can just let Ruthie know where and when and how."

Jared is quiet a second. "I'll have someone send over all the information. Have Floyd double check all the contracts, and then get back to me."

"Of course. Thank you, Jared." He's done me a real solid here, and that money . . . That alone is worth it.

"Don't thank me, thank Ruthie. She's the one who advocated for you. Demanded a deal, actually." His voice sounds off, despite the praise. He even sighs after he finishes. "We'll talk soon."

"Great." We hang up, and I return to the kitchen, watching Ruthie plate food for Tulane, who is seated in the converted highchair-turned-toddler stool.

"How'd it go?" she twists only enough to glance at me over her shoulder, but I take the spoon from her hand and set the bowl in her other hand on the counter.

Then I cup her cheeks and kiss her with all I have. My tongue sweeps through her mouth like she's the flavored drink I'm about to represent. I want every drop of her.

When I pull back, Ruthie follows my retreat, like she wants more of me and a strange image comes to my mind.

That girl from the kiss experiment leaning toward me, chasing after me like she wasn't ready to let me go. It's the oddest thing to think about considering I've just kissed my wife.

I drop my forehead to hers, listening to her breathe heavily.

"What was that for?" she chuckles lightly, the sound curious while flustered.

"Jared told me what you did. Thank you." I give her another quick peck. "Thank you for pushing me on him, or standing up for me, or whatever you did."

Ruthie giggles again. "I only want you to get what you deserve out of these next few years. I want you to know you're worth more than some guy playing a game."

She knows that's how I view myself. What I worry people will think of me once I leave the sport. If people will ever think of me again.

With my hands on her jaw, I lean down and kiss her again, expressing with every tug on her lip and touch of my tongue, how grateful I am that she's here.

As long as she finds me worthy, I'm a complete man.

35

[Ruthie]

Since Bolan has been gone a week and had a few night games upon his return home, I leave him to give Tulane her bath and tackle bedtime routines. When he finishes, I'm in the bathroom, staring at myself in the mirror.

The soft rap of his knuckles on the door does not distract me. "You okay in there?"

"Yep. Why don't you head downstairs? I'll be down in a minute."

I just need another few seconds to talk myself into what I'm about to do.

Seduce my husband.

Not that I think Bolan isn't attracted to me. Not that I believe he doesn't want me on some deeper level. I'm just feeling a tad raw after that night in Cleveland. It wasn't that I distrusted Bolan, but the situation did trigger old haunts and feelings. I had to talk myself through the emotions warring within me, and I recognized that Bolan admitting to me what happened, being forthright about it, at least once we were together, said something about him.

I could trust him. The panic in his voice. The fear that he'd mess *us* up. The earnest way he wanted to prove he was nothing like my late husband.

Tonight, I wanted to prove something to myself. I am desirable. I am worthy of the truth, and I accept it.

And after he repeated Valdez's comment, I want Bolan to know how I feel about him in return. I accept him. I desire him.

Focusing on my face in the mirror, I take in the smokey shadow around my eyes. The red lipstick covering my lips. The hint of color on my cheeks and the outfit I selected to wear.

I cannot remember the last time I wore something like this. I'm not certain I've *ever* worn something this risqué before.

Taking a deep breath, I exit the bathroom and tiptoe down the dark hallway. From the top of the stairs, I can tell Bolan has the television on but no other lights. Taking my time to walk down each step, I inhale another reassuring breath.

When I reach the bottom step, Bolan is draped over the couch cushions like he tossed himself onto the furniture. His arm extends behind his head. His feet are kicked up, ankles crossed, and he turns his head to glance at me.

I pause and watch as he slowly sits upright, not taking his eyes off me.

"Flower." He chokes, rubbing his hands down his jogger-covered thighs. "You are going to be my undoing."

Looking at me like he is, I know he means that in the best way.

"That outfit." He digs his teeth into his lower lip. Those green eyes almost solid gold as they roam from my hair to my chest to my toes. My breasts are covered by the thinnest red lace. The nightie hangs only to the tops of my legs, exposing all my skin to my feet. Only a scrap of material covers me in a place that's already pulsing and damp from his appraising gaze.

He doesn't move. He might not even be breathing. His fingers fist on top of his thighs as he watches me saunter closer to him.

Anxiety catches up to me and I smooth a hand down the thin fabric over my belly before I stop directly in front of him. Where he's spread his knees to make space for me. "I was thinking, maybe we could be reckless red again."

"I'll be any color you want, baby." His voice strains. His gaze roams over me once more. Those fists stay clamped on his legs, letting me be the one to lead this show.

I comb my fingers through his hair, and I swear he whimpers. Like the slightest touch makes him shiver. He also looks like a lion held back from pouncing on his prey. And he's vibrating with the need to pounce.

"Touch me," I command.

His tense fingers unclench, and he runs his fingertips along the outsides of my knees, climbing higher over the curve of my thighs until he reaches my hips. He pauses on the thin strap of ribbon around each hip, tucking his finger inside it, like he's testing its elasticity. Then he continues his journey, palms skimming up my sides and forcing the material of my nightie to lift until he's underneath my breasts, nudging them upward in the space between his finger and thumb.

"Sweet red." He leans forward and covers one breast, lace and all, with his mouth. His gaze flick upward, watching me while I watch him swirl his tongue over the sheer material and then bite me. Hard.

My eyes close and my hips buck forward.

While he moves to the other breast, one of his hands lowers down my belly and straight between my thighs. He pulls back from my breast and watches where his finger skims over the silky scrap.

"Cherry red," he whispers, pressing against me, forcing the fabric to crease into the damp folds. His concentration is focused as he slips both hands behind my backside, fingers tucking into the strap between my cheeks and tugging. The wet silk against my clit tightens and I tip back my head at the sensation that's strangely delicious.

With the silk taut, he lowers his head and breathes between my thighs, then swipes his tongue against the covered place.

"Flower," he hums, using his teeth to drag aside the material. The first stroke of his hot, thick tongue causes me to buck forward again. Quickly, he removes my panties and returns us to our position.

My hands come to his shoulders to hold me steady, and without warning, Bolan is falling to his back, taking me with him by cupping my ass. He moves me by my hips until I'm almost straddling his head.

"Get on my face, flower."

"Bolan." The strained chuckle gives away my nerves. I've never done something like that before and I worry I'll smother him.

My hesitation doesn't deter him as he scoots down the couch and positions me over him. I place my hands on the armrest for balance, unprepared for that first lick.

"Bear," I growl, as my head tips back again and something inside me turns wild. My hips start to dance under his insistence. My body slithers and rolls.

I cup one of my breasts and play with the nipple.

"That is so fucking hot," he says, offering only a second of reprieve before returning his attention to my clit. I glance down at him between my thighs, the sight unlike anything I've seen before. His eyes are wide and watching me.

One of his hands curls around my backside again, his

fingers slipping between the crack. He tickles down the crease until his forefinger presses at that puckered hole. I tighten my thighs, rocking forward, which clenches my ass.

"Bolan?" I question, not only what he's doing, but how it makes me feel.

He slides those fingers forward, dipping them into the mess he's making between my thighs before pulling back to his original position.

"Want to take you everywhere, flower. Want to make you feel all the things."

He has no idea how many places I already feel him. My head. My heart. My soul.

As his tongue continues its torturous flicking, his finger slowly breaches me from behind. The pressure intensifies everything.

My breath hitches but somehow my body relaxes, welcoming just the tip of his finger, while the tip of his tongue flutters against another sensitive spot.

Quickly, I'm tipping over the edge, digging my nails into the armrest and clenching my thighs around his head. Tightening my ass and spilling over his lips.

"Bolan," I cry out, not caring about a toddler sleeping one floor up or neighbors below us. Let the world know this man, and only this man, can take me to these heights. Make me soar and fly.

I'm coming hard and fast until Bolan pulls back. He shoves me down his body to rock my center over his hard length, freed from his joggers when I hadn't noticed.

He hisses at the contact as I continue to ride out my orgasm. Then he's notching at my entrance and slipping inside, and the sparks that have hardly turned to embers, ignite again.

"Bolan." I rock on his hard cock. His balls against my ass. His pubic bone kissing my clit.

"That's it, baby." His fingertips dig into my hips, guiding me back and forth as I hug him inside me. "Fuck me like you love me."

My gaze flings down to his face to find him watching me. Watching us and how I take him into me. My movements never falter as I lift and drop, lost to my own arousal, found in my desire for him.

I settle at his base and go off once more, fingernails scraping down his chest.

Bolan hisses. "I love it." Then his hips turn wild, bouncing upward, dropping back, dipping into me so all I feel is him.

"Home," he whispers, like he's finishing a sentence he hasn't spoken out loud.

"What?" I chuckle, only momentarily stumbling in rhythm.

"You are my home, Ruthie." He continues moving like he hadn't spoken. Then starts muttering again. "Why do you feel so good? Every kiss. Every touch. So good, baby. So good."

His fingers tighten almost painfully on my hips, and he settles me over him. Pressing me down as he thrusts up and holds. I feel every pulse and pump inside me. He's as deep as he can get and yet it doesn't feel deep enough.

"You consume me," he grunts. "Forever." Everything from his mouth sounds like an incomplete thought, but I don't question him.

Instead, I collapse over him, breathing in his leather and cinnamon scent mingled with the hint of me over his face. He kisses me. The kiss promising and possessive, and a punctuation on this moment.

"I think you got me pregnant," he teases, joking again by repeating what he once said, and breaking the intense, intimate tension.

I chuckle as I lie over him, shaking my head and rubbing my nose against his. What a ridiculous man. What a deliciously, lovable man.

"I hope you got me pregnant," I whisper, kissing the tip of his nose. "I think I might like forever with you."

Bolan cups my head, pushing it upward so he can look at me. Those eyes dance. His nostrils flare.

And then he's kissing me again, like forever with me is all he's ever wanted.

36

———

[Ruthie]

For the next ten days, the Anchors are home, and Bolan and I fall into a blissful swirl of family life. He goes off to play baseball. I take care of Tulane. And when he's home, we sneak in sex whenever and wherever we can. Tulane's nap time is particularly productive and creative.

One morning, Bolan fucked me up against the drawers inside our walk-in closet, when I was trying to put away laundry. Afterward he told me that being domestic made him horny. He also praised how I decorated the duplex. The little touches like plants and pictures. The bigger statements like the easy chair in the office and a dining table with six chairs.

Life is good.

Although, Bolan is set to leave on another long stretch of away games. He'll have three in Philadelphia, then back to Arizona for another set of three. I don't want to have concerns about our separation. I don't have any doubts about him. He's my future.

Even if he can be a hot mess. He's been scrambling around the duplex, looking for his bag, which is already at the top of the staircase, ready for his trip to the airport. He's standing in front of the fridge, looking at his phone, hand lifted like he's about to open the appliance. Tulane is still sleeping in the early morning hour, and I am waiting to say our goodbyes.

But then, Bolan lowers his raised hand and swipes something on his phone. His thick brows dip inward, the crease deep.

"What's this?" The growl in Bolan's voice makes the fine hairs on the back of my neck rise. "Just what the fuck is this?"

He swings his head in my direction, eyes passing through a wave of emotions. Shock, fear, disappointment. And then anger.

He steps toward me, flipping his phone in my direction, screen outward and points with this other hand at the display. "What the fuck?"

A female speaks on the video, her words projected on the screen as she talks:

"Bolan Adler paid me a million dollars to pretend to be his wife but then he settled on a consolation prize for his fake wife instead."

Glancing up at Bolan, I'm not certain I fully register what I'm seeing. I drop my gaze once more to his phone, the device nearly vibrating in his hands.

My eyes fall on the familiar, pretty face of Melody Cross who is explaining how Bolan proposed to her but within days of their engagement announcement, he broke the promise and asked a second-string woman to pretend to be his wife, claiming she was the financially cheaper of the two options.

The *she* is me.

I glance back at Bolan, dumbfounded. "I thought she signed an NDA."

Bolan glares at me, causing an uneasy feeling to stir in my belly. Like he somehow thinks I'm at fault.

"But wait. There's more." Sarcasm drips from his tone. He taps at his screen and produces a second video.

Something called a stitch appears, where Melody has split the screen, her face showing on half the image as she points at a video on the other half.

The caption reads: **Is that her?** I can almost hear the implied disgust as my gaze falls on the opposite video.

The one where two people are kissing. The film is black and white. The couple are young, college aged. He's wearing a backward baseball cap. She's wearing a backless shirt, and—

"Shit," I whisper.

In addition to Melody's caption, she mouths, *She kisses like a fish*. Then mimics the opening and closing of a goldfish's lips. The hit stings.

Bolan flips the phone toward himself to take a second glance at the video, then turns the device back toward me.

"That's us, isn't it?" Confusion and upset strangles his voice. "You fucking knew who I was after all, didn't you?"

When I glance at those forest-green eyes, the ones ablaze with flames, I swallow thickly. "I can explain."

Bolan continues to stare at me. The anger crackling in those eyes turns to something more desperate. Hurt.

He stands taller while slowly lowering his phone to his side. His eyes search my face for something, anything, but defeat seems to settle in. He rolls his shoulders back.

"Seems a little late to tell me the truth." His gaze is scorching. "That's if you *ever* planned to tell me the truth."

I step closer to him, but he jerks back. My heart sinks. "I didn't know it was you. Not at first." The dark ballroom. My thoughts on Clifton and the ocean.

"But when you kissed me . . ." I bite my lower lip. The truth was in that kiss.

"When I kissed you . . . What?" His shoulders lower, in direct conflict with the pain in his eyes that narrow. "You thought you'd get laid by *Bad-ler*?"

My back stiffens at the mention of an old nickname he told me about. My hands turn to ice. "I'm not going to dignify that question with an answer." Defending myself on this point is moot. Bolan knows sleeping with him was the furthest thing from my mind when we first reconnected.

He continues to stare at me, his mind computing something else. "You said Clifton and you took a break in college. He'd been unfaithful to you." His brows lift. "Had you been unfaithful to him first?" He lifts the phone and points at it. "Did you cheat on him with me?"

"No! No, absolutely not." The wound he's inflicting on me goes deeper. Bolan knows how I feel about cheating. Knows my experience with it from Clifton. I'd never do that to someone. Never do that to him.

"I went into that experiment—"

"That damn experiment." Bolan visibly bristles cutting me off, reminding me that he'd been blackmailed into participating. His future on the college team was linked to that moment. Heck, his entire life might have rested on that experiment. If he failed psychology. If he was kicked off the team. He might be upset with me from keeping the truth for him, but he isn't angry at me *because* of the experiment. That moment meant two different things to us, individually, but I need him to know what it meant to me.

"That experiment meant—"

"Was this some kind of revenge?" he counters, slicing off my words again, like his brain skipped ahead.

"Revenge for what?" I blink at him.

"I don't know." He tosses his arms out to the side, like he understands the statement is ridiculous. "Clifton maybe. Were you pissed at him, so you used me?" His expression is stricken, like that might actually be a possibility.

Staring at him, he reads my face. The one with guilt written on it but not how he thinks.

"You did," he whispers.

"It wasn't like that." I hold my breath expecting him to interrupt me once more.

When he lowers his head, eyes no longer able to look at me, I begin. "When Clifton wanted that break, I was relieved." I exhale, thumping my chest and blinking back the tears "I needed a break as well." Our love had been hard and fast, and too much at times. And he'd really hurt me when he'd been the one person I trusted.

"I didn't want to randomly hook up with someone. I didn't want to date someone else. I just wanted to kiss somebody."

"Just a little taste," Bolan snipes, narrowing his eyes while pinching his forefinger and thumb within an inch of each other. "A sample of another."

I shake my head. "I just needed to know if Clifton was the only one for me." The tears fall. Bolan stares at me and I lick my lips. "And that kiss proved to me he wasn't."

His eyes widen but his shoulders are still tight.

"I've held onto that kiss my entire life." My voice cracks and I blink harder as the tears fall faster. "And I knew someone like you wouldn't be interested in me. Wasn't ready for someone like me."

"Someone like you?" he echoes back, as if I'm insulting him. As if I'm better than him, but that's not what I mean.

"Someone quiet and shy and looking for a family. Looking to start one and be part of one."

Bolan continues to watch me. The anger in his eyes cuts deep, but within that anger is also hurt. I lied to him, although I hadn't outright. I'd omitted, and guilt eats at me just the same.

"You knew who I was," he finally states, reminding me of the rules. No contact. No seeking out the other.

"You were hard to miss on campus. Once I'd had that kiss from you, it felt like you were everywhere. Star athlete with a reputation as a ladies' man." I swallow thickly, the tears clogging my throat. "You would have never picked me." I shrug, knowing the truth is, if I'd approached Bolan back then, despite the rules, he wouldn't have wanted a serious, committed girlfriend, and I wasn't interested in being his one-night stand.

"You don't know that." His brows pinch again, softer than his earlier crease. "You didn't give me the chance."

Sighing, I accept that he's right.

"I kissed you for me," I clarify. "And something inside me came to life." I clutch one hand over the other against my chest. "I'd never done anything like that before. Never felt anything like that moment. Those sixty seconds. Not before. Not after. Not until I kissed you again in that ballroom. That's when I knew. Because I knew only you could kiss me like that. And I've been holding onto that first kiss all this time."

Bolan turns his head. His lids blinking suddenly. He squeezes his thumb and forefinger across them before facing me again.

"You went back to him." His tone is dark and growly once more.

"I went back to him." There isn't any way to dispute this truth. I accepted Clifton's apology and his groveling, and we were a couple again. Because I was still that young, foolish girl who wanted a family. Wanted to be the center of his world, and while I thought I was, I learned too late I wasn't. Then I just felt stuck.

"What about the ballroom? That night you—"

"I was lonely and melancholy. All this bullshit about Clifton. People praising him like he was a saint when he was just a man. A sad, depressed man who had demons I could not help him chase away." And dear God, had I tried. Suggestions of therapy. Constantly monitoring his mood. His behavior. Trying to navigate him day after day in those final years.

"In that ballroom, I would have never gone further with you if we hadn't shared a kiss first. When I knew it was you."

Bolan licks his lips, his shoulders falling finally. "Was it retaliation then? Were you angry at me for my past? For our college days?"

I'm shaking my head before he finishes the question. "No." The tears in my eyes nearly blind me. "I just wanted a second chance."

"A second chance at what?"

Love. Although I don't know that I thought it then, standing in a dark ballroom, kissing a stranger. Because I hadn't known then who Bolan Adler really is. Not his reputation. Not his past. But who he is now. The father to a sweet girl. A good person trying to right his name. The man I call my husband.

Who kisses me like no one else ever has, and now I worry he never will again.

I make a fist at my lower belly, pressing into the ache that feels like a cement block in my stomach.

Bolan's eyes catch on the motion, but he quickly looks to the side again. He licks over his top teeth before his jaw clenches.

His phone beeps in his hand. A reminder. It's time to leave. He has a plane to catch and games to play states away for the next week or so.

"The last thing I need is another scandal." His voice is hard, even and steady. He lifts his phone, shaking it in my direction. "As my agent, you'll need to do damage control on this."

The words cut. As if I'm nothing more than an employee. As if having a child with him would be one more mistake. As if holding onto an experimental kiss from college had been foolish and reckless, and not the fun kind of reckless, but something spiteful, something regretful.

Like he regrets me.

The hurt runs too deep, and I can hardly breathe.

"Me?" My breath hitches. "You spoke to Jared, right?" Jared called the other day to finalize discussions about the milk campaign. Surely, they discussed other things.

"You're assigned to me. *You* speak to Jared."

"Actually, I'm not."

"What?" Bolan narrows his eyes. His phone beeps again. Another reminder.

"I quit ISM."

Those eyes widen as big as baseballs. "When?"

I swallow, knowing the truth only digs my guilt deeper. "The day I arrived in California."

Bolan lifts his hand, ticking off against his fingers like he's counting back the days or weeks since I'd been there. Or possibly the infractions against me. Then he lifts his entire hand, palm outward, fingers spread, as if five is an important number. "That was weeks ago."

"I know. Jared promised me he'd talk to you. As Imperial Sports Management represents you, he told me he'd reach out to say you'd been reassigned to him."

In all the excitement of coming to Chicago early and then Bolan returning home, the fine detail of no longer being his agent slipped my mind. I hadn't been acting as his agent anyway other than suggesting to Jared that Bolan should have sponsorships and then I proposed a few brands I thought Bolan might represent.

"But Jared told me you brokered the deal for the milk campaign."

"I simply made a suggestion on your behalf."

Bolan continues to stare at me, and I wish I could read his

thoughts because his eyes are now hollow. The inviting forest is gone; in its place, is empty, solid black.

"Was this about the money?"

"This?" I question. Does he think I kissed him for money?

"Our marriage." He swallows thickly.

My mouth falls open, as if I've been struck by a fast ball. The unexpected hit so hard I'm speechless a second before the pain settles in.

"Was anything the truth between us?"

"Yes, Bolan." I step closer to him, but again, he steps back. "I —" *I love you and I didn't mean to hurt you.* I'd never hurt him like he thinks—intentionally, for gain. Marrying him for money. Kissing him for retribution.

"*I* got a nice deal with the Anchors." He points at his chest. "And now I have sponsorships, and you get a cut."

The tears on my face have shifted from guilt and grief to hot anger. "A cut?" I choke. "Did you even read the contract you signed with me?"

"Right. Because *we* have a contract."

His phone beeps with another reminder notification.

Suddenly, I'm done with this conversation. He isn't listening. While I see the hurt in his face, he apparently doesn't see the hurt in mine. And too often, I let my late husband walk over me in similar situations.

"We don't have a contract, Bolan. We're married, remember? And I'm here for you. You and that precious little girl." I glance in the direction of the stairwell and point, implying the second floor.

"You're here as the second string. And I'm your ticket to the game."

My head whips back in his direction. I register the wounded tone of his voice, but his words are the final strike. *Out* and sent back to the dugout.

"You didn't read the contract, did you?"

His phone dings one more time.

"That's a low blow, Ruthie. You know I don't read well."

Shaking my head, I grit my teeth. "No, a low blow is this: Fuck you, Bolan." Fuck him and his insinuations and misunderstandings and not offering me grace when I gave it to him.

He was my green.

"Good luck at your games." That's not my phrase, but I no longer care. "You need to go."

There are no more reminders to pop up on his phone. I know because even though I'm not his agent, assistant, or manager, I've still set the notifications for him. I've still been taking care of him, so he gets where he needs to be when he needs to be there.

Because I care about him.

To my surprise, Bolan turns and chucks his phone down the back hallway. The distinct crash of it hitting the back door and cracking before dropping to the floor echoes back at us.

Then he turns and leaves without saying goodbye.

37

[Bolan]

How the hell did everything get so fucked up so fast?

One minute I'm preparing to say goodbye to my wife for a week and the next I'm blindsided by Melody's video.

Someone sent me that damning clip. The one going viral of me and my wife kissing. Back in college. During an experiment.

I knew she felt familiar.

My wife and my mystery girl are one in the same and yet they are completely different people. I don't even know my wife anymore. The woman who kisses me like I'm her lifeline. Like I'm the air she needs to breathe, the same as she's become oxygen for me.

Was it revenge at first? Was it for the money now? I didn't want to believe either, but in the moment, anger overruled everything.

My commitment-white had become a lie.

I would have called Floyd on the way to the airport, but I'd tossed my damn phone, pitching it at the back door of our duplex. I regret that decision. That outburst of anger. And the mess I've left in its wake, because Ruthie will need to pick up the shattered pieces, so Tulane doesn't find any and hurt herself.

The device felt like it was scorching my hand.

Damn notifications. Damn social media. Damn Melody.

She was in breach of our non-disclosure agreement and if *she* thought she was getting a penny from me, she was wrong.

A thought trickles forward. What was all that Ruthie mentioned about our contract? The one between her and me?

My brain instantly flips to more important thoughts. Our vows to one another. The ones I'd taken seriously, promising patience and love. Respect and honesty.

Why hadn't she told me the truth? If our first kiss during that experiment meant so much to her why hadn't she reminded us both of that moment when she saw me again?

On the plane ride to Philadelphia, these thoughts fire through my head and the second I take my seat, I jam my headphones over my ears and close my eyes, ignoring the stares and whispers of my teammates. By now the video has spread like a wildfire among them, but I'm trying to quell the rage and confusion inside me.

What I did with Melody. What I did with Ruthie.

Once we land in Philly, we take a bus to our hotel.

As I sit on the bus, head tipped against the cool glass of the window, I'm given a wide berth by my teammates, certain the vibe coming off me says I'm ready to throttle anyone who comes near me.

The Bear is angry, but also restless. The unsettled sensation has more to do with Ruthie. The hurt in her eyes. The accusations I flung at her. The ache in her voice when she spoke.

"I'd never felt anything like that moment. Those sixty seconds. Not before. Not after. Not until I kissed you again in that ballroom."

Her words were my sentiment, and I tap my head against the window, berating myself for not recognizing her sooner. Not finding her on that college campus. Not realizing who she was in that ballroom. Not listening when my gut said there was something familiar about her.

My memory had been fleeting, though.

I can only hope social media is the same. Unfortunately, they are vultures, looking for the next riff in a team or wrong move by a player. The press will have a field day with this one.

Bolan Adler takes a wife and pays her to pretend.

I close my eyes again, stumbling over scene after scene of Ruthie and me. And Tulane.

At no time did anything feel fake between us. Ruthie is as real as I thought a person could be. Sweet and kind. Thoughtful and inspirational. She's everything and so much more. And the way she is with Tulane. The idea that we would have more children together.

"Looking for a family. Looking to start one and be part of one."

Ruthie has no idea that I've longed for the same thing. She didn't give me the chance to prove myself. Then again, she isn't entirely wrong. I wouldn't have been ready for her when I was in my young twenties. I was too self-absorbed. Too full of piss and vinegar and drive. Too wild and impulsive.

"You wouldn't have picked me."

Like selecting kids for your team before a pick-up game, I'd pick Ruthie first. She'd always be my number one choice. Now and for the future. I cannot change the past.

I cannot change that she went back to Clifton, and I lost out on an opportunity. And I really need to know what she means about our contract.

Startling me, Ross Davis swings into the empty seat next to me. He's quiet for a second. We haven't had much interaction after my altercation with Valdez other than the coach-player dynamic. After my plea for him to do something about the troublemaker on the team. Looks like I might be the next one under the spotlight.

"Gotta let social media roll off your back," he starts, staring toward the front of the bus. "Shit's never half the truth."

I snort, keeping my head pressed against the window, gazing out the glass, but not focusing on any one thing. "Which means the other half is the truth."

Ross chuckles. "Half full versus half empty concept?"

"Something like that."

He huffs, being thoughtful a second, before asking, "Which part is true?"

I swallow thickly, knowing that as much as I've accused Ruthie of being dishonest, I haven't exactly been truthful either. At least not with the Chicago Anchors.

"I didn't pay that woman a million dollars." Melody Cross hadn't gotten a dime from me. Only a verbal agreement. Not even a romantic one. "And we were never officially engaged."

"Ah." Ross is quiet another second. "And Ruthie?"

My head whips in his direction. "She's my wife."

However, my proposal to Ruthie hadn't been any more romantic than asking Melody if she'd agree to a fake marriage.

Yet, Ruthie is the whole truth. We *are* married. She quit her job and she's in Chicago for me. She's caring for Tulane right this minute.

"I'm here for you and that precious little girl."

You don't do that unless you love someone. Two someones.

My head falls back to the window.

"Then that's all that matters," Coach says, in response to my declaration. "Love her through the thick and thin. Because there will be thin moments that test everything in you, but thick moments that remind you why you picked her in the first place. Why you love her. Most of the time, it's because she still loves you during the thin."

I nod, appreciating his advice.

Ross pats my knee like I imagine a compassionate father might before pulling himself up to stand by using the back of the seat in front of us.

"All those emotions you're feeling, let it out on the field tomorrow. It's never good to keep everything bottled up inside." He nods once and steps away, leaving with advice my granddad used to give.

Maybe Ross is more grandpa than father figure.

My thoughts instantly drift back to Ruthie.

"I knew no one else could kiss me like that but you. And I've been holding onto that kiss all this time."

She's been bottled up for years, at least a decade or more, and the thing she'd been holding onto was me. My kiss.

I recall how I searched for her back in college. How I'd asked for her phone number and wanted a chance at kissing her again. A *second* chance.

How I left it up to Fate to bring us together. Or not.

Instantly, I reach for the *omamori* around my neck. Glancing down at the silver medal, I rub my thumb against the Japanese letters. The place where Ruthie kissed. I've touched the charm so often her kisses are now gone.

But had Fate responded after all? Had it pulled me into an empty ballroom to find my future standing there?

I tip my head back on the seat and blink up at the bus ceiling.

Her final words ring through my head. The deep ache, like I'd plucked my flower without care for her roots. I crushed her, dammit.

Gripping the top of the seat in front of me, I tug myself upright like Ross did and reach over the back of the seat, surprising Flynn Royal, the rookie pitcher who has the same lawyer as me.

"Dude, let me borrow your phone."

It's been a long day of travel and by the time we reach the hotel, I'm emotionally drained. The last thing I expect after checking into our hotel rooms is a message from the front desk that I have a package. Not wanting to put the staff out, I offer to go down to the lobby and claim whatever has been sent to me.

The bag presented is recognizable. A note inside reads: *So you can see Tulane.*

Guilt slams into my chest. I left without a final check on my baby girl. Without a final kiss. I'm such a horrible father.

Further feelings slap me in the face when I realize this gift is one more way Ruthie is thoughtful.

She bought me a new phone and had it sent to the hotel for me.

Within minutes, I have the thing powered up and find a missed text message. Only one.

A video of Tulane fills the screen. Ruthie's voice is in the background, her face notably not on camera.

"Tell Daddy you love him. Wish him good luck." That isn't our phrase, though. I need Ruthie to wish me to catch all the catches.

And as Tulane struggles with the l-sound, she hasn't mastered the phrase I love you.

I don't want to read deeper into the message. Find some subliminal meaning behind it, but I really want it to be Ruthie saying she loves me.

I want her apology, and I have one for her as well. Because I'm so, so sorry, suddenly.

Tulane places her tiny open hand over her mouth, then pulls it away. "Yuck," she says, no *l* in sight.

"Yuck. Yuck," she says again between what is supposed to look like her blowing kisses. Her hand covers her lips and then she tugs it away from her mouth, showing me her palm.

Yuck. It's how I feel right now. Crummy, crappy, shitty.

I wish Ruthie was on the screen. I should call her, but I'm clapped on the shoulder, startling me.

"Dinner," Cyrus says, holding onto my shoulder and catching on my eyes.

"I need to make a call."

He watches me a long second. "Not yet."

"What? Why not?"

"Because you need to let go of a few more feels before you make a call you'll regret."

Cyrus couldn't be more wrong. There is nothing I regret about Ruthie.

Nothing.

38

[Ruthie]

Bolan didn't call me last night. I don't have much to say to him anyway, but I'm relieved he got the phone I had sent to him. I didn't like that there was no way to connect with him, for Tulane. The message we sent now reads as seen, so at least I know he saw her and her wishes for him.

I don't bother watching the game that day. I'm baseball-ed out at the moment, needing a break from one particular player. Instead, I take Tulane on a walk through our neighborhood. Chicago is divided into so many diverse areas, and I haven't explored our little corner enough.

As we head to Roscoe Avenue, I make a stop in a romance only bookstore. The Last Chapter Book Shop is the cutest place, with all my favorites on the shelf, even if I'm not feeling romantic in my life right now. Still, I pick up two new releases, hoping to escape into someone else's happily ever after.

From there, we wander down the block, popping into some

of the other boutique-style shops before stopping at a BBQ chicken place. Tulane devours the chicken nuggets.

Eventually accepting that I've stalled as much as I can, we return to the duplex and meander through Tulane's nightly routine of bath and book reading.

While I treasure this time, tonight feels especially lonely. I miss Bolan. Emptiness exists in the unknown. Will he stay mad at me? Will he ask for a divorce? Will I be forced to give up both him and Tulane?

I'd like to believe marriage means we can work this out. It was a simple misunderstanding. A secret I held onto a little too long because it never felt like the right time to share it. There was no malicious intent in keeping the truth, though. No vengeance or vendetta or agenda.

I'd simply kept that first kiss to myself.

When Tulane finally settles into her crib, I decide to take a bath, and read the first few chapters of one of the romances I'd purchased earlier in the day. Unfortunately, my heart hurts too much to handle meet-cutes and one-night stands, and I eventually get out of the tub, and make the mistake of scrolling my phone.

The top news story reads:

Chicago Anchors. A sinking ship.

Rumors of inappropriate behavior and nefarious superstitions.

THE PICTURE beneath the caption shows Ross Davis, the coach, leaning toward Romero Valdez who is in a stronghold by my husband.

∾

Despite trying to reach Bolan, I don't. Eventually, I call Jared who is two hours behind Chicago time. He answers on the second ring.

"We're looking into the situation. Wondering what the allegations might be. What the result might mean for Bolan."

Suspension. Removal from the team. Forced retirement.

My heart sinks.

"What happened?" I ask, as if Jared was in the locker room where the explosion between teammates happened.

"I don't know exactly."

In the silence that ensues, I question Jared on a different matter. "Why didn't you tell Bolan I'm not his agent anymore?"

More silence follows before Jared says, "I was hoping you'd change your mind. That you'd come back to us."

"Jared." I sigh. "I didn't abandon you." Not like your son did to me. Like the soft plea in his voice reminds me of said son.

"You moved across the country and married a stranger."

"I moved because it was time to put some distance between me and the memories. And I married someone I'd known back in college." Not completely the truth, but the word is out now. Bolan and I met years ago.

"Why didn't you mention you knew Bolan?"

"Why didn't you mention he was family?" Clifton's cousin. Joanna's abandoned son. The black sheep according to Bolan.

"It didn't come up."

Just like so many other things within this family. Things I'll still take to the grave to protect the dignity of a man who does not deserve it.

"Jared, my resignation is firm. I'm not coming back to ISM. In fact, I'm not coming back to California." With or without Bolan, I'm staying in Chicago.

"It's time for *me*, Jared, and I hope you and Nylah can respect that. I gave almost eighteen years to Clifton. It's my turn."

I don't know if Jared understands. If he recognizes that as a woman I have as much value as a man. That I deserve a life of adventure like his son took. I deserve to live my dreams, hold my hopes, and follow my own path. Not theirs. Not his. Mine.

"We love you, Ruth."

"I know. And I love you, too." I do love them. Faults and all, which are nothing compared to my own parents.

The ones who called earlier, like they'd heard the news.

I married a man for money, but that isn't even half of the truth.

BOLAN CALLS me in the morning.

"Hey." His voice is quiet. His tone somber. "It's been a real shitshow here. I can't really talk but I wanted to check in. How is Tulane? How are you?"

I lower to the edge of the bed. I didn't sleep well last night. He doesn't sound like he slept at all.

"More importantly, how are you?"

"Well." He chuckles bitterly. "I'm not suspended, and I'm not kicked off the team. But I heard rumors about trades." He exhales heavily. "I fucked up, flower."

"It will be okay. I know you want to play for the Anchors because of your granddad, but he'd be proud of you no matter who you play for or where you play."

He scoffs. "I mean, I fucked up with you."

I'm quiet a second, uncertain what to say. How to tell him I'm sorry for my part in our mess, and I appreciate the remorse in his voice. I don't want him to be sad or feel hurt from me, but I appreciate that he sounds sorrowful. It gives me a sprig of hope. Couples fight. They disagree. Misunderstandings happen. If only we could talk, but he doesn't have the time now.

Other things feel weightier and more important than us at the moment.

"Fucking Valdez. We lost that game hard, Ruthie. And Valdez was muttering about everyone else but himself and his errors. Then he started in on Coach, commenting about his girlfriend. Something about superstitions and propositions. I told him he crossed a line, disrespecting our coach like that, and he turned on me. Said fuck you and your fake wife, and I just cannot tolerate when someone talks about you, flower."

A soft smile curls my lips.

"There's nothing fake about you, Ruthie. Nothing fake about us."

I had so many questions, but I know he needs to head out for his next game.

"We can talk when you get home."

"That's seven more days," he reminds me, as he needs to finish out the Philadelphia series and then heads to Arizona.

Seven more days.

"You'll be there?"

I hate the hesitation in his voice.

"I'm here, Bolan." I'll be right here. "Now, go catch all the catches."

Bolan huffs through the phone, the sound a bit lighter than the apprehension lacing his question.

"See you soon, flower."

"See you soon, honey."

39

[Ruthie]

Bolan arrives home late from Arizona. When he falls into bed beside me, I'm holding my breath a second until I feel him scoot closer to me.

"You sleeping, baby?"

I'd only been dozing, waiting on him to get home.

"I'm awake," I say groggily.

He presses a kiss to my shoulder and wraps his arm over my waist. "Is it okay if I hold you, flower?"

"I'd like that."

Quiet fills the dark room, and soon Bolan is fast asleep.

In the morning, he spends time with Tulane, and we tiptoe around one another, knowing whatever has to be said, needs to wait. Tulane hasn't seen her father in over a week, and Bolan surprises me by saying he's going to take Tulane to the park for a while.

"Just give me a minute. I'll go with you." I'd been doing

laundry again. Little ones might be little, but they go through lots of clothing.

"Actually, why don't you take a break? Hang out. Enjoy the quiet." He jostles Tulane on his hip and presses a kiss to her cheek. "We'll be back in a little bit."

Confused by the sudden rush to head out, I'm caught in a war with myself. A toss-up of hurt that he wants private time with Tulane, and possibly not me, and gratitude that he's giving me a moment to myself. Parenting is hard work, and while I regret nothing, I *could* use some time to myself.

While they are gone, I get three calls from my father and tell myself if he calls one more time, I'll answer.

Thankfully, he doesn't, and I try to put him out of my head.

More important thoughts are swirling up there.

Because Bolan's game is a night one, he asks me to get a sitter. He wants us to go out to talk afterward.

I've met a local high school girl who is smitten with Tulane, and I had her over last week to give myself that break Bolan suggested. I went to a movie and stared aimlessly at the screen, wishing Bolan and I had had more dates. More time. More of anything.

I haven't attended one of his games without Tulane, so when I took a seat in the WAG section beside Lacey Sawyer, it felt like I was forgetting something.

"Hey, girl. Long time, no see," she teases, wrapping her arms around her chest to protect herself from the chill of the early May evening.

"Yeah. It's been a bit crazy lately. My California blood is struggling with this Midwest weather." Not that I want to make small talk about the weather, but it is cool this evening and growing up on the West Coast, I've had some adjustments to make. I like it in Chicago, though. The easier pace than L.A. The friendliness of the neighborhood. The location with quick access downtown.

I walked to the stadium tonight, knowing I'll meet Bolan after the game.

Lacey and I chat about her boys and Tulane while intermittently watching the game. We skillfully bypass a discussion about the social media video, Bolan and my marriage, or our history with that kiss.

"Bolan's hitting so well for this team."

His stats have been impressive. He's one of the top hitters on the Anchors this year and he mentioned how he thought they might move him into the designated hitter spot, a valuable position, especially if he can't keep catching. There are talks of bringing a third catcher to the team.

"He looks good," I state casually.

"Mm-hm. That's how you talk about your man," she jokes, and my face heats.

When I glance out at the field, I catch Bolan watching me as he walks back to the dugout at the end of the inning.

During the fifth inning, the jumbotron shares birthday wishes, anniversaries, and the rare proposal. It's a favorite time of mine at the ballpark, and it's always fun to scan the crowd for the newly engaged couple. Only this fifth inning holds something extra special, and the fans go wild as I'm tapped on the shoulder.

"Miss Avery," the security man in a red T-shirt addresses me.

"Mrs. Adler," I correct, a prickle of unease skittering over my skin.

"You've been invited to a box."

I don't like the sound of this. "By who?"

"Graham Avery."

I hang my head.

"Who is that?" Lacey asks from the other side of me, her stance suggesting she's ready to take someone down if she needs to.

I glance toward the field, finding Bolan on the edge of the diamond, whistling and clapping for his Coach, who is kissing a woman on top of the dugout roof.

Bolan doesn't look up at me, so I turn toward Lacey.

"My father."

40

[Bolan]

I watched as Ruthie is escorted by security personnel up the aisle and away from the WAG section. Instantly, my heart races, concerned for Tulane. Had Ruthie gotten a call? Is everything okay?

I scan the seats for Lacey Sawyer, who was sitting next to Ruthie, I see her turned, her back to the field, watching Ruthie's retreat.

A strong sharp whistle comes from beside me and I turn my head toward Cyrus who is also looking toward the stands. When I glance back at the WAGs section, Lacey is pointing at me, shrugging her shoulders and lifting her hands like she's questioning something, then pointing up at the suites two levels above the lower level.

I can't possibly see that far, so I don't know what to look for, nor do I understand anything other than Ruthie possibly headed up to a suite for some reason.

The rest of the game is a blur. I can't concentrate, and I'm actually pulled in the seventh after two dropped catches in a row.

"What's going on with you?" Dalton Ryatt asks me as I take a seat on the bench.

"I don't know." I glance toward the WAGs section that I can't see from my position. Then I climb up to the railing, dangling over it by casually leaning against it, so I can see the seat Ruthie vacated. She hasn't returned and I'm not liking her absence.

When the game finally ends, I head for the field, not the tunnel and beckon Lacey down to the sideline.

"Where did Ruthie go?" I rush to ask her.

"Hi, Bolan. Nice to see you again."

"Lace," Cyrus groans. I wasn't aware he was behind me.

"I don't know. The security guy came and asked Ruthie to follow him to a box. I guess her father is up in the suites."

"Her father?" Ruthie hasn't mentioned him recently. Then again, I've been so focused on other things, I can't recall asking if the man was still calling her.

"She asked me to tell you which suite she's in. Said you should meet her there. She didn't look too pleased."

Players never rush the stadium seats, and I'm breaking all kinds of protocol, but I don't have time to race through the tunnel and exit through the locker room.

Everything in me says my wife is in trouble.

Taking the aisle stairs two at a time, I bypass well-wishers. Fans calling out my name. People stepping in my path to ask for an autograph. When I hit the concourse, I sense I've made a grave mistake. I'm working against the flow of traffic. Like a stream full of salmon swimming upstream when I want to go downstream.

I worry that too much time passes before I make it up two major levels and then take my chances that Ruthie is on the first base line and not the third base one.

Running from room to room, I brush past fans exiting them, desperate to find Ruthie.

Still in my uniform, I stick out like a sore thumb and since I'm certain I've broken a hundred rules, I'm probably kissing my contract with the Chicago Anchors goodbye.

But nothing is more important than finding Ruthie.

Thankfully, on the sixth room, I find Ruthie inside standing near two men.

One is Floyd Everest.

The other is a man I assume is her father.

There is something vaguely familiar about him. An air about him. It's probably the haughty way he holds his head and the slip of his hands into his slick pants' pockets.

"As I was saying—" Floyd cuts off as I stumble into the room, my cleats catching on the carpet.

"What's going on?" I glare at my *former* lawyer. The one who got me out of Japan but into a bind in the U.S. by proposing I marry his niece in a scheme to become a Chicago Anchor.

Ruthie rushes to my side and I wrap my arm around her shoulder, pulling her tight against me.

"Bolan Adler." The man with strange familiarity about him, reaches out his hand. His smile is too wide, held too tight. Arrogance covers every inch of him. "Graham Avery," he introduces himself.

It takes me a moment to process the name. Not that his name doesn't give him away as Ruthie's father, but that his name in general is important.

"You don't happen to be Graham Avery, world champion catcher for New York in the late eighties."

He smiles wider. "One and the same."

The man is a legend in the industry. Countless records. Three championship rings. And Ruthie's father. A man who ignored his child.

We shake hands, but I'm not feeling so honored nor awe-inspired by him.

"What can I do for you, sir?" I glance at Ruthie, giving her an extra squeeze beneath my arm.

"Seems we have a common interest. My daughter."

I snort, returning my gaze to him, knowing this man has had very limited interest in his daughter over the years.

"And as such, sounds like the two of you are in quite a pickle lately."

"A pickle, sir? No, I actually love pickles." I wink at Ruthie, who fights a smile, warring with the corner of her lips.

"My friend Floyd here told me about your predicament."

I dislike my father-in-law even more with the reference to Floyd.

"My predicament?" I sound like a fucking parrot as I glance toward Floyd, who I fired a week ago.

"You married my daughter to get on this team."

I turn back to Ruthie but answer this pompous asshole. "With all due respect, sir, I married your daughter for lots of other reasons." I arch a brow because I'm not about to tell my worthless father-in-law how I feel about his daughter without telling Ruthie first, privately.

"What do you want?" I glance back at the man whose gaze narrows on his adult daughter.

He nods toward Floyd. "You owe my attorney money, for the sale of my daughter."

I let go of Ruthie and rush the older man, but Ruthie catches my elbow, pulling me back to her.

"You watch your fucking mouth speaking about my wife like that," I snap, pointing a finger at him. "Your daughter isn't an object, and she wasn't for sale. She's a loving, kind, generous human being, and you're shit if you think you can bully her or me."

I turn on Floyd. "And you, you sack of shit, cowering behind this guy. I knew there were a few things wrong with you, but this is a new level. *Your* niece broke a legal and binding contract. And you did as well, and I should be asking you for compensation, instead."

My ex-attorney has broken about a million confidentiality laws.

Finally, I gaze at Ruthie. "As for any contract." I pause, staring into her eyes. "I don't know what you're talking about. I married Ruthie Avery because she agreed to be my wife. There is no contract."

"That's a bold-faced lie. You signed a contract with this woman, and I get a cut."

"Did you even read the contract?" I snark.

I learned the truth from Jared after asking him to forward me a copy of the papers that I hadn't bothered to read over, simply signing my name because I blindly trusted Floyd.

And, well . . . I don't read well.

Jared explained that Ruthie asked him to cross off all transaction fees. The dollar amount for any agreement was zero. Ruthie hadn't married me for one red penny. She wasn't looking to enforce a legal document. She willingly married me.

And I'm a fucking idiot.

He also explained how Ruthie quit the day she arrived in California, and while he held out hope she'd change her mind, he could tell that Ruthie was changed in general.

She looked happier. Sounded lighter. And he owed it all to me and Tulane.

Since Jared Jacobson and his wife Nylah love their daughter-in-law, they were willing to set her free.

"Whatever cut you think you deserve, you don't."

"I'll ruin you," Floyd points at me.

He can't. Because the only things of value in my life are Ruthie and Tulane. And one of them is tucked into my side, holding me back from strangling both these men.

"Gentleman, with all due respect . . . Fuck off." With my arm over Ruthie's, I turn us toward the door, but her hand on my belly stops me. She looks up at me, scared but strong, and turns back toward her father.

"I think it's best if you continue to pretend you don't have a daughter. And ignore me for the remainder of my life, like you've done for most of the beginning. I'm going to do the same to you." Her voice quivers. "And I take great solace in knowing I will never treat my children like you treated me. And he"—she points at me and then I point at myself, raising a brow and loving the thorns on my flower—"he will be twelve times the father you ever were."

I chuckle at the reference to my jersey number.

Ruthie turns her back on them and I slip my arm around her again, turning only to glance over my shoulder and point down at her.

"My wife. She's hot when she turns reckless red."

This isn't sexy reckless, this is just standing up for herself red, and I am here for it.

Once we hit the corridor leading to the upper level exits, I spin Ruthie, cup her cheeks and kiss her with all I have. My tongue deep in her mouth, my lips nearly swallowing her. Pulling back almost as quickly as we start, Ruthie follows my retreat, just like she did when we first kissed.

During that experiment.

And I return to kissing my wife, because she's more than sixty seconds in my life.

She's my forever.

～

"That was insane," I whisper, lowering my forehead to hers, as we stand beside my truck beneath the covered parking lot for the team and staff.

I'd been reamed out for my actions. Sprinting up through the stands that way, I could have been mobbed, injured or worse, according to Dalton Ryatt, who kept rubbing his forehead, muttering about how he wanted to keep me on the team and how I was a prospect for a coaching position. But he couldn't help me if I kept acting like a fool.

At the casual mention of a coaching position, Dalton had my full attention. However, my wife was waiting in the hallway, and I needed to get back to her, not wanting to leave her side while we were both so raw.

I am her green. And I wanted her to feel nothing but safe and loved by me.

Eventually, Dalton dismissed me.

"Do you understand now why I ignore my father's calls?" Ruthie asks, toying with the jacket only partially buttoned up my chest.

Rubbing my hands up and down her shoulders, I say, "How can he be like that with you? And why didn't you tell me Graham Avery was your father?"

Another secret.

Ruthie shakes her head. "Because he wasn't worth mentioning."

I nod, agreeing with the sentiment, then playfully pointing at her, swiping down her nose. "But no more secrets, baby."

"Bolan, we've only been married a few months. We can't possibly fit years into days."

I chuckle. "Okay. But let's start here." I lick my lips. "That kiss." I exhale. "That fucking wonderful kiss all those years ago. I don't know what happened back then, but it rocked my world, and I searched everywhere for you. Cafeteria. Bars. Even went into the library."

"Not the library," she jests, giving me a slow smile.

"I couldn't believe you just disappeared. I mean, the campus was only so big." I sigh, searching her eyes. "But then you were just gone, and out of sight, I guess, out of mind." I tap the side of my head because she knows I'm a bit of a slog up there.

"But when I saw you in that ballroom. Do you remember how I asked you if I knew you? Like there was something between us."

In the silence that follows, Ruthie nods. "I remember."

"Because there *is* something between us, Ruthie."

"I felt it, too," she whispers, tears filling her eyes.

"I'm so sorry it took me so long to find you again, flower."

Ruthie chuckles, the sound soggy as a tear slips from her eyes. "I'm sorry, too. For all the time we missed. But also, for not telling you right away, when I knew you were you. I should have told you who I was. It's just that as time went on, I didn't know how to slip it into conversation. And I eventually convinced myself it didn't matter. It was in the past. And I love you now."

My eyelids flap wildly. My heart stammers.

"Say that again, Ruthie." My voice doesn't even sound like my own. Like I've been hit in the chest with a fast ball and had the wind knocked out of me. I've never felt such pleasurable pain.

"I love you," she says a little stronger, those dark eyes wide and watching me.

"I love you, too, baby." God, I love her so much, and I've never said that phrase to anyone before. And I never plan to say it to anyone else again. Not like this. Only her.

"I don't want to lose you, Ruthie. Not ever."

"I'm not going anywhere." Then she clutches my jacket and pulls me toward her, kissing me like I'm fresh air, just like she's that deep breath I haven't taken in years.

MID-SEASON
EPILOGUE

[Ruthie]

As Bolan pulls up in front of the city college, I'm confused.

"What are we doing here?" I ask, staring at the large building beside the visitor's parking lot.

"Just trust me."

I turn to look at him. "Always green," I whisper.

I do trust him.

He smiles and holds out his hand. I take it and he pulls my fingers to his lips, pressing a kiss to my knuckles before hopping out the driver's side and coming around his truck to open my door.

We've been talking about my future lately. I told Bolan how I'd been thinking about going back to school and earning a teaching certificate. However, I'm no longer certain that's the path my life should take.

Bolan is too giddy about wherever we're going that I don't

have the heart to tell him I might have changed my mind. But I will tell him. No more secrets.

First, I just want to let him revel in whatever surprise he has in store for us.

As we wander down the hallway, classrooms lining each side of the campus building, I don't miss the sign on the wall marking the psychology department.

"Wait right here," he says, holding up both hands outside an office. "No peeking."

As I don't know what I'm *not* supposed to be peeking at, I giggle. Within seconds, Bolan steps back into the hallway and takes my hand again, leading me to a classroom. He pulls a key for the room from his pocket, and he opens the door, locking it behind us once we enter.

The room is dark, but from the hallway light streaming into the space from a narrow rectangular window in the door, I can see the desks are pushed to one side of the room and a photography lamp is set up in the opposite corner.

Bolan walks over to the lamp and clicks it on.

"What's going on here?" I chuckle, noting how the set-up is very similar to the first time I met Bolan, minus a video camera and a college professor. Instead, a tripod is positioned a few feet from the photography light that looks like an umbrella with a lightbulb in the center.

Bolan holds out his hand again and leads me to a mark on the floor. "Stand here, please."

His voice is formal while he's dressed in a T-shirt and jeans, plus his signature baseball cap. As I stand in position, smiling wide and giddy, Bolan rounds the tripod, sets his phone in the holster, and taps the screen a few times.

"Okay. *And.* Ready."

He steps over to me and stops directly in front of me.

"Ruthie Adler, welcome to the reenactment of our first kiss. We'll have sixty seconds on the clock. No groping." He playfully points his finger at me. "Nothing below the belt. No boob play." He pouts.

"But we kiss. No breaking lips." He rubs his fingertip along my lips. "Now. Just look into my eyes. And breathe."

My breath hitches. I'd told him that I remembered him saying these words all those years ago, but I didn't expect him to remember them now.

Bolan clicks a clicker in his hand, slips it in his pocket and cups my face.

And we kiss like we did fifteen years ago. The connection instant. The energy intense. With a clock winding down, we try to take in as much of each other as we can. But in the back of my head, I know we have more than these sixty seconds.

Bolan Adler is more than a moment.

He's a lifetime.

When the timer beeps, Bolan abruptly pulls back, but I follow his retreat as I often do. My body craving more of his.

He rushes to turn off the timer and then takes giant steps back to where I stand, still a little breathless, still thoroughly kissed.

"Any questions?" he jokes, wiggling one brow.

"What's your name?"

"*Our* name is Adler." He winks at me. "But I'd like to know if I can have your number?"

I hum. "My favorite number is twelve."

He gives me a quick peck, smiling against my mouth.

"Well, Mrs. Adler. I have another question for you." Bolan slowly lowers to one knee and my breath hitches once more. He pulls from his pocket a beautiful diamond solitaire ring on a silver band.

"Will you do me the honor of *staying* married to me and *continue* to be my wife?"

With my hand over my mouth, as if it can contain my smile

or my shock, I nod vigorously. "Yes, I would love to remain your wife."

"I love you, flower. You're my first pick. Every time. Like kids picking other kids for sandlot teams, I'll always want you on my side."

"I love you, too." Tears stream from my eyes. Happy tears.

"Now, I have another question for you."

Bolan slowly stands, kissing me before I can ask him mine. "Anything."

"How do you feel about February for a baby?" I lower my hand and cover my belly.

Bolan leans back, looking down at my stomach, then back up at my face. Suddenly, he bends at the knees, wraps his arms around me and lifts me up beneath my backside.

"Are you serious?"

My hands land on his shoulders. "Never been more serious." Or in love with this man.

He sets me down, steps back, and glances down at my belly. Placing his hand over my stomach, he says, "I say yes to that."

Then his hands are on my face, and he's kissing me again. The crackle between us will never grow old. The spark\ I look forward to each time our lips connect. The electricity zapping through me, which was all just a sign of what was to come.

Bolan is my happily ever after.

And I'm his.

I look forward to every kiss (and more) with him.

Thank you for taking the time to read CATCH THE KISS.

Please consider writing a review on major sales channels where ebooks and paperbacks are sold and discussed.

Want an extra inning of Bolan and Ruthie?
How about The Chocolate Milk Commercial.

The Chocolate Milk Commercial

Want to know more about the sexy silver fox coach Ross Davis? You can read his superstition proposition in ELEVATOR PITCH where a writer-blocked romance author meets her sports' crush.

Turn the page for a sample.

Are you curious about sexy single dad Ford Sylver? You can read his enemies-to-lovers, professional baseball player meets country music sweetheart in STERLING STREAK.

Turn the page for a sample.

ELEVATOR PITCH - SAMPLE

Offseason
November
[Vee]

"Hold the elevator."

My heels clack against the tile floor of the Autumn Hotel's lobby as I race for the elevator. I can't wait to take off these shoes and the constricting panties beneath my dress.

A masculine hand grips the closing door, triggering it to re-open, and I skip into the lift. Collapsing against the back wall, I tip up my head and let out a sharp, singular laugh.

I made it.

With my heart racing from the sprint, I'm breathless when I say, "Eleven, please."

The doors close and I lower my head, giving a cursory glance at my elevator mate and dismissing him. Then I do a double take.

Holy cow! I mean, Holy. Speckled. Cow. Baseball legend Ross Davis is standing in the elevator with me, staring at his phone. Baseball cap slung low over his eyes. Three-quarter zip shirt. Dress slacks. Not going to lie. I totally objectify his back-side in those pants that curve around his firm ass and outline muscular thighs.

With my back to the interior wall, I plaster myself even tighter to the panel. The gold-colored rail lining the space jabs into my lower spine. My gaze drifts to the shiny chrome bank of floor numbers, finding eleven is the only button glowing.

That isn't as consequential as the fact I'm standing—*alone*—with not only a present icon in baseball but someone I have the biggest sport-celebrity crush on.

Some people have book boyfriends. I have a baseball boyfriend.

Ross Davis was the pitcher for the Chicago Anchors when they won the World Championship eight years ago. As a die-hard fan of the royal blue and red, he stood out in the league because of his age. He was thirty-nine back then, making him forty-seven now.

However, I'd recognize him anywhere. Hidden beneath the ball cap on his head is the buzz-cut of salt-and-pepper hair but the beard on his jaw is what distinguishes him. Silver, gray, and white in an artful blend on a man with a fuller face. He's very tall up close with mile-wide shoulders and a solid stance.

Ross Davis as a fantasy in my head is nothing compared to Ross Davis in the flesh. My hands grow clammy, my mouth sticky like caramel corn. My heart rate is slightly more erratic than usual.

When he left the Anchors, he took a year off before becoming manager of the Philadelphia Flash. Neither of us are near our home states as we stand in this elevator in downtown Houston on the final night of the current championship series. The last game of the season for his team.

I'm here for a writers' conference.

And again, I'm the only person in the elevator with him.

I should say something. Then again, I shouldn't say

anything. The game was rough. He's clearly focused on his phone. He probably doesn't want to be interrupted. Definitely does not want to be fangirled over. Although, since I'm forty-five, I guess I might be called a fan*woman*. However, I'm not a ball chaser. The women who toss themselves at baseball players for their fame and status. Not to mention, any overzealous attention from me might make me look like a stalker.

But I'm absolutely crushing on him.

Suddenly, the elevator jolts. The lights flicker. A grinding sound *kathunks*, and the lift abruptly stops.

With my fingers clutching the railing behind me, I glance at Ross, who lifts his head, and squints at the electronic square that blinked through the once-ascending numbers.

"What the fuck?" he mutters under his breath. He presses the number eleven, but we are obviously not moving. Next, he jabs at the emergency call button. Nothing happens. We wait in silence. He triple-jabs the offensive button. *Poke-poke-poke*. Still, nothing.

"Maybe you should use your phone."

His shoulders stiffen, head lifting higher, before twisting only his upper body to face me. With the device in his hand, he stares at me like he'd forgotten someone else was present.

His eyes narrow before he gazes down at his phone and rapidly types out a message.

With his head bowed, he shakes it side to side. "No service."

The elevator jolts. My knees buckle and I clutch the railing harder. We seem to rise a few feet and then abruptly halt, rocking the lift.

Dear God, I'm going to die. In an elevator. With Ross Davis.

There could be worse ways to go but plummeting to my death still wasn't on my bingo card. As we rapidly descend to the end of our lives, I'm going to scream like I'm watching a horror flick, pee myself, and then die in a pool of urine at the feet of Ross Davis.

Graphic. I get it. My overactive imagination is what makes me a great writer.

And the thought of peeing sparks the urge.

No. Just no, no, *no.* My weak bladder is not allowed to kick in right now.

I. Do. Not. Need. To. Pee.

The mental command only stirs more urgency. My palms sweat on the railing. I can smell the tainted mixture of metal and perspiration. Or maybe that's me, as my pits are beginning to moisten as if I hadn't already been a little damp from my race to the elevator.

My pajamas, a lush bed, and a good romance novel were calling my name.

Trapped in an elevator would make a great meet-cute, but this was not romantic.

Peeing myself in front of Ross Davis is not the fluff of fantasies.

Lifting a hand, I fan my face, which has no effect but I'm internally telling myself it helps.

"Are you alright?" Ross asks, finally acknowledging my presence.

"Is it hot in here?" *Mother of baseball, this can't be happening.* On top of the sudden need to pee, panic is setting in, triggering a hot flash. Not that the scorching-curse can be called forth. The devilish hormones inside me have a mind of their own and they've chosen this moment to strike, adding to my discomfort. Starting at my shins, heat rises up my body like the vines of the ivy wall in the iconic Chicago Anchor stadium. My skin goes up in flames. Steam is probably wafting off my flesh.

Ross stares at me as I frantically wave one hand in front of my face while clinging to the railing with my other hand. The restrictive, uncomfortable, possibly size-too-small spandex I'm wearing is making everything worse. My stomach is tight, pressing down on my bladder. Once I shed these control-top panties, I plan to never wear them again. I bend a little at the knees, clenching my thighs together. Any second now, the full-on *I've-got-to-potty* dance will commence. Momentarily, the hot flash is distracting me. I'm certain the additional heat turns my face Anchor red.

"You're not claustrophobic, are you?"

Now that he's mentioned it . . . "Maybe a little bit." *Are the walls getting closer in here? Is the oxygen lessening?*

"Fuck." He tips back his head and glares at the ceiling for a second before tugging off his baseball cap and rubbing his thick hand over his head. I have never in my life had a thing for tattooed or nearly bald men until this man. And with that silvery beard and the winning smile I've seen him give a crowd of cameras, he's panty-melting.

Only I don't need my panties to melt. I need them to stay intact.

"It will probably only be a few minutes."

"Yep." I dig my teeth into my lower lip as I continue the hand-fanning, knee-bending, thigh-clenching dance.

"Rough game tonight," I add, then mentally curse myself. Now isn't the time for small talk. In fact, it might be best if he goes back to ignoring my existence and I peacefully die a slow death unacknowledged by him.

"You a baseball fan?" He resettles the cap on his head.

"Go Anchors," I muster.

"Shit," he mutters, lowering his head again. He played for our team for six seasons before that record breaking one. We were sad to see him go when he'd announced his retirement after a personal tragedy. He was a worthy coach, though. Players adored him. Front offices respected him.

He lifts his head again, tipping it back to stare at the ceiling. "I miss Chicago."

"Oh, yeah?" I grasp for something more intelligent to say. "What do you miss?"

His shoulders lift as he inhales deeply. He removes his cap again, scrubs over his head, and replaces the covering once more. "I miss the fans."

"For baseball," I interject, dropping my gaze to the Philadelphia logo on his shirt. Of course, he means baseball. Isn't that the topic?

He tilts his head, confusion scored in his expression. "Yeah."

"What else do you miss?" Maybe small talk won't be so bad. Keep him chatting. Then maybe he'll ignore the perspiration dampening my neck and the excessive wetness at my pits as I fight through the hot flash, the need to pee, and the onset of my height-phobia which involves additional sweating on my palms and feet.

"Walks along the lakefront in the summer. Hell, even the frigid temps of winter. Although my bones appreciate springtime in Florida." The Flash's spring training takes place in the sunshine state.

"Summer in the city is the best." Still not the most conversational statement but the truth. Chicago has this strange dichotomy of beachfront town and major metropolis divided by a famous highway, still affectionately called Lake Shore Drive.

"Ever done the polar plunge, though?" Ross shivers.

The idea of throwing myself into the frigid winter lake isn't helping with my need-to-pee emergency.

I cross my legs and bounce once. Ross notices. His brows cinch tight. He rubs his forefinger and thumb around his mouth, circling his lush-looking lips before drawing them together along the thick edge of his chin. His eyes are blue which I've only ever seen on a screen. Up close, they are the same royal shade as my beloved baseball team.

"Hello?" A scratchy voice projects through the emergency call speaker.

"Yes. Hello." Ross quickly turns toward the box and bellows louder than necessary for such a small space. "We're stuck." He glances at the floor numbers, none of which are lit to tell us where we've stalled.

"Sir, it should only be another minute."

"Someone in here is on the verge of a panic attack. If she goes into cardiac arrest, it will be on your conscience."

Oh my. "Was that necessary?" I demand, surprised by the sharpness of his tone and the terse insult to someone only trying to help us remain calm. Not to mention, he's calling out *my* verge-of-hysteria. The only heart attack I'll have is if my bladder gives out.

The elevator thuds, rumbling the lift before a loud clacking occurs, and we move again. I drop my fanning hand to my lower belly and squeeze my thighs tighter together. Knowing I'm *this close* to exiting this thing and reaching the safety of my room has the urge to pee ratcheting sky-high.

The sweat lingering on my skin is no longer related to the hot flash but to the potential mortification of *not* making it off this elevator and into my room in time.

Suddenly, the doors whoosh open.

Without a word to my *former* celebrity crush because he'd just lost all his points by reprimanding the elevator attendant, I rush toward my room. I have a vague sense of him turning in the same direction as me but I'm hyper-focused as I fumble with my room key. My hands tremble as the plastic card swipes over the electronic lock.

Red.

Red.

I flip the card over.

Red.

What the hell?

My hips rock. My knees knock. My thighs are pressed together tighter than a ballpark hotdog in a bun.

"That's my room." The masculine voice, embodied by the man standing beside me, watching me struggle to enter a hotel room, only irritates me further.

Glancing at the marker beside the door, I read the number. 1113.

Shit. I step to my left, forcing Ross Davis out of my way, and swipe my card over the keypad for my room. 1111.

Green. *Click.*

Without a glance backward, I step inside, allow the door to slam behind me and enter the bathroom. The potty dance continues as I struggle to roll down my nude-colored shaper briefs and settle on the toilet. Relief hits instantly and I bow my head, resting my forehead in my hand with my elbow on my thigh.

Holy cow, that was close.

Taking a deep breath, I linger on the porcelain throne as sweat cools on my skin. Pushing the body-contouring torture garment over my knees, I let it fall to my ankles. After kicking off my heels, I jiggle my feet for the final stage of removing the underwear.

With another deep exhale, freedom comes for my once constricted belly while I wiggle my toes, now released from my pinching shoes.

Placing both hands on my thighs, I lean forward, shaking my head back and forth.

No one else. To no one else would such a moment happen. I nearly peed myself in an elevator in front of Ross Davis.

Who really wasn't a conversationalist, nor was he particularly polite. Not to mention he sort of threw me under the bus without compassion, like I was one hand wave away from smacking myself or dropping to the floor in a frothing panic.

I hate when you learn your crush isn't really *all that* in the end.

Sitting upright, I reach over my shoulder and attempt to lower the zipper on the back of my dress.

Single-Woman Issue 171: Zipper lowering. Equally as difficult as zipper lifting.

My arms don't bend behind my back quite like they once did to operate zippers on a dress. I only have the closure lowered a few inches before I take care of personal hygiene and stand from the toilet. With my shaper on the floor, I push the garment aside with my foot and wash my hands, taking a second to stare at myself in the mirror.

My blonde hair shows evidence of finger combing throughout the long day of attending seminars. My eyes are bloodshot from straining to read in low-light ballrooms, plus, I've had two glasses of wine. Reaching for a washcloth, I wet it and scrub my face with the warm terrycloth, removing any remaining makeup.

As I wring out the washcloth, a knock comes on my hotel room door. Being that I was kind of in a hurry to enter the bathroom, I hadn't bothered closing the privacy slider. Plus, I'm the only one staying in my room. Either way, I haven't ordered room service, and someone evidently has the wrong room. I pause, waiting out the sound.

But another knock occurs, a little harder, a little more insistent.

Setting aside the washcloth, I pick up a hair band and tuck my hair into a messy bun at my nape while I cross the room for the door.

Peeking through the peephole, a sight I never in a million years imagined seeing stands in the hallway.

Even with an overactive imagination, I couldn't make this situation up.

And for a full minute or more, I stare at the peephole, as if I have imagined him. My stomach ripples like stands full of fans attempting The Wave. Unhindered, I observe him. Even though he was rude in the elevator, the tilt of his head gives a vibe of bone-deep weariness. A vulnerability that has me stepping back.

I tug at the loose twist of my hair then smooth my hand over my belly, hoping to calm the fluttering within me. I'm highly conscious that my dress is partially unzipped. *And,* I'm not wearing underwear.

With a flourish, I open the door and stare into the hall.

Ross Davis's gaze drops to a cut-crystal bottle of amber-colored liquid he cups in his hand. "I was saving this for tonight." He lifts the container. "For the big win."

I nod, suddenly sympathetic. Nothing excuses his tone or behavior earlier, but I instantly recall he's had a tough night. Maybe rougher than getting stuck in an elevator with a woman fanning herself, but not quite as desperate as my near-urination emergency. I will not concede the direness of *that* situation.

"I'm sorry about the loss."

Yep. Ross Davis and the Philadelphia Flash lost the biggest night in baseball in a gut-wrenching sixth game match up with Houston. The game came down to the ninth inning with bases loaded and a double play when the centerfielder caught a fly ball and then threw to the second baseman, who tagged the runner for the game ending out. In a mediocre game, the play was a major blow.

Ross nods once. His demeanor melancholy as he lowers his gaze again to where his thick fingers circle the neck of the crystal container, which he cradles like a prized possession. Albeit a poor substitute for a championship trophy.

For some reason, I envision what it would look like to have those thick fingers wrapped around me in some way. My thighs. My wrist. My throat.

"And I'm sorry for my behavior in the elevator. I called the front desk to apologize to the kid." He lifts the bottle in his hands and shrugs, the subtle movement almost bashful. "Anyway, I wondered if you'd like to share a drink with me. Even though, I can't promise to be the best company."

Holding onto the door, I shift to one leg and rub my bare foot over my ankle. Ross watches the motion. He's no longer wearing his team's three-quarter zip shirt or those ass-complementing dress slacks, but a plain black sweatshirt made of waterproof material and athletic pants.

We might be total strangers to one another but the aura of defeat around him has me stepping back and silently waving him inside. A hint of freshly-showered man mixes with a splash of spicy, masculine cologne as he passes me.

Was I really sitting on the toilet long enough for him to shower? Then again, I remember the days when Cameron could shower in under five minutes and be prepared to go in a total of eight. It's a man-thing.

However, the man-thing I'm most curious about right now is why Ross Davis wants to share a drink with me and how we're doing it in my hotel room.

Continue reading ELEVATOR PITCH.

Elevator Pitch

STERLING STREAK - SAMPLE

Offseason
[Ford]

I wake with a raging hard-on in an empty bed, although I'm certain I went to sleep with someone beside me last night.

While my head thumps to a wicked beat, I roll it on the hotel pillow. The space beside me is rumpled. The sheet tossed back. The extra pillow creased. Someone else was definitely in my bed. But who?

Candy? Cassidy? Something along those lines.

Lifting my hand to squeeze my forehead takes effort. Thinking is more difficult than it should be this late in the morning.

Then again, the purpose of last night was to *not* think. To shut down my recall of what I'd seen yesterday afternoon, moments before I was scheduled to leave my home in Chicago for my brother's wedding.

Closing my eyes, I press my finger and thumb into my lids as if I'm able to scrub from my vision what now resides in my mind.

Nope. Not going to go there yet.

Instead, I'm going to lay here and try to pull up an image of the woman I'd met last night. The one singing to herself in a corner of Randy's Bar, hosting a private concert for one. She peered at me under half-lidded eyes, the brim of her cowboy hat working as a shield for her face and covering her hair.

I didn't need to fully see her. I didn't have to remember her. There was just something about her. A recognizable sadness resonated around her.

I'd had a disguise of my own last night. A baseball cap pulled low. My head down; my collar up. I could have gone to Milton's Roadhouse in the center of Sterling Falls, but I'd have been recognized by everyone in this town. My hometown.

Randy's was the place a man went when he wanted to get lost and didn't want to be found.

For once, I didn't want to be noticed.

Later tonight at my brother's wedding rehearsal dinner, I'm not going to have a choice. My brothers will give me that look. The one that's a lethal combination of sympathy and I told you so. Vale, my sister, will be the one filled with concern. I love my family but there's a reason I stay away from them. There's also a reason I need them now more than ever.

Rolling to my side, I slide my hand over the cool, vacant hotel sheet beside me.

Did we fuck?

What I do vaguely remember is she matched me shot for shot last night. In a game of who can drink the most tequila, she won. And I hated losing.

Every inch of me demands I be a winner.

In my profession.

In my personal life.

And yet, I'd been on a losing streak lately. One I needed to turn around before I lost everything important to me.

With a heavy head and a stiff body, I press on the mattress to sit upright.

Jesus. If I didn't know better, I'd say I was roofied. My brain is foggy. My memory wiped clean. However, something tells me, the woman from last night wouldn't do such a thing.

Suddenly, my phone buzzes beneath my pillow.

"Fuck," I cry out. The sharp reaction hurts my head as much as the annoying trill blasting through the room. As I answer, I snap, "What?"

"Daddy?"

Shit! "Hey, Zelle." I hold the phone outward to read the caller ID. Vale's number.

"Daddy, you sound funny."

"I . . . I have a headache." I massage my forehead again, scrubbing at my skin as if I can cleanse my mind. "What's going on, Zelly?"

"Aunt Vale asked me to call you. Where are you?"

Good question. Glancing around the room, I find an unmarked pad of paper on the bedside table, which offers no clue as to the name of the hotel I'm in, if I'm even in a hotel, and not some seedy rent-by-the-hour motel. A phone number is written across the top sheet.

Fuck. Am I any better than my ex at this point?

"I'm getting coffee and donuts," I announce a little too hopeful I'm not too far outside of Sterling Falls to make my excuse legitimate. There's no way I drove last night.

Is my Escalade still at Randy's? What a clusterfuck.

"Give me a half hour, Zelle. Tell Aunt Vale I'm good."

"Okay, Daddy." My eight-year-old pauses a second. "You're coming back, right?"

Fuck, again. And fuck Felicity for putting doubt into our children.

"Yeah, baby. I'll be back to Aunt Vale's soon."

What I need is a liquid IV, something instant and deliverable, but being that I don't know where I am or how I got here, that's out of the question. Coffee it is this morning, a gallon's worth and stat.

Shifting my legs off the side of the bed, I balance on the edge a second. Even with my feet firmly planted on the floor, my knees bounce. My hand holding the phone shakes. My left arm feels worthless.

"Be a good girl for Aunt Vale, baby. I'll be there in thirty."

"I'm counting backwards, starting now. Thirty, twenty-nine—"

"Love you, sweet girl." I hang up and bitterly chuckle.

Guilt hits me like a ninety-seven mile per hour fast ball to the elbow. I wanted so much more for my girls. More than a cheating mother and a losing-it father.

Tipping back my head, I stare up at the ceiling a second.

Just one bat at a time, Ford. I could swing and miss as long as I learned from each misstep.

I'm not certain what lesson there is to be learned when one finds his wife—correction *ex-wife*—with another man from your team. A fellow player. A brother in sport.

Shaking my head because I don't have the bandwidth for Felicity this morning, I notice my SUV fob and wallet on the desk across the room. Over the back of the chair are my jeans, neatly folded in half, along with my T-shirt and jacket from last night. Glancing down at my briefs, my dick is still pitching a tent in the material.

I didn't fuck anyone last night.

I couldn't have, right?

It's been so long since I've had sex I'd remember the act.

But I don't.

+ + +

Thankfully, I was outside Sterling Falls and quickly able

to make good on my promise of donuts before returning to my sister's home soon. As I stand inside Curmudgeon Bakery, the bake shop owned by my youngest brother, a female presence stands too close to me near the counter while I wait on my order. I do not have the energy to encounter a fan. Not yet.

Turning only my head, the bluest eyes meet mine and a wide, lush feminine mouth curls in recognition. "Hey you."

I cringe at the cheerful familiarity in her voice. I also notice she's wearing a Chicago Anchors baseball cap. Wisps of light brown hair dangle from beneath the hat around the long column of her neck.

I grunt in response.

Staring back at me, her eyes dance like little blue flames. Like she holds a secret or is about to let loose a laugh. Her head tilts the slightest bit, like she's waiting on more than a disgruntled noise from me.

"Look, I don't really want to sound like a dick, but I don't want to sign any autographs today. I'm here for a family thing. Can you respect that?" My tone is a bit sharper than necessary, but my point is made. While everyone in this town might know me, I don't want to be acknowledged this weekend.

Her dancing eyes dull. The crooked smile on her face falls, but I bury the guilt because I just want to be left alone.

I want to be Ford Sylver, brother to Sebastian Sylver, who owns the Curmudgeon Bakery. Not Ford Sylver, center fielder for the Chicago Anchors baseball team, otherwise known as The Streak. Rookie of the Year when I started fifteen years ago. A two-time Golden Glove recipient and countless times an All-Star player.

Quickly looking away from her, I sigh as I reach for my wallet in my back pocket and pull out my credit card for the bill.

The woman beside me continues to stare, standing a little

too close and smelling a little familiar. Something citrusy. Grapefruit, maybe?

I wrinkle my nose as if I can distinguish the scent. *What the hell am I doing?*

As the bakery clerk tells me my total, I snort. "What happened to the friends and family discount?"

"It doesn't apply to dickheads." The deep masculine voice has me turning toward the back of the shop where my younger brother is exiting his office.

Fuck! I'm not ready to see Sebastian, especially when I'm wearing yesterday's clothes, sweating out tequila, and this woman is still standing too close to me.

"Hey, man." I open my arms, and Sebastian and I embrace in an awkward one clap on the back motion that doesn't allow our chests to meet, before pulling apart like we singed one another. "Should you be working today?"

"I work every day." His gruff voice suggests there's something more he wants to say on the subject of working, but at the same time, he's smiling a goofy grin. My little brother is getting married tomorrow. He's in love and I've heard his future wife is a treasure. I haven't met Enya, the woman who changed Sebastian's life, yet.

I huff but Sebastian is already looking around me at the woman behind me.

"Hey, Cadence," he states.

Cadence? Fuck, why does that sound . . .

Slowly, I turn to glance over my shoulder. The spark in her gemstone blue eyes has shifted to the iridescence of a blow torch, and she wants to incinerate me. Reaching for a napkin in the holder on the counter, she snatches one free. A bright purple marker appears in her other hand, and she leans forward, signing something on the flimsy paper.

When she stands upright, she slaps the napkin against my chest with a hard pat.

"Here. How about taking my autograph as you clearly lost my number?"

My mouth falls open.

Sebastian lets out a choking cough.

"Cadence," I repeat the name like it is foreign on my tongue but familiar in my head.

"C-A-D-E-N-C-E. Seven letters like the number of digits in a phone number *and* the number of shots I drank to your . . . what was it?" She taps her chin like her memory needs a minute. Then she stands straighter. "Oh right, your four. Alliterative with your name, Ford. Or is it four, as in the number of inches in your . . .?" Her coolly amused eyes flicker to my crotch, those lush lips of hers kicking up on one side again in a wicked grin.

Harsh. Closing my eyes a second, my foggy memory clears a little. A woman singing in the corner of the bar. Her voice somber and sad. My offer to buy her a drink. She bought me one instead.

The thought of alcohol makes my stomach roll.

When a strong pat comes to my shoulder, my lids pop open. Sebastian rounds me and Cadence.

"Yeah, I'm not gonna touch that." He chuckles harder as he walks around the glass bakery display case and steps behind the counter.

"Met your brother last night," Cadence announces, looking away from me and toward Sebastian. "Pity party of one."

Wow. Way to spill my secrets.

Wait? Did I tell her my secrets?

I don't ask. I can't do anything but stare at her, taking in the brightness of the acorn-colored hair curling in subtle waves along her neck and the smoothness of her skin.

Did I fuck her? Please say I did.

No . . . don't say that.

Still, my body jolts like some kind of awareness is happening. Or maybe that's the fact she boldly took the napkin she wrote on and is now tucking it into my front jean pocket.

Fuck. I'm such an idiot.

"And how do you know each other?" I question, pointing between my brother and this woman, giving away how lost I am in this encounter.

Sebastian glances from Cadence to me and back. His chin lifts in her direction.

"This is Cadence Calloway. Enya's sister."

Her sister? Did I know that Enya had a sister? Did Cadence mention the relation last night? Does she know who *I* am to Sebastian?

"That's Cadence only to you, my friend." Acidic sass fills the command as she steps toward the counter, picks up a to-go cup of coffee from my order of three and pops the lid. Taking a sip, her plum-colored lipstick marks the paper mug. She grimaces.

"What self-respecting American drinks their coffee plain?"

My mouth falls open, ready to argue that I do, and many others as well, American and otherwise.

But she wiggles her fingers at Sebastian who absentmind-edly hands her four sugar packets. I watch as she pours the sweetener into the cup, stirs it with the bottom half of her purple marker, and then takes another sip.

"Better." She sighs, smacking her lips before holding up the mug in salute like she's thanking me for the coffee I didn't offer her. "See ya 'round, cowboy."

Cowboy? I'm no fucking cowboy, which has me glancing at her cap again.

My baseball hat on her head.

Before I can demand she give it back, she's already turning on the heels of her eggplant-purple boots, forcing me to notice her long legs peeking out from a short denim skirt. As she walks away, I can't seem to take my eyes off her. The flexing of her toned legs. The sway of her hips. The way that skirt hugs her ass.

"What the hell, man?" Sebastian grouses.

Only I don't drag my gaze from Cadence's exit. My heart continues to thump. My body leans forward as if I'm drawn to her, being pulled to follow her. Like a ball connects with a bat. *Crack!*

Instantly, I stand taller, holding myself back and mentally shaking my entire body.

Fuck. I think I slept with my future sister-in-law last night.

Continue reading STERLING STREAK.

Sterling Streak

MORE BY L.B. DUNBAR

<u>Sterling Falls</u>
Seven small-town siblings muddle their way through love
over 40.
Sterling Heat
Sterling Brick
Sterling Streak
Sterling Clay
Sterling Fight
Sterling Touch
Sterling Stone

<u>Chicago Anchors</u>
When your eyes are on the silver fox coach more than the ball.
Elevator Pitch
Catch the Kiss

Parentmoon
When the mother of the groom goes head-to-head with the
single father of the bride.

__Holiday Hotties (Christmas novellas)__
Holiday novellas certain to heat the season.
Scrooge-ish
Naughty-ish
Grouch-ish

__Road Trips & Romance__
Three sisters. Three destinations. All second chances at love over 40.
Hauling Ashe
Merging Wright
Rhode Trip

__Lakeside Cottage__
Four friends. Four summers. Shenanigans and love happen at the lake.
Living at 40
Loving at 40
Learning at 40
Letting Go at 40

__The Silver Foxes of Blue Ridge__
Small mountain town, silver fox brothers seeking love over 40.
Silver Brewer
Silver Player
Silver Mayor
Silver Biker

__Sexy Silver Foxes__
When sexy silver foxes meet the feisty vixens of their dreams.
After Care
Midlife Crisis
Restored Dreams
Second Chance

Wine&Dine

Collision novellas
A spin-off from *After Care* – the younger set/rock stars
Collide
Caught

The Sex Education of M.E.
The original sexy silver fox.
When a widowed professor decides she'd like to date again,
and a local fireman volunteers to give her lessons.

The Heart Collection
Small town, big hearts - stories of family and love.
Speak from the Heart
Read with your Heart
Look with your Heart
Fight from the Heart
View with your Heart

A Heart Collection Spin-off
The Heart Remembers

BOOKS IN OTHER AUTHOR WORLDS

Smartypants Romance (an imprint of Penny Reid)
Tales of the Winters sisters set in Green Valley.
Love in Due Time
Love in Deed
Love in a Pickle

The World of True North (an imprint of Sarina Bowen)
Welcome to Vermont! And the Busy Bean Café.
Cowboy

Studfinder

THE EARLY YEARS

<u>Legendary Rock Stars Series</u>
A classic tale with a modern twist of rockstar romance and suspense.

<u>Paradise Stories</u>
MMA romance. Two brothers. One fight.

<u>The Island Duet</u>
Intrigue and suspense. The island knows what you've done.

<u>Modern Descendants – writing as elda lore</u>
Magical realism. Modern myths of Greek gods.

ABOUT THE AUTHOR

www.lbdunbar.com

L.B. Dunbar loves sexy silver foxes, second chances, and small towns. If you enjoy older characters in your romance reads, including a hero with a little silver in his scruff and a heroine rediscovering her worth, then welcome to romance for those over 40. L.B. Dunbar's signature works include women and men in their prime taking another turn at love and happily ever after. She's a *USA TODAY* Bestseller as well as #1 Bestseller on Amazon in Later in Life Romance with her Sterling Falls, Lakeside Cottage, and Road Trips & Romance series. L.B. lives in Chicago with her own sexy silver fox.

To get all the scoop about the self-proclaimed queen of silver fox romance, join her on Facebook at Loving L.B. (Dunbar) or receive her monthly newsletter, Love Notes.

+ + +

CONNECT WITH L.B. DUNBAR